DEATHBED WARNING

The old man did not respond at first, but then, all at once, his whole body stiffened. The eyes opened, but what they saw was not Adam or the room beyond.

"The treasure of the Temple!" he rasped hoarsely. "The Seal guards the secret. Adam, it *has* to be recovered, do you hear me? The Seal *has* to be recovered . . . !"

PRAISE FOR THE ADEPT SERIES

"Admirable, elegant . . . A constantly absorbing story that features excellent pacing, a frequently compelling sense of place, and an equally compelling emotional impact."   —*Booklist*

"One of those rare books that, once you start reading, you can't stop."   —*SFRA Newsletter*

THE ADEPT

BOOK THREE: THE TEMPLAR TREASURE

KATHERINE KURTZ
and
DEBORAH TURNER HARRIS

ACE BOOKS, NEW YORK

This book is an Ace original edition,
and has never been previously published.

THE TEMPLAR TREASURE

An Ace Book / published by arrangement with
Bill Fawcett and Associates

PRINTING HISTORY
Ace edition / July 1993

ISBN: 0-441-00345-1

Ace Books are published by The Berkley Publishing Group,
200 Madison Avenue, New York, NY 10016.
The name "ACE" and the "A" logo
are trademarks belonging to Charter Communications, Inc.

PRINTED IN THE UNITED STATES OF AMERICA

10 9 8 7 6 5 4 3 2 1

For
Dr. Sheila Rossi,
who taught Adam Sinclair
much of what he knows about hypnosis,
and also for
Christine Hackett and Suzanne Eberle

ACKNOWLEDGMENTS

Grateful thanks are owed to the following people, whose assistance was invaluable in filling out much of the rich background for this book:

Ms. Kirsty Beck, for technical information concerning not only Hebrew art objects of the First Temple Period but also archaeological methods of dating such artifacts;

Cantor Alwyn Shulman, Dublin and Terenure Hebrew Congregations, and Dr. Jay Barry Azneer, D.O., for insights into Jewish funeral practices;

Mr. Donald Little, administrator of Fyvie Castle on behalf of the National Trust for Scotland, and his wife, Liz, for their generosity in allowing us to spend five hours of their precious time exploring Fyvie;

Mr. Brian Nodes, administrator at Blair Castle, for opening up Earl John's Room after the end of season and allowing a private look at Bonnie Dundee's breastplate and morion;

Dr. Martin Hardgrave, for sharing with us a resident's knowledge of the city of York;

Dr. Ernan J. Gallagher, Ireland, and Dr. A. V. Davidson, Scotland, for technical medical advice;

Dr. Richard Oram, for his continuing guidance on questions of Scottish history;

Mr. Kenneth Fraser of the St. Andrews University Library, for his ongoing assistance in matters of general research;

And the staff of the St. Andrews Tourist Information Bureau, for their cheerful readiness to dig up all manner of information not covered by the guidebooks.

PROLOGUE

THE Yorkshire home of Professor Nathan Fiennes was fitted with the latest in household security systems. Ritchie Logan even knew what kind, because the company installing it had seen fit to publicize the fact by fixing a bright red box to the gable end of the house, marked with their company logo. Such displays were intended to deter casual thieves—and maybe they did deter amateurs and opportunists—but Logan was a professional. As far as he was concerned, knowing in advance that the house was wired only served to make his job easier.

But then, the promise of easy pickings had been one of the attractions of this job. Besides being offered a handsome cash retainer merely to breach the house's security and open the safe, Logan had been assured that he might have his pick of the jewellery and other valuables kept there. The man who'd engaged him for this job, sitting in the passenger seat of the rented Volvo, was after something else entirely—some kind of archaeological artifact.

Logan cruised slowly past the cul-de-sac where the house lay, and noted with satisfaction that nothing had changed. Half an hour before, from a vantage point on the main road, he and his employer had watched the owners and their dinner guests leave, all of them dressed for the theatre as anticipated. If no one returned in the time it took to make one more long orbit around the city walls, Logan felt reasonably confident that the house would remain empty for at least another two to three hours. As he swung into Monkgate, heading toward the city, he stole a sidelong glance at the man sitting next to him.

He still had not figured out Monsieur Henri Gerard. The Frenchman looked nothing like the sort of man likely to hire a professional cat burglar. Had Logan seen him on the street, he would have pegged Gerard as someone hoping one day to make a name for himself in law or politics—conservatively well dressed and respectable-looking, probably approaching forty, with sleek, dark hair brushed straight back from a high forehead and a dapper moustache trimmed pencil-thin in a style reminiscent of a young Maurice Chevalier. This Gallic impression was heightened by the continental cut of his dark suit and the fact that he spoke English with a Parisian inflection.

He was an odd duck, Logan decided, as he eased the big car along Lord Mayor's Walk and then swung left into Gillygate, skirting the city's medieval walls. From the very beginning, Gerard had made it clear that his sole purpose in coming to England was to acquire an antique bronze seal currently in the possession of the owner of the house targeted for tonight's venture. According to Gerard, the seal was of value only to a historian like himself. If that was true, it would confirm Logan's suspicion that the Frenchman was one of those academic fanatics who would do literally anything in order to steal a march on a rival scholar—in this case, Dr. Nathan Fiennes, a distinguished philosopher presently lecturing at the University of York.

None of this had anything to do with Logan, of course. And even if Gerard was lying, and the seal was worth more than he was letting on, Logan was prepared to let him have it, provided that the rest of the takings were as lucrative as the Frenchman had made out. Finding a suitable buyer for a stolen museum piece was always a time-consuming enterprise, requiring far more work than Logan was willing to invest when there were much quicker profits to be made on more conventional commodities.

The only real catch in the arrangement was that Gerard had insisted on taking part in the burglary. Logan would have much preferred to do the job alone, but the Frenchman had argued with some heat that he had to be present to authenticate the seal, on the chance that Fiennes might have had a copy made. Logan could think of no reason why Fiennes should have wanted to do anything of the sort; but then again, academics of Gerard's caliber were seemingly a breed apart. And since, in any case, Gerard was already paying for the privilege of sharing the risks, Logan had resigned himself to the necessity of having the Frenchman along for company.

He just hoped that Gerard wouldn't do anything stupid that might risk their getting caught.

They crawled past the vast, floodlit pile that was York Minster, with the delicate tracery of its spires and towers bright against the starry backdrop of a mid-September night. On through the night-hushed streets they wove, emerging through the Monk Bar Gate and picking up speed as they headed back along Monkgate again. Half a mile northeast of the historic city center, as Logan made the turn into the darker, quieter streets of an established residential suburb, Gerard sat forward, apparently unaware how his eagerness showed.

"Just relax," Logan told his employer. "From here on out, we've got to look like we belong to this neighborhood. We don't want to do anything to draw attention to ourselves."

The Fiennes house was one of three detached stone villas that stood at the bottom of a crescent-shaped cul-de-sac. Alert but relaxed, Logan drove on around the corner into the adjoining street and parked the Volvo at the curb in an island of shadow between two streetlamps. The two men alighted unhurriedly from the car and set off up the sidewalk at a leisurely pace. A casual observer, noting their conservatively cut trenchcoats and expensive leather briefcases, would have taken them for two businessmen out to pay a social call on a friend.

They used a public footpath to cut back in the direction of their goal across the narrow, grassy common that ran between the two opposing rows of back gardens. The Fienneses' property was enclosed by a high wall, but the lock on the garden gate yielded readily to Logan's expert manipulations with a lock pick. He let himself inside and swiftly beckoned Gerard to follow, pulling the gate to but not latched. Crouching low in the shrubbery flanking the wall, the two paused to don black balaclava helmets and tight-fitting surgical gloves before making their way stealthily up the flagstoned walk to the conservatory at the rear of the house.

Gerard watched in tight-lipped anticipation as Logan took a specialized assortment of implements from his briefcase and set himself to disabling the alarm system, his work illuminated by a tiny pencil-flash held between his teeth. In less than a minute they were inside the conservatory. A glass sliding door leading into the house yielded in a matter of seconds, after which Logan led his employer stealthily into the narrow confines of the downstairs hall, where a small lamp glowed on a side table. Gerard made a darting movement toward the foot of the staircase, only to feel Logan's restraining hand catch at his sleeve.

"Not so fast," the thief whispered. "The stuff in the safe isn't going anywhere, is it? Then slow down, and let's do this thing according to plan."

Nodding somewhat sullenly, Gerard dropped back to let Logan precede him up the stairs, toward where an overhead light dimly illuminated the upstairs landing. The upper regions of the house were silent except for the hollow ticking of a grandfather clock standing against the wall just outside the study. An ornate mezuzah of finely wrought silver graced the right-hand lintel of the study door, and Logan grinned thinly to himself as he pried it off and slipped it into his pocket. The door swung back on silent hinges as Logan led the way across the threshold into a large square room redolent of pipe tobacco and book bindings.

Light spilled from the landing through the open doorway. The room's only window lay directly opposite, with a large desk set before it. The curtains were standing open, affording a darkling view of the garden below.

"Get the curtains," Logan ordered, moving to the left, where the entire wall was taken up by an immense built-in bookcase. When Gerard had complied, Logan shone the beam of his electric torch along the fourth shelf from the top until its light picked up a mousy-looking set of commentaries on the Talmud.

"I've found the benchmark texts you said to look for," he reported in a clipped undertone, turning to set his briefcase on a corner of the desk. "Come and hold the light while I lift them out."

As keen as his associate to get on with the job, Gerard made haste to comply, setting his own case on the desk's chair. Logan removed the books from their place and set them aside on the desk. The cavity left behind on the shelf was backed not with walnut panelling, but with the metal door to a small wall safe fitted with an old-fashioned combination lock.

"Well, well, this thing's practically an antique in itself," the thief exclaimed in tones of scornful satisfaction. "Let's arrange for a little more light on the subject, and we'll be in and out before you know it."

There was a goosenecked reading lamp on the desk. Logan angled it round so that the shaded bulb was pointing toward the safe before switching it on. Then, taking a stethoscope out of his case, he pushed back his balaclava helmet and donned the earpieces with workmanlike efficiency.

"Go out in the hall and keep watch," he directed over his shoulder. "If you hear anything suspicious, sing out."

Much as it galled him to take orders from his English hireling, Gerard knew it was a sensible precaution. Suppressing a pang of irritation, he retreated to the hall while Logan gave his attention to dialling up the opening combination. The seconds ticked away with what seemed like maddening slowness. Gerard was about to inquire sharply how much longer the operation was likely to take when there was a muffled exclamation of triumph from inside the office.

"Got it!"

Gerard rushed back into the room to find Logan opening velvet-covered jewellers' boxes into his briefcase. A diamond tiara and a necklace dripping with diamonds and emeralds already gleamed in the glancing light of the goosenecked lamp, and a pair of diamond clips and a string of pearls quickly joined them, their boxes tossed onto a growing pile on the floor as Logan riffled through a sheaf of negotiable bonds with obvious satisfaction. Lying next to the briefcase was a battered wooden box the size of a small, thick book, its lid inlaid with Hebrew characters.

"Is that what you're looking for?" Logan said drily at Gerard's gasp, indicating the box with a jerk of his chin.

Heart pounding, Gerard pounced on the box and flipped it open. Inside, pillowed on faded crimson velvet, was an oval of age-blackened bronze nearly the size of a man's palm, pivot-mounted between the arms of a heavy arc of the same dark metal. The device deeply etched into the face of the disc was that of a six-pointed star made of interlocking triangles, surrounded by a serpentine scroll of Qabalistic script.

Almost reverently Gerard allowed himself to touch the seal with one trembling forefinger. It still staggered him to reflect that the seal—*the* seal—had been in the Fiennes family for so many generations without any of its keepers even suspecting the incalculable potency vested in the object they had in their possession.

"Oh, yes," he breathed, licking his lips like a wolf who scents meat. "But I must be sure."

All but quivering with eagerness, he took a jeweller's loupe from the breast pocket of his suit coat and adjusted it in his eye, at the same time lifting the seal from its box with his free hand and moving over into the light. A brief examination of the face of the seal confirmed that the design had been etched with a tracer rather than a graver—circumstantial evidence, at least, that the piece had been crafted prior to 800 B.C. But the real proof Gerard was looking for was a recent telltale scratch on the inside of the mounting.

To the sound of more loot going into Logan's case, Gerard rotated the seal in the glare of the lamp. His breath caught in his throat as his searching gaze found what he was seeking—the scratch he himself had made a few months back, in the course of taking a sample shaving of the metal. Subsequent photomicrographic analysis of the shaving had confirmed the seal's genuine antiquity. And now it was in his hands at last!

"We can go now," he murmured, smiling almost dreamily as he laid the seal reverently back in its box and closed the lid. "This is, indeed, the piece."

In that same instant, Logan suddenly stiffened in a listening attitude, his manner all at once apprehensive and alert.

"What is it? What's wrong?" Gerard demanded in a startled undertone.

"Car in the driveway," Logan muttered.

"That's imposs—"

Logan gestured vehemently for silence. An instant later, they heard a pair of car doors open and slam, and then the patter of footsteps coming up the front walk, high heels and leather soles, making for the front door.

"Must've been a bad show," Logan said, already snapping his briefcase shut and heading for the door, pulling his balaclava back into place. "We've got maybe forty seconds to get the hell out of here!"

His hand was already on the study door. Gerard looked stunned, but likewise went into action. Gripping the wooden box tightly in his right hand, he made a clumsy left-handed grab for his own carrying case, but his gloved fingers miscued and it slipped from his grasp, striking the carpet with a muffled thud and bouncing out of reach under the chair.

Logan fetched up with a virulent whispered curse as Gerard scrambled to retrieve the case. From downstairs came the rattle of a key being turned in the front door lock. Showing teeth like a pit bull terrier, Logan gently closed the study door as the one below in the vestibule creaked open. A woman's voice, slightly muffled, floated up to them from the ground floor in tones of indulgent reproof.

"Honestly, Nathan, you really shouldn't have let David Wolfson talk you into having burgundy with the meal. I probably shouldn't even keep it in the house any more. You know perfectly well what red wine does to your digestion these days!"

Gerard recognized the voice as that of Rachel Fiennes. Her admonition drew a rueful groan from her husband.

"I know, I know," the intruders heard him say. "I was hoping that just this once— But I'm far more distressed that I made you miss out on the second half of the performance."

"Don't give it another thought, my dear," came Rachel's amiable reply. "To tell you the truth, I've never been all *that* fond of Ibsen anyway. You'd probably better have a couple of your stomach tablets, though. Where are they, in your desk upstairs? All right, you go on into the parlor and sit down, and I'll go fetch them for you."

As soft footbeats mounted the stairs, Logan made a dive for the study lamp and switched it off. Catching Gerard by the sleeve, he hurried them both over to the wall on the blind side of the doorway, shrinking back as Mrs. Fiennes drew even with the threshold outside. The porcelain knob turned over with a rattle, and the door swung open.

Light spilling in from the hallway showed up the opened safe and the tumble of books on the desk. Seeing it, Rachel gave a startled gasp and faltered abruptly to a standstill. In the same instant a lithe, dark figure lunged at her from behind the door and grabbed one wrist, jerking her into the room. She had just enough presence of mind to utter a shriek of alarm before her captor dealt her a heavy backhand blow that hurled her bruisingly against the inside wall.

In the parlor below, Nathan started up at the sound of his wife's scream. He heaved himself up out of his armchair and rushed out into the hall as two men in dark suits and balaclava helmets came thundering down the stairs. Both of them were carrying briefcases, and the taller of the pair was clutching a small wooden box to his chest with one gloved hand. With a sudden, terrible clarity of perception, Nathan recognized it as the box in which he habitually kept the seal he had inherited from his father.

Not thinking of the possible consequences, he snatched his walking stick from the stand by the door and charged forward in a desperate attempt to stop the thieves. The blow he aimed at the man with the box went wide by a whistling inch. Before he could swing again, the second intruder slammed him in the temple with a sharp corner of his briefcase and wrenched the stick from his hand. Even as Nathan recoiled with a cry, instinctively flinging up an arm to the pain, the intruder took an overhead swing with the cane and dealt him a brutal crack across the back of his head.

Red agony exploded inside his skull. With a choked moan, he reeled aside and collided with the stairpost. Before he could catch his balance, the intruder struck him a second blow with the cane and shouldered him roughly out of the way. As Nathan crumpled to the floor, still clinging to the stairpost, he heard their footsteps clattering past him out the door and down the front path.

The throbbing pain in his head was like repeated thrusts from a red-hot dagger. He put a hand to his temple and it came away sticky with blood. Groaning aloud, he made an effort to pull himself up only to slump down again in defeat. All but blind, he sensed movement above him, coming down the stairs, and heard his wife calling his name on a frantic note of inquiry. Clinging to consciousness with all the strength of will he could muster, he gasped out, "Rachel, the Seal! The thieves took the Seal!"

Rachel dropped to her knees beside him. He could hear her sobbing distractedly as she tried to loosen his tie.

"Nathan, be still! Please don't try to talk!" she begged. "Just stay there and don't move while I call an ambulance."

"No, wait!" Sensing she was about to move away from him, he groped for her hand and clung to it. "Rachel, you *must* listen!" he rasped, hoping with all his heart that his strength would hold out long enough to get this vital message across. "Things about the Seal you don't know—dangerous things. It's *got* to be recovered, at all cost! Call Sir Adam Sinclair and tell him what's happened. Tell him I've got to talk to him. Promise me you'll call him *tonight*. . . ."

His hold on awareness was slipping as he spoke. Rachel's voice came filtered through the haze, tearful and pleading.

''I will, Nathan. I'll do anything you ask. Just please, *please* lie still and let me go call for help.''

Nathan struggled a moment longer, striving for the strength to reassure her. But this time the darkness won out and overwhelmed him.

CHAPTER ONE

"HYPNOTIC age regression," said Sir Adam Sinclair, "can be an exceedingly useful diagnostic tool for the psychiatric physician. If we accept that the majority of psychiatric disorders, whether neurotic or psychotic in their intensity, are to some degree rooted in the patient's personal past, then the value of gaining access to that past becomes immediately apparent. At the very least," he continued, keenly surveying the youthful upturned faces of his listeners, "hypnotic regression provides for the detailed retrieval and review of a wide range of personal data that might otherwise be inaccessible to the individual concerned, if only through the natural and inevitable clouding of the memory owing to passage of time. At its most useful, regression can provide the very key with which to unlock the shackles of a mind fettered by its own repressions."

He was lecturing to his regular Monday afternoon class at the Royal Edinburgh Hospital, a mixed bag composed mainly of white-coated junior doctors on their psychiatric rotation but also including two social service workers, a retired university lecturer, and a woman deacon training for chaplaincy in the Episcopal Church. Their expressions reflected a gamut of reactions ranging from sober acknowledgement to skepticism, the latter of which was only to be expected and even encouraged, especially right after lunch.

"Dr. Sinclair," said a stocky, bespectacled young man sitting in the first row, as he flung up a hand. "I can see the possible usefulness of regressing a patient to an earlier age, but—is it true that you've even managed to regress some of your own patients as far back as other previous *lives*?"

The question generated a minor stir of excitement. The dashing and elegant Dr. Sinclair had a reputation as something of an adventurer in the field of psychiatric therapy and practice, no doubt enhanced by his occasionally sensational association with Lothian and Borders Police as a psychiatric consultant. Had his audience known the true range of his knowledge and experience in the field now under discussion, the excitement might have turned to amazement, disbelief, and even fear.

Adam smiled indulgently. "It's certainly been my experience that such regressions are possible," he acknowledged easily.

His questioner looked astonished to have gotten an affirmative answer.

"Well, did you set out deliberately to induce these past-life regressions?"

"Yes, Mr. Huntley, I did," Adam said mildly. "And you needn't look so scandalized. I am certainly not the first hypnotherapist to do so."

"But—"

"Let's review a few notable case studies, shall we, and then you can draw your own conclusions," Adam offered, coming around to sit informally on the front of the desk. His crisply starched white lab coat was open casually over a three-piece navy suit of impeccable cut, with the mellow glint of an antique gold watch-fob swagged across the front of the vest. With his classic good looks and dark hair silvering at the temples, he might have been a media personality rather than the eminent psychiatrist he was.

"I'll first mention the studies carried out in the seventies by Arnold Bloxham and Joe Keeton," Adam went on. "Bloxham was able to regress one of his subjects, a woman named Jane Evans, through no fewer than *six* previous lives, including that of a medieval Jewess named Rebecca who was killed in a pogrom that took place in York in 1190. 'Rebecca' was able to render a graphic description of the church crypt in which she and her child were trapped and subsequently murdered by the angry mob. After listening to a recording of 'Rebecca's' account, Professor Barrie Dobson of the University of York ventured the opinion that the church most closely answering her description was St.

Mary's Castlegate—except for the fact that the church didn't have a crypt.''

"I've heard of that case," said a white-coated young woman in the back. "The BBC featured it in a special exploring the possibility of reincarnation."

"Leave it to the Beeb to waste good airtime on rubbish," said an intense, sharp-featured young man beside her. "They didn't take it seriously, did they?"

"Actually, they concluded that the evidence was inconclusive," his classmate allowed. "Six months later, however, a workman doing some renovation work on the church accidentally broke through into a previously unknown chamber that might well have been a medieval crypt."

"I remember reading about that in the papers," said one of the social workers. "Didn't the chamber, or crypt, or whatever it was, get bricked back up before any archaeologists could come and take a closer look?"

"An unfortunate bureaucratic glitch," Adam agreed, easing back into the exchange. "Perhaps one day, that part of the investigation will be completed. Nonetheless, the circumstantial evidence would still seem to suggest that Jane Evans, through 'Rebecca,' had access to historical information unknown to present-day authorities."

One of the students in the front row was tapping her pen against her front teeth. "Wasn't there also an American psychiatrist from Virginia who did a lot of work on spontaneous past-life regressions in very young children?" she asked.

"That's right," Adam said. "His name is Dr. Ian Stevenson. His most celebrated case involved a five-year-old Lebanese boy whose people claimed he was the reincarnation of a man called Ibrahim, who had died recently in a neighboring town. When Stevenson examined the boy, he found that the child possessed an inexplicably intimate knowledge of Ibrahim's personal life, besides exhibiting certain behavioral traits which Ibrahim's surviving family swore were consistent with those of their deceased relative. Stevenson later published this and other findings under the title *Twenty Cases Suggestive of Reincarnation*."

"What a load of bunk!" exclaimed one of the students in

the front row. "How can he call himself a serious scientist?"

"I assure you that Stevenson did not use the term lightly," Adam said mildly. "In his estimation, the evidence was strong enough to constitute a case for speculation, at very least."

"Evidence for reincarnation . . . ," another of his students mused. "Is that what you're looking for when you attempt to do past-life regressions with your own patients?" she asked bluntly.

"What I'm looking for," Adam said with a droll smile, "is information that will help me arrive at an effective diagnosis. If the unconscious can allow me access to vital information by couching it in terms of past-life experiences that have bearing on the patient's present problems, then it behooves me, as a physician, to treat 'memories' of these past-life experiences *as if* they were real, and to deal with the patient accordingly. I think that no one would argue that experiences of the mind are any less 'real' than experiences of the physical body. Indeed, in some cases, they can be more vivid, as in the instance of phantom limb pain, long after an amputation."

"But that's a physiological reaction of damaged nerveways," a young man objected.

"In part, perhaps," Adam agreed. "But who is to say exactly where the lines are drawn between body, mind, and spirit?"

A striking brunette in the front row rolled her eyes and put down her pen.

"I knew it was only a matter of time before someone came up with one of the 's' words," she muttered, then glanced at the woman deacon in friendly challenge. "Lorna, care to tell us what the God Squad has to say about spirit, or soul, and the matter of reincarnation?"

"Certainly," Lorna replied, "though I'm not certain I have any answers. Would you prefer an Eastern or a Western bias?"

"Perhaps you might share both points of view," Adam said.

"Very well." As all eyes flicked briefly from Lorna to Adam and back again, she settled herself composedly in her chair, collecting her thoughts. Her very name, Lorna Liu, proclaimed her mixed Scottish and Asian heritage, and her appearance combined the most graceful attributes of both, enhanced by the clerical collar she wore with her conservative grey suit.

"I'd be less than honest if I said I wasn't impressed with the way the case for reincarnation is being argued," she said amiably, "but I think it's time that someone pointed out that the question is not so much a scientific issue as a theological one. Let's take Buddhism and Christianity, since those are my background. While the two theologies have many views in common, especially with regard to ethics and morality, they differ rather drastically in their respective concepts of personal salvation."

Seeing that she had the attention of the rest of the room, she went on in the same reflective tone.

"Buddhists believe that the whole material world is nothing but mere illusion—*maya*—and can only be transcended in most cases at the cost of repeated lifetimes spent in pursuit of personal enlightenment. Sometimes this is visualized as a wheel, escape from which becomes the goal of the enlightened individual.

"Christians, by contrast, believe that matter and spirit are inextricably bound together as a consequence of divine creation, and are likewise simultaneously eligible for redemption—not through some long-drawn refining process of repeated existences, but as a direct consequence of divine atonement through the sacrificial death and resurrection of Christ, the God Incarnate. As a Christian, I must confess I see no logical way of bridging the gap between my religious convictions and the concept of reincarnation as a fact of existence. If anyone else can suggest a means of resolution, I would be very grateful to hear what he or she might have to say."

Thoughtful silence settled for a few seconds as the rest of the group wrestled with the problem, after which the bespectacled Mr. Huntley said bluntly, "I don't see how there can be a resolution. One point of view or the other has got to be wrong.''

''If not both,'' said the retired lecturer with a touch of skepticism. As all eyes turned to him, he added, ''I admit quite freely to being an agnostic, Dr. Sinclair. But whether or not there's a spiritual dimension to our existence, I find the notion of reincarnation messy and illogical. Where, for example, do souls get stored when they're not in use? When a given soul attains enlightenment and escapes from the wheel, is another soul immediately created to take its place? If so, who or what determines whether a newly conceived infant receives a virgin soul or one that has been around for a while? If not, will we one day run into a shortage of souls? Do souls get recycled more quickly when there's a population explosion, as there is at the moment?'' He broke off with an ironic gesture of disclaimer.

''Maybe not everyone gets reincarnated,'' a new voice said thoughtfully. ''Maybe it only happens in special cases.''

Adam glanced toward the speaker and raised an eyebrow. Avril Peterson's academic standing might not be the highest in her class, but this was not the first time he had seen her display a flash of intuitive insight.

''Ms. Peterson, I do believe you may have offered us a possible solution to this theological paradox,'' he said, his smile warming. Transferring his attention to the group at large, he went on to elucidate.

''Allow me to acquaint you with a possible key to be found in Judaic tradition associated with the Qabalah, which is a body of Jewish mystical doctrine. A very learned friend of mine who is a scholar in such matters once confided to me that a true knowledge of the inner meaning of the Qabalah was not to be acquired through the study of books, but rather through the agency of special ministers whose sacred office it was to transmit 'the teaching' from one generation to the next. According to apocalyptic Hebrew legend, mankind was first instructed in the Qabalah by the archangel Metatron, who is legendarily identified as the transfigured Enoch—the man who, according to Genesis, 'walked with God' and did not taste death. Metratron is said to have subsequently manifested himself throughout history as various great teachers, including Melchizedek, the priest-king whose encounter with Abraham foreshadows the Eucharist, because he offered bread and wine.

"By more conventional reckoning," Adam went on, "we might regard Metratron as an archetypal figure—a symbol, if you like, of all others of his kind. There's a rather fascinating passage at the beginning of the sixth chapter of Genesis which speaks of there being intercourse between 'giants'—a tantalizing reference to beings apparently infe-rior to God, but superior to humankind—and the 'daughters of men.' The children born of these liaisons are described by the King James Bible as *mighty men which were of old, men of renown.*

"If we accept that such legends, along with myths and the contents of certain dreams, are expressive of nonempirical truths—truths known to the psyche, but inaccessible by empirical means—then it becomes feasible to consider as a possible vehicle of truth Ms. Peterson's notion that reincar-nation is confined to a selected handful of individuals recruited by the angels and thereafter entrusted with the task of imparting sacred knowledge, generation after generation.

"These individuals thus become bearers of the divine light of truth, in the Promethean sense," he concluded, "but the lifetime experiences for such individuals might well be likened to the projections thrown off through the apertures of a magic lantern—emanations of light manifested in different places, but derived from the same common source. What is withdrawn at the death of the physical body is the projection, rather than the essence. The light itself continues to burn undiminished, until another aperture opens in the fabric of time."

His audience had been listening with rapt fascination, caught up in the near hypnotic intensity for which Dr. Adam Sinclair was famous, and now the old lecturer nodded grudging approval.

"You appear to have thought the matter through very thoroughly, Dr. Sinclair," he admitted. "Are we to take it then, that you personally subscribe to the belief you've just outlined in such poetic terms?''

"You may take it," Adam said lightly, "that we have come as close as we can to providing Ms. Liu with the theological resolution she was seeking. Speaking more clinically, from the standpoint of a psychotherapist, I would say that whatever we may personally come to believe about the nature of past-life regressions, when we encounter such regressions in our patients, it behooves everyone concerned to treat such memories as a valid aspect of the patients' total experience.''

He would have continued but for a rap at the lecture room door. He glanced in that direction as the door opened and one of the hospital administrators poked his head around the door frame.

"Sorry to interrupt your lecture, Dr. Sinclair, but I have a telephone message for you. They said it was rather urgent.''

Coming forward, he handed Adam a folded piece of hospital memo paper. Inside, written in a neat secretarial hand, was a single sentence: *Sir Adam: Humphrey requests that you phone home immediately.*

Conscious of a sudden feeling of foreboding, Adam consulted his pocket watch, then directed his attention back to his class as he stood.

"My apologies, but it seems I'm going to be obliged to cut this lecture short," he said smoothly, pocketing watch and note. "Please feel free to carry on in my absence, but we'll plan to resume the discussion next time.''

Five minutes later, seated behind the desk in his office, he was listening soberly as Humphrey, his butler and personal valet, relayed the news about Nathan Fiennes.

"Mrs. Fiennes said that emergency surgery was performed during the night to alleviate pressure on the brain, but his condition is deteriorating,'' Humphrey concluded. "Apparently he asked for you immediately after the attack. Mrs. Fiennes was quite agitated that you should come, if at all possible.''

The account, as it unfolded, struck Adam as oddly coincidental, for though he had not thought about his old mentor in some time, it had been Nathan to whom he was referring when he spoke of the Qabalah during his interrupted lecture. He had to wonder whether the old man's worsening condition, coupled with his specific request for Adam's presence, perhaps partially explained why Adam should have been thinking about Nathan only minutes before.

"Thank you for relaying that, Humphrey," Adam said, when Humphrey had finished. "I'll go, of course. I don't suppose you had time to check with the airlines to see what flights are available?"

"As a matter of fact, I did, sir. Air UK has a four-fifteen flight into Leeds-Bradford, which is the airport nearest to York itself. There were still seats available ten minutes ago. Shall I book you one, sir?"

"Yes, do that, please," Adam said. "On second thought, book two seats. If Inspector McLeod can get away, I'm going to ask him to accompany me. Since there's a police aspect to this, it may be that he can facilitate interface with the Yorkshire constabulary."

"Very good, sir. Shall I pack you an overnight bag and meet you at the airport?"

Adam glanced at his gold pocket watch and grimaced. "Good idea. It's going to be tight to make that flight. See you when I get there, Humphrey."

His next phone call was to the Fiennes residence in York, but there was no response. After the seventh ring, Adam abandoned the attempt and dialled the number assigned to police headquarters in Edinburgh.

"Good afternoon. Sir Adam Sinclair calling. Please put me through to Detective Chief Inspector Noel McLeod."

He did not often invoke his title, but as usual, it got him the desired result.

"Hello, Adam. What can I do for you?" came a gruff, familiar voice.

"Hello, Noel. I've had something rather unusual come up," Adam said. "Are you busy?"

"Not unless you count the usual backlog of paperwork,"

McLeod replied. "Given half an excuse, I'd gladly play hooky for the rest of the afternoon."

"How about a whole excuse, and play hooky tomorrow too?" Adam replied. "I'm afraid that what I have to offer is hardly in the nature of a pleasant diversion, but it *is* police business, and it isn't behind a desk. How good are your contacts down in York?"

Adam heard the muffled squeak of chair springs as McLeod pulled himself upright. "What's happened?"

Briefly Adam outlined the situation as Humphrey had relayed it to him.

"Nathan Fiennes is an old and dear friend," he concluded. "I read philosophy with him when I was down at Cambridge, and we've maintained the friendship ever since. I would have been happy to go to him in any case, but the fact that he's asked for *me* in particular suggests that there may be more to this situation than meets the eye. Your assistance would be welcome on a number of fronts."

"Shouldn't be too difficult," McLeod replied. "If all else fails, I've got some personal leave time coming to me. When were you planning on leaving?"

"I've had Humphrey book seats for us on the four-fifteen flight to Leeds," Adam said. "I realize that's cutting things a bit fine at your end, but the alternative is to drive, which wouldn't put us in much before midnight. I'm not sure Nathan has that much time."

"Don't worry about me," McLeod said sturdily. "How do you want to handle this, logistic-wise?"

"Why don't I meet you there at your office in about half an hour?" Adam said. "Humphrey will be at the airport ahead of us to pick up the tickets. I drove the Jag in this morning, so I'd rather leave it in the police car park than here, if it's going to sit for a few days. If you don't mind, we can take your car from there, and swing by your house on the way to the airport to collect your kit."

"Aye, that ought to streamline things a bit," McLeod agreed. "I'll call Jane and have her pack me a bag. See you when you get here."

Several more phone calls handled the arrangements to

cover Adam's duties at the hospital for the next few days. Then he put a call through to York District Hospital.

"Yes, Dr. Adam Sinclair calling with regard to a patient named Fiennes. He would have been admitted last night for emergency surgery. I expect he's in ICU."

After several transfers of his call, Adam found himself speaking to one of the on-call physicians in intensive care.

"I'm afraid the professor's prognosis is very poor, Dr. Sinclair," the woman concluded. "He was still conscious when he came in last night, but a hematoma developed during the night and we had to go in to relieve it. Unfortunately, he hasn't regained consciousness since the surgery. I wish I could say there was much hope that he will."

"I see," Adam said. "I don't suppose Mrs. Fiennes is there in the ICU, by any chance?"

"No, I don't see her—though I'm sure she hasn't gone far. I think her son finally persuaded her to go down to the hospital cafe for a cup of coffee. She's been here all night, and he came in first thing this morning. Shall I have one of them return your call when they come back?"

"No, I'll be on my way to the airport by then," Adam said. "Just tell Mrs. Fiennes that I've received her message and that I expect to be joining her there at the hospital in a couple of hours. Will you do that? Thank you very much."

CHAPTER TWO

A DAM made the drive across town to police headquarters
in a mood of somber reflection, skirting west of the
castle mound and into Princes Street, then winding up
around Charlotte Square and on along Queensferry Road.
He could not escape the growing conviction that something
beyond a mere burglary and assault lay at the root of what
was now unfolding.

The headquarters complex for the Lothian and Borders
Police Department was a multistorey confection of glass
and steel, bristling with radio antennae on its roofs and set
back from Fettes Avenue, northwest of the city center.
Pulling around into the visitors' car park, within sight of
McLeod's black BMW, Adam parked and locked the dark
blue Jaguar and headed for the main entrance. One of the
officers on duty at the desk recognized him and waved him
on through, rather than asking him to wait for an escort to
come down and fetch him, and he made his way purpose-
fully up a back stair. As he headed through the large
open-plan office toward McLeod's door, which was ajar,
he nodded recognition to several officers working there. He
could hear McLeod's voice through the gap as he approached.

"Yes, thanks, Walter. That's all I can think of at the
moment. Right. We'll talk again when I get there. In the
meantime, thanks for all your trouble."

There followed the click of a telephone receiver being
returned to its cradle, just before Adam gave a light rap at
the door to announce his presence.

"Enter!" McLeod called.

Adam pushed the door open. McLeod was at his desk,
gold-rimmed aviator spectacles pushed up on his forehead

and his tie askew, looking like a man in no mood to
welcome interruptions. As soon as he caught sight of Adam,
however, his expression eased to a grin of welcome, the
wiry grey moustache bristling above a glint of white teeth.

"Hullo, Adam. Sorry about the bark. I thought for a
moment it was one of my confounded juniors determined to
bollix things up at the last minute."

"I take it, then, that you're free and clear?"

"At least for the rest of today and tomorrow," McLeod
said with a grim nod, getting to his feet and reaching for his
coat. "I've just been on the phone to a colleague down in
York, who's going to find out what he can. Someone will
meet us when we arrive. On the surface, at least, it appears
to have been a professional job: household alarm effectively
disabled—safe opened, not blown—no identifiable prints
left anywhere, other than those of the victim and his wife.
There were two perpetrators, but they were wearing balaclava masks and surgical gloves. York Police are still
interviewing possible witnesses in the neighborhood, but
they haven't got any leads. It doesn't look very hopeful at
present."

As he did up his tie, a fresh-faced young man in civilian
clothes appeared in the doorway—Donald Cochrane, one of
McLeod's most able assistants, recently promoted to the
rank of detective.

"Oh, there you are, Donald," McLeod said. "Did you
finally get through?"

Cochrane grinned, just missing a salute. "Yes, sir. Mrs.
McLeod apologizes for tying up the phone, and will have a
bag waiting for you by the time you get there. Anything else
you'd like me to do?"

"Can't think of anything," McLeod replied. "You have
the con till I get back. Keep things ticking over smoothly,
will you? I don't want to come home to find half a dozen
crises on my desk."

"Aye, sir," Cochrane returned with a grin. "See you in
a couple of days."

On the way out to McLeod's house in Ormidale Terrace,
Adam gave the inspector a concise briefing on Nathan
Fiennes' medical condition.

"No wonder Walter and his lads are frantic, down in York," McLeod said when Adam had finished. "A burglary with assault is bad enough, but if the case gets compounded with a murder charge, they're really going to have their work cut out for them."

"If the charges extend to murder," Adam said grimly, "the perpetrators are going to have more than the Yorkshire police to contend with."

They picked up McLeod's bag and made it to the airport in time to rendezvous with Humphrey a good twenty minutes before flight time. The intrepid Humphrey had already checked them in, and handed over tickets and boarding cards along with Adam's overnight bag before bidding them farewell. The flight itself was uneventful, touching down at Leeds-Bradford within a minute or two of its appointed arrival time.

With only carry-on luggage, Adam and McLeod disembarked along with the rest of the passengers and made their way into the arrivals lounge. Here they were intercepted by a short, wiry individual in a dapper three-piece tweed suit and sunglasses. McLeod's look of intense scrutiny transformed immediately into a grin of recognition.

"Hello, Walter!" he exclaimed. "I didn't expect you'd come in person."

His associate shrugged and smiled.

"I figured I might as well, and save time all around. My driver's waiting outside in the car. We can talk on the way back to York. Do you have any luggage?"

"No, just what we're carrying," McLeod replied. "Walter, I'd like you to meet Sir Adam Sinclair, special psychiatric consultant for Lothian and Borders Police. As I mentioned earlier on the phone, he's a longtime close friend of Nathan Fiennes, and Fiennes apparently asked his wife to call Adam, right after the assault. Adam, this is Superintendent Walter Phipps, whose men are following up on the investigation."

"I'm grateful for any assistance you and your men can render, Superintendent," Adam said, taking stock of his new acquaintance as he and the Yorkshireman traded handshakes. Half a head shorter than McLeod, Phipps was lean and active-looking, with short-cropped fair hair and a crisp moustache, both lightly touched with hints of silver. Steady grey eyes returned Adam's gaze with shrewd regard, then crinkled slightly at the edges, as if their owner was favorably impressed by what he saw.

"Your reputation precedes you, Sir Adam," Phipps said with a tight-lipped smile. "And please call me Walter, if you're a friend of Noel's. I seem to recall that you're the man Scotland Yard called in several years ago to construct a psychiatric profile of the man they eventually arrested as the so-called Scarborough Slasher. Nobody looks for a miracle like that to come along every day, but maybe you can come up with some leads in the present case—because I'm afraid we haven't much to go on, so far."

"I'll certainly do whatever I can," Adam promised, as they headed out to the curb and a waiting black Ford Granada. "Right now, however, I'd like to get to the hospital as soon as possible. I gather that Professor Fiennes' prospects are not good, and I'd like at least to *attempt* to speak with him before time runs out."

"Well, I don't know how successful you're going to be in that," Phipps replied, opening the boot so McLeod and Adam could stash their bags. "He was still unconscious when I left York, three-quarters of an hour ago, though at least he was holding his own. It doesn't look good, though." He got into the front, next to the uniformed constable who was driving, and McLeod and Adam piled into the back.

It was twenty-three miles back to York. On the way, Phipps briefed them on the essentials of the case to date. The police car pulled up at the main entrance to York District Hospital shortly before six o'clock. As Adam prepared to get out, Phipps produced a business card from his breast pocket and scribbled some numbers on the back.

"I expect you'll want to be here for a while," Phipps said, handing the card to Adam. "This is the extension at my office, and the other one is my home number. Noel and I will pick up a bite to eat on the way to headquarters, but then we'll be at this number or thereabouts for the rest of the evening. If it gets too late, we may come to check on you. Incidentally, you're both welcome to stay at my place, if you haven't made other arrangements.''

"Thank you," Adam said with a nod. "I'm not sure sleep is in the cards for me tonight, but I'll try to give you a call later this evening, when I know more. See you later, Noel.''

Once inside the building, Adam made his way up to the intensive-care unit. The sister in charge of the ward greeted him with an air of reservation at first, but her manner thawed at once when he produced one of his business cards listing his credentials.

He skimmed over Nathan's chart with growing dismay, returning it with a word of thanks. He was just turning to go into the ICU when a tenor voice hailed him from farther up the corridor.

"Is that Sir Adam Sinclair? Oh, thank God you're here!"

The speaker was Nathan's elder son, Peter, a muscular, dark young man in his mid-thirties, wearing an impeccably cut grey pin-striped suit and round horn-rimmed glasses that made him look studious. After graduating with a first-class law degree from Oxford, Peter Fiennes had gone to work for one of the most prestigious corporation legal firms in London and quickly earned his barrister's credentials. Recent rumor had it that he soon would take silk as a Queen's Counsel. At the moment, however, little in his manner suggested the cool, levelheaded barrister. Instead, he looked tense and grief-stricken and far younger than he was—a man already in mourning for a father whose grasp on life was growing weaker with every passing hour.

He hurried forward to clasp the hand that Adam held out to him, allowing himself to be drawn briefly into an embrace of commiseration. Feeling the tremor in the younger man's shoulders and hand, Adam said quietly, as they drew apart, "Peter, I can't tell you how sorry I am that this should have happened. Naturally, I came as quickly as I could. How's your mother holding up?"

Peter shrugged and shook his head. "She's exhausted; I don't think she's gotten more than an hour or two of sleep while Dad was in surgery early this morning. He's always

meant the world to her. Right now, all she can think about
is that she's losing him. And there doesn't seem to be
anything anyone can do about it.''

"Peter, I'm so sorry," Adam repeated. "How about your
brother? Have you gotten through to him?''

Peter nodded. "He'll be in in a few hours. He's flying in
from Tel Aviv. The orchestra's getting ready to go on tour,
but they drafted the second flute to move up to first. She's
thrilled at the chance, but sorry for the circumstances, of
course—a really nice girl. I hope Larry marries her. Anyway, that means that he'll be able stay as long as—as he has
to.''

"As will I," Adam said quietly. "As long as I'm needed.
Where's your mother just now?''

"Keeping watch over Dad," Peter said, gesturing with
his chin toward the glass-windowed double doors. "She's
hardly left his side since he came back from surgery. Come
with me and I'll take you to her.''

The intensive-care unit, like most facilities of its type,
was a gleaming, antiseptic wilderness of light-panels, con-
soles, and life-support installations. Several of the other
patients confined there had relatives in attendance, in
addition to physicians and nurses circulating among them,
and the big room breathed with the susurrant murmur of
lowered voices above the hum and ping of the electrical
equipment. Adam and Peter drew one or two token glances
as they entered from the corridor, for both were striking-
looking men, in different ways, but it was clear that the
other visitors present were too wrapped up in their own
concerns to pay much heed to what was going on elsewhere
in the unit.

Nathan Fiennes occupied the bed farthest to the left of the
room, his supine, white-draped body wired up to a battery of
monitors. His face beneath the alien white skullcap of
surgical bandages was grey and bruised-looking, more like
the face of an effigy than that of a living man. As Adam
drew closer, he could hear the older man's breath whistling
as it sawed in and out between slack, dry lips. A nasal
oxygen tube of transparent greenish plastic snaked back

over his head to disappear among the orderly tangle of other tubes and wires. Even without a knowledge of what was recorded on Nathan's medical chart, Adam would have known at a glance that his old friend was not likely to recover from his injuries.

Rachel Fiennes was slumped exhaustedly in a chair between her husband's bed and the next, which was empty, her back to the doorway. Her head was bowed, either dozing or praying, but even from across the room, Adam could see the tension in the lines of her body as she clung fast to one of her husband's slack hands. His other hand, confined by a cuff, was connected to an I.V. drip. Together they made a study in tragedy.

Shaking his head sorrowfully, Peter Fiennes went up to his mother and laid a hand lightly on her shoulder. When she started up, he soothed her with a pat and said gently, "It's all right, Mother. Sir Adam's here—just as Dad wanted."

Rachel Fiennes' haggard gaze flew beyond her son to the tall, dark figure standing a few feet behind him, at the foot of her husband's bed, and a tremulous smile touched her lips.

"Adam," she breathed softly. "Thank you so much for coming."

"I only wish it were under happier circumstances," Adam said quietly. "I'm not sure why Nathan asked for me in particular, but now that I'm here, I hope I can be of some service."

Wordlessly Peter Fiennes brought up a chair for Adam beside his mother, then took another for himself on the other side of the bed, facing them. As Adam settled beside Rachel, she reached out to take one of Adam's hands with her free one.

"I can't tell you how relieved I am that you're here, Adam," she whispered. "If only you knew how guilty I've been feeling."

"Guilty?" Adam said. "Whatever for?"

"For not telephoning you sooner," she replied. "Nathan wanted me to call you last night. Right after the incident, before he lost consciousness, he made me promise to call you *at once*. I gave him my word, fully intending to do as he wished, but I could see he was desperately in need of medical attention. My first call was to summon an ambulance and the police, and after that—'' She made a helpless gesture.

"You were doing your best to save your husband's life," Adam said quietly. "You were entirely right to regard everything else as secondary."

"No, I don't think you understand," Rachel insisted. "The thieves, whoever they were, took the Seal—the one that's been in Nathan's family for goodness knows how many generations. You know the piece I'm talking about?"

"Not the one he used to refer to as the Solomon Seal?" Adam said, seeing it in memory and suddenly flashing on a twinge of greater uneasiness.

"Yes, that's the one. I'm sure he must have shown it to you."

Adam nodded. "He did—but that was many years ago. It certainly was very old—though I wouldn't know about it having been Solomon's Seal."

"I don't know that either," Rachel said. "I think it was more than just old, though. I do know that research surrounding it had occupied a great deal of his time and energy, these last few years. And just before he passed out, he said—he said, 'Things about the Seal you don't know— dangerous things. It's *got* to be recovered, at all cost. Call Sir Adam Sinclair and tell him what's happened. . . .'"

"Indeed," Adam said, cocking his head. "Do you know what he was talking about, saying there were dangerous things about the Seal?"

She shook her head.

"I see. Tell me this, then. Do you think the thieves were after the Seal in particular?"

Rachel shook her head again. "I don't know," she said tersely. "If they were, they didn't hesitate to take all my jewellery as well. And they would have been welcome to every gaudy scrap of it, if only they'd left me my Nathan, safe and sound!"

As tears welled up and she stifled a sob, releasing his hand to wipe at her eyes with the back of her hand, Adam took a fresh handkerchief of monogrammed linen from the breast pocket of his suit coat and offered it to her. She nodded her thanks and dabbed at her wet cheeks, sniffling miserably, and Adam exchanged a sympathetic glance with Peter.

"Rachel, from what you've told me," Adam said, "it's obvious that the Seal has acquired a far greater importance of late than it had all those years ago—or at least Nathan had become aware of a greater importance."

As she nodded, he went on.

"The fact that Nathan asked for me, in conjunction with his worry about the Seal's theft, also suggests that he intended me to devote my attention specifically to the problem of locating and recovering it before any harm can result from its theft. I have no idea what kind of harm that might be, but I'll certainly do my best to find out and to carry out his wishes. Tell me: Besides myself, how many people outside the family would have known about the existence of the Seal?"

Rachel gave him a blank look and turned to her son for inspiration. Shaking his head, Peter gave a helpless shrug.

"I suppose that any number of people might have known *something* about it," he said. "Dad's never been a particularly secretive man. If you're talking about anyone having specific knowledge—"

"How about *recent* and specific knowledge," Adam prompted, "perhaps in the last year or so?"

Peter grimaced and sighed. "I suppose I ought to give you some recent background first, then," he said. "Since Dad showed you the Seal, he probably also told you that it's always been something of a family mystery. When I was little, my grandfather used to tell me stories about how the Seal used to belong to the royal house of Israel, and how it had the power to stamp out evil spirits. You know the kinds of tales that grown-ups sometimes tell kids, to embellish."

Adam nodded, his face impassive, but the mention of evil spirits had triggered a new apprehension.

"Anyway," Peter went on, "over the years, Dad had been trying to find out more about the Seal—probably sparked by the tales *his* grandfather had told him when *he* was a boy. It started out as a kind of academic game, I think—and you know how tenacious he can be when he gets his teeth into a research project—but a new factor entered the equation about eighteen months ago."

"What happened eighteen months ago?" Adam asked.

"Well, Grandfather Benjamin died. It wasn't unexpected— he was eighty-seven, and he went in his sleep, like *that*." He snapped his fingers. "After the funeral, Dad went up to the old house in Perth to clear away the last of Grandfather's personal effects. While he was about it, he came across a whole chest full of old family papers stored in the attic. Among them was a really battered old parchment document. It was badly yellowed, and the writing was faded brown with age, practically illegible, but Dad was able to make out enough to tell that it was in Latin, and seemed to refer to a seal of some kind."

"The Solomon Seal?" Adam asked.

"So he believed. The possibility was enough to make him drop everything and head across to St. Andrews University to see if anyone in the medieval history department could decipher it for him. The document turned out to be a promissory note for a bronze seal pledged in pawn to one Reuben Fennes of Perth, by somebody named James Graeme, dated 1381!"

He directed an inquiring look at Adam, as if inviting comment, but Adam only shook his head.

"This is all news to me," he said. "I gather, by your expectation, that the Seal had been pawned for a substantial sum."

"I'll say," Peter replied. "It was practically a duke's ransom. The figure cited was so extraordinary that Dad was keen to find out who this James Graeme might have been, and why the Seal should have been worth that much money to our distant forebear."

"And did he?"

"That, I don't know," Peter said. "It was about that time, however, that he started seriously ferreting through all manner of medieval archives, not only in the U.K. but also on the Continent. It got to be quite an operation. I'm sure he must have used research assistants to help him sift through some of the documentary material. Isn't that right, Mother?''

"Oh, yes," Rachel agreed. "There have been several dozen, over the years. He loved to involve his students in his work."

Adam smiled. "I can attest to that. Tell me, do you suppose you might be able to draw up a list for me?"

"Dear me, you don't think—"

"Unfortunately, it's far too soon to tell you what I think," Adam said easily. "A list of people who know about the Seal is a good place to start, though. Peter, do you think you might be able to give your mother a hand?"

Peter shook his head. "I don't have any direct knowledge, Adam, but maybe Dad's personal notes would give us some clues. They should be locked up in his desk at home, shouldn't they, Mother?"

Rachel's face brightened. "Yes, of course," she said. "And fortunately, the thieves didn't tamper with the desk."

She might have said more, but at that moment, the injured man in the bed stirred and groaned aloud.

CHAPTER THREE

INSTANTLY attentive, Adam and the others leaned in toward the bed. Nathan Fiennes stirred again. His bruised eyelids fluttered, then opened a painful chink, the gaze wandering unfocused.

"Rachel?" he muttered hoarsely.

Suppressing a small sob, his wife bent down and clasped his hand more closely. "I'm right here, Nathan. So is Peter. Larry's going to be arriving shortly. And Adam—Adam Sinclair. You asked me to call him."

A crooked smile touched the injured man's bluish lips. "All here," he mumbled drowsily. "That's good. Always nice when the boys come home for the holidays. . . ."

Rachel directed a wordless look of dismay toward Adam, who said softly, "This is not unexpected, I'm afraid. It's very common in the case of head injuries for the patient's memory to wander."

"Is there anything you can do to help him focus?" Peter asked. "He was so adamant that Mother call you."

Considering, Adam gave a cautious nod. "It's just possible that he might respond to hypnosis, that he's at least partially aware of his surroundings."

"Yes, but would it work in a case like this?" Peter wondered. "The surgeon says there's been localized brain damage."

"Let me answer your question with yet another question," Adam said. "Do you believe that your father has an immortal soul?"

The query brought Peter up short. He gave a blink, then said, "Yes. Yes, I do."

"Then believe me," said Adam, "when I tell you that the

33

true seat of memory lies there, in the realm of the spirit, not in the perishable physiochemical structures of the brain.''

Even as he spoke, the man in the bed heaved a heavy sigh.

''Sure hope this flu passes off soon,'' he murmured, his head moving restlessly from side to side. ''Promised the boys we'd drive up to Perth . . . all go camping. . . .''

Rachel lifted her head, her expression one of anguished tenderness. ''He's talking about an incident that happened nearly twenty years ago,'' she said softly. ''You remember, don't you, Peter?''

Her son nodded without speaking.

''Those were happy times,'' Rachel said, her voice quivering on the edge of a break. ''He's there now, in memory. Do we have the right to call him back to the present—to the pain, and the realization that he's almost certainly dying?''

''That's your decision, of course,'' Adam said quietly. ''But given the apparent urgency of his request that I should come, I'd like to at least try to question him. I promise you that nothing I intend will harm your husband in any way, either physically or spiritually. Indeed, it may even be possible to alleviate some of his pain, make him a bit more comfortable.''

There was a moment's silence, broken only by Nathan's labored murmurings as his mind wandered aimlessly about its chambers of memories. Then Rachel drew a deep breath and squared her shoulders with an air of decision, her hand tightening on her husband's.

''Forgive me, Adam. I wasn't thinking of Nathan's wishes. He's always trusted you. You must do what you think best. Were I to interfere with this last confidence he wanted to impart to you, I would be less than true to the trust he and I have shared for most of a lifetime.''

Adam smiled gently and patted her hand. ''Thank you, Rachel. I know that was not an easy decision. Do you think you and Peter could give me a few minutes alone with him? This is going to require maximum concentration on my part, and the fewer distractions, the better.''

"I think a breath of fresh air might be exactly what Mother and I need," Peter said, getting to his feet. "Maybe something to eat as well. Can we bring you anything, Adam? A cup of coffee, maybe? Tea?"

Adam shook his head as he stood. "Not just now, thank you. Give me twenty or thirty minutes, would you?"

"Of course."

As mother and son left the ICU together, arm in arm, Adam moved closer to the head of the bed and casually drew the curtain partway between Nathan's bed and the rest of the room, thus shielding them from casual observation by the family gathered two beds down around an unconscious older woman. Nathan was still vaguely conscious, if rambling, but there was no telling when he might lapse back into coma. Adam knew he had to act with dispatch or risk losing what might be his one and only chance to question Nathan and learn whatever it was that the old man wanted him to know.

His action had drawn no untoward attention from the nurses tending patients at the other end of the room. After making an understated show of checking Nathan's pulse and glancing at the readings on the life-support monitors, he reached into the inside breast pocket of his suit coat and unclipped a small, pencil-sized flashlight. For a quick trance induction, its beam would catch and hold Nathan's wandering attention far better than the usual, more indirect focus of his pocket watch, and also be less conspicuous.

Leaning in close over the bed, he turned Nathan's face gently toward him and directed the light first at one pupil, then at the other, beginning a rhythmic oscillation between the two.

"Nathan," he called softly. "It's Adam Sinclair. Listen to me, Nathan. Would you look at me, please?"

The injured man's distracted gaze slowly gravitated toward the light and the sound of Adam's voice. He blinked twice, then focused with an effort on the strong face beyond the moving light.

"Adam. . . . It *is* you, isn't it?" he mumbled with a fleeting attempt at a smile. "Always a pleasure to see you.

My, but you're getting grey—but I suppose medical school does that to a man. What can I do for you?"

"Nothing terribly difficult, Nathan. I've come to help you." Adam's voice deepened slightly as he went on. "I want you to relax. If you can manage it, I'd very much like you to look at the light I'm holding in my hand. Can you see it?" He continued to move it back and forth, flashing it first in one eye, then the other.

"That's good. Just relax, my friend. Listen to my voice and follow the light. Back and forth . . . that's right. Relax. Listen to my voice and feel yourself starting to float. Very relaxed. That's good, Nathan. Tell me, how do you feel?"

Nathan's pale lips twitched, his eyelids starting to droop as he continued to track the moving light.

"No too well," he murmured. "Head hurts damnably. Flu, I think. . . ."

"No, it isn't flu," Adam said softly, his voice taking on a soothing, singsong lilt. "But I think we can do something about the discomfort. Imagine that the pain in your head is like a hat that's on too tight. Imagine yourself taking the hat off and putting it to one side. Once you've taken it off, the pain will ease up and your mind will be clear. It will be like floating on a quiet pool—no noise, no trouble, only peace. Take off the hat, Nathan. . . ."

He waited a moment, watching Nathan's taut face. After a few heartbeats, the trembling eyelids closed and the lines of pain and stress began to smooth out.

"That's good, Nathan," Adam murmured, switching off his light and returning it to his breast pocket. "The pain is gone. You're very relaxed. Tell me, are you floating now?"

"Yes . . . floating. . . ."

"Very good," Adam said. Dropping his voice till it was scarcely louder than a whisper, he said, "Nathan, I want you to picture something in your mind's eye—a familiar object. It's a bronze seal engraved with the star of Solomon. Can you see it?"

"Yes."

"I knew you could. Nathan, there was something you

wanted to tell me about this Seal, something you were having trouble remembering. I'm taking hold of your wrist, and I'm going to count backwards from five to one. When I reach the end of the count, I'll give your wrist a tap. At that moment, the clouds will lift from your memory and you'll be able to recall the message you wanted to convey to me. Are you ready? Five . . . four . . . three . . . two . . . *one.*"

He tapped Nathan's wrist lightly just below the base of his thumb. The old man did not respond at first, but then, all at once, his whole body stiffened. The eyes opened, but what they saw was not Adam or the room beyond.

"The treasure of the Temple!" he rasped hoarsely. "The Seal guards the secret. Adam, it *has* to be recovered, do you hear me? The Seal *has* to be recovered!"

Adam tightened his clasp reassuringly about the older man's wrist, his other hand brushing soothingly across the forehead. "I hear you, Nathan, but I don't yet follow you. What does the Seal guard? What secret? What treasure? And what Temple?"

"Solomon's treasure," Nathan murmured, "from the Temple in Jerusalem. The Seal came from there . . . part of a sacred trust. Great power and great danger . . . royal legacy of the House of David."

Beneath his calm exterior, Adam's mind began to work furiously. What Nathan seemed to be hinting was that the missing Seal was, in fact, the legendary Seal of Solomon himself! Tradition had always ascribed to Solomon power and authority over evil spirits, and Adam found himself wondering if some measure of that controlling influence might have been vested in this Seal of which they were speaking. If that was so, there might well be some who would be willing to steal and even kill to obtain it.

"Nathan, what was the purpose of the Seal?" he asked softly. "Do you know?"

"It was a key," Nathan whispered. "A key to keep a deadly evil locked away from the rest of the world. But the Seal is only part of the secret. I think . . . the Knights knew. . . . The Knights of the Temple knew. . . ."

"The Knights of the Temple?" Adam repeated. "You mean, the Knights Templar?"

Nathan drew a labored breath, nodding weakly. "So I believe. The Seal came in pledge. . . . Pawned to my ancestor . . . 1381 . . . Graeme of Templegrange. . . ."

The significance of the name was not lost on Adam. The appearance of the word "temple" in many a Scottish place name generally indicated that the site had once been associated with the Knights of the Temple of Jerusalem. Indeed, the Templars figured prominently in Adam's own family history. The ruined tower of Templemor, now being restored on a hilltop overlooking Strathmourne Manor, had once been a Templar outpost.

"Then, you think the Templars guarded this secret?" Adam asked.

"I think so. . . . Many connections," Nathan whispered, his breathing starting to quicken. "I was getting so close. . . . Try Dundee. . . . Dundee may provide more of the answers. . . ."

Nathan's voice broke on the last word, and his pulse suddenly gave an irregular, ominous flutter beneath Adam's fingers. In the same heartbeat, the gauges on the monitors beside him came alive with blips and warning lights as the old man's pulse rate soared. As if sensing that his body was nearing the limits of its endurance, Nathan made a struggling attempt to raise his head off his pillow.

"Find the Seal!" he muttered hoarsely. "Stop those who stole it! The evil they can loose. . . . Adam, you must stop them! Please, Adam, for the love of God. . . ."

"I understand, Nathan," Adam said in a tone of quiet authority, gently pressing him back against the pillows and trying to calm him. "That's enough for now. I'll do what must be done. You've told me what I need to know. Stop fighting now and relax. Stop struggling and be at peace. This need not concern you any more."

Under the influence of his voice and the stroke of a soothing hand across his brow, Nathan's agitation gradually subsided. His pulse rate slowed, though it remained very weak, and the monitor readings somewhat stabilized, but his condition clearly was deteriorating. Nathan had not much time, and Adam knew he must try to ready the way for the soul's passing.

"You're doing just fine now, Nathan," he continued softly, as nurses and an ICU physician converged on them and he fended them off with a glance and a shake of his head. "Let go all thoughts of the Seal. Let go all thoughts of strife. Feel yourself floating without pain now on a tranquil stream. Feel the pull of a gentle current carrying you backwards in time. Somewhere in the past a safe haven is waiting to receive you—a place of gentleness and peace and joy. Find a moment of your own choosing, and say to that moment, *Stay*. . . . And there abide in peace until the door opens into Light. . . ."

"*Light . . . ,*" came Nathan's faint and unexpected whisper, hardly more than a sigh.

"Yes, Nathan," Adam murmured, heartened to have gotten any response at all, and suddenly aware what final thing he still might do, that would mean much to his old friend. "The Light will embrace you and hold you safe. Listen to me now, and try to repeat what I say. This is very important. You taught me yourself. If you can't speak the words, then offer them up in the temple of your own heart. *Shema Yisrael.*"

Nathan's eyelids fluttered, and his hand tightened slightly in Adam's.

"*Shema . . . Yisrael . . .*"

"*Adonai Elohenu.*"

"*Adonai Elohenu . . .*"

"*Adonai Echad.*"

"*Adonai . . . Echad. . . .*"

Nathan Fiennes slipped gently back into a coma shortly thereafter, and did not rouse a second time. Though apparently in no discomfort, his vital signs became more and more depressed as the evening wore on. His physicians held out little hope that he would last the night.

His son Lawrence arrived shortly after ten o'clock, white-faced and anxious, fetched from the airport by Superintendent Phipps and McLeod, the latter of whom remained at the hospital to wait for Adam. Nathan lingered until just before midnight, surrounded by his wife and sons and the friend he had called both to witness his passing and to carry out his final wishes. Adam watched over his old friend's bedside like a knight keeping vigil at the altar, bowing his head when, at the end, a grieving Lawrence pulled a small prayer book from his pocket and began to read, beginning in Hebrew and then shifting to lightly accented English.

"*Shema Yisrael, Adonai Elohenu, Adonai Echad*. Hear, O Israel, the Lord is our God, the Lord is One. . . . Go, since the Lord sends thee; go, and the Lord will be with thee; the Lord God is with him, and he will ascend."

As Lawrence intoned the exhortation twice more, his voice choking toward the end, Peter reached across and gently took the prayer book from him, continuing to read as Adam quietly slipped an arm around the shoulders of the younger son in comfort.

"May the Lord bless thee and keep thee," Peter read. "May the Lord let His countenance shine upon thee, and be gracious unto thee. May the Lord lift up His countenance upon thee, and give thee peace. At thy right hand is Michael, at thy left is Gabriel. . . ."

Adam lifted his head at the recitation of the angelic names, for though the order was slightly different, the calling of the four archangels was common to his own tradition.

"Before thee is Uriel, and behind thee is Raphael, and above thy head is the divine presence of God," Peter went on. "The angel of the Lord encampeth round about them that fear Him, and He delivereth them. Be strong and of good courage; be not affrighted, neither be thou dismayed; for the Lord thy God is with thee whithersoever thou goest. . . ."

When it was over, Adam spoke briefly with the attending physician, who had slipped in beside him during the final moments to watch helplessly as the life-support monitors faded, then joined McLeod in the corridor outside, to give the family a few minutes alone with their grief.

"He's gone, then?" McLeod said, as Adam appeared, his tie loosened and his suit coat over one shoulder.

Adam nodded, his expression somber. "I don't suppose one could wish for a gentler passing, under the circumstances. It was premature, though. He should have been allowed another decade or two, to see his grandchildren well grown and to carry on his research."

"Well, we'll see if we can't find those responsible," McLeod said. "Did you find out more about this stolen Seal?"

Adam glanced back at the glass-windowed double doors leading into the ICU.

"Yes, I did; and Nathan's urgency apparently was well founded." His expression was grave as he drew McLeod farther along the corridor from the nurses' station, where they would not be overheard.

"I'm afraid Nathan was out of his depth," he said quietly. "I wish he'd come to me sooner, but I doubt he really knew what he had. He had come to believe that the Seal guarded a treasure or a secret somehow connected with King Solomon and the Temple in Jerusalem. I'm left with the distinct impression that it kept something powerful and dangerous locked away—whether in Jerusalem or someplace closer to home, I couldn't begin to guess. The Knights Templar figure in the story somehow, perhaps as guardians of the Seal. According to his son, Nathan has a document from the late fourteenth century that's a promissory note for money borrowed against the Seal by someone called James Graeme. Nathan referred to him as Graeme of Templegrange."

"Sounds like a Templar place name, all right," McLeod rumbled. "But isn't that a little late for Templars?"

"Aye, at least half a century late," Adam agreed. "But don't forget that the papal decree dissolving the Order was never publicly proclaimed in Scotland. Even in England, it was months before the authorities made a halfhearted attempt to enforce the decree. This James Graeme could have been a Templar, or a descendant—and Templegrange certainly suggests a former Templar connection of his estate, just like Templemor.''

"But what would Templars be doing with the Seal of Solomon?" McLeod asked.

"Maybe they brought it with them from Jerusalem, when they moved their headquarters to Paris," Adam said lightly. "I don't know. For that matter, I don't know that it's actually Solomon's Seal. He also mentioned Dundee, and I also don't know what connection the Templars had with that. I never had the impression that their holdings were extensive in that area, but I never had reason to investigate specifically, either. I know a lot about Templemor, of course; and there's the village of Temple, down by Gore-bridge, which used to be the main Templar preceptory for Scotland. I don't think there's much left standing, though—''

He broke off as a shaken-looking Peter Fiennes came out of the ICU, glancing in their direction and then heading toward them.

"There you are," Peter said. "I wasn't sure where you'd gotten to. You must be Inspector McLeod," he added, offering his hand to McLeod, who shook it. "Thank you for coming along with Adam.''

"I only hope I can help your local police find the culprits," McLeod said. "I'm very sorry for your loss, Mr. Fiennes. I wish I'd known your father. I've heard Adam speak of him often, and in glowing terms.''

"You're very kind," Peter said, obviously restraining his emotions only with an effort. He returned his gaze to Adam and drew a fortifying breath. "Adam, if you and the inspector haven't made other plans, I'd be very grateful if you'd both come and stay at my mother's house tonight. You'd have to share a room, I'm afraid, but I'd feel better if you're there for her in the morning, when some of the shock begins to wear off.''

Adam glanced at McLeod, who gave a sober nod.

"Whatever you think best, Adam. We have an offer from Walter as well, but it sounds like you might be needed more with Mrs. Fiennes.''

"If you're sure it won't be an imposition," Adam said to Peter. "You'll have heavy family obligations in the next few days. I wouldn't want to intrude."

"It's no intrusion, believe me," Peter replied. "Besides, if you stay at the house, you can start going through Father's papers first thing in the morning. One always feels so helpless at a time like this. At least maybe something in his notes will help with the police investigation."

CHAPTER FOUR

T HEY were at Nathan's files shortly after ten the next morning, following a substantial breakfast served up by Peter's wife. Rachel was still asleep, thanks to the light sedative Adam had persuaded her to take the night before, and her younger son, Lawrence, had assumed responsibility for arranging the funeral, which would take place the following morning. As the house began to buzz with the bustle of callers coming to offer their condolences downstairs, Peter conducted Adam and McLeod up to Nathan's study and gave them a quick briefing on the general form of his father's research notes.

"There're these two boxes of index cards," Peter said, thumping the two green file boxes on the desktop, "and then there's three—no, *four* hard-backed notebooks." He pulled these from a bottom desk drawer and slapped them down beside the boxes. Nathan had kept the notebooks in ballpoint pen, and the pen's impression on the thin paper had made the pages bulge slightly from between the grey marbleized covers.

"Here's some more stuff," Peter went on, pulling out a slim stack of file folders and large manila envelopes. "One of these ought to be—yes: photos of the Seal. I knew these were around here somewhere. He sent me one, years ago, and I used to keep it thumbtacked to my bulletin board at college. Of course, I had no idea how old it was, in those days. Neither did Dad, I suppose."

Adam glanced at the photo Peter held out, gesturing for him to show it to McLeod, and picked up one of the notebooks at random, riffling experimentally through its pages.

"At least it looks like he kept his notes in plain English,"

44

he observed. "I was half-afraid we might find ourselves having to grapple with some kind of personal cipher."

"Well, there may be something worse than that," Peter said, delving into another desk drawer and lifting out a very compact laptop computer. "I know he'd started using this the last couple of years. I'd be willing to bet that most of the recent material is in here."

As he set it on a clear spot on the desk, McLeod positioned his aviator spectacles more squarely on his nose and gestured toward the chair before the desk.

"May I?" he asked, also including the machine in his gesture.

"Of course."

Sitting, McLeod opened the screen and turned the computer on. A series of standard commands got the system booted up and running, and finally produced a directory listing such intriguing headings as *Britmus, Dundee, Resasst,* and *Tmplgrng,* but it also demanded a password to gain further access.

"I don't suppose you know what your father's password was for these files?" McLeod asked Peter, as he tried, first, SEAL and then SOLOMON and failed to get in.

Peter shook his head. "I'm afraid I don't. It's possible Mother might know, but I doubt it."

"Well, I don't know about Noel," Adam said, "but I'm afraid my computer skills aren't up to hacking into protected files without some expert assistance. Would you mind if we take this away with us, Peter?"

"Not at all, if you think it will help," he said. "Good Lord, that must be maddening, to know there's possibly useful material there, and not be able to get at it." He glanced at the boxes and notebooks. "Do you think these will be any help?"

"We'll have a quick scan through them and see," Adam said, as McLeod shut down the computer and closed its screen. "Meanwhile, if you want to go and see if your mother has stirred yet, or your brother needs help—"

"I can take a hint," Peter said with an awkward smile.

"I'll leave you two at it. Let me know if I can help you with anything else."

When Peter had gone, closing the study door behind him, Adam pulled another chair closer and resumed his perusal of the least thumbed of the notebooks. McLeod had already shifted his attention to the first file box, and was flipping through the cards in it.

"What do you think?" Adam said.

McLeod shook his head. "It isn't going to be easy. This is right out of my league."

"You may surprise yourself," Adam said. "What have you got?"

"Well, these appear to be bibliographical references," McLeod replied. "He's got books, articles, manuscripts, and other miscellaneous documents, mostly about biblical archaeology and a lot on the Knights Templar and the Crusades. A good many of the citations seem to come from libraries on the Continent.

"Ah, now, this may prove interesting," he said, pulling out a card and holding its place with a finger as he tilted the card toward the light from the window. "Look here, in the lower right-hand corner. Would you say those are initials? Maybe the initials of the researcher who made the citation?"

Adam glanced over at what he was doing and gave a nod.

"That would be my guess. Are there many different sets?"

Returning the card to its place and fingering farther along the stack, McLeod made an affirmative grunt.

"Looks like there could be a dozen or so. The entries themselves have been typed on a variety of machines, apparently over quite a span of time. Some of these cards look pretty old and dog-eared. Shall I try to pull a list of initials?"

"Yes, and it wouldn't hurt to see if you can match any of them to names in Nathan's address book, if we can find that," Adam replied, setting aside the notebook he had been looking at and leaning in to open the desk drawer. As he bent to peer inside, feeling toward the back among the untidy piles of envelopes and index cards, McLeod conducted the same sort of search in the drawers on the left.

The elusive address book turned up in the top drawer on the right. Adam flipped through it briefly, illogically hoping that a name would pique his attention, then handed it to McLeod.

"See what you can do with that," he said, picking up the stack of notebooks. "If you can come up with a list of initials in the next hour or two, I'll ask Peter to have a look at it when we break for lunch. Meanwhile, the address book may provide some preliminary guesses."

As McLeod moved a yellow pad closer and pulled a pen from an inside coat pocket, Adam took the stack of notebooks over to an armchair nearer the window, where he settled down for a serious read. The most recent one had only half a dozen entries, mainly having to do with background on seals similar to the one until recently in Nathan's possession. Apparently Nathan had recently received confirmation of his own Seal's antiquity.

Prepared for a long and probably fruitless search, Adam set the notebook aside and picked up the next most recent one. As he flipped to the end, intending to work backwards from the material he had already read, the notebook fell open to a letter-folded piece of paper tucked snugly into the crease of the binding. It proved to be a photocopy of a letter from a Dr. Albrecht Steiner, in the art history department of the Sorbonne, to someone named Henri Gerard at a Paris address. It was dated the previous March.

"Noel, do the initials 'H.G.' appear on any of your cards?" Adam asked, as he skimmed over the typewritten French with growing interest.

"Yes, quite a few," McLeod replied. "What have you got?"

"A copy of a letter to a Henri Gerard from the Sorbonne," Adam replied. "It appears to be a report on a metal sample taken from Nathan's Seal and sent to their labs for—well, now."

McLeod looked up. "What does it say?"

"Well, unless my French has totally failed me, the man

who wrote this letter dates the piece from around 950 B.C.—what's known as the First Temple Period. He apparently was working from detailed photographs of the Seal. And listen to this,'' he said, translating. "Chemical analysis of the sample provided is compatible with bronze samples taken from the prehistoric mineworks at Tell el-Kheleifeh, more popularly know as King Solomon's Mines.''

"King Solomon's Mines?'' McLeod repeated. "Adam, do you think the stolen Seal really *is* the Seal of Solomon?''

Adam shook his head. "I wouldn't go that far, based on the evidence I've seen so far. But I wouldn't rule out the possibility, either. I wonder what other intriguing tidbits we're going to find. Oh, Nathan, I wish you could have told me more about what's going on. . . .''

They carried on with their research for the remainder of the morning, until Peter Fiennes came to summon them downstairs for lunch. Lawrence had gone to the airport with Peter's wife to collect Nathan's sister and her family, so they were only four at table.

"What can you tell me about Henri Gerard?'' Adam asked, over green salad and grilled cheese sandwiches washed down with a crisp Riesling. "I gather that he was one of your father's researchers.''

Peter exchanged a glance with his mother, who was looking reassuringly composed as she settled into her first full day of widowhood.

"What makes you ask about *him*?'' Peter replied.

"Just that I found a copy of a letter to him. Apparently he had lab tests run on a metal sample taken from the Seal.''

He showed the letter around while he related the general findings of the report.

"Aside from the information being very interesting, though, it's the name that interests me,'' he said, as he took the letter back. "Henri Gerard is the first name we've come up with, who we know is connected with Nathan's research. Noel has compiled a list of initials he'd like you to look at, after you've finished lunch, to see if you can assign names. We suspect they're other researchers who have worked with your father, and the police will probably want to talk to some of them, to start forming a profile of who might have wanted to steal the Seal.''

''Well, I can't imagine any of them would be involved in something like that,'' Peter said. ''Gerard's a little older than most of the assistants Father worked with, over the years—a bit of an eccentric, in the manner of many dedicated scholars, but I'm sure he's harmless.''

''He probably is,'' Adam replied. ''How did he and your father meet?''

Peter gave a halfhearted shrug. ''Gerard spent a sabbatical here a couple of years ago, right after a team of archaeologists uncovered a previously unknown burial ground in the medieval Jewish quarter of the city. At the time, he was pursuing some crackpot theory that the Knights Templar had been making an in-depth study of Jewish necromancy. That's what I meant by 'eccentric,''' he added at Adam's look of surprise. ''The trial of the Templars is his area of special expertise. He was hoping the grave sites might yield up some support for his theory. He needed some help with some Hebrew translations, so the site supervisor put him onto my father.''

''*Was* there evidence of Jewish necromancy?'' Adam asked.

''Of course not. So far as I know, that research never came to anything. But he got interested in what Dad was doing, that summer he was here, and he sort of became Dad's continental contact for tracking down obscure references. I know he has access to parts of the Vatican Archives that most people can't get at. Can't tell you much more about him, though.''

''Well, that's probably sufficient on him for now,'' Adam said, glancing at McLeod. ''How about taking a look at Noel's list of initials, and seeing if you can supply us with some more names?''

''Sure. Let's see,'' he said, turning his attention to the list McLeod passed him. ''Ah, 'N.G.' That would be Nina Gresham. She was a dear. She did a Ph.D. under Dad's supervision a couple of years ago. I think she's at some private institute in Italy now. She isn't Jewish, but her Hebrew is almost as good as Dad's. I don't know where she picked it up. She has six or eight ancient languages. Works with documents from the time of the Crusades.''

"What about this 'T.B.'?''

"That would be Tevye Berman. He's Israeli, was working on a dig in Jerusalem near the site of the old Temple. A good guy. I think he's dead now, though.''

"And 'M.O.'?''

"Couldn't tell you.''

"How about 'K.S.'?''

"Karen Slater, maybe. Or it could be Keith Sherman. They've both worked for Dad, over the years.''

In the next quarter hour, Peter Fiennes was able to assign names to almost all of the initials McLeod had gleaned from the file cards, with his mother supplying a few he had not known. After coffee, Adam and McLeod went back upstairs to continue their research and leave the family their privacy.

Most of the names matched those McLeod had been able to glean from Nathan's address book, compiled on a second list with addresses and telephone numbers. The ones that matched, McLeod ticked and copied onto a master list, while Adam continued to read in Nathan's notebooks. By four, when it was clear that McLeod had done about all he could at this end, he rang Walter Phipps at York Police headquarters to arrange for transportation to the airport for the 5:50 flight back to Edinburgh.

"There's really no point in my hanging around here for the funeral, since I didn't know your Nathan,'' he said, when he had made the call. "I can probably do a whole lot more from home. When Walter collects me, I'll give him this copy of the names and addresses of the research assistants, and let his lads follow up on the conventional aspects of the case. Meanwhile, I'll have a go at cracking those computer files tonight.''

"That might save us some time,'' Adam agreed. "There's nothing in the last notebook since spring, so it's quite possible that some of his recent correspondence is in there—anything that might give us a clue what we're up against. What about this Henri Gerard? Am I grasping at straws, just because Peter said he was a bit eccentric, or do you think he figures in the case? There *is* a Templar connection.''

McLeod sat back in his chair and pulled off his glasses with a sigh, to massage the bridge of his nose.

''I think he may be a player, Adam. Call it a cop's sixth sense, if you like, but to use a cop term I picked up in the States, there's something 'hinky' about him.''

''You think so too, eh?''

''Good, then. I'm glad it isn't just me,'' McLeod said. ''When I get back, I'm going to make a couple of calls to Paris. My friend Treville at the Sûreté owes me a favor or two. I'd like to see whether he knows anything about our man.''

He replaced his glasses and put the lids back on the two file boxes, then pushed them farther toward the back of the desk. ''You planning to catch the same flight tomorrow night?''

Adam nodded. ''The funeral's at eleven, so the timing's just about perfect. A lot of people will be coming back to the house afterwards, so I shouldn't have any trouble getting someone to run me to the airport. If you could call Humphrey and alert him when you get back, I'd appreciate it.''

''Will do.''

When McLeod had gone off with Phipps, Adam returned to join the Fiennes family for the soothing and civilized ritual of afternoon tea, made more formal by the subdued clothing and conversation of those partaking. Members of the Fiennes clan had been arriving all afternoon, from far-flung corners of the world, and Rachel and Risa, Peter's wife, were diverting their sorrow by catering to their guests. After tea, to give the family some privacy, Adam took himself off for a walk into the ancient city of York, with notice to Peter that he would find his own evening meal. He needed time to assimilate what he had been reading, and space apart for an hour or two, to deal with his personal sorrow at Nathan's passing.

His meanderings soon took him into the grounds and then the rear entrance of the cathedral, which was in the midst of Evensong. Especially drawn by this offering of thanksgiving and praise after the sorrow of the past twenty-four hours, he slipped inside and sat listening quietly in the back, for he did not wish to intrude on the service in progress. Heard down the length of the great nave, the pure sound of the boys' voices floated poignant and sweet. As Adam settled back to actually listen to what they were singing, he realized that they could not have chosen better, had they known that they marked the passing of Nathan Fiennes.

"Remember, Lord, how short life is,
How frail you have made all flesh.
Who can live and not see death?
Who can save himself from the power of the grave . . . ?"

Much moved, Adam slipped to his knees and offered up a silent prayer of thanksgiving for the life of Nathan Fiennes, knowing that his old friend would not mind that it was given in a Christian place of worship. The actual words of the scripture readings that followed did not carry well to where he was seated, so he let the drone of the reader's voice simply carry him deeper into communion with the All. After a while, kneeling there with his eyes closed, he found the image of Nathan's Seal before him in his mind's eye, dispelled only when the choir began to sing the *Nunc dimittis*. "Lord, now lettest Thou Thy servant depart in peace, according to Thy word. . . ." That, too, was a fitting farewell to his old friend.

After the service was over, Adam lingered for a little while to savor the beauty of the cathedral, strolling up as far as the transept to crane his neck backwards and gaze up at the soaring vault of the lantern tower, the largest of its kind in England. Shortly thereafter, vergers began quietly herding visitors toward the door, so he drifted outside to mount the city wall at Bootham Bar and stroll along its esplanade, gazing out over the city by the light of the dying day.

After tea so late in the afternoon, he did not feel like

eating dinner, so he returned to the Fiennes residence at about half past nine and, after inquiring whether there was any way he could assist the family, declared his intention to head up to bed for a proper night's sleep after the short hours of the night before. Before retiring, however, he paused at the phone in a niche at the foot of the stairs to make a brief call to McLeod.

"Hullo, Noel," he said without preamble, when McLeod himself answered. "I know you've only been home a few hours, but any progress?"

"None on Gerard," McLeod replied, "though I did talk to Treville. He's supposed to get back to me sometime tomorrow. I had some luck with Nathan's computer, though. Have you got a minute?"

"What did you find?"

"Well, he's got some very interesting files in here," McLeod said. Adam could hear the gentle click of the keyboard as McLeod called up material on his screen to refer to it. "A lot of it is diary-type entries, probably similar to what you were reading in the notebooks, but he's got some actual transcripts and translations of some of his documents as well. Do you want to hear some of this?"

"Give me a sampling," Adam replied, pulling a notepad closer and taking out a pen. "I don't want to tie up this line too long, in case relatives are trying to get through to the family, but it might give me something to work on while I sleep. I don't know about you, but I'm exhausted after last night's late hours."

"So am I," McLeod agreed, to the accompaniment of more keys clicking. "I nodded off on the flight home, slept right through the landing. I've never done that before. Anyway, I'm looking at a chain of references that appears to link the Templars with our Graeme of Templegrange, who pawned the Seal. A minor demesne called Templegrange is mentioned in a letter of 1284 from King Alexander III to the Bishop of Dunkeld. The wording leaves it uncertain whether Templegrange belongs to the King or the bishop, but Nathan cites later evidence suggesting that the property was probably a minor Templar commandery at the time of the Order's dissolution in 1314. The Order had a lot of land in Scotland, as you know.''

"Yes, Templemor has a similar history," Adam said, jotting down notes. "Go on.''

"A little later on, Nathan references a grant of lands by Robert the Bruce to a Sir James Graeme of Perthshire, in gratitude for support given to the King at the Battle of Bannockburn the previous year. There's no transcription of the document itself, but even I remember that Bannockburn was also 1314. After that, something else is obviously missing, but Nathan somehow makes the connection that Templegrange was the particular land granted to Sir James Graeme, and concludes that this same Sir James may have been an ancestor of the Graeme of Templegrange who pawned the Seal in 1381. Have you got all that?''

"It seems like a straightforward chain of logic, if it's all supportable," Adam replied. "The important thing is the Templar connection—though we'd supposed that, from the name Templegrange.''

"There's more," McLeod continued, "and you're going to feel really foolish over this one. I certainly did.''

"Go on.''

"Well, I also cracked the Dundee file. I think Nathan meant the person, not the place—as in 'Bonnie Dundee,' whose full name was—?''

"John Grahame of Claverhouse, Viscount Dundee," Adam supplied, feeling foolish as predicted—though how the Seal of Solomon and a Templar secret connected with a seventeenth-century Cavalier general, he had no idea.

The man remembered as Bonnie Dundee was perhaps one of the most flamboyant and controversial figures of the early Jacobite period of Scottish history. Known to every educated Scot as the victor of the Battle of Killiecrankie, fought in 1689 against a superior force of English soldiery, Claverhouse had been feared by his enemies as "Bluidy Clavers" and adored by his Highland followers as their "Dark John of the Battles." Though he had not survived his famous triumph, his undoubted courage and gallantry had made him the hero of many a song and story—none, so far as Adam knew, with any connection to Knights Templar or mysterious seals. It briefly occurred to him to wonder whether Nathan's whole story might be just as fanciful as the historical fantasies of Henri Gerard—except for the urgency of Nathan's dying declaration.

"I know you're probably hunting for a connection, the same as I've been doing," McLeod said, intruding on Adam's brief speculation. "Other than the link of the names—Graeme and Grahame—I haven't a clue what that connection might be, since the Seal was pawned well over three hundred years before Dundee died. And it's been *another* three hundred years since then.

"But Nathan obviously thought there *was* a connection," McLeod went on, "or he wouldn't have cluttered up his hard disk with all these Dundee files. We have to assume that Graeme of Templegrange never redeemed the Seal, since it ended up in the Fiennes family; so where does John Grahame of Claverhouse come in?"

Adam shook his head, even though he knew McLeod could not see it.

"I haven't the foggiest idea," he said truthfully. "Not even an inkling. There's nothing in all that Dundee material to suggest anything?"

"I honestly don't know," McLeod replied. "It took me a while to hack into these files, and I've only had a chance to skim through. Would you like me to print out what's here? I could have Donald run the hard copy out to Strathmourne tomorrow, so it'll be waiting for you when you get in. I'll have to stick close to the office myself, to wait for that callback on Gerard."

"I think that might be a good idea. Yes, do that."

They parted on the understanding that Adam would try to check in again between the funeral and leaving for the airport. Meanwhile, he had been given much new food for thought. As he headed upstairs, he chided himself again for missing the Dundee connection with John Grahame of Claverhouse.

And how did the Jacobite hero connect with the Templars and the Seal of Solomon? That was not at all clear. Dundee had been a staunch supporter of the Stuart cause—but again, how did that connect to Templars?

He let his brain mull the questions as he brushed his teeth and readied for bed, and found a traditional, haunting melody running through his head, accompanied by the immortal words of Sir Walter Scott:

> To the Lords of Convention 'twas Claver'se who spoke,
> 'Ere the King's crown shall fall there are crowns to be
>   broke;
> So let each Cavalier who loves honour and me,
> Come follow the bonnets of Bonnie Dundee.

The melody stayed to haunt him as he drifted off to sleep, with snatches of the lyrics weaving in and out of consciousness until at last he sank beyond awareness. The first few hours were dreamless, as he made up for the night before. But then images of increasing vividness began to tease at semiconsciousness.

The source of the initial impressions was not difficult to determine: glimpses of Dundee astride a great, plunging bay steed, sword in hand as he urged his followers on—the archetypal Cavalier hero. Then, gradually, the buff-coated Highland cavalry following him became crusader knights charging into battle, red crosses emblazoned on their white surcoats and the black and white beauceant banner of the Order of the Temple fluttering overhead in the bright sun of desert climes.

But there was a tension building. Suddenly the equestrian images yielded to a ghostly apparition of King Solomon himself, bearded and potent, majestically robed in flowing vestments of scarlet adorned with Qabalistic symbols, and crowned with a shining golden diadem that looked like a six-pointed star with the points bent up. In his left hand he held up what was surely Nathan's Seal like a protective talisman. His right hand wielded a sceptre or wand, its tip so brightly glowing that Adam could barely look upon it.

Adam's dream-self flung up an arm to shield his eyes, but a word of command from the great King bade him look where the Sceptre pointed. Trembling, Adam obeyed—to find himself being drawn toward a roil of churning yellow cloud, alive with sickly flickerings of greenish-yellow light. From within the clouds came waves of such dread as to make his stomach turn.

He woke in a cold sweat, gasping, his heart pounding as he instinctively drew on deep protections to envelop and protect him. He did not turn on the light, for by the sliver of light leaking underneath the bedroom door from the hall, he could see that there was nothing physically there. But certain it was that the dream had been a warning—whether merely from his unconscious, embroidering on what he had been reading about Nathan's speculations regarding the missing Seal, or from some external source, he could not tell.

But this was not the time or place to find out, alone and in unfamiliar surroundings, without even a clear picture of the problem yet, much less the solution; and certainly not under the added tension of the palpable grief in the Fiennes house. The urgency was unmistakable, but more active investigation must wait until tomorrow, when he returned home, and as more of the background became clearer.

Yet the residue of menace lingered, so much so that eventually he got up and fetched from the pocket of his suit coat a handsome gold signet ring set with a dark sapphire. Slipping it on his finger as he padded back to bed, he simultaneously offered up a formal prayer for protection and then touched the stone to his lips in salute. The ring was an outward symbol of his esoteric calling, and sometimes a tool of that vocation, and the little ritual grounded him firmly back in the realms of reason.

Further ritual before he lay back down again made of his bed a focus of celestial protection—a simple rite known as Sealing the Aura, which called upon the great archangels to guard the quarters and was sealed at last with a six-pointed star. His sleep thereafter was undisturbed by dreams, but he still slept lightly, as a part of him kept watch and pondered what had surfaced.

CHAPTER FIVE

NATHAN Fiennes' funeral took place shortly before noon the following morning, in the presence of his family and scores of friends and colleagues who had come together in shock and grief to mourn his passing. In keeping with Jewish custom, the service was starkly simple and unpretentious, all the more poignant for the weight of ancient tradition that shaped its form. Adam, sitting directly behind the family in the chapel adjoining the burial ground, was struck, as always, by the commonalities that united all men and women of goodwill, especially at a time of loss.

"O Lord, what is man that Thou dost regard him, or the son of man that Thou dost take account of him?" the officiating rabbi read. "Man is like a breath, his days are like a passing shadow. Thou dost sweep men away. They are like a dream, like grass which is renewed in the morning. In the morning it flourishes and grows, but in the evening it fades and withers. . . ."

Following along in the service book, caught up in the cadences of ancient ritual, which alternated between Hebrew and English, Adam was yet aware of the physical setting of this farewell and memorial to his departed friend. The chapel itself contained no religious symbol of any faith. Its focus was the plain and unadorned wooden coffin set before the congregation, covered with the pristine wool drapery of a *tallit,* such as all observant Jews customarily wore at their devotions. This one, Adam knew, had been brought by Lawrence from Jerusalem, in hopes that he might wear it in thanksgiving at his father's recovery; now it lay in tribute upon his father's coffin. Nathan's own *tallit* would have been lovingly wrapped around his shrouded body before laying it in the coffin, with one of the fringes cut to render it no longer fit for use—for Nathan no longer had need of it.

A single candle burned behind the coffin, but no flowers adorned coffin or chapel, for Jewish custom did not deem this appropriate in a time of sorrow. The men all wore *yarmulkes* on their heads, as did Adam himself, out of respect for Jewish custom.

"O God, full of compassion," the rabbi prayed, "Thou Who dwellest on high, grant perfect rest beneath the sheltering wings of Thy presence, among the holy and pure who shine as the brightness of the heavens, unto the soul of *Natan,* son of *Binyamin,* who has gone unto eternity, and in whose memory charity is offered. May his repose be in Paradise. May the Lord of Mercy bring him under the cover of His wings forever, and may his soul be bound up in the bond of eternal life. May the Lord be his possession, and may he rest in peace. Amen."

Following a brief but moving eulogy and more prayers, Adam was among those who joined Nathan's sons in shouldering his coffin to bear it out into the cemetery, their halting procession accompanied by the cantor's solemn recitation of the beautiful and moving ninety-first Psalm.

"He that dwelleth in the shelter of the Most High abideth under the shadow of the Almighty. I say of the Lord, He is my refuge and my fortress; my God in Whom I trust. For He shall deliver thee from the snare of the fowler, and from the noisome pestilence. He shall cover thee with His pinions, and under His wings shalt thou take refuge. . . ."

The graveside rites were as bleak as the wind that sighed in off the Yorkshire downs.

"Tzidduk ha'din. . . ." The Rock, His work is perfect, for all His ways are judgement: A God of faithfulness and without iniquity, just and right is He. . . . The Lord gave, and the Lord hath taken away; blessed be the name of the Lord. . . . May he come to his place in peace.

The coffin was lowered into the earth with simple finality. After that, beginning with Peter and then Lawrence, those wishing to pay their final respects came forward to turn three shovels of earth onto the coffin; the shovel was not passed from one to the next, but left upright in the mound of earth beside the grave. Earlier, briefing Adam on what to expect, Peter had explained that the symbolic gesture expressed the prayer that the tragedy of death not be passed on.

The silence was broken only by the hiss of the shovel being thrust into earth, occasionally ringing against stones, and the thump of falling earth, first hollowly on the wooden coffin and then, as the grave began to fill, the softer, more solid patter of earth on earth. When Adam's turn came, he made of each of his oblations of earth a prayer as well, drawing on his Celtic heritage for the words of his own silent farewell.

> *Blessings in the name of the Father of Israel,*
> *Blessings in the name of the Rabbi Jesus,*
> *Blessings of the Spirit Who brooded on the waters—*
> *Thus may you be blessed as you travel on your*
> *way. . . .*

He thrust the shovel into the mound of earth beside the grave with bowed head and stood back, melding into the crowd.

The process continued until the grave had been completely filled in, the men taking turns with the serious business of shoveling earth, once the token gestures had been made. Then, after the rabbi had offered another short prayer and led the assembled mourners in recitation of a Psalm, Peter and Lawrence stepped forward to offer Kaddish for their father for the first time—an ancient prayer Adam had learned from Nathan many years ago, and which he now offered in company with those around him, giving somber response to Nathan's sons.

"*Yisgadal v'yiskadash sh'may rabbah,*" the two read, "*b'olmo d'hu asid l'is-chadosho. . . .*" Magnified and sanctified be His great name in the world which He will renew, reviving the dead, and raising them to life eternal. . . . May He establish His kingdom during your lifetime, and during the life of all the House of Israel, speedily; and let us say, Amen. Let His great name be blessed for ever and to all eternity! Blessed, praised, glorified, and exalted; extolled, honored, magnified and lauded, be the name of the Holy one, blessed be He. He is greater than all blessings, hymns, praises and consolations which can be uttered in this world; and let us say, Amen. May there be abundant peace from heaven, and life for us and for all Israel; and let us say, Amen.

"Oseh shalom bimeromav, Hu ya'aseh shalom, alenu v'al Kol yisroel; v'imru amen."

"Amen," the congregation replied, in affirmation of the final exhortation.

When the last prayer had been offered and the last Psalm recited, those present formed a double line through which the family passed, offered comfort by ancient formula: *"Ha'makom yenachem et'chem b'toch she'ar avelei Tziyon vi'Yerushalayim."* May the Omnipresent comfort you together with all the mourners of Zion and Jerusalem.

Adam held back a little as the rest started to disperse slowly toward the cars, watching as some of the attendees plucked grass and cast it behind them. Several more paused to set small stones on the grave, bowing their heads in what Lawrence had told him was an Israeli custom, asking forgiveness for any injustice they might have committed against the deceased. Bowing his head, Adam added his own silent promise to Nathan to persevere in the task set before him, even though it seemed overwhelming at present. He had just turned to join the rest, heading toward the car in which he had ridden with several of Nathan's distant relatives, when Peter Fiennes detached himself from the immediate family, leaving his mother in the care of his brother, and came to fall into step beside Adam.

"Thank you again for being here," he said quietly. He hesitated slightly, then added, "I didn't realize you were so familiar with Hebrew ritual. Your accent is almost better than mine."

"I owe my instruction to your father," Adam said with a faint smile. "When he and I were both at Cambridge, a close friend of mine was drowned in a boating accident, and

I asked your father to teach me to pray Kaddish in Hebrew for him. It's one of those universal prayers that speaks from the heart of mankind. Nathan always maintained that a common thirst for communion with the Divine was what united all truly spiritual people, whatever their formal religious affiliations might be.''

Peter accepted this tribute with a wan smile. ''That sounds like Dad, all right. He was lucky to have you for a friend. If anyone can recover the Seal for him, I know you can. I wish there were more I could do to help, besides just drive you to the airport in a couple of hours.''

''Just pray for our success,'' Adam said, ''and I mean that quite literally.'' He smiled and added, ''Actually, there is one, more concrete thing you could do, and that's to let me take the rest of your father's notes away with me for further study. It's beginning to look like we need to speak with Henri Gerard, but we still don't know exactly what we're up against. Also, if anything else should turn up in the next few days, or you should think of anything that might have bearing, please let me know.''

''I'll do that, of course,'' Peter agreed. ''And do take the notes, by all means. In your hands they may do some good.''

''I devoutly hope so,'' Adam said. In his own mind was the thought that if Nathan was to rest easy in his grave, he and McLeod were going to have their work cut out for them.

Back at the Fiennes home afterwards, where many of those present at the funeral had retired to offer their condolences and share a light repast of bagels and coffee, Adam excused himself to go upstairs and pack, then moved into Nathan's study where, after packing up the rest of Nathan's notes in a briefcase he found there, he rang McLeod at his office, charging the call to his home number.

''Hullo, Noel,'' he said without further preamble. ''Any progress on Gerard?''

''A bit—for all it's worth,'' McLeod said without enthusiasm. ''The address and telephone number we found for him are good, but Gerard isn't there. To make a long story short, he's supposedly gone off to Cyprus on a four-week camping holiday."

"That's convenient."

"Yes, I thought so," McLeod agreed sourly. "According to my friend Treville, our boy purchased a round-trip air ticket to Nicosia and picked it up from the travel agent's on Monday of last week. He paid for it with a credit card. His bank records show that he drew a substantial amount of money from his standing account the selfsame day."

"How substantial?"

"Nearly ten thousand pounds—more than he'd need for any camping holiday," McLeod replied. "But Gerard is known to be a collector of antiquities. It could be argued that he simply wanted to have sufficient cash on hand, in case he ran across any irresistible finds while on holiday. Treville's men are still trying to find out if he bought any camping gear recently, but again it could be argued that he already had what he needed in the way of kit. So you be the judge."

"If it's a cover story, it's a reasonably useful one," Adam allowed. "I wouldn't fancy having to track down the whereabouts of a camper on the move. Has anyone verified that Gerard actually made the trip?"

"Treville had Interpol check it out," McLeod said, "and they checked with the Cypriot authorities. Both the airline and the passport-control people show in their records that on Wednesday the eleventh, a Monsieur Henri Gerard got on the plane in Paris and got off again in Cyprus. But you and I both know that doesn't necessarily mean anything. With enough cash and a forged passport, our boy could have bought another ticket out to London within hours of his arrival on Cypriot soil, and departed thence without anyone in Nicosia being the wiser."

"So much for that lead, then," Adam replied. "What next?"

"Oh, I'm not finished," McLeod said. "Bearing in mind what Peter Fiennes said about Gerard being something of a nutter, I asked Treville if he'd get somebody to look into Gerard's psychological background. He made the inquiries himself, and it turns out that our boy has a history of emotional instability. His colleagues in French antiquarian circles say that Gerard's interest in the Knights Templar amounts to something of an obsession; he's fanatically convinced that all the charges laid against them were true, and has set himself to prove as much. He bases this assertion on the belief that he is, in fact, the present-day incarnation of a medieval French nobleman who lived to witness those events.''

"Very interesting," Adam murmured. "Very interesting, indeed. If there's more to this assertion than mere romantic fantasy, it could explain a great deal. I'd be curious to know whether or not he has a psychic past. If his interest in Nathan's Seal dates back to a previous lifetime, we may be dealing with someone far more dangerous than a mere eccentric."

"That was my thought too," McLeod replied. "I don't suppose you've had any more insights about the Seal itself? What it was for, and so on?''

"Not yet, but I'm working on it. I had an interesting dream that I'll tell you about when I get back. Meanwhile, I think it might be safest if we proceed on the assumption that Gerard is actually here on British soil. At very least, I'd like to know what he tells the York Police about his movements two days ago, if they can turn him up. Have you relayed your information to the authorities here in York?''

"All the conventional information, yes. And Treville is faxing me a photo later on. What do you want to do about the other?''

"Just sit tight until I get home," Adam replied. "Did you send those printouts to the house?''

"Yes, Donald's just gotten back. I took the liberty of having him deliver the packet to Peregrine, with instructions to read it, if he had a chance, and see what kinds of cold impressions he might get. You don't mind, do you?''

"Of course not. I should have thought of that myself. I have the feeling we're going to need him on this, before it goes much farther." He glanced at his pocket watch. "Anything else? I ought to head downstairs and be sociable for a little while before Peter runs me to the airport.''

"No. Talk to you when you get home.''

*   *   *

The Edinburgh flight out of Leeds left at 5:50. This time, as well as his overnight bag, Adam had a leather briefcase crammed full of Nathan's research notes. He arrived to find no Humphrey waiting at the gate, but as he came out of the terminal building, he spotted his silver-blue Range Rover standing by at the curb with Humphrey at the wheel.

"I'm afraid I misjudged the traffic, sir," Humphrey said, as he alighted to open the back so Adam could toss in his meagre luggage. "I would have met you at the gate as I usually do, but I only just got here."

"Not to worry, Humphrey. Let's swing by police head-quarters so I can pick up the Jag."

"Very good, sir."

They were home by a little after seven. After putting the Jaguar away and dropping off Nathan's briefcase in the library, Adam went upstairs for a quick shower while Humphrey took himself off to the kitchen to prepare a quick evening meal. Twenty minutes later, refreshed and relaxed in a clean white shirt and grey slacks under his quilted blue dressing gown, he was heading back down to the library to sort through the mail on his desk before eating.

Most of the mail was not urgent, but one item, in particular, caught his attention—a formal invitation printed on stiff cream card stock, with the shield of the present-day Order of the Temple of Jerusalem emblazoned at its head. He gazed at it for several seconds, absently running a thumb over the raised engraving, then picked up the telephone at his elbow and tapped in the number printed below the line that read, *RSVP Chev. Stuart MacRae.* He knew MacRae through their mutual interest in restoring castles. MacRae lived in a partially restored castle farther to the east, near Glenrothes, and had been giving Adam ongoing advice on the restoration of Templemor. He was also an expert on Templar history.

"Hello, Stuart, this is Adam Sinclair," Adam said, when the hearty bass voice of MacRae himself answered the phone. "I hope I'm not interrupting your dinner."

"Not at all!" came MacRae's genial reply. "I was

hoping I'd hear from you soon. Did you receive your invitation to the investiture?''

"I did, indeed," Adam said. "Forgive me for not getting back to you sooner, but I was called away unexpectedly on Monday, and I've only just gotten back. I'll try to make it on Saturday, but a lot depends on how things have gone at the hospital while I was away. I haven't even checked in yet. I'm not sure I want to know."

A hearty chuckle erupted from MacRae's end of the line. "I can appreciate *that,*" he replied. "But don't worry about us. Come if you can—and if you can't, then send your good wishes. I still keep hoping that, since you're restoring a Templar castle, we'll eventually be able to persuade you to join the Order."

"Well, I'm honored that you keep asking, but I already have too many claims on my time," Adam replied easily. "However, you may certainly count me as a friend of the Order. And I hope to affirm that friendship in person on Saturday."

"Well, so do I."

"In the meantime, I'm calling because I've got something of a mystery on my hands," Adam went on. "It has to do with Templar history, and I'm hoping you may be able to give me some information."

"Ah, well, then," MacRae said. "That's something I do know something about. What did you want to know?"

"I need a connection," Adam said, choosing his next words to be carefully neutral. "Have you ever heard tell of any dangerous Templar secret connected with Dundee?"

"I assume you mean Bonnie Dundee, not the town," came MacRae's prompt reply, making the human connection immediately, as Adam had not. "You know, of course, that he was Grand Prior of Scotland at the time of his death?"

"Indeed?" Adam said, jotting down *G.P. Scotland* on the back of an envelope. "Tell me more."

MacRae gave a knowing chuckle, obviously delighted at the chance to confide his knowledge to a receptive and appreciative listener.

"Well, some of this might be considered crypto-history by more conventional scholarship, but there's a strong tradition that when Grahame of Claverhouse fell at Killiecrankie, he was wearing a Templar cross around his neck. What became of the cross after the battle isn't certain, but it's mentioned as being in the possession of a French priest named Dom Calmet some years later. I'd guess that he got it from David Grahame, Dundee's younger brother. I'd give a lot to know where it finally ended up," he finished, rather wistfully. "That's the sort of thing that really ought to be in the custody of the Templars of Scotland."

Adam was silent a moment, his mind racing. MacRae's disclosures had thrown a whole new light on the investigation.

"Is there anything else you'd like to know?" MacRae asked.

"No, you've given me ample food for thought just now," Adam said. "But tell me, where might I find out more about this Claverhouse/Templar connection?"

"Well, if you've been following the books by Michael Baigent and Richard Leigh—I'm sure you're familiar with their *The Holy Blood and the Holy Grail,* with Henry Lincoln—they talk about a lot of this in a book called *The Temple and the Lodge.* It came out a couple of years ago."

Adam's gaze had already shifted upward to scan the bookshelf on his right, and he stood to tip down a book in a black dust jacket, with the square and compass of Freemasonry between the red of its title and the white lettering of the authors' names on the spine.

"Yes, I have a copy right here," Adam said, trapping the receiver between shoulder and ear as he sat and flipped back to the book's index. "Thanks, Stuart. This may be exactly what I needed."

"Glad to be of service," MacRae replied. "Do you think you might let me in on what you're up to?"

"Just a bit of research," Adam said neutrally. "It may not come to anything. I'm thinking of writing an article," he added, to allay any further undue curiosity.

"Ah, well, then. Let me know if I can help you with anything else."

"I certainly will."

With a final word of thanks and the hope that they would, indeed, see one another on Saturday, Adam rang off, already settling back to devour the material on John Grahame of Claverhouse. He had skimmed through the entire volume when it first came out, but then he had focused on later sections having to do with his own family's Sinclair connections with the founding of Freemasonry in Scotland, and their role in the building of Rosslyn Chapel, south of Edinburgh. Now, while he ate the light supper Humphrey brought him on a tray, he read the pertinent sections on Claverhouse's Templar connections.

When he had finished both, he pushed his tray aside and went back to his bookshelves to look for something more specific on the life and times of Bonnie Dundee. Of all the books on his shelves dealing with various aspects of Scottish history, only one was a detailed biography of Dundee. Adam pulled it from its place and went over to his favorite chair by the fireside to have a read of it, grateful for the fire Humphrey had started while he ate.

The book was an old one, as witnessed by the fact that the bookplate on the inside bore the name of Adam's father. The date of publication was 1937. Making himself a mental note to obtain something more recent, Adam checked the index for any reference to Templars—there were none—then set himself to reading the account of Dundee's last battle and its aftermath. He was just finishing it when the telephone rang, so he let Humphrey answer it in another room—though he was not surprised when Humphrey buzzed it through. Holding his place with a finger between the pages, Adam went over to the desk and answered.

"It's Mr. Lovat on the line, sir," Humphrey said.

"Thank you, Humphrey. Put him through, please."

He sat as a series of clicks told of the call being transferred.

"Hello, Peregrine," he said, turning back to the frontis-piece of his book—a faded black-and-white photo of a portrait of a handsome young Cavalier. "I was just about to ring you. Did Donald Cochrane drop by this afternoon, with some computer printouts from Noel?"

"As a matter of fact, he did," came the light, cheerful voice. "It's fascinating stuff. Makes me want to start painting portraits of John Grahame of Claverhouse. But what's all this business about a stolen seal?"

"It's a long story," Adam said. "If you'd like to run that material up to the house, I'll tell you all about it. The matter's likely to require your services anyway, probably sooner rather than later, so I might as well bring you up to speed."

"Super!" Peregrine replied. "I'll be right up. I assume this is apt to take a while?"

"I'm afraid so," Adam replied. "Did you have other plans for the evening?"

"Not at all. I was just confirming that it'll be worth my while to bring along a suitable libation. I finished that portrait of Janet Fraser over the weekend, and Sir Matthew gave me a bottle of hundred-year-old port that's just begging to be sampled. Julia doesn't care for it, and it's far too nice to drink alone."

"Hundred-year-old port?" Adam said with an appreciative chuckle. "Would you like me to send Humphrey down in the Bentley to collect you and it? I shouldn't want to even *think* of it being jostled or disturbed."

Peregrine laughed. "It's well packed in straw, but I promise I'll drive very slowly. Anything else you need?"

"As a matter of fact, there is one thing you could bring," Adam said, glancing again at the book in his lap. "Have a look at your art books and see if you have any of the Dundee portraits. I've got one here, but it's the Melville one, done when he was in his early twenties. A charming portrait, but I'm looking for a later one, that will show him more the way he would have looked about the time of his death."

"You'd want the Glamis Portrait, then," Peregrine said. "That's the one you usually see. I'm sure I've got a print of it around here somewhere. I'll see what else I can find. See you in fifteen or twenty minutes."

CHAPTER SIX

IT was more like half an hour before Peregrine arrived, with an oversized art book and large manila envelope cradled in one arm and a look of eager anticipation on his face. Humphrey followed him with the dark green bottle of vintage port in its straw basket, bearing it with a stately reverence usually reserved for holy relics.

"Ah, there you are," Adam said, smiling as he rose to shake the younger man's hand. "And I see that Humphrey has been entrusted with the grave responsibility of carrying the port. Shall we allow him to do the honors?"

"By all means," Peregrine said with a grin, depositing his own burden on the table before the fire, where Adam was clearing a space. "And pour one for yourself as well, Humphrey."

"Thank you very much, sir," Humphrey replied, a pleased smile touching his usually impassive features.

As the butler retired to deposit the port on a Jacobean sideboard and began assembling the necessary requisites of corkscrew and crystal glasses, Peregrine settled in the chair opposite Adam and set aside the manila envelope and a slender booklet on paintings housed in properties owned by the National Trust for Scotland. Taking up the large art book, he ducked his head to search for the place he had marked.

Peregrine Lovat was a slender, fair-haired young man of middling height and graceful carriage. At just thirty, he had already carved out a niche for himself as one of Scotland's most important young portrait artists, with increasingly prestigious commissions coming his way. His attire reflected an artist's instinct for color and texture—a nubby Fair Isle sweater in muted greys and creams over a cream silk shirt and tan slacks, subtle foil for the pale hair worn longish in the front. The hazel eyes behind gold wire-rimmed spectacles shone with a joy and sense of purpose that had grown and emerged steadily in the year since he and Adam first had met.

For Peregrine Lovat also possessed the gift of Sight, the ability to focus his artist's eye on a scene of past psychic intensity and bring images to mind—and to sketch or paint those images while in trance. Such visions had been disturbing enough, before he learned to control them; but far more devastating had been the emergence of a parallel talent for sometimes seeing into the future—a shattering experience when it involved glimpsing the deaths of some of his sitters.

Despondency over one such death was what had driven him to seek Adam's help in a professional capacity, almost a year ago. Since then Adam had helped him learn to channel his gifts, so that they now emerged only on command, and mainly when working with Adam and McLeod as a very special kind of forensic artist. The ability to catch glimpses of prior events at the scene of a crime was of inestimable value when teamed with the unique sort of law enforcement in which Adam and McLeod—and now Peregrine—were so often engaged.

"Here we go," Peregrine said, opening the book to a full-page color plate and turning it for Adam's inspection. "I think that's the one you'll want."

Adam nodded and pulled the book onto his lap, studying the man who gazed back at him from the page. The face in the picture, somewhat stylized in the manner of all late-seventeenth-century portraits, was that of a dashing cavalier gentleman swathed in brunette silk-velvet, with full white shirt sleeves, a bunch of lace at his chin, and the gleam of an armor breastplate just visible at his waist. The oval face, handsome and refined, was framed in lustrous auburn curls, the sensitivity of the finely modelled mouth effectively countered by the challenge lurking in the heavy-lidded dark eyes. The legend beneath the plate identified the subject as

John Grahame of Claverhouse, Viscount Dundee, by Sir Godfrey Kneller.

"That one's more commonly known as the Glamis Portrait," Peregrine said, "on account of it being part of the collection housed at Glamis Castle. It was painted in London, only two years before his death. I found a print of another one that's kept at Fyvie Castle," he went on, opening the smaller booklet and laying it atop the first book. "This is a pretty small photo, and it's in black and white, but you get the general idea. I've seen the original. It's by a relatively obscure Scottish artist named John Alexander, who copied it from an original by Sir Peter Lillie. I couldn't find any further mention of the Lillie portrait in what I've got at home, but if it's important, I can always go into Edinburgh tomorrow and take a poke about in the arts section of the university library."

Adam turned the second reproduction to a better angle in the light. It showed a slightly younger version of the same face surmounted by a painted wreath in the shape of an oval. Of the two versions, the second was less polished in terms of technique, but more human in its limning of the features.

"No, these are sufficient, I think," he murmured, sitting back in his chair as Humphrey came bearing a silver tray with three ruby-filled glasses shaped like crystal thistles. "Neither shows what I was really looking for. And the Melville portrait, which I've already seen, is far too young. Ah, thank you, Humphrey," he added, as the butler offered the tray first to Peregrine, then to Adam, himself taking the third and tucking the tray under his other arm as Adam raised his glass.

"May I offer a toast?" Adam asked Peregrine.

"Please do."

"To Sir Matthew Fraser, then—the giver of the gift," he said with a smile, "and to Peregrine, whose artistry undoubtedly deserved it, and whose generosity prompted him to share it."

"And don't forget Janet, Lady Fraser, whose beauty inspired the art," Peregrine added gallantly.

"Hear, hear," Adam agreed. "To everyone who had a

hand in bringing us this excellent wine—even Humphrey, who poured it. *Slàinte mhór!* To your very good health, gentlemen!''

All three of them sipped it appraisingly, contented expressions telling of their pleasure, after which Humphrey glanced at Adam and raised his glass in query.

"If there's nothing further, sir, I'll leave you and Mr. Lovat to your work. And may I add, sir, to your very good hunting?"

"You may, indeed, Humphrey. Thank you," Adam said.

They drank to that; and when Humphrey had gone, leaving the bottle on the tray at Adam's elbow, Peregrine glanced at his mentor expectantly, taking another sip of his port.

"So, what's Dundee's connection with this missing Seal?" the young artist asked. "And is it true that the Seal realized enough in pawn to finance the entire Peasants' Revolt?"

Adam raised an eyebrow in surprise. "Does Nathan connect the Seal with the Peasants' Revolt?"

"He certainly does." Peregrine tapped the manila envelope. "That's what part of this document is about. Didn't Noel tell you?"

Adam shook his head. "I don't think he'd had a chance to really read any of it in depth yet. Tell me more."

"Well. Your friend Nathan talks about a theory that secret survivors of the Templar dissolution had formed an underground of some kind, and were the driving force behind the Peasants' Revolt of 1381. There's evidence to suggest that the revolt was not at all spontaneous, and that many aspects were well planned in advance."

"What makes him say that?" Adam asked, setting his glass aside and drawing the manila envelope toward him.

"Apparently, a number of things. As just one example, many of the rebels wore livery, almost a uniform of sorts—a white hooded shawl with a red tassel. In one town alone— Beverly, I think it was—he mentions *five hundred men* wearing these. Think about what that alone would involve, even today. And six centuries ago, when all cloth had to be made from scratch, first spinning the yarn, then weaving the cloth, then assembling the things, sewing them by hand— And he points out the interesting similarity between these 'hooded shawls' and the white mantles with red crosses worn by the Templars.''

Adam had been opening the manila envelope as Peregrine spoke, and now he held up a hand for the artist to pause a moment while he pulled out the printout and began to leaf through it. He was reasonably familiar with the general background of the Peasants' Revolt. In June of 1381, overburdened by high taxes and unjust labor restrictions, the peasantry of England had risen up against their oppressive government and set the countryside ablaze with rebellion, led by a dissident priest named John Ball and another man of uncertain origins known only as Wat the Tyler. The peasant army had marched on London and taken it by storm, and might well have gone on to overthrow the English monarchy had Tyler not been treacherously slain during a parley with the young King Richard II and his ministers.

This was the gist of the usual history of the rebellion. But as Adam skimmed over what Nathan had written, making a mental note to check Nathan's source, a book called *Born in Blood,* by one John J. Robinson, a further interpretation began to emerge—that Templar technical advice and guidance had backed the rebellion, and Templar funds had bought equipment and information. The theory of intervention by successors of the Templars made sense, for no former Templar establishments had tasted the wrath of the marching peasants—though the men had gone out of their way to burn and loot holdings of the Knights Hospitaller, who had profited by the Templar dissolution and acquired many former Templar properties. And as for Nathan's Seal providing the funding—

"It does make sense," Adam murmured, lowering the pages. "We already know that Graeme of Templegrange, who pawned the Seal, held land that formerly had belonged to the Temple. If there *was* still an underground organization of former Templars and their descendants, and Graeme of Templegrange was part of it, it follows that he might have had orders from his superiors to pawn the Seal in order to raise the cash for a last attempt by the Templars to regain their former prominence.''

Peregrine nodded. ''Nathan seems convinced that was why the Seal was pawned—and why it was never redeemed, since the Peasants' Revolt failed. Our Graeme of Temple-grange may have been killed, and no one else knew where the Seal had been pawned. Or they might not have been able to raise the money. And that's how it came to be in the keeping of Nathan's family all these years.'' He sighed. ''But that still doesn't explain why the Seal should be so valuable, then or now. What *is* it? And what does it have to do with Grahame of Claverhouse?''

Adam settled himself more comfortably in his chair and laced his long fingers together, choosing his words with some care, for he was still working out much of it in his own mind.

''That last, I can't answer,'' he said. ''Claverhouse apparently was a Templar, but I can't yet make any connection between him and the Seal. As for the Seal itself—'' He glanced thoughtfully at the young artist.

''I gather that Noel filled you in on some of the story regarding the death of Nathan Fiennes. What he may not have told you—and what apparently didn't come through in what you read—is that the Seal of which we're speaking is no ordinary archaeological artifact. Nathan seemed convinced that it is the very Seal of Solomon himself.''

Peregrine blinked and gave a low whistle.

''Good Lord, do you think it really is?''

''That remains to be seen,'' Adam said grimly. ''Nathan spoke of a great power and a great danger, and described the Seal as *a key to keep a deadly evil locked away from the world.* He also intimated that the Seal is somehow bound up with a secret responsibility that, at one time, was the burden of the Knights Templar. He believed that the Seal possesses certain arcane powers.''

''What—kind of powers?'' Peregrine asked hesitantly.

''That also remains to be seen. Nathan was killed before he could find out. Based on a dream I had last night, little

would surprise me. Esoterically speaking, however, I can
tell you that there has always been a tradition that King
Solomon had authority and control over evil spirits. If that's
true, and Nathan's Seal *is* literally the Seal of Solomon, I
hesitate even to think what it might have been made to bind,
that its keeping should have been guarded through so many
centuries—and what might be lurking, ready to wreak
havoc, if someone were to loose what it binds. I simply have
no idea.''

"And the guardianship of the Seal and its secret was
given to the Templars?'' Peregrine asked after a few
seconds.

"So it would appear. Let me read you a short passage
from one of Nathan's diaries.'' Nathan's briefcase was
sitting on the floor beside his chair, and he pulled out one of
the volumes and opened it to a place marked by a slip of
paper.

"This is a reference to a document purported to be part of
a deposition by one Renault le Clerque, a witness for the
French Crown testifying against the preceptors of the
Knights Templar in Paris. Nathan got it from someone with
the initials 'H.G.,' whom Noel and I believe is Henri
Gerard, one of Nathan's researchers. The police are trying
to locate him for questioning. Anyway—'' He turned his
gaze to the text before him.

" 'H.G. arrived this morning,' '' he read, '' 'bringing with
him a copy of the promised manuscript fragment relating to
the Renault le Clerque deposition. In the main, Renault
merely gives evidence in support of those oft-repeated
allegations that the Templars practiced the usual vices of
idolatry, the *Osculum Infame,* sodomy, devil-worship, and
the all-encompassing sin of heresy. But there is one tantalizing piece of new information—to wit, an assertion that
the preceptor general of the Order *had made contracts in
writing with evil spirits, formalizing those contracts with a
bronze seal of great antiquity, bearing an arcane symbol.*

" 'The accusation itself is fantastical, but nevertheless
would seem to contain one significant grain of truth,' ''
Adam continued to read, glancing at Peregrine to be certain

he was listening—and he was. " 'Though Renault does not describe the seal in any great detail, there seems little doubt that the Templars *were* keepers of an ancient seal of some kind. Taking into account everything I have been able to find out since embarking on this investigation, I am increasingly convinced that the Seal my ancestor obtained so long ago from Graeme of Templegrange is the same one referred to in Renault's deposition, brought here with other Templar treasures when the Templar fleet departed La Rochelle shortly before the arrests of 1307.

" 'Which still leaves us with many intriguing questions remaining yet unresolved. What was the original purpose of the Seal? What did it guard? If the Seal did not originate with the Templars, where did it come from? And how did these military monks come to be its keepers?' " Adam looked up.

"He goes on to tell about how Gerard proposes to send a metal sample from the Seal for testing—and I actually found a copy of the letter he got back from the Sorbonne on this, and it *does* support the antiquity of the Seal. Of course, it proves nothing about whether it did, indeed, belong to Solomon," he concluded.

As he closed the notebook and set it aside, Peregrine gave a soft sigh and shook his head.

"Well. That puts the entire matter far beyond simple burglary, doesn't it?" he said. "It could certainly explain the Templar link. But where does Dundee fit in?"

"I keep asking myself the same question," Adam said. "Other than the fact that Dundee apparently was a Templar, there's a three-hundred-year gap between him and the Seal that I haven't yet been able to bridge."

He went on to render a brief account of what he had learned from MacRae concerning Dundee and the Templar cross he had worn into his last battle. By the time he had finished, Peregrine's hazel eyes were wide as an owl's behind his gold-framed spectacles.

"There's nothing about any of this in the material I read," he said. "I wonder if Nathan was even aware of that connection."

"I'd guess that he was at least heading in the right direction," Adam said. "He certainly believed that Dundee figured in the puzzle somehow. Even if it weren't for all of this"—he indicated the printout with a gesture—"his last words had to do with Dundee somehow being or having the key. At the time, I thought he meant the town. Come to think of it, there *is* a castle in Dundee that's associated with him: Claypotts Castle."

"Well, I think it's clear that he meant the person," Peregrine said.

"Probably true," Adam agreed. "But let's follow this Templar association further. If Dundee *was* Grand Prior of Scotland at that time, it follows that he might have had knowledge—perhaps even *sole* knowledge—of the Order's most privileged secrets. If those secrets included any information relating to the Order's collective office as guardians of the Seal of Solomon—or what *it* guarded— then our Bonnie Dundee might, indeed, have the answers we're looking for."

"Are you thinking to attempt contact with the historical persona who was John Grahame of Claverhouse?" Peregrine asked.

Adam nodded. "That's the most direct approach that occurs to me—though that, in itself, presents something of a challenge. As you know, the most efficient way of approaching such a proposition is via some material focus to link us into Dundee's personal past."

"Like, for example, the Templar cross Dundee was wearing when he died." Peregrine made it a statement.

"Or, failing that, some other personal object closely associated with Dundee," Adam agreed, gesturing toward the open books. "That's partly why I wanted the portraits: to see if there was anything—some piece of personal jewellery or item of equipment—which Dundee might have favored wearing at all times. Unfortunately, as you can see for yourself, the three portraits show no common features of that kind."

"But surely a man of his stature must have left *something* behind, in the way of personal mementoes," Peregrine said.

"Agreed," Adam replied. "But what? I know of two, if we don't count the Templar cross—which may not even exist any more. A breastplate and steel morion cap alleged to be Dundee's are kept at Blair Castle. I've seen them several times. Unfortunately, the original items were stolen from his grave within a few years of his death. Eventually, they were recovered, but their provenance was broken. Hence, it isn't altogether certain that the artifacts now on display at the castle are genuine."

"I see your point," Peregrine acknowledged with a grimace. "What about other items that might have been associated with him? Is it possible we might be able to locate the Templar cross you mentioned?"

"That's a good question," Adam said, leaving his chair to head for the telephone. "To answer it, I think we need the advice of someone intimately acquainted with the world of British antiquities and their collectors."

Whomever Adam was calling, Peregrine noticed that he didn't need to refer to his address book before tapping in the number. After a brief double *chirrup* of the line ringing came a muted click, followed by the remote murmur of a woman's voice. Adam's resigned expression indicated that the call was being handled by an answering machine, as did his tone as he spoke briskly into the receiver.

"Lindsay, this is Adam. I'm trying to track down any personal relics you may know of that are associated with John Grahame of Claverhouse, more commonly known as Bonnie Dundee. I'm especially interested in finding out what may have become of a Templar cross which Dundee supposedly was wearing at the time of his death. Does such a cross still exist, and if so, who is now its keeper?

"Failing information concerning this particular artifact," he went on, "I would welcome news of any other related items you may know of. I'm already aware of the breastplate and morion at Blair Castle. Please get back to me on this matter as soon as possible. I believe the matter may be of some urgency."

He returned the receiver to its cradle and went back to his chair by the fireside. Peregrine had picked up the book with

the Kneller portrait and was gazing thoughtfully at the
serene face of Bonnie Dundee.

"I've been thinking," he announced, as Adam reclaimed
his seat. "Your Lindsay may take a while to report back,
and even then, there may be nothing to report. Why don't I
drive up to Killiecrankie tomorrow and have a look around
the battle site? Who knows? I might be able to pick up some
visual resonances centering on Dundee, maybe even verify
whether he was wearing a Templar cross that day. I could
use one of these portraits as a focus."

Adam considered the offer, then shook his head. "I have
a better idea," he said. "You're on the right track regarding
technique, but let's focus it on St. Bride's Church at old
Blair. That's where Dundee was buried. It's in the grounds
of Blair Castle. If we could be sure of the exact spot at
Killiecrankie where he died, that might be the better
choice—but even then, I'd tend to be wary, because of the
general residuals of a major battle like that."

"I hadn't thought of that," Peregrine allowed.

"Only because you didn't know where he was buried,"
Adam said with a smile. "If you like, we can have a look at
the breastplate and morion, since we'll be there anyway. In
either event, whatever images you might pick up there are
apt to be far more controlled and specific than any you'd be
likely to encounter at Killiecrankie itself."

Peregrine was nodding avidly. "All right, Blair it is. How
early would you like to be off in the morning?"

His unabashed enthusiasm made Adam chuckle in spite
of himself.

"Steady on. Some of us have morning rounds to make,
before we can go anywhere. Remember, I've been away for
two days. Besides that, I'd like Noel to come with us, if he
can get away. Let me check with him just now and see what
his schedule's like for tomorrow. We can rendezvous here
for lunch before heading off, whether or not he's able to join
us."

CHAPTER SEVEN

SHORTLY before noon the next day, Peregrine Lovat slung a fawn-colored leather jacket and a lightweight portable sketchbox onto the passenger seat of his Morris Minor Traveller and set out up the beechwood drive to the manor house. There had been a time when he had regarded the visionary insights of his artistry as a curse, and in those dark days he had avoided carrying any sketching materials with him, hoping thereby to avert any casual invoking of the deep sight he feared.

Since then, with Adam's help, he had learned how to control—and value—those selfsame faculties of perception. Nowadays, he rarely left home without taking at least a pocket sketchbook with him. Especially when he was going on an outing in the company of Adam Sinclair.

He pulled up in the yard in the shadow of the manor house and left the Morris parked on the gravel outside the entrance to the stableyard, where Adam's cars and his own Alvis drop-head were garaged. He had room for only one car down at the gate lodge, and the aging green Morris Minor was his everyday workhorse. The Alvis he had inherited from a wealthy patroness who was fond of him—Lady Laura, Countess of Kintoul, who had first introduced him to Adam and whose death had been the catalyst for him to seek Adam's help. He poked his head into the garage to admire the old car, mentally thanking Lady Laura, wherever she was now, then presented himself at the side door which was commonly used by Adam's close friends and acquaintances. He was admitted at once by Mrs. Gilchrist, Adam's efficient and motherly housekeeper, who had a soft spot in her heart for "young Mr. Lovat" and offered him tea and scones before ushering him into the library to wait for Adam. Peregrine reluctantly declined the offer, for lunch would not be long in coming, once Adam arrived with McLeod; and they must be off fairly quickly afterwards, if they hoped to have sufficient time at Blair Castle before the light failed.

Twenty minutes later, the deep purr of a powerful car in the driveway announced the impending arrival of Adam himself, in the Jaguar. Going to the library window to watch the car pass, on its way to the garage to be changed for the more practical Range Rover, Peregrine saw a familiar broad-shouldered figure sitting in the passenger's seat which could only be Inspector Noel McLeod.

Peregrine considered the two men as he went out on the front steps to await their arrival. An outsider would have regarded them as unlikely companions and associates. Sir Adam Sinclair, baronet, psychiatrist, and antiquarian, was a model of graceful propriety, tall and well proportioned, always elegantly dressed and possessed of an understated poise that Peregrine had never seen desert him, even in the most stressful situations he had known them to encounter. McLeod, by contrast, was wiry and muscular and sometimes gruff-spoken, with a peppery turn of temperament that had made Peregrine slightly wary of him until he'd gotten to know the inspector better.

But under the surface the two were more closely allied then anyone outside their fellowship might ever have suspected. Both of them were Huntsmen of redoubtable skill and proven prowess, dedicated to the pursuit of an order of justice not normally recognized by conventional law enforcement authorities. Peregrine, though he now had often joined them in the field, suspected he had yet to fathom the full scope of their powers and jurisdiction. As the most recently recruited member of the Hunting Lodge, he was not even certain he had met all the peripheral members of the group.

One thing *was* clear, however, and that was that the job came with its share of attendant dangers. But then, danger was the accepted complement to the challenge of the Hunt.

Adam and McLeod joined him shortly thereafter, Adam

withdrawing briefly to change from his three-piece suit to cords and a tattersall shirt with knitted tie, much as Peregrine was wearing. McLeod's tweed suit already had a country look to it, and would easily see him through whatever the afternoon might bring.

"Sorry to keep you waiting," Adam said, as he came into the downstairs parlor where Humphrey had set the table for lunch.

Over Tandoori chicken, kedgeree, and salad, with a single glass apiece of white Zinfandel, McLeod related what had transpired during the night regarding the search for Henry Gerard.

"So far, the Cypriot police haven't been able to verify Gerard's presence on their turf," he informed his listeners, pulling a folded sheet of paper from an inside pocket and passing it for Adam and Peregrine to see. "Treville from the Sûreté was able to fax us this photograph of Gerard taken from passport records. I've had it blown up and duplicated, and sent copies along to Phipps down in York, as well as the airport security people at Heathrow, Gatwick, Manchester, and Prestwick. It's a long shot, I admit, but someone might just have spotted our man in passing. Provided, of course, that we aren't simply barking up the wrong tree. He may still be camping innocently on Cyprus."

Adam dismissed the suggestion with a shake of his head. "My instincts say otherwise."

"Mine too," McLeod agreed, "but we're going to need more than instincts to get us where we need to go with this case."

When they had finished lunch, a twenty-minute run up the A90 brought them skirting Perth to the west. From there they continued north and westward toward Pitlochry on the A9, gradually climbing up into the Highlands. The day was bright and dry, and the Range Rover ate up the thirty miles in as many minutes. Just past Pitlochry, they came down off the A9 to take the secondary road that parallelled it, passing through the Pass of Killiecrankie and skirting the green fields that once had reeked of battle.

"You can see that there's nothing much to use as a focus

out there," Adam said, pointing out the hillsides as they
sped by. "There's an exhibit about the battle at the National
Trust Visitor Center, but it wouldn't have been much use for
what you had in mind."

Just past Killiecrankie, the road crossed under the A9 and
brought them into the village of Blair Atholl. A few minutes
later, they were turning through the main gates of the Blair
Castle estate of the Duke of Atholl, who was also hereditary
Chief of Clan Murray. The castle rose regally beyond the
lime trees lining the main avenue, its dark slate rooftops and
snowy harling giving it a dazzling, fairy-tale appearance
that belied grim centuries of history. The bright blue and
white saltire of Scotland floated from a flagstaff high atop
one of the castle's towers, but not the ducal banner,
indicating that the duke himself was not at home.

With the ease of familiarity, Adam swung the Range
Rover into the visitors' car park and brought the big car to
a halt very near the walkway that led up to the visitors'
entrance. Clambering out of the car behind Adam and
McLeod, Peregrine drew a deep breath of fresh, wood-
scented air and decided to put on his leather jacket. It was
warm enough in the sun, but he had worked on commissions
for enough noble and landed families by now to know how
chilly it could be inside their stately homes. A small sketch
pad and a selection of favorite pencils already resided in the
jacket's inner pocket, obviating the need to take his sketchbox for this part of the afternoon's excursion.

Adam led the way up to the visitors' entrance. Before he
could identify himself to the young woman at the desk as a
sponsor of the National Trust, an older man wearing a kilt
in the dark green and blue of the Murrays of Atholl came
bustling out of the rear office, his face lighting with a broad
smile of recognition as he spotted Adam.

"Sir Adam Sinclair! I had no idea you were planning to
stop by. How are you keeping?"

"Very well, thank you, Davy," Adam responded pleasantly as they exchanged handshakes. "Good to see you
again. Noel, Peregrine—this is David Alexander, the castle's assistant administrator. Davy, let me introduce you to

two friends of mine: Detective Chief Inspector Noel McLeod, from Edinburgh, and Mr. Peregrine Lovat, whose portraits may well hang here at Blair Castle one day, if His Grace is as shrewd a judge of artistic talent as I think he is.''

"A pleasure to meet you, Inspector. And you also, Mr. Lovat," Alexander said, as he shook hands with both men. "I'm afraid that you've missed His Grace by a good few hours, Sir Adam. He took off this morning for a long weekend in London, and he won't be back before Monday.''

"Not to worry," Adam replied. "I wasn't expecting to find His Grace at home. Actually, if I might make a confession, the three of us are out playing tourist today. Peregrine wanted to do some sketching. I wonder if we might simply take a wander about the place with the rest of the visitors?''

"Of course you can. Nothing easier," Alexander said affably. "Was there anything in particular that you wanted to look at? I'd be quite happy to act as your guide.''

"That's very kind," Adam said. "Peregrine?''

"As a matter of fact, I *would* rather like to see the mementoes of Bonnie Dundee," Peregrine replied, taking his cue smoothly. "I understand that you've got his breast-plate and helmet here at the castle. He's always been something of a hero of mine.''

"Right you are," Alexander said, nodding. "Those are on display in Earl John's Room. Come with me and I'll take you there.''

The room in question was smallish and rather dark, dominated by a large bed hung with ancient red velvet. A fine collection of portraits adorned the walls, including one of Earl John himself, an ardent royalist of his day, and another of the Marquis of Montrose who had raised the King's standard at Blair in 1644. The Dundee relics, wired to the left-hand shutter of one of the windows, consisted of a tarnished morion and a battered breastplate pierced by a bullet hole which Peregrine knew had actually been added by one of the later Dukes of Atholl in the somewhat misguided belief that it made the armor look more authentic.

A plaque fixed to the shutter beneath the helmet gave details of authentication.

Another group of visitors was there ahead of them, but moved on almost immediately. To give Peregrine some privacy in which to inspect the relics, Adam contrived to draw David Alexander aside with questions about a handsome, plainly finished grandfather clock in the room's far corner. As Peregrine moved closer to the window, McLeod trailed along with the others, casually interposing his body between Peregrine and their guide.

Closing his ears to the politely lowered voices of his companions, Peregrine took a moment's brief pause to compose himself, then focused his attention more closely on the pieces of armor in front of him. His passively receptive gaze could detect no ghostly visual resonances. Summoning up a visual picture of Dundee, as portrayed in the Kneller portrait, he waited again to see if some more lively impression suggested itself. For a brief moment, he saw the breastplate whole, without the cosmetic addition of the bullet hole, but he could detect no trace images of the man who might have worn it. Disappointed, he drew another deep breath and briefly closed his eyes to allow his sight to readjust to the material world.

"It's a pity these old relics can't speak," he observed out loud. "Still, it's interesting to be able to look at them."

Adam turned to glance in his direction, obviously aware, from these casual remarks, that his younger associate had observed nothing to engage their interest.

"Have you seen enough, then?" he asked jocularly. "In that case, let's move on."

For form's sake, they allowed David Alexander to complete a quick tour of the castle. They never seemed to hurry, but Peregrine had to admire the way Adam was able to direct the conversation to keep them briskly on the move through the many rooms that were open to public view. The tour ended half an hour later at the Larch Passage, so named for the wood in which it was panelled, where Adam politely declined Alexander's invitation to partake of tea.

"I thank you for the offer, Davy, but I'm afraid we really must be going," he said in tones of courteous regret. "I particularly wanted Peregrine to see the old kirk where Dundee is buried, and we'll lose the light if we don't head down there. It's been good to see you again, though."

Reclaiming the car from the car park, they set off along a narrow, wooded back road pointing them in the direction of the old factor's house and St. Bride's Kirk, the latter now a ruin. The shadows were, indeed, lengthening as they parked again and entered the old churchyard. A few other visitors were inspecting gravestones farther across the yard, but they seemed engrossed in their own activities. As Peregrine followed Adam and McLeod out across the grass among the grave markers, this time carrying his sketchbox, he was suddenly conscious of a subtle prickling in his senses—and the distinct feeling, absent at the castle, that he now was on the right track.

His heartbeat quickened as they wound through the burial ground and approached the western front of what remained of the little church, a lichen-studded enclosure open to the sky. Ducking through the round-arched doorway, they made their way along the narrow line of paving slabs set where the center aisle had been, heading for a memorial plaque mounted on one of the stones to the right, just before a doorway leading out to the yard to the south.

"Here's the memorial marker," Adam said, checking in his stride and pointing to the stone with its chiselled inscription. "The actual burial would have been in the crypt below here." He indicated a steel trapdoor set into the paving just before it, closed with a heavy padlock.

Peregrine glanced at the trapdoor, then turned his gaze to the stone plaque, reading it aloud as an exercise to begin focusing his attention:

"Within the Vault beneath are interred the remains of John Graham of Claverhouse, Viscount Dundee, who fell at the Battle of Killiecrankie 27th July, 1689, age 46. This memorial is placed here by John, 7th Duke of Atholl K.T. 1889." Peregrine glanced at Adam. "Was he really forty-six? I always thought he was younger than that."

"Actually, the most recent scholarship suggests that he was born in the summer of 1648," Adam replied. "That would have made him just forty-one."

Nodding, Peregrine swept his gaze around the chapel, returning finally to the trapdoor at his feet.

"This is about as close as you're going to get, I think," Adam said. "Go ahead and get yourself up, and we'll see what you can See. Noel, why don't you fend off interruptions, at least until he gets started?"

As McLeod retreated wordlessly up the aisle, Peregrine handed his sketchbox to Adam and opened it to take out a drawing pad and the book containing the Kneller portrait of Dundee. There was a low, rounded stone like part of the top of a tombstone set against the wall under the memorial plaque, and Peregrine sat on it gingerly, facing the trapdoor that led down into the crypt, as Adam set the sketchbox on end beside him and crouched down alongside. After opening the art book to the appropriate page, Peregrine balanced it across his knees and turned to a fresh sheet in his drawing pad, situating that on the opposite page as he groped in an inner pocket of his leather jacket for a favorite pencil.

"Ready when you are," he said, glancing over at Adam.

"All right, we'll do this a little differently from what we usually do," Adam said quietly. "You're going to use the portrait as a focus, to help you zero in on Dundee's connection with this place. Fix your gaze on the portrait and tell me what you see as you gradually let your focus move *through* the image."

Peregrine drew a deep breath, shifting into the floating twilight of light trance.

"I see a man standing in the midst of a dark forest," he murmured softly after a few seconds. "His name is John Grahame of Claverhouse, Viscount Dundee. He's arrayed like a gentleman soldier, in armor and lace, and his face is bright against the shadows."

As he spoke, he felt Adam's light touch on his brow. He took another sighing breath and felt normal waking perceptions recede, leaving him alone with the image of Claverhouse, Dark John of the Battles. . . .

"Dark is the wood through which you must travel," came Adam's quiet voice, softly singsong in his ears. "Bright is the face of the man you seek there. Enter the wood where he stands waiting. His face shines before you like a beacon, drawing you to him amid the shades of his own lifetime. . . ."

A landscape of shadows took hazy shape before Peregrine's entranced vision. Anchored by Adam's voice and the sense of his presence, the young artist let his perception move tentatively forward among the shadows. As he did so, the shapes before him sharpened and clarified. He was still surrounded by the stones of St. Bride's Kirk, but the scene was of another age.

The burial vault gaped open. Beyond it, a small group of armored men holding torches stood clustered around a rough wooden coffin resting on two wooden hurdles. Several tartan plaids had been spread in the coffin to receive the body, spilling over its edges, and Peregrine felt his gaze drawn to the figure laid out within their woolen folds.

The pale, still face was very like the one in the Kneller portrait, but it retained yet the suggestion of the dashing younger Dundee of the Melville depiction. The lace at his throat harked back to both paintings, and the dark hair had been carefully arrayed in curling ringlets on his shoulders and chest. He was wearing in death the same buff cavalry jacket and thigh-high leather boots described in eyewitness accounts of the battle at Killiecrankie. In the dancing torchlight, Peregrine could see clearly the dark, rust-red stain and ragged hole marring the jacket on the dead man's lower left side to show where he had taken his death wound, two hand-breadths within the area the breastplate would have covered.

Without consciously willing it, Peregrine's hand began sketching what his deep sight reported. The faces of the mourners meant little to him, but his reading of the accounts of the burial suggested identities for several of those present. One of them, a well-favored man in cavalry buff like Dundee himself, Peregrine judged to be the brave and loyal Earl of Dunfermline, James Seton, who had been one of Dundee's staunchest supporters and closest friends. Another he supposed to be Lord Murray's factor, Patrick Steuart of Ballechin, in whose house the body had lain before bringing it here.

The one whose identity was little in question, both by his resemblance to the dead man and by the depth of his grief, was David Grahame, the brother of Dundee. Grahame was openly weeping, his lean face wet with unregarded tears. But what drew Peregrine like a magnet was something clenched tightly in Grahame's right hand—something small and bright that winked crimson as he brought the closed fist to his lips and pressed a kiss to what lay enclosed within.

Pencil poised to draw what he was seeing, Peregrine moved closer in spirit to see what the object might be. With a small thrill of excitement, he realized it was a red-enamelled cross, perhaps three inches in length and breadth, fixed to a sturdy gold chain.

Even as another part of his mind registered this discovery, his hand moving to sketch it, his trance-self watched raptly to see what would happen next. As the mourners began to draw the plaids over the body, preparatory to closing the coffin and transferring it to the vault, the Earl of Dunfermline abruptly signaled a delay. His look of grief was almost as poignant as that of the dead man's brother. Taking a small, sharp blade from a sheath at his wrist, Dunfermline bent down and reverently cut away a long, curling lock of the dead man's hair. He wrapped it in a silken handkerchief as he nodded to the others to proceed, and slipped it inside the breast of his buff jacket as he watched them lower the coffin into the crypt.

As the coffin disappeared from sight, Peregrine's view of the scene blurred and dissolved into obscurity. His hand kept sketching automatically for several minutes, finishing what he had started, but as it finally became motionless, pencil merely poised over the paper, he found himself drifting in temporary limbo. It seemed like too much effort to do anything about it.

After a few more seconds, he heard Adam's voice softly calling to him as from a great distance. Obedient to the summons, he took flight out of the depths of vision, winging upward in slow spirals toward the threshold of awakening. As he surfaced, he felt Adam's strong fingers grip his wrist briefly in a touch that signalled his release from trance-state. With a sigh like a sleeper awakening, he gave himself a slight shake and blinked.

Adam was still crouched beside him, and McLeod was standing over him, bent with his hands braced on his knees, watching him expectantly. The concern left their faces when they saw he was once more aware of his present surroundings, and McLeod likewise dropped to a crouch beside Adam. Feeling more than a little drained, Peregrine summoned a wan grin and lowered his gaze to the sketchbook in his lap. He was mildly surprised to see that he had managed to fill three whole pages with images.

"Aye, you've been a very busy lad for the past twenty minutes," McLeod observed with a faint smile.

Peregrine's fingers were trembling slightly, as they usually did when his visions demanded that he draw at speed, and he pocketed his pencil and shook his hands lightly to relax them as he allowed Adam to turn back to the first page. The first sketch showed an overall scene of the funeral gathering, with quick cameo portraits of several of the mourners around the edges and a study of Dundee himself, lying in his coffin. The next showed David Grahame with the cross in his hand, and a life-sized detail of the cross itself—a cross *formée,* slightly flared at the ends, a form of insignia worn by the Templars at the time of the Crusades rather than a Maltese cross or the patriarchal cross worn by modern-day Templars.

"Well, there's your cross," Peregrine said softly. "It almost has to be the one he's supposed to have been wearing at the battle. I guess this tends to confirm his affiliation with the Templar Order."

"Indeed," Adam agreed. As he turned to the last page, his own gaze was arrested by the attendant drawing of the Earl of Dunfermline taking a lock of Dundee's hair. That incident seemed to him to have a significance equal to that of finding a Templar cross in the possession of the Grahames of Claverhouse. The feeling was strong enough to convince him that the matter might be worth further investigation. In the meantime, the shadows were lengthening. And Peregrine was looking decidedly in need of sustenance.

"I think we've garnered all the information we're likely to get here," Adam told his two companions. "Let's pack up and go see if we can find some place that serves high tea. We'll review the content of the drawings in greater detail once we get back home to Strathmourne."

CHAPTER EIGHT

ADAM and his companions stopped off for tea in Blair Atholl village before embarking on the drive home. Peregrine was silent for most of the way back. Now that the elation of the moment had worn off, he realized that they were still no closer to finding the answers they were seeking regarding the stolen Seal of Solomon. They had confirmation of the existence of Dundee's Templar cross, but that was of little practical value unless they could lay hands on the artifact itself. The cutting of a lock of hair suggested another possible avenue of inquiry—it was apt to have been preserved as a precious relic—but hair was far more perishable than metal. Whether cross or hair might have survived for more than three hundred years was by no means certain.

Yet only with some sort of physical focus such as the cross or lock of hair could they hope to make contact with the spiritual essence that once had been John Grahame of Claverhouse, and obtain directly from him whatever knowledge he once had held concerning the Seal. Peregrine wondered briefly about the possibility of centering such an inquiry on the tomb where Dundee's body had been laid to rest, but almost as soon as the notion occurred to him, he dismissed it as being both technically and morally dubious. For one thing, the tomb was known to have been disturbed by grave-robbers at least once, and perhaps twice. One tradition even claimed that Dundee's bones had been moved to a church at Old Deer, up in Aberdeenshire, in the 1850s. The very existence of such a tradition called into question the identity of any bones that still rested there.

And even assuming that the spirit of Dundee was willing to participate in a dialogue on those terms, to be called back via a body now no more than bones, Peregrine's own soul shrank from the thought of even attempting such a thing. He had not forgotten how, less than a year ago, a rogue lodge of black magicians had conjured the spirit of the wizard Michael Scot back to Melrose Abbey, leaving it trapped there in the ghastly prison of its own mummified corpse until Adam had contrived to release it. Even though, in this instance, Dundee would be under no such horrible compulsion, Peregrine still found the associations too uncomfortable for his liking.

"Adam, what happens if we can't locate any artifact associated with Dundee?" he asked, as they came off the M90 and began winding along the surface roads toward Strathmourne. "And can we afford to wait as long as it's likely to take, even if such an artifact still exists?"

"I've been thinking about that," Adam replied. "We won't give up on Lindsay yet, but there's a place with a strong connection. I mentioned Claypotts Castle, over in Dundee town. It's essentially as it was when he lived there—at least the fabric of the building is essentially intact. None of the furnishings are the same, of course."

"So we'd go there and—what?" Peregrine said. "Try to focus him in through Noel as a medium? Is that possible?"

"Oh, it's possible," McLeod replied. "Not easy and not pleasant, but with sufficient intent, it could probably be done. I *hope* Adam has that at the bottom of his list, though."

"He does," Adam said. "But I wanted to mention it now, so you both can be getting used to the idea, in case it becomes necessary. We'll give Lindsay a couple of days before we start to panic—and meanwhile, see what else turns up on our M. Gerard by conventional police methods."

It was getting dark by the time they turned in at the gates to Strathmourne. Having invited Peregrine and McLeod to join him for dinner, Adam drove on past the gate lodge without stopping and carried on up the beech-lined drive. As they came around the last bend, he was just reaching for the dashboard remote to activate the outside house lights when he realized they were already on, illuminating another vehicle pulled up before the front steps of the manor house. Peregrine's eyes widened as he took in the exotic lines of a sleek Italian sports car, all swooping wings and glittering chrome and rich cream coachwork.

"Good Lord, that's a *serious* piece of auto design!" Peregrine breathed. "Who do you know that goes in for custom-made race cars? A descendant of the Dukes of Lombardy?"

Adam chuckled. "Would you be very much surprised if I told you it belongs to an antique dealer of my acquaintance?"

"I'd be flabbergasted," Peregrine said frankly, as they pulled in behind the car. He paused, blinking as the mental connection fell into place. "Not your friend Lindsay?"

"None other," Adam said, switching off the ignition. "And if she's taken the trouble to come here in person," he continued, "that can only mean she's found information that she was unwilling to entrust to the telephone. Bring that sketchbook, Peregrine, and we'll go find out what she's got to say."

Humphrey had installed Adam's visitor in the library with a drink. Taking the car as evidence for what Lindsay might be like in person, Peregrine decided that almost anything was possible. Even so, his first glimpse of her was as eye-opening as his first glimpse of her mode of transport. So struck was he by her appearance that he only belatedly realized that they were being introduced. Seizing on her last name as Adam pronounced it, he stammered, "I'm enchanted to make your acquaintance, Ms. Oriani."

Lindsay Oriani, he reckoned, was perhaps an inch short of six feet tall, and slim as a thoroughbred racing filly, an impression that was accentuated by the elegant cream trouser suit she was wearing. As if that were not enough, her shoulder-length hair was a vibrant titian red, in dazzling contrast to the deep, cool blue of her eyes. Returning his gaze with a wry glint of amusement, she replied, "I'm pleased to meet you too, Mr. Lovat," and offered him an elegant, long-fingered hand.

His first impulse was to raise it to his lips, but before he could do so, she turned the gesture deftly into a handshake. The clasp of her hand, despite its slenderness, was firm and sure as a man's. Though her femininity was manifested to stunning advantage by her manner of dress, there was an ambiguous undercurrent of something else in her demeanor that he was slightly at a loss to interpret. But before he could refine his impressions, Adam stepped in with the suggestion that they should all be seated.

Together they moved toward the fireside, where Humphrey had kindled a fire. Humphrey remained on hand to serve up drinks to the new arrivals before retiring to the kitchen to supervise dinner arrangements. Two fingers of The Macallan in a cut-crystal tumbler made a start at restoring Peregrine's composure. Lindsay allowed Adam to freshen her Campari and soda. By the time Adam turned the conversation to business, Peregrine had made the necessary adjustments and was ready to listen to what the fabulous Lindsay might have to say.

"As you've no doubt guessed, I have information for you," she informed Adam, her attention focused on him alone. "I've managed to locate two artifacts associated with the person of John Grahame of Claverhouse. I cannot vouch personally for the authenticity of either piece, but I offer the information for what it may be worth.

"The first item is a ring containing what purports to be a lock of his hair, owned by a Miss Fiona Morrison, who lives in Inverness. The other piece is a gold cross overlaid with red enamel, which closely matches the description of the one you were inquiring about. This is in the keeping of a cadet branch of the Graham family down in Kent, specifically, a retired brigadier general named Sir John Graham."

Adam's face was very keen in the reflected light from the fire on the hearth. Peregrine's jaw had dropped at the mention of the ring, and he continued to gape as Lindsay described the cross.

"Excellent," Adam murmured, flicking Peregrine an amused glance. "Have you approached either of these people?"

"Yes. I've spoken to both of them over the telephone," Lindsay said. "Since Miss Morrison lives in Scotland, I contacted her first. Having acquainted her with my own credentials, I told her that I was acting on your behalf to locate certain hitherto unpublicized Dundee relics which you are hoping to examine, preparatory to completing a learned article on Dundee for the Royal Society of Antiquaries. The Society would welcome such an article, I feel sure," she added with a droll smile, "thus preserving your reputation as a gentleman of your word. Miss Morrison has agreed to let you see the ring, upon our joint assurances that no liberties will be taken."

This quaint indirect rendering of what were evidently Miss Morrison's own words drew a snort from McLeod, but he subsided again without further comment.

"And what about this Sir John Graham?" Adam asked Lindsay.

The elegant woman sitting opposite him smiled somewhat grimly.

"Sir John Graham is another matter entirely," she said. "I was of two minds whether or not to contact him without first conferring with you."

Adam raised an eyebrow. "Why so circumspect? You should know by now that I have absolute trust in your discretion."

"You have yet to hear the whole story," Lindsay said mildly, with a sultry flash of her sapphire eyes. "The name rang a bell, so I made some very discreet inquiries. It seems that Sir John is far more than a much-decorated military man retired to the country. He's ex-intelligence, for one. Also, my initial contacts were reluctant to be very specific, but gave me to understand that he has worked in a number of esoteric disciplines."

"Indeed?" Adam's brow darkened as he considered this report. "Do you mean to imply that he sides with the Opposition?"

"Not at all," she replied. "Further inquiry revealed that he generally prefers to work in an altogether different tradition from ours, but my sources assure me that his allegiance is pledged unreservedly to the Light. His overall abilities are said to be formidable, but his integrity is above reproach. However, he is not a man to be trifled with.''

"And what's at stake here is no trifling matter, either," Adam said. "I hope you were nothing less than candid in speaking with him."

This observation earned him another sea-change flash from Lindsay's deep blue eyes.

"I told him what I know of the matter—that you are interested in examining this relic of his for reasons that may prove of some urgency outside the conventional bounds of the law. What more he may have inferred for himself I can't say. It may be that he has heard of you as well, at least in a professional capacity. He declined to commit himself to a meeting without first speaking to you—and who can blame him, under the circumstances?—but I gathered that he is favorably disposed, provided this conversation is to his liking. He indicated that he would be at home to take a call from you this evening, but he will be away for the weekend."

Adam glanced up at the carriage clock on the mantel, smiling grimly. "Whatever we choose to confide in one another, I'd probably better not keep the gentleman waiting for my call, then, especially since it's I who want a favor from *him*. Have you got his telephone number with you?"

"Of course." She was already slipping a well-manicured hand into the pocket of her jacket to produce a business card. As she passed the card to Adam, Peregrine saw that there were two telephone numbers neatly pencilled on the back.

"The first one is Sir John's," she said. "The other is Miss Morrison's."

Adam glanced at the numbers and nodded as he rose.

"No time like the present. If the rest of you will excuse me a moment, I believe I'll go ring up both parties. Peregrine, why don't you show Lindsay the sketches you did this afternoon? Let her have a good look before you explain. I've *told* you he's good, Lindsay," he added, pointing at her for emphasis as he went out of the library.

While Adam retreated to another telephone to make his call, Peregrine opened his sketchbook to the first of today's pages without a word and handed the pad to the exquisite Lindsay. As she settled back to look at it, serene and tranquil as she turned the pages, Peregrine sat back to look at her. Under cover of polishing his glasses, he narrowed his gaze and allowed his deeper perceptions free rein. Not at all to his surprise, the ensuing flicker of overlaying images suggested that he was dealing with someone with multiple past lives. What did surprise him was that the dominant visual impressions he was receiving from Lindsay Oriani were masculine, rather than feminine.

The force of the gender bias was unexpected. Where Adam Sinclair's preeminent historical identities included an Egyptian priest-king and a Templar knight, both quite in harmony with his present incarnation, Lindsay Oriani's most potent anterior persona seemed to be that of a lean, powerful man in the uniform of a Hussar officer. The accompanying aura of masculinity was strong enough to color the personality and even some of the mannerisms of the present female incarnation. All at once Peregrine began to wonder whether that explained why Lindsay had deflected his impulse to kiss her hand.

It did make sense. In the early days of their acquaintance, he and Adam once had discussed the matter of gender identity with respect to reincarnation. On that occasion, Adam had asserted that it was not uncommon for the gender of a single historical individual to vary between one lifetime and the next. Since then, Peregrine had seen that assertion borne out in the case of the wizard Michael Scot, whose present-day incarnation was a young girl by the name of Gillian Talbot. It seemed likely that Lindsay Oriani was another example of the principle at work, except that the gender resonances of her past lives seemed to be unusually strong.

What strain those resonances might impose on her present female personality, Peregrine could only imagine. It made him wonder if perhaps, like himself, Lindsay had initially been driven to seek Adam out for professional reasons, to deal with that strain. If that were so, Peregrine felt quite certain she would have found comfort and counselling there, along with a unique degree of understanding. If anyone could help somebody deal with a problem of that kind, Adam Sinclair was the individual to do so.

"These are very interesting, Mr. Lovat," she said suddenly, looking up at him with her sapphire gaze. "You anticipated my finds precisely. It's quite obvious that we're playing on the same team."

Peregrine smiled and shrugged. "It's what I do," he said. "It's a gift I can appreciate now, but it took Adam to teach me how to use it, instead of letting it rip me apart."

"He's good at that," Lindsay allowed, a small smile sketching at her lips. "And you're good at *this*. I assume that you knew about the cross before you went out to Blair, since Adam specifically asked me about that artifact, but did you know about the ring with the hair?"

As Peregrine shook his head, Adam returned from the telephone.

"Well, we're in luck so far," he announced. "Sir John was waiting for my call, and he's very graciously invited us to call on him on Monday. Noel, can you get time off? We'd better plan on two days, just to be safe."

McLeod nodded. "I'm due in London for a conference over the weekend, but I can meet you at Gatwick on Monday."

"Good. Peregrine, how about you?"

Peregrine grinned. "I was hoping you'd ask."

"I'll take that as a yes," Adam said with a droll smile.

An amused chuckle from Lindsay reduced Peregrine to blushing silence.

"What about trying our luck with Miss Morrison in the meantime?" McLeod said, heading them back to business.

"I phoned her as well, but there was no answer," Adam said. "I'll try again after dinner. Lindsay, can I press you to join us? Humphrey says it won't be more than five minutes."

She gave a decided shake of her titian head and tossed off the last of her drink.

"Thank you, but no. I must be heading back to Glasgow. Val and I have made plans for a romantic dinner at home, and I've promised to be on time."

"Well, far be it from me to stand in the way of romance," Adam said with a smile. "Do give Val my fondest regards."

She smiled and gave another restless toss of her fiery hair. "I'll do that," she said. "And if there's anything else I can do for you, call me. I *do* check the machine regularly. You needn't bother to see me out. And nice to finally meet you, Mr. Lovat. *Ciao,* Noel."

Peregrine watched her go with eyes that were still somewhat dazzled.

"What a woman," he murmured, when he had heard the front door close. "And whoever this Val is, he's a damned lucky man!"

"Yes, Lindsay has certainly found a lover worthy of her," Adam said. "They've been together for many years."

His tone was studiously devoid of expression. Belatedly it occurred to Peregrine that "Val" might just as easily be a woman's name. His eyes widened at the thought, but of course it made sense, in light of his earlier observations.

"I see you've guessed the right of it," Adam said. "Does the notion bother you?"

"Bother me? No, not really," Peregrine said, a little surprised to discover he was speaking the simple truth. "I could see her background in her face. But . . ."

"Are you wondering why she should be haunted by her past in quite that way? I'm not sure I know myself," Adam said. "But she understands and accepts herself as she is, and has gone on to find a measure of joy in this life. For any human being, that is no inconsiderable triumph. Shall we go in to dinner?" he finished brightly. "I believe Humphrey is about ready for us."

CHAPTER NINE

WHILE Adam and his associates were dining at Strathmourne, a slightly built man with sleek dark hair and a pencil-thin moustache presented himself at the door of an Edinburgh bed-and-breakfast establishment and requested accommodation for the night. Once the particulars had been arranged and the owner had departed back downstairs, he locked his door and drew the drapes before making a move to open the light valise he had brought in with him from his rented car.

The subdued light of the sixty-watt bulb overhead picked out the initials "H.M.G." in brass lettering on the lid of the valise. The name recorded in the residents' registry book in the lobby was Hilaire Maurice Grenier, but the initials in fact stood for Henri Marcel Gerard. He laid the case flat on the bed and took stock of his surroundings. The room, with its plain furnishings and slightly outmoded decor, was nothing like what he would have chosen, had present circumstances not compelled it, but it would serve for a few nights. If all went well, it would not be long now before he had the means to command all the luxury that always should have been his due.

With this consoling reflection, he opened the case and took out a pair of striped pajamas and a leather kit-bag containing his shaving paraphernalia and other personal items. Carefully packed among the rest of his clothes were two heavy leather-bound books and a weighty, palm-sized object wrapped in several thicknesses of silk handkerchief, which he removed and set on the coverlet beside the case. His agile fingers lingered briefly on the silken bundle before he straightened to take stock of the rest of the room.

Besides the single bed and a bedside locker with lamp,

the room boasted a mirrored wardrobe, two mismatched armchairs, and a cheap, functional coffee table. These latter were arranged before the hearth of a small fireplace which now housed a modern electric fire. After moving the two volumes to the coffee table, Gerard switched on the heating, lingering with an extended hand until he was sure it was starting to warm up, then went back to reclaim the silken bundle. Carrying it over to the fireside, he chose the more comfortable-looking of the two chairs and sat down, allowing himself to indulge old dreams as he felt what it contained through the folds of rich silk.

Its acquisition marked the culmination of many months of scheming. Ever since Gerard had determined the Seal's history and significance, he had desired it as he had desired nothing else so ardently in all his thirty-six years of life. It was, he told himself now, a criminal miscarriage of fate that Nathan Fiennes and his family should have possessed such a treasure for so long in swinish ignorance of its value. Thus it was only just that he, Henri Gerard, should have stepped in to relieve them of it.

Surely so powerful an artifact as the Seal of Solomon belonged rightfully in the hands of someone who would know how to employ its powers to some good purpose. Nathan Fiennes had been a fool to try and stop them from taking it—all the more so because, like the proverbial dog in the manger, he had been trying to retain possession of something that was no use to him personally. It was only equitable that he should have been forced to give it up. If the old man had gotten more than he deserved in the process, the fault for that was to be attributed to Logan. Gerard certainly had never intended Nathan to die; in that regard, his own hands were clean.

Even as he repeated these assurances to himself, his mind conjured up an unbidden image of Nathan Fiennes crumpling to the floor with blood streaming from a broken contusion on one temple. To purge that image from his thoughts, Gerard took refuge in contemplating the wealth and power that would soon again be his, in glorious fulfillment of a dream from the past.

That dream, which had first occurred to him in childhood, had repeated itself so often that he had come to regard it as an oracle. In The Dream, he had figured not as a humble scholar of limited means and reputation but as a powerful advisor to kings. He even fancied he knew the name he had borne in that other life: Guillaume de Nogaret, Keeper of the Seals and trusted advisor to King Philippe le Bel of France. A man of incalculable wealth and far-ranging influence, de Nogaret had been feared and courted by all lesser men, his political powers such that no one had ever succeeded in defying him with impunity.

Not even the Knights Templar.

His were the promptings that had emboldened Philippe le Bel to launch his assault on the Order, a campaign which had resulted in its official dissolution. Within the revelations of The Dream, Gerard/de Nogaret had presided over the trials and torments of many a Knight Templar, and had heard the testimony which convicted a number of them of sorcery and sodomy. Waking as well as sleeping, Gerard had come to believe unshakably in the Templar's guilt, and had shaped his academic career accordingly in this life. Little had he suspected that there might be more to the story—until his association with Nathan Fiennes revealed the existence of the Seal, and his further research for Fiennes had prompted him to go looking for new documentary material that might pertain specifically to Templar treasures denied to Philippe and de Nogaret centuries ago, but perhaps still accessible to Henri Gerard.

The Dream had hinted at such wonders—and had led Gerard not only to the hitherto undiscovered testimony of Renault le Clerque, which he foolishly had shared with Fiennes, but to two additional unpublished depositions Gerard had since discovered, wherein both the witnesses in question had sworn to the existence of a mysterious coffer which the Templars had guarded with ceaseless vigilance since the days of their founding. This coffer, they asserted, was sealed shut by magic, and could only be opened by the guardian of the Seal. One of the witnesses had speculated that the coffer contained a small trove of choice treasures more valuable than all the rest of the Templars' property put together: books of magic and implements of sorcery which had enabled the Order to become the single richest, most powerful organization in all the known world.

De Nogaret would have been aware of the depositions; perhaps, Gerard allowed, their promise of wealth was part of what had led de Nogaret to urge the King to attack the Order. But no coffer or any other great Templar treasure had ever been found. When the seneschals of the French King broke into the former Templar strongholds, they had found the treasuries empty. Apparently no one, not even de Nogaret himself in those days, had suspected what Gerard had since discovered—that the Seal of Solomon and the secret and treasure it guarded were the key to the mystery. After a lapse of nearly seven hundred years, Gerard was about to succeed where he had failed as de Nogaret—and his fortunes were to be raised to a height even beyond that of his predecessor.

For he had the Seal. Now all he needed to do was locate the casket. Between the research Nathan Fiennes had carried out and the information Gerard had since been able to assemble, all the evidence indicated that the coffer and its contents, like the Seal itself, had been spirited away to Scotland for safekeeping when the Templar fleet fled France. Gerard was convinced that he was getting close now. So far he lacked any specific clues to its whereabouts, but fortunately there were ways of getting at the truth without resorting to Nathan's painfully pedestrian methods of investigation. Gerard had not spent all his time merely poring over obscure, mouldering manuscripts for historical snippets; he had studied as well, with some of the finest if most amoral minds on the Continent.

He rewrapped the Seal in its silken swaddlings and laid it in front of him on the coffee table. Then he reached for the topmost of the two ancient books he had brought with him. It was a treatise, in Hebrew, on the art and practice of Qabalistic divination. Nathan Fiennes, he knew, would never, ever have profaned the Qabalah as he proposed to do.

But Nathan was dead, and Gerard had staked his remaining fortunes on the success of this present, all-important gambit. . . .

CHAPTER TEN

THE next day was Friday. Up at Strathmourne, Adam finished his usual light breakfast while he cast his eyes over the headlines in *The Scotsman*, waiting for a decent hour to phone someone he did not know, then dialled the Inverness number of Fiona Morrison at nine o'clock precisely. There had been no answer the night before, but a woman's voice answered cheerily on the third ring.

"Oh, yes, Sir Adam," she said, when Adam had identified himself. "Miss Oriani said you'd be ringing. If you tried last night, I'm sorry I missed your call. I'm a light sleeper, so I unplug the phone before I go to bed. I understand you'd like to see the Dundee ring."

"Indeed, I would, Miss Morrison," Adam replied. "I believe Miss Oriani may have mentioned that I'm writing an article for the Royal Society of Antiquaries. I wonder, would it be convenient if I drove up this afternoon to have a look at the ring?"

"Oh, no, I couldn't possibly let you do that," she replied. "My niece is bringing her children over after school, and I haven't seen them for months. Besides, I was already planning to be in Edinburgh at the weekend for a Templar investiture," she added, just as Adam was drawing breath to try another tack. "Perhaps we could meet somewhere and I'll show it to you. You do know, of course, that Dundee was a Knight Templar? It's said he was wearing the Grand Cross of the Order when he died at Killiecrankie."

"Yes, I'd heard that story," Adam said, "and if you're already coming down to Edinburgh, that would be absolutely splendid. As a matter of fact, I'd been planning to attend that investiture myself. It's the one at St. Mary's Cathedral tomorrow afternoon?"

"Yes, that's the one. Yes, of course I'll bring the ring to show—oh, dear, there's someone at the door. I'll have to ring off now, Sir Adam, but I'll see you tomorrow at St. Mary's. I look forward to meeting you."

She hung up before Adam could say yea or nay, but as he hung up at his end, he reflected that a day's delay probably wasn't going to make that much difference, especially since he couldn't see the Templar cross until Monday anyway. Besides that, the fortuitous coincidence of Miss Morrison's already planned trip to Edinburgh seemed to confirm that he probably was being led in the direction he was supposed to be going.

Meanwhile, there were more mundane responsibilities that required his attention after a two-day absence from his professional duties. Resisting the temptation to fret over the enforced lag in the investigation, Adam drove in to the hospital and spent the morning attending to the needs of his patients and students. A late morning call to McLeod revealed that the inspector had put out an advisory police bulletin on Henri Gerard and was awaiting responses that might not come, similarly obliged to press on with some of his more conventional police work while he marked time. Peregrine had planned to start a new commission this morning, so at least had something to occupy his attention for the day.

After lunch saw a resumption of the lecture Adam had been forced to curtail on Monday. Even so, the afternoon seemed to drag by, only briefly leavened by a lively tutorial session with some of his brighter students. Four o'clock came and went without bringing any further word from McLeod, by which Adam inferred that there must be nothing new to report. Overruling an impulse to phone up his Second on general principles, he wound up his day at the hospital with a 4:30 staff meeting, then went home to shower and shave.

At least the evening promised some diversion, though not as originally conceived. Weeks before, he had made plans to attend an advance review performance of *Die Walküre*, scheduled for tonight at the Playhouse Theatre. Those arrangements had included a pre-theatre dinner engagement with Sir Matthew Fraser and Janet, his wife, who were friends of long standing—a comfortable threesome, even though Janet's ongoing attempts to find a match for one of Edinburgh's most eligible bachelors occasionally wore on Adam's nerves.

He had counted on Matthew's presence to keep Janet from pressing the matter too stringently, but with Matthew unexpectedly called away to fill in at a medical conference in Boston, Adam had promptly invited Peregrine and Julia along to swell the party, so that Janet could exhaust some of her matchmaking energies on the two of them. The pair had been keeping company for nearly a year now, and Adam suspected that marriage was an eventual probability. It had been agreed that the two couples would meet up in Edinburgh for dinner, and proceed from there to the theatre.

Adam had Humphrey drive him in the Bentley. They collected Janet at the Frasers' elegant home near Dunfermline, then continued on to the Caledonian Hotel, where Adam had booked a table overlooking the lamplit sweep of Princes Street and the Princes Street Gardens. Peregrine and Julia had not yet arrived.

"This must be one of the most romantic views in all of Edinburgh!" Janet exclaimed, as she slipped gracefully into her chair and laid aside her beaded evening bag. "However, it really does seem a waste that you should be sharing it with me. Fond as I am of your company, Adam, I can't help thinking it's a great pity that your lovely Ximena isn't here in my place. But then, I suspect that you're probably thinking much the same thing," she added archly, picking up a menu.

A stillness came over Adam's chiselled face at the reminder of recent disappointment. "You make me out to be very uncivil," he said quietly.

"Not at all," she replied. "I make you out to be what you are: a man with a lady on his mind. Now, let's see what's on offer tonight. Do you suppose it's too early in the season for venison?"

As she turned her attention to the menu, Adam pretended

to study his own. The lady of whom Janet spoke was Dr. Ximena Lockhart, an American surgical specialist who, up until three months ago, had been working in Edinburgh on contract as a consultant advisor in emergency room practice and procedure. Adam had met her the previous December in the emergency room at Edinburgh Royal Infirmary, when an auto accident had brought him in as a casualty. Their attraction for one another had flourished from the outset, giving rise to the first intimately romantic relationship Adam had allowed himself to enjoy in many a long year. They had even spoken of marriage, though there was no disguising the difficulties that must be resolved to accommodate their respective careers.

Since then, she had been obliged to cut her contract short and return to California, because of the terminal illness of her father. The relationship now hung in limbo, though at least the almost ghoulish process of waiting for her father to die forced a time of mutual reevaluation. Unfortunately, too, most of the onus was on Ximena; for though Adam's qualifications as a psychiatrist would have enabled him to practice virtually anywhere in the Western world, the ties that bound him to Scotland were such that he could not break them without violating a commitment as solemn and inviolable as the ordination vows of any priest. He had not yet broached this aspect of his requirements to Ximena.

"Well, there's no venison on the menu," Janet said brightly. "And sitting there mooning isn't going to bring her back, Adam."

A wistful smile tugged at one corner of his long mouth as Janet's words brought back to him all the bittersweetness of loss and longing. Rather than let her see the depth of his feelings, he took refuge in a wry shrug of his shoulders.

"I won't deny missing Ximena's company," he said lightly, "but life must go on."

Janet started to pout at this apparent piece of flippancy, but then she took a closer look at Adam's eyes.

"You really oughtn't to let her get away, you know," she told him quietly. "All your friends would like to see you happily married—even to a colonial, if that's what you truly want.''

It was spoken in all sincerity. As Adam groped for a suitable response, somewhere in the back of his mind he could hear an echo of his mother's voice.

"The way of an Adept is sometimes fated to be solitary," Philippa had told him, early in the days of his initiation. "It is not a road you can easily tread in company—as much for the sake of those you love as for the sake of the Work that must be done. It can be done, but only if both parties are willing to make considerable sacrifice."

Experience since then had taught him that his mother had been speaking nothing less than the truth.

"What I want," he said aloud, "is not the only thing at issue here."

"That's certainly true," Janet observed with a sisterly tinge of asperity. "But your wants *are* important. I suppose you'll tell me next that there are a hundred and one other things that have to take precedence. Granted that you may be right, I'd still like to see you just once try putting yourself first."

It was rare for Janet to speak with such intensity. But before Adam was obliged to answer, he was saved by the approach of the maître d', with Peregrine and Julia following close behind.

"Julia, you look radiant tonight," Adam said lightly, rising to take her gloved hand and kiss her cheek as a beaming Peregrine greeted Janet and the maître d' seated them.

Like Adam and Janet, the two were attired in evening wear: Peregrine in black tie and dinner jacket, Julia in a full-length frock of pale blue silk-crepe with white kid gloves. As the couple settled in their chairs and the maître d' departed, Adam sensed that the pair of them had been up to something. There was a shared gleam of mischief in the looks they exchanged across the table, which Janet apparently noticed too.

"You two look like a pair of Siamese cats who've just jointly eaten a canary," she exclaimed. "Are you going to confess of your own volition, or have Adam and I got to tease it out of you?''

Grinning, Peregrine glanced over at Julia. ''Will you tell them, or shall I?''

The twinkle in Julia's blue eyes was a match for the sparkle of the sapphire hair clips holding back her red-gold curls.

''I'd rather just *show* them,'' she told Peregrine, and drew off her left-hand glove.

The flash from the dainty heart-shaped ruby set round with diamonds proclaimed their news better than any mere words.

''You're engaged!'' Janet exclaimed delightedly, as Adam nodded, his smile a little wistful. ''When did this come about?''

Peregrine grinned through a rising blush. ''We've been toying with the idea for quite some time, but it just became official this afternoon. The ring was my grandmother's engagement ring.''

''Oh, how lovely for you both!'' Janet said, leaning over to give Julia's hand an impulsive squeeze. ''Have you given any thought to a wedding date?''

''Sometime in the spring, we think,'' Julia said, ''though we haven't yet fixed a day.'' Diverting another laughing glance over at Peregrine, she added, ''We'll be sure to let you know, the moment it's decided.''

Adam had kept silent during the past exchange, but now he rose and smilingly offered Peregrine his hand.

''Congratulations, my friend,'' he said warmly, ''and I mean that with all my heart. And Julia, my dear,'' he continued, turning to kiss her again on the cheek, ''I'm very happy for you both. Whatever the future may bring,'' he said, resuming his seat and signalling for a waiter, ''I do believe that tonight calls for champagne. . . .''

The ensuing dinner assumed a hitherto unanticipated air of festivity that lasted through the meal and saw them into the theatre. Until the lights went down, Adam was able to let himself be carried along on the tide of his young friends' high spirits and good fortune, refusing to let himself dampen the mood by dwelling either on his own romantic frustrations or on the uncertainties of the task currently set before them. But the tumultuous music of *Die Walküre* drew him back to his own concerns, and he found himself brooding inescapably on the dark responsibility still hanging over him.

The Seal still missing, and Gerard still at large. Two of the many reasons why he could not afford the wondrous distractions of the heart, especially when there was nothing he could do right now to resolve his own situation. And yet the thought of Ximena stayed with him, like the echo of a musical phrase.

He carried that thought home with him later that night. Once he and Humphrey had seen Janet back to her house and were on the final stretch back to Strathmourne, he could not stop himself from comparing this evening to the many others when it had been Ximena sitting next to him in the darkness, drinking in the magic of the music, or merely enjoying one another's presence in the same room. Her image in his mind made him suddenly, exquisitely aware of the silken resonance she had left behind her in the car, in his house, everywhere that the two of them had been together, haunting as a lingering breath of rare perfume. As Humphrey pulled in at the gates to the manor, he found himself calculating the eight-hour time difference between Scotland and California.

Declining his butler's offer of tea, he went upstairs to his bedroom and sat down on the bed. He gazed for a moment at the bedside telephone, then impulsively reached for the receiver. A quick tattoo of his fingertips over the buttons elicited the sound of a telephone ringing on the far side of the North American continent.

He let it ring three times, then abruptly forced himself to hang up. Just now, there were more urgent priorities at stake. Indulging a loneliness that could not be satisfied, at least at present, would only blunt his edge for the confrontation to come—and there *would* be a confrontation with whoever had stolen the Seal. He only hoped that he and his could find the thief before irreparable damage was done, both to that individual and in a larger sense. The potential for disaster, if Nathan's Seal really was the Seal of Solomon, and guarded what Adam feared it might, was so awesome as to be almost unthinkable.

CHAPTER ELEVEN

THE Saturday of the Templar investiture dawned fair, but by noon, as Adam was completing his hospital rounds, a wind had picked up and the clouds had rolled in, bringing with them a dour possibility of showers to come. The uncertainty of the weather was reflected in a general mood of restlessness among Adam's patients, but with gentleness and the skill of long practice, he was able to allay the signs of disturbance where he found them. After a quick lunch with two of his fellow consultants, he was able to quit the hospital in good time to drive back to Strathmourne for a fast shower and a change into attire more appropriate for the afternoon's activities.

The measure of the rest of the day's success was going to depend on the Dundee ring, and whether or not Miss Morrison could be prevailed upon to loan it to them. This presumed, of course, that the lock of hair preserved in the ring had, indeed, been cut from the head of Dundee. If so, since hair came from the actual physical body occupied by a soul during a given lifetime, the lock would provide one of the most potent possible links for attempting to make an esoteric contact across the abyss of the astral void. Only blood was more potent—and obviously impossible to procure, since the body once known as Dundee had been dead more than three hundred years. Still, the prospect of utilizing such a relic presented the most immediate and likely means for possibly gaining access to whatever knowledge Dundee might have had of the mysterious Seal of Solomon and what it guarded.

And if Miss Morrison declined to let the ring out of her custody? That would complicate matters, but they still might salvage *some* insight. Whether or not they gained private access to the ring, Adam's backup plan called for Peregrine to examine the ring on the spot with his Sight, and later draw whatever resonant images might come to light. At least that was a procedure not likely to elicit unwelcome attention or comment—though if the artifact proved to be genuine and they *were* denied useful access, that made the Dundee cross even more important in their reckoning.

He was considering such alternative plans of action as he headed down to the gate lodge to collect Peregrine. Since the weather was not yet totally deteriorated, he had left the Jaguar's soft top down for the drive into town. A greyed tweed daywear jacket and vest muted the red of the Sinclair tartan of his kilt, and a Balmoral bonnet with a red and white diced band confined his hair, twin eagle feathers behind the Sinclair cap badge proclaiming his status as a chieftain. Close by his right hand, tucked into the top of his grey kilt hose, the pommel of his *skean dubh* sported a pale blue stone the size of a pigeon's egg. The *skean dubh* itself was a common enough accoutrement to be worn with Highland attire, but this one was also a familiar working tool of his esoteric vocation, as was the sapphire signet ring on his right hand.

He tapped on the horn as he drew up beside the door of the gate lodge, and the door opened almost immediately.

"'Lo, Adam," Peregrine said cheerily, tucking a zipper portfolio under one arm as he pulled the door shut behind him.

He cut a dapper figure as he came down the steps, impeccably turned out in a tan tweed daywear jacket and vest with his kilt of brown Hunting Fraser tartan. After tossing his portfolio into the backseat, he dropped his door keys into his brown leather sporran, then opened the car door and eased himself into the passenger seat.

"Well, I see that I've chosen the correct uniform of the day," he observed with a grin, as he shifted briefly to adjust his kilt pleats under him.

"You have, indeed," Adam replied. "There's a cap behind the seat, if you want it. We'll put the top up before we go in, but it seemed a shame to lose what may be the last nice afternoon for a while.''

With a nod of thanks, Peregrine retrieved the indicated cap and put it on, adjusting it to a rakish angle in the mirror on the visor and then buckling up as Adam eased the Jaguar out onto the road, heading for the motorway several miles away.

"So," Peregrine said, as he settled down with one arm braced along the top of the doorsill. "I've never been to anything quite like this before. Any pointers on protocol I should hear before we get there?"

"Not really," Adam said, smiling. "It's basically a church service, as I recall—all pretty straightforward." He glanced over his shoulder toward the zippered case. "I see you've come prepared."

Peregrine grinned. "That's only the official arsenal. I've also taken the liberty of squirrelling away a pocket sketch-book and a couple of pencils in my sporran. I wasn't certain whether it might put people out of countenance if I sketch during the investiture itself."

"I shouldn't think so," Adam said with a chuckle. "It's certainly no more obtrusive than taking photographs—less, actually—and I don't think there's any problem with that. Besides, I know you'll be discreet. Quite frankly, most of the knights of my acquaintance would take your artistic interest as a compliment."

"Good, because aside from the serious work we have to do, events like this are a treasure trove of inspiration for an artist," Peregrine said. "It's like stepping onto the stage of a historical costume drama, and all in living color!"

"I suppose one *could* look at it that way," Adam agreed.

They went on to discuss the general game plan for the afternoon as they sped across the Forth Road Bridge and on along the sweeping curve of the Queensferry Road, mostly ignoring the good-natured glances they attracted en route—for the sight of the open sports car bearing two attractive Scottish gentlemen in traditional dress invariably turned heads and occasionally elicited waves from appreciative ladies of all ages.

A light mist had started to descend by the time they threaded their way southward into Palmerston Place, which fronts the Gothic splendor of the Episcopal Cathedral of St. Mary. They were fortunate to find another car just pulling out of a choice parking space in an adjoining side street, and Adam waved an appreciative half-salute in the other driver's direction before whipping the Jaguar into the space just vacated.

Tossing their caps into the back of the car, he and Peregrine made short work of putting the top up and locking up the car, then headed briskly back toward the cathedral's front porch. Peregrine, with his zipper case under his arm, was already in his element, happily noting details of attire of the other guests arriving. Almost all of the men were kilted, but many of them sported Highland finery of earlier times, recalling the real history underlying such romances as *Rob Roy* and *The Master of Ballantrae*.

They strode up the main steps under a grey sky increasingly threatening serious rain. As they entered through the great doors, passing through the narthex into the cathedral's spacious interior, Peregrine immediately became aware of a sense of reverent expectancy charging the air with unseen energy, different from any of his previous visits to the cathedral. Off to his left, in the receding shadows of the north aisle, he could see the beginnings of a procession forming up. He decided that the handful of men and women who formed the leading ranks of the procession must be postulants, for they wore no regalia as yet. But behind these, he caught glimpses of other figures moving to and fro in a shifting panoply of white mantles emblazoned at the left shoulder with the red Templar cross—members of the Order's existing chivalry.

He slowed in his tracks, intent on catching a better look, but at that point, a big barrel-chested man appeared around the corner of the choir screen and hailed them with a wave of a meaty hand.

"Ah, there's our host," Adam said, heading them in that direction. "Come and let me introduce you to Stuart MacRae."

MacRae, Peregrine decided, would have made a striking subject for portraiture. Tall above average, and stout as an oak tree, he wore the red tartan of his clan with the informal assurance of a born Highlander. The effect was further heightened by the fact that his grizzled chestnut hair was pulled back in a queue, in the style of a Jacobite laird, tied with a velvet ribbon. White teeth gleamed in a broad smile through a luxuriant thatch of chestnut beard as he came forward to pump Adam's hand.

"Ah, *there* you are!" he said heartily. "Welcome, Sir Adam! Glad you could make it!"

"So am I," Adam responded. "Stuart, I'd like you to meet Mr. Peregrine Lovat, one of my associates. He's also a very fine artist, and hoping to find some inspiration here today. Peregrine, Stuart MacRae."

"Well, then, welcome, Mr. Lovat," MacRae said, offering Peregrine a hearty handshake. "I think I've heard your name before."

"Only good things, I hope," Peregrine responded, smiling. "I'm very glad that Adam let me tag along. I've been looking forward to it."

"Well, I hope we don't disappoint you," MacRae said cheerily. "In any case, I'm always happy to meet a friend of Sir Adam's. He did tell you, I hope, that the date of this investiture commemorates a very special Jacobite connection to the Templars?"

"No, I don't think so," Peregrine replied, glancing at Adam, who shrugged minutely.

"Ah, well then. On September 27, 1745, Prince Charles Edward Stuart received Scottish Knights of the Order of the Temple at a special reception in the Palace of Holyrood, at which time the Prince himself became a Templar. There's a braw painting in one of the Queen's galleries that I like to think was meant to depict the event. Being an artist, ye may know it, Mr. Lovat. It shows the Prince flanked by Lochiel and Pitsligo, the Chiefs of Clan Cameron and Clan Forbes—a broody, darkling picture."

"If it's the same one I'm thinking of, I know it well," Peregrine said. "The artist was John Pettie. It's one of the more dashing paintings I've ever seen of the Prince, but as an artist, I've always been more intrigued by the other two faces. The background is very dark, as you say, but there they are—loyal and stalwart at their Prince's back. The faces are intriguing.''

"Aye, that's the one," MacRae agreed. "Ye *do* know it! Anyway, we'll be holding a formal reception later this evening to commemorate that event—the Soirée of the White Cockade, it's called. We do it every year. You're both welcome to come along, if you like.''

"I'd like to, Stuart, but I'm afraid we'll have to pass," Adam said easily. "Mr. Lovat's just gotten himself engaged to a most attractive young lady, and I'm trying to wind up some research for an article I'm writing. Which reminds me, I'm supposed to meet a Miss Fiona Morrison here. Could you point her out to me, and perhaps introduce us?''

"Och, aye, but I think it'll have to wait until after the service," MacRae said. "She's back in the vestry, giving some last-minute help with decorations and mantles and the like, and it's nigh on time to start.''

"So it is," Adam replied with a glance at his pocket watch. "Perhaps we'd better go claim our seats, then. We'll catch her afterwards.''

"I'll see that she doesna get away," their host agreed.

MacRae's summons produced a white-mantled usher, who conducted Adam and Peregrine to choice seats in the upper choir stalls, far over to the right. Perhaps two dozen people were already seated in the choir facing the center aisle, mostly friends and members of the families of those present to be invested. The seats farther forward, in the chancel itself, remained empty, reserved for the participants about to enter. Peregrine had just time enough to get himself settled with pencil and pad in his lap when there was a heightened stir on the far side of the choir screen, back where the procession was forming up in the north choir aisle.

A current of unspoken excitement swept through the body of the cathedral, like a rising gust of wind. Touched by the breeze as it passed, Peregrine experienced an unlooked-for thrill of mystery along with anticipation.

The service commenced in solemn silence as the white-mantled column passed quietly along the long north aisle toward the back of the church, then turned to process down the center aisle. The waiting congregation rose to acknowledge and receive the procession as the first knights mounted the two steps onto the choir level—the Order's sword-bearer, carrying a great claymore, followed by the paired standard-bearers of the various Templar commanderies all over Scotland.

Next came the processional cross of the Order, followed by a knight bearing a case containing what appeared to be a badly rusted spur and a blackened bit of metal that might have been part of a sword blade—Templar relics belonging to the Order, Adam guessed, at Peregrine's glance of query. Clergy of half a dozen different religious denominations followed the relics, preceding five solemn-looking postulants who shortly would receive the accolade, the sign and seal of knighthood. The three men wore kilts, the two women kilted skirts. The looks of rapt intent on the five earnest faces reminded Peregrine of the occasion of his own initiation into the ranks of the Hunting Lodge, not yet a year ago, though his had been on a slightly different scale from this. Marching by twos after the postulants came the chevaliers themselves, forty or fifty of them, men and women alike, arrayed in their white mantles emblazoned with the red cross of the Order.

Last of all came the Grand Prior, together with the bearers of his personal standard and his sword, escorted by eight mantled knights with drawn swords. The dignity of the procession was heightened by the slow, silent tread of the participants, the panoply of the bright banners, and the sweep of white mantles over the multi-colors of the kilts, settling to an expectant hush when the last person had filed into place in the chancel and lower choir stalls.

The service began with an opening hymn—most fittingly, "Onward, Christian Soldiers." Lifting his voice with all the rest, Peregrine was struck by the singular fitness of the third verse:

Like a mighty army moves the Church of God.
Brothers, we are treading where the Saints have trod.
We are not divided, all one body we,
One in hope, in doctrine, one in charity. . . .

The words, at once simple and rousing, seemed to underline a truth Peregrine had already come to realize in his own vocation as a Huntsman—that there was an essential unity among all those called to the service of the Light, defying all external accidentals of form.

"Just as all the colors of the spectrum are unified in a beam of pure light," Adam once had said, "so are all souls of good and noble intent brought to resolution by Light Divine. Thus every man who serves that Light is at one with us, and we with him."

The kinship evoked by that unity was strong in Peregrine's mind by the time the hymn swelled to a close. As the organ accompanied the final *Amen* and everyone was seated, he found himself overtaken by a sense of wider reverberation, as if the voices of this gathered assembly had wakened echoes beyond the range of normal sound. Like the full range of harmonics generated by the plucking of a single harp string, the resonances seemed to linger in the air, felt rather than heard.

The texture of echoes seemed all at once rich and deep, denser than it had any right to be from this relatively small, select congregation. It was a texture Peregrine associated with packed assemblies of singers—echoes from a cathedral crowded to capacity, not three-quarters empty as this one was at the moment. All the same, he could not shake off the odd feeling that the cathedral was somehow fuller than it looked. He even glanced back toward the doors at the far end of the nave, half expecting to see a whole crowd of late-comers come spilling across the threshold; but beyond the confines of the choir stalls and sanctuary, there was nothing to be seen but empty chairs. The sense of imminent presence continued to haunt him throughout the ensuing prayers and Bible readings.

That sense of imminent presence teased at the edges of

Adam's perceptions as well, intensifying as a stir among the unmantled postulants signalled a shift into the actual ceremony of investiture. As the first of the five candidates was escorted forward to kneel and receive the knightly accolade, head bowed before the Grand Prior and hands resting on an ancient volume of Sacred Scripture, Adam felt within him the stirrings of a kindred affirmation that had its roots in memories of a deep and distant past of his own.

Without the aid of a properly focused trance, which was inappropriate in his present circumstances, the past itself was beyond the immediate reach of his conscious mind, but its sensory resonances played about him like breezes blown in from the incoming tide, striking a resonance in his very soul as the sword was lifted in the Grand Prior's hands and flashed downward to dub the kneeling candidate on each shoulder and on the head.

"Sois Chevalier, au Nom de Dieu. Avances, Chevalier. . . ." Be thou a Knight, in the Name of God, Arise as a Knight. . . .

As the neck cross was fastened around the neck of the new-made knight and the mantle was laid about his shoulders, Adam briefly knew the weight of a similar mantle on his own shoulders, and felt the grip of a sword hilt within the compass of his right hand. Unbidden, his heart rose in martial response to a distant call of arms. Though only its echoes reached his outward senses, those echoes were enough to hold him spellbound, like a rumor of distant battlesong.

Suspended on the threshold of trance despite his intentions, Adam was aware of being suddenly one of a great company stretching back many centuries. Though he turned no physical gaze from the new knight now retiring to be replaced by the next candidate, he found himself suddenly aware of a veritable sea of mailed and white-robed forms that shone before his eyes and all around him, like mist in sunlight. The knightly host was so vast that it filled his vision, as if the cathedral's interior, by some mystical transformation, had been somehow enlarged by their presence. It was as if all the Knights Templar who had ever lived were somehow manifested here today to welcome these newcomers into their ranks.

When the last new chevalier had received the accolade, Adam closed his eyes and made his will one with their predecessors in offering up a communal prayer for the welfare and guidance of these new-made champions of the Light. His prayer was compounded by the solemn reading of the ancient oath of fealty of the knights of the Scottish Temple. Tradition held that the oath had first been administered to knights of the Scottish Priory in the year 1317, three years after fighting alongside King Robert the Bruce at the Battle of Bannockburn. Though the language of the text had since been updated, that oath had never been rescinded, either by papal bull or by order of any Grand Master. The knight who read it now for the affirmation of the incipient new knights did so in fellowship with thousands who had gone before them:

"Inasmuch as the ancient Realm of Scotland did succor and receive the Brethren of the most Ancient and Noble Military Order of the Temple of Jerusalem, when many distraints were placed upon their properties, and many heinous evils upon their persons: the Chevaliers of the Order do here bear witness.

"Chevaliers of the Order do undertake to preserve and defend the rights, freedoms, and privileges of the ancient and sovereign Realm of Scotland. Further, they affirm that they will maintain, at peril of their bodies, the Royal House of the Realm of Scotland, by God appointed.

"Chevaliers will resist with all their might, attempts by any person, or bodies of persons, wherever or however authorized outwith the Realm of Scotland, to take unto themselves the ancient Realm of Scotland, or any portion thereof.

"As we Chevaliers do fear the perils to our immortal souls, upon our Knightly Honours, we attest the foregoing, and before God we so swear."

"We so swear," the assembled knights repeated in unison, newly made and veterans alike.

Affirmed by them all before the altar, in the presence of

the Grand Prior and all the assembled company, the oath set the seal upon their dedication to serve sovereign and country. By extension, it was also a promise to serve a higher realm and a higher order of sovereignty, for the ultimate Master of these earthly knights was God Himself, and all these were sworn in His service.

The deeper meaning of the oath touched Peregrine too, standing at Adam's side, and he glanced obliquely at his mentor as the oath concluded. The image that met his eyes startled him almost into crying out, and did drive him back a step, for in that split instant of perception, Adam appeared to him not as a modern-day Scottish gentleman but as a bearded knight in chain mail, wearing the white surcoat and scarlet cross of a Knight Templar.

It was not the first time that Peregrine had Seen Adam take on a historical change of aspect. But on those previous occasions, the historic imaging had been semi-transparent, like a photographic negative superimposed on a fully developed print. This time, the visual transformation was all but complete—as if, rather than donning a costume, Adam had unconsciously lowered his mask of the present to allow a hidden aspect of himself to shine forth. In a sudden glimmer of insight, Peregrine realized that the emergence of Adam's Templar persona must be in direct response to the investiture ceremony itself.

It was a striking demonstration of the evocative power of ritual. At the same time, it was indicative of the strength of Adam's historical bond with the Order. Whether or not Adam was consciously aware of the change that had come over him just now, Peregrine had the feeling that it might be worth remembering. As they sat, the oath completed, he took a fresh grip on his pencil and again began to draw. . . .

CHAPTER TWELVE

THE investiture service concluded with a succession of prayers for the welfare of the Order and the world at large and then a final hymn. Afterwards, a rousing organ postlude accompanied the knights' recessional back down the center aisle and up the north side, where the participants dispersed.

When Peregrine had put the finishing touches to his last sketch and zipped up his portfolio—Adam had drifted down into the aisle to chat with an acquaintance—the two of them headed back into the nave, where Stuart MacRae was deep in converse with a stout, rosy woman of indeterminate years, with a shelf of lace on her ample bosom. Her sturdy, strong-minded appearance put Adam very much in mind of one of his great-aunts on his father's side of the family, and the green and blue tartan of her long kilt skirt convinced him that she could only be the redoubtable Miss Morrison.

This supposition was confirmed when MacRae performed the introductions. She offered a firm handshake, first to Adam and then to Peregrine, inspecting both of them with her shrewd, bespectacled gaze.

"Yes, you *are* who I thought you were, Sir Adam," she observed with a smile, her bifocals winking up at him. "Oh, we've never met, but you're a supporting member of the Royal Scottish Preservation Trust, aren't you?"

Raising an eyebrow in some surprise, Adam smiled at his interrogator and said, "Guilty as charged, Miss Morrison. May I take it that you likewise have an interest in the Trust?"

"I have, indeed," said Miss Morrison. "I make it a point to attend their sponsored lectures whenever I can. You spoke at Gleneagles last year on the relationship between intuition and archaeology.''

"I hope you enjoyed it," Adam replied, genuinely impressed. "You have an excellent memory."

"It was a memorable lecture," she countered. "One of the most interesting I can recall offhand. I was intrigued by your central thesis, that intuition is a valid tool for archaeological research."

"Well, I'm very pleased to hear that my rather cockeyed ideas were well received in at least one quarter," Adam said with a chuckle. "I'm afraid quite a few of the Trust's more conservative members are inclined to regard me as something of an eccentric."

"More shame to them, then," Miss Morrison said stoutly. "If it's being eccentric to take an interesting new angle on some of the issues and problems related to historical research, then all I've got to say is that we could probably do with a bit more eccentricity in our ranks."

She cut herself short with a cluck of her tongue. "But, listen to me, wittering on when what you're really interested in is this ring of mine! Here, let me get it out and show it to you."

So saying, she snapped open the sporran-like purse on her arm and took out an embroidered white handkerchief wrapped around something small and lumpy. As she unwrapped it, Peregrine wordlessly sidled closer to look on over Adam's shoulder. Light from the chandelier overhead reflected richly off a heavy gold ring, which she laid expectantly in the hand Adam extended to receive it.

The design of the ring, together with the size of its band and its weight of precious metal, suggested that it had been fashioned to be worn by a man rather than a woman. The band was broad and plain, supporting a cabochon oval of transparent rock crystal mounted on a solid bezel. Beneath the crystal, pressed flat against the gold of its backing, was a tightly wound lock of dark hair. After giving it a moment's close scrutiny, Adam passed the ring to Peregrine for his comment.

"It certainly seems to be of the period," he said, as

Peregrine likewise inspected it. "What can you tell me about its provenance?"

"Well, it's been in our family for about a hundred years," Miss Morrison said placidly, as Peregrine narrowed his gaze, hoping to catch a telltale flicker of ghostly resonance. "Traditionally, it's been the legacy of the eldest son, but there were only girls in my generation, so my father—God rest his soul—passed it on to me. He knew, you see, that I was the one most interested in historical artifacts and curiosities."

"A hundred years," Adam said, as Peregrine handed the ring back to him with a faint shake of his head to indicate that he had picked up nothing from it. "That's a fairly long time, but it doesn't begin to take us back to Dundee's days. How did your family happen to come by the ring in the first place?"

"Oh, that's simple enough. My great-great-grandfather acquired it with the contents of a house he purchased up in Huntly. That was in the 1880s. I should perhaps mention that the previous owner of the house had been an elderly gentleman by the name of Mackintosh, supposedly of the same branch of the family that fought alongside the Duke of Argyll in the 1715 Rebellion. It was family tradition that a Mackintosh brought the ring to Scotland from France at that time. Remember that it hadn't been that long since Killiecrankie. Plenty of people in those days would have regarded such a ring as a luck-token, since it contained a lock of the hair of the famous Bonnie Dundee."

For just an instant, Adam flashed vividly on the drawing Peregrine had done at Blair Castle, of James Seton, the Earl of Dunfermline, tearfully cutting a lock of his slain friend's hair for the sake of remembrance. It could well have ended up in a memorial ring, as a lucky talisman. But so far, there was still ample room for doubt.

"Forgive me if this next question sounds impertinent," he said apologetically to Miss Morrison, "but I find myself obliged to ask what grounds you have for accepting that the lock of hair under the crystal is truly Dundee's—aside from family tradition."

Miss Morrison pursed her lips thoughtfully. "Well, for one thing, the ring is mentioned in a number of wills pertaining to this particular family of Mackintoshes as 'Dark Johnny's Taiken.' You won't need me to remind you that Dundee's Highlanders liked to refer to the viscount as their 'Dark John of the Battles.' Beyond that, the dating on the wills confirms the family's ownership of the ring at least as far back as the period between the '15 Rebellion and the Rebellion of 1745. Admittedly, some professional historians might regard the evidence as a trifle soft. Speaking for myself, however, I'm prepared to go along with my intuitions and assert that the ring is a genuine artifact."

Adam did not immediately respond. As he turned the ring this way and that to examine it from all sides, he was simultaneously aware of a tingling sensation in his fingertips. The sensation grew more pronounced the longer he held the ring in his hands. It seemed to him almost as if his personal touch might be activating some hitherto dormant resonances associated with the ring's history. And yet, Peregrine had indicated no particular reaction to the ring.

The apparent contradiction was enough to whet his curiosity to a cutting edge. Masking his true level of interest, he returned the ring to the handkerchief Miss Morrison handed him and summoned a smile.

"If you're going to invoke intuition, I see I'm in danger of being hoist on my own petard," he said lightly. "I can hardly challenge your position without compromising some of my own arguments."

Miss Morrison gave an appreciative chortle. "If I invoke intuition, Sir Adam, it's only in the nature of giving credit where credit is due."

"I shall take that as the compliment I hope is intended," Adam said with a chuckle. "Tell me, do you suppose I might impose on you so far as to borrow the ring for a few days? Besides taking some photographs for the article I'm writing, I'd like Mr. Lovat here to study the ring in greater detail and make an artist's assessment of the workmanship."

All at once Peregrine found himself the target of a disconcertingly penetrating pair of blue eyes.

"So you're an artist, are you, Mr. Lovat?" Miss Morrison observed. "I've just remembered that you were at Sir Adam's lecture too. I was rather wondering if you might be a psychic of some kind."

Peregrine just missed letting his jaw drop. "I hope you're not disappointed," he said, summoning his most ingenuous smile.

"Only a little," she replied. "I've often thought it would be interesting to hear what a psychic would have to say about this ring of mine."

"I can arrange that, if you're really serious," Adam said with an easy chuckle. "I know a psychic or two. In the meantime, *would* you be willing to part with the ring for a few days?"

"Oh, I think so, since it's you," she said. She watched as Adam took a pen and business card out of his pocket and began writing out a receipt. "I'd need it back before next Saturday, though. Could you really introduce me to a psychic?"

Smiling, Adam handed her the card.

"Of course. Let me think about it a few days. And I promise you shall have the ring back before next Saturday. If I can't return it in person, my valet will act as my courier."

"That would be splendid," said Miss Morrison. "Actually, you or your man could save either of us a round trip between here and Inverness if you deliver the ring to the National Gallery here in Edinburgh. They're doing a special exhibit of Jacobite memorabilia, and I'd already agreed to let them include the ring in their display."

"Well, then, I'll have it delivered back to the National Gallery no later than—say—Thursday," Adam said, tucking the ring and its handkerchief into a jacket pocket. "Will that suit them?"

"Oh, I'm sure that will be fine," Miss Morrison replied. "And you won't forget about the psychic?"

Adam restrained a grin far better than Peregrine, who had to cover his own amusement with a feigned cough.

"Oh, I shan't forget," he assured their benefactress. "We'll make the arrangements after the exhibition is over."

After parting company with Miss Morrison, he and Peregrine stayed on long enough to let Stuart MacRae introduce them to the Grand Prior and some of his officers before taking their leave. As they made their way back to the car through a light mist, Peregrine could hardly contain himself.

"Good God, that was almost too close to home for comfort!" he exclaimed with an owlish glance over his shoulder. "Do you suppose Miss Morrison had any inkling of the truth?"

"I'll certainly grant her more than a fair share of intuition," Adam said with a faint smile. "For what it's worth, that fact probably worked out to our advantage. Still feel up to working this evening?"

"Of course," Peregrine said. "I'm not sure how much I'll be able to get, though. Not much was coming through before, but that may have been because Miss Morrison was there, and I didn't really feel confident opening up. *You* were looking a little odd, though."

"Was I?" Adam said.

"Oh, not that anyone else would notice," Peregrine assured him, as they got back into the Jaguar. "I didn't know you were able to pick up things from objects."

"Ordinarily, I don't," Adam replied. "I'm not even sure I did just then. But we'll see what *you* pick up first, when we get home. And maybe I'll give it a try as well."

They arrived back at Strathmourne shortly after six o'clock. Adam learned from Humphrey that McLeod had phoned from London in their absence, but the news was disappointing: still no sign of the elusive Henri Gerard. Suppressing his frustration at the thought of what the Frenchman might be up to, Adam led the way into the library, shedding his jacket and loosening his tie as he gestured Peregrine to his customary chair before the fireplace.

It was too warm for a fire, but Adam moved a candlestick

from the mantel down onto the rosewood table Peregrine set in front of his chair, lighting it before retrieving the Dundee ring from his jacket pocket. He avoided touching it as he unwrapped it from its handkerchief and set it on the table at the foot of the candlestick. Peregrine had already begun to compose himself in silent meditation, sketchbook on his lap and eyes closed behind his gold-wired spectacles, but he stirred slightly as he sensed Adam sitting in the chair to his left, his eyes opening to fix immediately on the candle flame.

"I can see that you're already one step ahead of me," Adam said, quietly assessing his subject. "Are you ready to go deeper?"

With a faint nod, Peregrine murmured, "Yes."

"Take a good deep breath, then," Adam said, and reached out to lightly touch Peregrine's left wrist.

Impelled by that now-familiar signal, Peregrine let go his hold on present time and place and slipped effortlessly into trance. As always, the change in his perceptual orientation brought with it a sense of immanent depths. All at once he was aware of dimensions beyond the normal apprehensions of his conscious mind, through he was not yet quite deep enough to See them.

He never came this far without feeling like an archaeologist poised at the entrance to an unexplored pyramid—half-afraid, half-exhilarated, at the prospect of plumbing the unknown. He took an unhurried moment to calm and center himself, drawing another deep, relaxed breath and then slowly exhaling. As his heartbeat and respiration slowed and steadied, Adam's resonant baritone intruded from the borders of normal perception.

"You're ready to go deeper now. On my signal. . . ."

As if in slow motion, the hand that had touched his wrist lifted now to press lightly across his forehead. Eyes closing, Peregrine knew a brief, swooping sensation in the pit of his stomach, and a fleeting psychic sensation as of walls falling away from him on all sides. Liberated, his astral self took flight like a hawk springing airborne off the fist of its falconer. Adam's voice was in his ears as he spiralled aloft and hovered, seeking a grounding point below.

"Open your eyes and focus on the ring now," Adam urged quietly. "Let the ring be your beacon in time."

He could not but obey. A circle limned by burnished gold swam slightly out of focus before his entranced gaze. Like the peregrine breed for which he was named, he homed in on it. The circle seemed to expand until it filled his field of vision, so that he found himself looking through it, as through a porthole. Gradually the roiling shapes beyond took form and held their focus.

It was dark night under a canopy of trees. A tall man in a riding cloak stood at the crossing of two woodland paths, an unshuttered lantern glimmering on trampled ground at his feet. The dim glow of the lamp underlit the man's face beneath a broad-brimmed chapeau with a sweeping white plume. Peregrine knew him even before he lifted his head, half turning so that the light fell full upon his features—the patrician nose, the firm, sensitively modelled lips above a strong chin—and upon a Templar cross against the froth of lace at his throat.

Bonnie Dundee!

Even as the Cavalier general turned his noble head in query at a sound, he was joined at the crossroads by two women so heavily cloaked that nothing could be seen of their faces until they shook back their hoods. Both of them were young and slender, with heavy dark hair and darker eyes in their pale, finely drawn faces. Even by the dim light of the lantern, Peregrine judged them to be sisters, so close was the resemblance between them.

Dundee greeted the elder of the two with a kiss, his expression so solemn that it was clear that the gesture had little or nothing to do with mere courtly convention. As the younger girl stepped forward and lifted her face to receive the viscount's salute, Peregrine was struck by a sudden, potent conviction that she was someone he knew. The pang of recognition, sharp as a knife thrust, was enough to make him catch his breath. But before he could frame any clearer impression of her aspect and identity, she was drawing back into the shadows, leaving Peregrine to focus on Dundee. It was only then that he realized that the viscount was holding something concealed beneath his cloak.

Dundee crouched down beside the lantern, the girls kneeling with him, and Peregrine's gaze was drawn to the viscount's gloved hands as he drew out a lightweight bundle wrapped in white silk. With a care approaching reverence, he presented it to the sister who had been first to greet him. She allowed him to place the bundle in her hands, then lifted her eyes to meet his, her expression one of wondering inquiry. When he nodded unspoken encouragement, she folded back the wrappings, revealing something that shone with warm, metallic luster in the lantern light.

It seemed to be a crown of some kind—a diadem whose broad, textured circlet was surmounted by six tall, upturned points of beaten gold. The simplicity of the design and the quality of the metal together bespoke immense antiquity.

Fascinated, Peregrine attempted to get a closer look at it. As he narrowed his focus, the diadem all at once seemed to come to life, shimmering as if infused with an inner heat of its own.

The shimmer brightened to a molten glow. Haloed in that glow, the gold itself seemed to liquefy, racing and flowing without losing its shape. Each point seemed to dance like a tongue of fire, spreading outward, molten light tracing two interlocking triangles that pulsed with a rhythm that echoed Peregrine's own heartbeat. Dazzled by the orient blaze of fiery metal, he lost himself in ardent contemplation of its refined and fluid symmetry . . . until a voice recalled him sharply by name.

"Peregrine." The authority of the voice sufficed to pull back a tenuous link with the world beyond his vision. "Peregrine, whatever you're seeing, try to let your perceptions channel through your hand. Don't try to analyze. Just let the images flow through your hand, and draw what you see."

Obedient to his guide, Peregrine drew a deep breath and made the conscious shift, feeling the faint twitch in his right hand as the transition became complete, hardly blinking lest he lose the images of what his hand began to sketch. It felt vaguely different from what it usually did when he attempted to capture resonances from a *place* of psychic import. This was more compelling, less under his control. Having embarked, he was not certain he could have pulled back, even had he wished. The crown held him in its thrall—urgent, potent. . . .

And Adam, leaning forward to observe as images now began to appear under Peregrine's quick pencil strokes, found his own attention increasingly caught and held by the same compulsion that drove his young colleague.

CHAPTER THIRTEEN

THE first few strokes of the pencil established the general setting—the bold impression of three kneeling figures, one of them Dundee, by the suggestion of strong profile and the unmistakable shape of a Templar cross amid the lace at his throat. But it was what Dundee and his two companions regarded that quickly caught and held Adam's attention as Peregrine's efforts focused in on it, more confident now, smoother and more sure, taking on the deliberate fluidity of automatic writing.

The picture that eventually took shape under Peregrine's pencil might almost have been a detail from a heroic painting by Rembrandt: an oriental diadem clasped firmly, almost protectively, by two outstretched hands. They were definitely a woman's hands—and that seemed like it should mean something to Adam—but it was the design of the diadem that drew his gaze like a magnet. The six upturned points of the Crown were like the half-furled petals of the wildflower known as Solomon's Seal.

The realization catapulted Adam briefly back into the dream of Solomon, the night after Nathan's death. Surely the crown of Peregrine's sketch was not the crown of his dream. What had John Grahame of Claverhouse to do with King Solomon's Crown? And yet, before his stunned and captive gaze, a ghost-image of the crown in his dream seemed to superimpose itself above the drawing of the crown—two interlocking triangles forming a six-pointed star as the points of the crown flattened out.

The crown in the sketch *was* Solomon's Crown. Suddenly Adam knew that with the same certainty by which he knew himself bound to find Nathan's Seal before those who had stolen it could unleash the terrible secret it guarded.

Somehow the Seal and the Crown were linked—and the revelation of the link had been invoked by the ring containing Dundee's hair, which meant that Dundee himself was somehow linked with the Crown or the Seal or both. The Crown now became a possible factor in recovering the Seal—or possibly in protecting what it guarded, if the Solomonic imagery held true.

He was pondering this possibility, in light trance himself, when Peregrine suddenly gave a heavy sigh and surfaced spontaneously, giving his head a shake as if to clear his vision and setting down his pencil to flex his drawing hand.

"Well, *that* was certainly different," he said, as Adam also blinked himself back to normal consciousness and glanced at him. "I wasn't sure what to expect, but it certainly wasn't that."

He cast a look down at the drawing in his lap, squinting and peering like someone trying to compensate for an eyesight deficiency.

"That's interesting," he went on. "I wasn't sure what the Crown looked like."

The remark made Adam wonder whether Peregrine's inner vision might have matched his own.

"You didn't draw what you saw?" he asked.

"Well, yes and no," Peregrine replied with a frown. "I—think this is what it looked like physically, but there was another reality to it. It was as if—as if there were another crown inside the one I drew. A bit like something from an Egyptian tomb, I thought at first—Middle Eastern, at least. Very ancient, almost primitive in its simplicity: a circlet of pure gold with six triangular points.

"Then it—*changed*. The gold—came to life, I suppose is the only way to describe it. It seemed almost to catch fire, but the fire held its shape. . . ."

His frown deepened. "Somehow it reminded me of biblical accounts of Pentecost—something to do with a visitation of Divine Wisdom."

This halting observation served to confirm the conviction that had formed in Adam's own mind.

"Solomon's Crown," he stated flatly.

Peregrine lifted his gaze and stared, openmouthed. "Good Lord."

"Good Lord, indeed," Adam agreed. "I dreamed about King Solomon and his Crown the night after Nathan died. I didn't think to mention it before, because it just as easily could have been an ordinary embellishment of images connected with recent events. I wasn't sure it had any direct bearing.

"But he was wearing *that Crown*." He tapped the drawing with a forefinger. "And he was holding what appeared to be the Seal in one hand and a sceptre of some sort in the other. There's the cross again too," he pointed out. "A pattern is starting to emerge, and Dundee is a part of it."

"Maybe so. I think you're right," Peregrine agreed. "But why would he have given the Crown to these two women?"

At Adam's look of sharp inquiry, the artist went on to relate what had transpired in the introductory phase of his vision.

"I can't tell you how I know this, but I'm certain Dundee was the keeper of the Crown, up to that point," he said. "When he handed it over to the elder of the two sisters, I had the distinct impression that he was entrusting it to them for safekeeping. I'm afraid I don't know what happened after that," he finished apologetically. "I got so wrapped up in looking at the Crown itself that I had no attention to spare for anything else. In a way, I'm amazed that I drew as much as I did."

"Well, I don't suppose that's surprising, under the circumstances," Adam said. "I would venture to guess that what you were Seeing was the aura associated with the Crown—the psychic image of its essential nature, if you will. The fact that your vision of it made such a profound impression suggests that the Crown is probably an object of considerable power—which it certainly could be if it is, indeed, the Crown of Solomon."

"But what does that have to do with the Seal?" Peregrine asked.

Adam shook his head. "I can't tell you that exactly, but

given what we've put together about Dundee, I would say that it's highly probable that he and the Crown are directly linked, historically and metaphysically, with the Seal we've been looking for.''

Peregrine's lips made an awed little *O* as he whistled low under his breath.

"Then, since we haven't yet got either the Seal or the Crown, it sounds like Dundee is still our best hope of finding out more. I don't understand about the ring, though," he went on, glancing toward where it lay glinting softly at the foot of the silver candlestick on the little rosewood table. "From the fact that I Saw him on the Astral, I'd guess that the lock of hair embedded in the bezel must be his. But if so, why didn't he manifest himself more directly? I thought hair and blood were supposed to be the most potent sorts of links.''

"There are two possible explanations," Adam said thoughtfully. "First of all, your principal receptive talents aren't those of a medium. Noel might have had an entirely different reaction—and we'll see about that when we have him work with the Templar cross down in Kent. It could also be that the associations of the ring itself are more strongly attuned to someone else who later owned the ring. Perhaps one of the women you mentioned.''

"Now, *that's* certainly a possibility," Peregrine said. "It would account for their images being so strong.''

"But you have no idea at all who they might have been?" Adam asked.

"None," Peregrine said frankly. "That bothers me, too, because the younger one seemed intensely familiar to me. I remember thinking that I must have met her before, but I just couldn't pin down where or when. I don't suppose there's any way to follow up on that?''

"Not without something more concrete than you've given me to go on," Adam said regretfully, for he had just been considering that same question himself. "I'll confess, this business of another identity impinging on the ring has me stymied. I've never encountered it before. Given time to think this through and do some research, I might be able to come up with an explanation, but the 'why' isn't really at issue here. Far more useful would be 'who' or 'what.' Realistically, though, I think we're going to have to hold off on those questions until we've got access to the cross—and Noel, to work with both artifacts and see if he can sort out anything.''

''But that isn't until Monday!'' Peregrine observed in some frustration. ''Anything could happen between now and then!''

''I'm well aware of that,'' Adam said. ''But I don't see how it can be helped.''

''Neither do I,'' Peregrine admitted, but his expression remained dogged. After a moment's thought, he said, ''Consider this: We've surmised that Dundee gave a crown—possibly King Solomon's Crown—into the keeping of the two sisters I saw. We've agreed that this crown may have been a Templar relic, possibly connected with the Seal. Is there any chance at all that Dundee might have passed on his knowledge to a successor before he died?''

''I would guess it highly unlikely,'' Adam said. ''It was both Dundee's glory and his folly that he paid little heed to any suggestion that he might be killed in action at Killiecrankie. Before the battle, his men begged him to hold back and not risk himself, fearing that if he was killed, the whole campaign would be lost—which, in fact, happened, even though they won the day. It was the beginning of the end for the Stuart cause. His only concession for the day was to change his customary red coat for a buff cavalry jacket under his breastplate—the one you drew up at Blair Castle.

''As for confiding his secrets to another Templar, we don't even have any evidence of who other Templars might have been at the time—or I don't know, at any rate—and certainly no evidence to indicate that he ever took the precaution of sharing any of the knowledge he held in trust. Perhaps he preferred the risk that his knowledge might be lost, to the risk of its surviving to fall into the wrong hands. Or maybe he had confided something to your two sisters when he handed over the Crown.''

Peregrine sighed and began leafing idly through the other entries in his sketchbook from earlier that day. "I can see that I'm going to have to try to draw them," he said. "It's more and more clear that they're key figures in the puzzle. You know, though, given the continuity of Templar tradition itself, it's a pity there isn't some way to arrange things so that some present-day Templar could communicate with Dundee on our behalf, on the strength of their communal bond within the Ord—"

He paused as his hand turned up the drawing he had made of Adam in the semblance of a Templar knight.

"I say, Adam," he murmured. "Something's just occurred to me. Take a look at this."

He passed over his sketchbook so that his mentor could see what he had drawn earlier that afternoon, and Adam scanned the quick study Peregrine had done of him as a Templar knight.

"This isn't the first time I've Seen you as a Templar knight, you know," he said, as Adam looked the drawing over. "We both know that you have historical connections of your own with the Order, both spiritual and hereditary. Might there not be some way to make use of those connections? After all, Dundee was only one of a long line of Templar Grand Priors. Even if he took his knowledge with him to his grave, what about all those who came before him? Is it possible that you yourself could have been one of them?"

"I very much doubt it," Adam said. "If I had been, and it had any bearing on our present situation, it's highly likely that such knowledge would have surfaced spontaneously by now."

"All the same, you apparently *were* once a knight," Peregrine persisted. "If you were to reveal yourself as such on the Astral, might not the Grand Master of your day and age be willing to communicate to you whatever he might have known about Solomon's treasures and their powers?"

"You assume that I would have been important enough to be entrusted with such information," Adam said with a smile. "Besides that, I think my Templar persona's demise somewhat predates the arrival of Solomon's treasures in Scotland—or at least *he* had no part in their relocation. Jauffre de St. Clair died in Paris, shortly before the last Grand Master, Jacques de Molay. That was in 1314. We know that the Seal was in Perth by 1381, to be pawned to Nathan's ancestor, and presumably whatever it guards was also somewhere in Scotland by then. But neither Jauffre nor his Grand Master would have had any knowledge of that."

"Then, what about your actual blood ancestor who took back Templemor after the suppression?" Peregrine asked. "That's later. He might have known something—maybe even just a rumor of whatever secret the Order was guarding. And maybe he'd tell it to a descendant, who'd also been a Templar himself."

Adam nodded thoughtfully. "It's a long shot, but it might be worth a try," he agreed. "With Noel away, we're really at loose ends until we head down to Kent on Monday."

"Shall we go up to the castle, then?" Peregrine asked. "I'd think that would be the natural place to make contact, if it's going to happen."

Adam nodded. "I agree. Several times, out at the ruins, I've thought I caught sight of a Templar knight standing in the doorway. I've always dismissed it as romantic fantasy, but maybe there's something to it. If I were to focus on a particular intent, it's just possible that something useful might surface. Are you free tomorrow?"

"I can be," Peregrine said. "When did you have in mind? Some friends of Julia's family have invited us to come for lunch after church, but I daresay I could beg off, if you want to make it a morning excursion."

"No, don't change your plans," Adam said. "You're newly engaged. It wouldn't be fair to Julia, when there's no need. The afternoon will do just as well—better, in fact, since it will give me the morning to do a bit of historical review. Just don't let your luncheon engagement drag on too late."

"That's no problem," Peregrine agreed. "What time do you want me here?"

"I think we'll ride up, to help set the mood," Adam said,

"so I'd like to be in the saddle no later than three. Actually, you can bring Julia along, if you like. You can show her how the restoration is progressing; bring those first sketches you did, when it was all still falling to bits. I'd like you there with your sketch pad, just on general principles, but I don't expect I'll need to call on you for anything she shouldn't see. She does ride, doesn't she?"

"Yes, she does," Peregrine said, "and weather permitting, I'm sure she'd enjoy that—as long as you're quite certain she isn't likely to come face-to-face with a Templar ghost in full battle armor."

He cocked an owlish look at his mentor, and Adam chuckled.

"I think you can rest easy on that account," he said with a smile. "As far as any visible demonstrations of our work are concerned, all Julia's likely to see is you making a few imaginative sketches while I daydream about the family past."

"I'll take your word for that," Peregrine said with a wry grin. "Now that I've finally convinced Julia's family I'm capable of earning a living with a paintbrush, the last thing I want to do is scare her off!"

True to his plan, Adam spent the better part of the following morning tracking down the names and locations of former Templar properties in Scotland. It was common knowledge to anyone with a background in Scottish history that most of the lands belonging to the Order of the Temple at the time of its suppression had ended up in the hands of the Hospitaller Order of St. John of Jerusalem. Of six baronies held by the Knights of St. John after the suppression of the Templars, five were former Templar sites: Thankerton, Denny, Temple Liston, Maryculter, and Balantrodoch, the latter of which had been the preceptory for all of Scotland.

There were scores of lesser sites as well. One source mentioned nearly six hundred Templar holdings in Scotland alone, and named a fair number of them. Running the names through his mind like beads on a string, Adam had to wonder whether any of these places might yield a clue to the mystery he and his colleagues were seeking to unravel.

Peregrine and Julia arrived shortly after two o'clock, both of them in breeches and boots and equipped with velvet-covered riding caps. As they headed out to the stableyard, Peregrine donned a day-pack containing his art supplies over his tweed hacking jacket. Julia, with her red-gold curls pulled back in a ribbon at the nape of her neck, looked almost the cavalier lady in her riding jacket of forest green, with a hunting stock tied close around her throat.

John, the former Household Cavalry trooper who looked after Adam's horses, had their mounts standing saddled and ready for them, and helped Julia get mounted up and adjust her equipment. Adam took the lead as they set out, mounted as usual on his tall grey hunter, Khalid, with Peregrine following after on Khalid's stablemate, a spirited blood-bay mare called Poppy. Julia brought up the rear on Crichton, a reliable, well-schooled dun gelding borrowed with permission from the daughter of one of Adam's tenant farmers.

The afternoon was bright and cool. Skirting a wide field full of golden hay stubble, they trotted decorously along a drainage ditch until they came to a gate at the edge of a rolling pasture. Once past the gate, they quickened their pace to an easy canter, making for the belt of mingled larch and fir trees on the far side. Above the firs rose the wooded slopes of Templemor Hill, surmounted at its crown by the twin turrets of Templemor Tower.

Even at a distance, Adam could appreciate the difference wrought by recent months of intensive restoration. A year ago, the tower house had been roofless and under siege by ivy, its stair turrets headless and jagged, with small trees growing from the first-floor vaulting. Since then, the gaps in the walls had been rebuilt, the tower reroofed, and the cap houses restored atop the stair turrets to present a picturesque skyline of crow-stepped gables and jutting dormers capped by grey-green slate. Most of the scaffolding around the chimneys had disappeared since his last visit. Much interior work remained yet to be done, but Adam was pleased with all that had been accomplished so far.

At the foot of the hill, he and his companions slowed as they struck a wooded bridle path that wound its way upward, in and out of shadow, like a thread laid down by a weaver's shuttle. The first time Adam had brought Peregrine up to see the tower, before restoration began, there had been no other way to approach it. Now a single-lane tarmacadam track ran up the back of the hill from a farm access road a quarter mile away—a necessity so that the men engaged in doing the reconstruction work could more easily bring in supplies and machinery, but once that work was complete, Adam hoped one day to see the unsightly lane transformed into a graceful private avenue.

The air grew fresher as they climbed toward the summit of the hill. At the top of the path, the trees parted, affording them a clear view of the tower house itself, its newly reharled walls whitely agleam. Down below the clearing on the other side of the hill, a parked earth-mover guarded the partially opened trench being dug to accommodate supply connections for plumbing, electrical, gas, and telephone service. The view in that direction, however, was effectively obscured by a thick screen of trees, their leaves only lightly touched with the beginnings of autumn color. Gazing around him as they dismounted, Adam was satisfied that there were no visible distractions to compromise the investigation he had planned for the next half hour or so.

The three of them tethered their horses at the edge of the clearing and left them to graze, Julia gawking delightedly as they continued on foot.

"Adam, this is really wonderful!" she exclaimed, tipping her head back to get a better look at the upper stories of the house. "It looks almost like something out of a fairy tale. Leave out the doors and the lower windows, and you'd have a proper artist's setting for Rapunzel."

Peregrine laughed. "If you'd seen it before the restoration started, you'd have said it looked like something out of a *horror* tale. It was really sad. Here, I'll show you."

He shrugged off his day-pack and drew out a largish binder bulging with plastic sheet protectors. As he opened it to the first sketch for Julia's inspection, Adam recognized one of the studies the young artist had made on his very first visit here. The collection as a whole represented Peregrine's first effective exercise of the esoteric talent he had since come to use so effectively in the service of the Hunting Lodge—a composite historical picture of Templemor Tower, based on what Peregrine had Seen of its past and its structure. The accuracy of those studies was reflected in the present-day reconstruction of the building.

"My architects found Peregrine's drawings extremely useful when they were drawing up their plans for the reconstruction," Adam said, watching Julia's face as she leafed through the pages in the notebook. "I have your future husband to thank for much of the success of this enterprise."

This remark bought a warm smile to Julia's lips. "He is *awfully* good, isn't he?" she confided with a mischievous twinkle. "Just don't say things like that too loudly in his hearing, or you'll make him terribly conceited!"

"Me? Conceited?" Peregrine exclaimed in tones of mock outrage. "Here I am, positively *pining* for a few kind words—"

He broke off with a muffled yip as Julia reached out and gave him a playful tweak on the ear.

"I can see you two are headed for a lifetime of marital bliss," Adam laughed. "Peregrine, why don't you go show Julia the layout on the inside, now that they've got the stairs rebuilt? I probably ought to go inspect the site farther down and see how they're coming on with the gas mains, but it's *not* a view I would recommend to anyone else."

"I agree," Peregrine said, covering his slight nod of comprehension with an easy grin. "Come on, Julia. Let's see if this gives you any ideas about what you'd like in the way of a dream house."

The two of them disappeared across the threshold, the cheerful echoes of their conversation floating after them as they moved off to explore the rooms that now made up the tower house's interior. Satisfied that he could count on being alone for the next little while, Adam turned his gaze briefly to the Sinclair crest painted on the lintel above the doorway, where vibrant color picked out the nearly obliterated carving of its original device: above a twisted torse of red and gold, a red Maltese cross surrounded by seven gold stars rather than the phoenix crest used by Adam's more recent branch of the family. The cross and the stars together suggested even more of an esoteric connection than had occurred to him on previous visits, even when watching Peregrine paint in the design some weeks before.

That anchor and link to the past gave him focus as he turned and withdrew to the edge of the clearing, seating himself on a large cut-stone block facing the entrance to the old keep. He was wearing his signet ring under his riding glove, and he clasped his left hand over it in physical affirmation of his intent as he briefly bowed his head in prayer. Then, mentally commending himself to the inspiration of the Light, he straightened and set both hands on his thighs with palms upturned and composed himself to settle into an effective working level of trance.

A sense of deep calm stole over him as he drew in a deep breath and let it out. Grounded in that calm, he called to mind the image of a knight in Templar array, standing in the open doorway of the tower. It was an image he had glimpsed before and never pursued, but now he made it the focus of his concentration. Drawing further in upon himself in spirit, he willed himself to even deeper levels of awareness as he framed a voiceless appeal to his knightly kinsman of bygone days.

The silence around him expanded, insulating him from all outward distractions, and a faint tingling in that stillness moved him to let his gaze drift outward. As he waited passively, a light that was not of the waking world or of the weakening afternoon sun manifested itself in the shadows of the tower's open doorway, gradually growing fuller and brighter until, shimmering on the threshold, it resolved into the luminous image of a knightly form.

The knight was accoutred for battle, with the red cross *formée* of ancient Templar usage bold on the front of his white surcoat. His gauntleted hands gripped the quillons of a great sword, its blade flickering like quicksilver along the length of his mailed legs. The face beneath the mail coif was bearded and stern, the eyes keen and compelling.

Who summons Aubrey de St. Clair? came the knight's sharp query, understood rather than heard. *Speak, for I may not tarry long.*

In vision, Adam met the other's piercing gaze without flinching. Drawing himself up, he gave back the reply.

I am Adam Sinclair, descendant of your blood and lineage and brother in spirit to your Order. In this time and place, I am also Master of the Hunt, with a task set before me that concerns the Order of the Temple. I dare to hope that you may have knowledge that will assist me in its execution.

The figure from the doorway was suddenly before him, close enough to touch, its brightness expanding to encompass Adam in its shimmer. In that instant, he became aware of a change in his own appearance, of a ghost-image of himself rising out of his entranced body, garbed not in the fashionable riding clothes his body wore, but the white mantle and gleaming mail of a Templar knight.

That change of aspect, he realized, betokened Aubrey's recognition and acceptance of their common bonds. As he clasped the gauntleted hands that Aubrey offered, Adam opened his mind to that of his Templar kinsman, sharing with him unreservedly all he had been able to learn so far of Solomon's Seal and Solomon's Crown. Nor did he hold back from communicating his fear that the thief who had stolen the Seal would find a way to track down the Crown as well, along with any other artifacts associated with it.

All I know at this point is that these Templar treasures collectively represent a power too dangerous to be let loose on the world, he informed his counterpart soberly, using thought-framed words to emphasize his own feeling of urgency. *If you have knowledge bearing on this matter, I entreat you to tell me.*

There was a brief pause, followed by a strong nonverbal surge of bleak regret from Aubrey de St. Clair. Then the other knight's thoughts crystallized briefly into language.

I have no information to offer. Certain it is that our fleet brought many treasures out of France, but nothing came to Templemor. Perhaps the preceptory at Balantrodoch holds what you seek.

Alas, Balantrodoch stands no more, Adam replied. *Is there some other location that might have served as a secret treasury? I* must *have a starting point.*

Again the regretful negative, and this time a note of restlessness, a pulling back.

Aware that the light surrounding him was starting to fade, Adam resigned himself to accept failure, at least in this attempt. Letting his feelings speak wordless thanks, he watched in dazed silence as the shade of Aubrey de St. Clair slowly dissipated. Just before it vanished completely, however, he was briefly aware of a gentle touch, like a benison, just at the back of his mind.

Then he was sitting alone on a hard stone block, blinking himself back to normal awareness in fading sunlight that now had a chill bite to it, heralding the dusk. Everything, it seemed, was going to depend on tomorrow's excursion down to England to meet the mysterious and reputedly formidable Sir John Graham of Oakwood.

CHAPTER FOURTEEN

FOLLOWING abbreviated rounds at the hospital the next morning, Humphrey having driven him in, Adam took himself and his overnight bag out to the airport in a taxi. An anxious-looking Peregrine was standing by at the gate, where most of the other passengers had already boarded, but his face lit up in a relieved smile as Adam approached.

"What a relief!" he exclaimed, handing over Adam's boarding card and ticket. "You're all checked in, but I was starting to worry that you might have gotten held up at the hospital."

"It *has* been known to happen," Adam conceded wryly, "but I seem to be in luck today."

Their flight to London was uneventful. They had a cold lunch in-flight and touched down at Gatwick shortly before one o'clock, right on schedule. McLeod was waiting for them at the gate, and briskly escorted them to the curbside, where a uniformed constable was standing by beside the red Ford Grenada McLeod had rented. With McLeod at the wheel, they sped eastward from the airport, eschewing the motorways farther north to strike out directly across country on the A264 toward Royal Tunbridge Wells. While they drove, Adam brought McLeod up to date on the events of Saturday and Sunday, especially regarding the Dundee ring and its apparent Templar connections.

"You have it with you?" McLeod asked.

For answer, Adam took the ring out of his coat pocket and put it in the inspector's outstretched hand. McLeod fingered it thoughtfully, barely taking his eyes from the road, then handed it back to Adam.

"This isn't really the time to take a close look, but it may be useful, if we get cooperation on the cross. And you say Peregrine's brought the sketches?''

''They're in the boot, with my overnight bag,'' Peregrine offered. ''Do you think you ought to see them before we get to Oakwood?''

''No, we'll see whether they corroborate *after* I've done my bit with the cross and the ring,'' McLeod said. ''That way, my experience won't be colored by any preconceptions.'' He sighed. ''Incidentally, would you two like to hear what I've found out about our Henri Gerard, after a whole weekend with access to all the resources of the various London police forces and Interpol?''

Adam glanced at him sidelong. ''Why do I get the impression that all these resources were for nought?''

''Probably because they were,'' McLeod returned sourly. ''Nothing. *Nada.* Zip. I feel it in my bones that he's somewhere in the U.K., probably in Scotland somewhere, but as far as proof—he might just as well have been snatched off the face of the earth by aliens from outer space!''

After that, he and Adam briefly returned to a discussion of possible approaches for what they hoped to accomplish at Oakwood, then settled into companionable silence as the car ate up the miles. Adam occasionally gave navigation advice from a road atlas, and Peregrine daydreamed.

Quickly the fields of Surrey gave way to the Kentish countryside. Their route followed the northern boundary of the Weald, formerly one of the most thickly forested areas in all Britain. Much of the land had been cleared in modern times to make room for orchards and farms, but more than a few local inhabitants still kept green the memory of those former days when Edward III had required the services of no fewer than twenty-two guides to conduct him safely from London down to Rye.

The countryside here was far different from the moorland vistas of the Scottish borders. Ensconced in the backseat with his sketchbook on his knee, Peregrine was charmed by the passing views of fragrant apple orchards and fields of golden hops, with here and there a row of oast houses with their distinctively funnelled roofs, where the hops were stored and dried. Where fields in Scotland were flanked by freestone walls, here they were marked off by hedgerows canopied by wild roses, honeysuckle, and brambles, the latter weighted down with ripe black berries at this time of the year.

As his gaze swept out across the fields, Peregrine found himself recalling the "green and pleasant land" of Blake's famous poem "Jerusalem," immortalized in that hymn of the same name which had become almost a second national anthem for the English. Briefly he wondered whether it was possible that, in ancient times, the feet of the "holy Lamb of God" had, indeed walked upon "England's mountains green." On days like this, it was not difficult to imagine the young Jesus treading here with Joseph of Arimathea, as the Glastonbury legends insisted He had done.

Nor had Peregrine any trouble appreciating where such celebrated English artists as John Constable and Samuel Palmer had derived their inspiration for more secular subjects. The rural tranquillity of farm cottages and tame woodlands was subtly offset by shifting changes in the light. Peregrine became fascinated with the transparent flow of shadows across the landscape, sometimes blurring, sometimes highlighting details at a distance. The ever-changing patterns were almost hypnotic. After a while all the colors blurred together, and he nodded off into a light doze.

He roused some time later to find they were driving along a single-track country road, flanked to the left by rolling green pastures and to the right by the shady slopes of a wooded park. Immediately to either side was the dense thicketry of ancient hedges bright with wildflowers, though not so tall as to obscure the views beyond. Drawing himself up with a slightly guilty start, Peregrine glanced at his watch and was surprised to discover that he had been asleep for the better part of an hour.

"The Sleeper awakens," McLeod said drily, grinning at Peregrine in the rearview mirror as Adam glanced back at him. "Have a nice kip?"

Peregrine pulled a rueful grimace. "I must have been shorter on sleep than I realized. Where are we?"

"About half a mile short of our destination," Adam said. "I'd suggest you straighten your tie. We'll be there in another few minutes."

The entrance to the Oakwood estate was marked by a pair of sphinx-like stone lions standing guard at either side of the massive wrought-iron gates, which stood open and looked as if they were rarely closed. The drive beyond was bordered by majestic oak trees, the intricate spread of their branches overlacing the road like a baldachin. More oaks dotted the grassy parkland on either hand, interspersed with groves of lesser trees, mostly birch and rowan. Beyond them rose the battlemented rooftops and chimneys of a handsome Tudor manor house.

From the moment they passed between the stone gate-posts, Adam was quick to sense a change in the air. As they progressed farther up the drive, he became aware of a deep, protective hush underlying the twitter of birdsong and the stirring of a light wind among the trees. Recalling what Lindsay had said regarding Sir John Graham's esoteric abilities, he was not surprised to detect the subtle presence of powerful wards set permanently in place to guard Oakwood and its occupants. The latent potential energy in the very air was such that no one with psychic gifts could fail to be aware of it.

McLeod cast a wary glance around him, like a hunter conscious of venturing into unknown territory.

"This is quite a place," he muttered under his breath.

Peregrine hunched his shoulders, just missing a shiver. "I'm glad we're coming here as friends." He opened his mouth as if to comment further, then gave an involuntary exclamation of admiration as they rounded the last bend in the drive and he caught his first unobstructed view of the manor house itself.

The central wing of the house presented a handsome façade of half-timbered walls and gables and diamond-paned bay windows embellished with ornamental mould-ings. Peering up at the upper story, Peregrine counted eight chimneys, each one carved differently from the others. The stonework had all been executed in native Kentish ragstone, the hue of wild honey. Rose-tinted tendrils of ivy curled and twined their way up trellised sections of the walls, gentling the angles of the building with delicate networks of bright color.

To the hiss of gravel beneath their tires, McLeod drove them under the arch of a two-storied gatehouse into an open Elizabethan-style courtyard, where he parked the red Granada beside a tidy-looking Fiat Panda, in the shadow of what once had been the carriage house. A King Charles spaniel came bounding out to greet them as they got out of the car, its joyful barking further heralding their arrival as they approached the front steps, though it did not accompany them to the door. A tug at the bellpull summoned an elderly butler in traditional striped waistcoat and black coat, who received Adam's card with the stately formality of an old family retainer.

"Good afternoon," Adam said, as the butler's eyes flicked over the card. "I believe Sir John is expecting us."

"He is, indeed, sir," the butler replied with a slight bow that included McLeod and Peregrine as well. "Come this way, please."

From the high-ceilinged entryway he led them through a vestibule passage and along the length of a long gallery, its walls hung with portraits and landscapes. Though the collection included choice works by Romney, Gainsborough, and Reynolds, some of which Peregrine had seen before in photographs, he found his eye drawn to an unsigned late medieval tempera painting of a noble-looking gentleman kneeling with joined hands clasped in homage between those of a man wearing a royal crown. It stopped him in his tracks.

The legend on the tiny plaque at the bottom of the frame identified the subjects as King Henry VI and David, Second Earl of Selwyn. Though much of the painting had darkened with age, the faces held something ineffably poignant in the look locked between the two. Rarely had Peregrine seen a clearer depiction of the almost sacramental relationship between sovereign and subject that was the mystical essence of kingship. He was not even aware that he had lagged to a halt until a strong hand clapped itself to his shoulder.

"Come along, lad," McLeod muttered in his ear. "Best not keep our host waiting."

Adam's attention, meanwhile, was focused on the impending interview. The Dundee ring was loose in his coat pocket, and his signet ring was on his finger, but it was the prospect of seeing the Dundee cross that drew him now— and meeting its apparently formidable keeper. Glancing ahead beyond the butler's shoulder, he could see a door at the far end of the gallery, its oaken panelling carved with a design of oak leaves and acorns.

Through this door the butler led them, briefly along another short hallway and then to a similar door, on which he rapped respectfully before opening it and stepping through.

"Sir Adam Sinclair, Miss Caitlin," he announced gravely, "along with his associates."

"Thank you, Linton. Please show them in," called a musical contralto voice from the room beyond.

With old-fashioned ceremony Linton ushered Adam and his companion inside. A willowy young woman with shoulder-length chestnut hair rose from the overstuffed chair before the Tudor fireplace and came forward to greet them. She looked to be in her early twenties, with skin as freshly translucent as apple blossom, simply dressed in a silk blouse open at the throat and an easy, calf-length skirt, both in a robin's-egg blue. A single strand of pearls lay outside her collar, and the hand she extended to Adam was ringless.

"Welcome to Oakwood, Sir Adam," she said, smiling with easy informality. "I'm Caitlin Jordan. Sir John is my great-grandfather. It's a pleasure to have you with us."

"It's a pleasure to be here," Adam said, smiling in his turn. "These are my associates, Inspector Noel McLeod, from Lothian and Borders Police, and Mr. Peregrine Lovat. I hope we haven't kept you waiting."

"Not at all," she replied. "I'm actually surprised you got

here so quickly. Oakwood is somewhat off the beaten track, so we always make allowances for first-time visitors. How do you do, Inspector McLeod? I'll bet you drove, and that's how you managed to find us so readily. Mr. Lovat, I hope you had a pleasant journey."

As she offered Peregrine her hand in turn, he found himself looking deep into a limpid pair of dark brown eyes. The sensation was like gazing down into a clear woodland pool, a mirror of mutable reflections overlaying hidden depths. For the space of a heartbeat the reflections seemed to rise up and encompass him, catapulting him backwards in time to a primeval glade ringed round with towering oaks. In place of the lovely Caitlin, he was suddenly confronted by the vision of a slightly older but no less beautiful woman, gowned in flowing white and crowned with mistletoe like a Druid priestess. . . .

He took a grip on himself and shut his eyes briefly. When he opened them again, his vision was back under control. Aware that she was gazing at him in quizzical expectancy, he gulped slightly and tried to recall the question she had just asked. Adam, glancing his way and perhaps guessing what had happened, came to his rescue.

"The drive was very pleasant, thank you," he said. "The Kentish countryside is particularly lovely this time of year."

"Yes, we who live here like to think so," Caitlin replied. "But may I offer you a drink, perhaps? Or tea?"

Adam smiled. "I'd prefer to meet the general first, if you don't mind. I don't wish to appear unsociable, but—"

She raised her hand and inclined her head with an answering smile.

"You needn't explain, and I'm not offended," she said. "Come this way, then, and perhaps I can tempt you to tea *after* you've seen Great-Grandfather. He's waiting for you out in the gazebo. He thought you wouldn't mind, since the day is so fine."

A pair of French doors let them out onto a sunny terrace commanding a wide view of well-manicured formal gardens. Near at hand, the close-clipped lawns were interspersed with beds of lilac and roses. Beyond lay a boxwood maze. Above the hedge tops at the heart of the labyrinth, the domed roof of an ornamental gazebo gleamed white in the sunlight.

Glancing back to be sure they were following, Caitlin led them briskly down a flight of dressed-stone steps onto grass cut smooth as a bowling green. Keeping pace with her as they made their way toward the entrance to the maze, Adam remarked, "It was very good of Sir John to agree to see us at such short notice."

"Well, you *did* intimate that the matter might be one of some urgency," she replied. "Fortunately, tonight's a full moon, so if you intend to do any serious work with the Dundee cross, tonight is the absolute best time."

Adam managed to mask his own surprise, but he sensed McLeod stiffening behind him, and caught Peregrine's faint but audible gasp.

"Oh, you needn't worry," she went on with a slight smile. "We know who you are, and very shortly, you'll know who we are. These days, Great-Grandfather rarely sees strangers unless he's checked them out first. He's ninety-two, you know."

As she continued blithely on ahead of them to open the gate to the maze, Adam glanced back at his colleagues in reassurance. Her comment confirmed what he had already suspected—that the lovely Caitlin Jordan, though young in years, had been an initiate in many past lives as well as this one, but it was still a little disconcerting to be told that he and his had been "checked out." The impending meeting now assumed a more momentous weight. Adam Sinclair might be Master of the Hunt in Scotland, but Sir John Graham clearly was Master here. Though that realization carried no threat of danger, not knowing what to expect could not but make him slightly apprehensive as they paused at the gate to the maze.

"This is the entrance to our maze," Caitlin said, smiling brightly as she opened the gate and stood aside with a gesture of invitation. "If you keep always to the right, you can't go wrong."

It might have been a simple piece of advice, but after her

earlier comments, Adam was prepared to look for additional meanings. In esoteric terms, references to the right referred to the Right-Hand Path, or the path of Light, as opposed to the path of Darkness. Hence, the comment might have been meant as reassurance. All the same, as he and his companions entered the labyrinth, Adam found himself fingering the band of his signet ring, and was glad to have McLeod, in particular, at his back. It also would be interesting to see how Peregrine perceived the maze, being junior of the three of them and having less experience.

Peregrine himself, meanwhile, was wondering why their host should have chosen to receive them out here in the open air rather than inside the house. It also seemed curious that the lovely Caitlin had abandoned them to find their way without a guide. The maze itself did appear almost childishly simple in comparison with others he had seen, such as the famous Tudor maze at Hampton Court Palace. At the same time, however, as they ventured deeper among the close-clipped hedges, he seemed to sense an underlying pattern of invisible energies held in dynamic suspension. It was almost as if the external form of the maze were but the outer shell of some complex lock, awaiting only a fine adjustment to the mechanism to set its inner forces free.

The air inside the maze seemed preternaturally still, the country sounds of birdsong and the sough of breeze among leaves oddly muted. The thrum of disciplined power in the air was like the throb of a distant dynamo. The deeper they penetrated the maze, the more difficult Peregrine found it to concentrate. His physical vision remained unaffected, but his thinking seemed sluggish, lethargic.

''Adam, what kind of a place is this?'' he whispered, setting a hand on Adam's sleeve.

Adam paused and turned, though he did not look particularly concerned. McLeod's expression was unreadable.

''I thought you might have guessed,'' Adam murmured. ''It's a magical maze—a formal pattern for storing and directing psychic energy. I've seen them before. I don't think the pattern we're walking is meant for working—more likely, a protective pattern, perhaps a screening device. Is it bothering you?''

Peregrine gave his head a dazed shake, not in negation but in an attempt to clear his senses. His physical vision was still clear, but his inner perceptions were becoming oddly blurred, almost as if he'd been dosed with a narcotic.

"Yes, it is," he managed to say. "Are we—in any danger?"

"Not at all," Adam assured him. "The energy here is certainly benign. Having said that, however, even benign energy can have a distracting effect on those not familiar with the patterning. Try putting on your ring. That should help you stay focused as long as we're subject to the maze and its influence. I suspect the effect will go away once we reach the center."

Only then did Peregrine take in the fact that both Adam and McLeod were already wearing their rings. He nodded mutely and drew out his own ring from his trouser pocket. Its sapphire was emerald-cut rather than oval like Adam's, set in a plain bezel on a wide band carved with Chinese dragons. When he slipped it onto his finger, the effect was like a switch being thrown.

"Better?" Adam asked.

Peregrine nodded. "Much."

The fog had lifted from his inner vision, but the low thrum of unseen power persisted as a background accompaniment as they continued on into the maze.

The last turning of the maze led into an open area paved with flagstones. At its center lay the gazebo itself, an elegant structure of white trellises overgrown with roses, in whose arched doorway stood an erect, silver-haired figure in black, silently waiting.

From his war record, they had known that Brigadier General Sir John Graham must be over ninety, and his great-granddaughter had confirmed ninety-two, but there was nothing about his appearance to suggest either infirmity or decline. On the contrary, the upright length of his lean frame proclaimed an enduring vigor, and the canted hazel eyes were keen as an eagle's in his still handsome face—a face lined more by care, Adam judged, than by years. He was dressed entirely in black, from the black polo-necked sweater and slacks under his well-cut black blazer down to the silver-headed ebony walking stick resting beneath his clasped hands.

Added to what Adam had already perceived, the stark visual image immediately conveyed to him both the authority vested in his host and the esoteric tradition he represented. By the symbolism of Britain's Old Religion, ancient long before Christianity reached these shores, the figure of the Man in Black was the direct representative of the Horned God, who was consort to the Great Mother, the Lady of the Moon. Together, the Lord and the Lady constituted a duality of Deity that had guarded the welfare of the Island of Britain and ensured its fertility since time immemorial. Such guardianship was held to have protected the Island of Britain from foreign invasion more than once, most recently during the Second World War. It even occurred to Adam to wonder whether Sir John might have had a hand in that, for he certainly was of an age to have done so.

In any case, General Sir John Graham quite obviously was a very senior Man in Black, perhaps subordinate to none other in England. The tight-leashed power contained in the upright figure was formidable, easily a match for Adam himself, if differently focused. Nonetheless, Adam sensed more to their reception than a mere show of strength—a growing conviction that, in choosing to present himself in his rightful guise, Sir John was also paying his guests the ultimate compliment of acknowledging them as companions in the same service of the Light, even if they chose to approach that Light from different perspectives.

It was a heartening gesture of courtesy, but it suggested an awareness of their real intentions and function that could not be explained by two brief telephone encounters, one of them with the always discreet Lindsay. Caitlin had spoken of them being "checked out," and Sir John Graham was known to be a former intelligence officer; but unless the general was far more perceptive than even Adam's skills might suggest on a parallel level, there was no way he could know exactly who and what they were. And yet, as his eyes met Adam's, he seemed to *know*.

"So," he said, smiling. "You're Philippa's son. I'm very pleased to finally make your acquaintance. Please enter, and be welcome."

CHAPTER FIFTEEN

THE mention of his mother's name clearly startled Adam, but apparently it also defused any uncertainty he might have had about the hint of a ritual bidding phrase Peregrine thought he caught in the general's invitation. Without looking at either of his companions, Adam inclined his dark head in graceful deference and mounted the four steps up to the gazebo entrance, at the same time making a small movement that might have been a screened gesture of his right hand.

"The invited guest always honors the rule of the householder," he stated quietly, lifting his gaze unflinchingly to that of their host.

A firm handclasp met him and drew him inside, hazel eyes meeting his in unspoken approval. As Adam turned to call his colleagues to him with a glance, McLeod moved forward, Peregrine following behind him.

"Sir John, may I introduce my Second, Noel McLeod," Adam said, in a display of candor that surprised Peregrine, based on so short an acquaintance. "And this is Mr. Peregrine Lovat—among other things, an artist of rare talent."

The general's handclasp was sure and firm as he drew Peregrine from the last step and bade him welcome with an enigmatic little smile. In the hazy shade beyond lay a glass-topped round table of white-painted wrought iron surrounded by four matching chairs with cushions of flowered chintz. The sunlight filtering through the rose-twined trellises of the gazebo's supporting walls laid patterns of shadow on the floor like a covering of forest leaves. The sheltering shade provided the same sort of easy sanctuary as a forest glade. The dynamo thrum at the back of Peregrine's awareness had ceased as he crossed the threshold.

"A formidable Hunting Party," Sir John remarked, still smiling faintly as he swept a hand toward the chairs. "Please be seated, gentlemen."

The open identification of who and what they were gave Peregrine a moment's pause, but neither Adam nor McLeod seemed concerned. As Sir John shifted one of the chairs slightly and prepared to sit, Adam chose the one to their host's right and directed McLeod to the one at *his* right, leaving Peregrine to take the remaining one, at their host's left hand.

"So," Sir John said, settling himself with his walking stick resting on the floor between his feet, hands clasped atop the silver head. "I see no reason to continue sparring, since we all know, at least in general, who and what we are. Perhaps I ought to clear up one mystery before we go any further. Adam—if I may presume to call you by your Christian name—you're no doubt wondering how I came to be acquainted with your mother."

"I confess to a certain curiosity," Adam said, carefully neutral.

"Don't worry, my boy. I'm not about to reveal any hitherto unknown details of a sordid past," Sir John said with a smile. "Without violating any confidences, suffice it to say that your mother and I had business in common during the war—a matter of gravest national security. Philippa was only young then—not even as old as Mr. Lovat here—but I had good cause to respect her courage no less than those other abilities of hers which I suspect you have inherited in full measure."

"You're very gracious, sir," Adam murmured, a little taken aback.

"No, I acknowledge simple truth," Sir John said with a slight inclination of his silver head. "At my age, one does not waste energy on platitudes. Without Philippa's contributions, on a variety of levels, the war might have gone quite differently than it did. The next time you speak with her, I hope you will convey to her my warmest regards."

He had not asked, Peregrine noted, whether Adam's mother was still alive or not; once again it seemed clear that

Sir John Graham knew more about some things than one might have expected, even of the senior Adept he obviously was. At Adam's silent nod of acknowledgement and agreement, the general continued.

"Thank you. On to business, then. When we spoke on the telephone on Thursday evening, you very wisely refrained from detailing the precise nature of your interest in the Templar cross which I have in my keeping. However, now that we appear to have established our bona fides to one another's mutual satisfaction, perhaps you would care to elucidate. I'm intrigued that our paths finally should have crossed, and I'd be delighted to help you in any way I can."

"I think neither of us can fault the other's display of caution," Adam said, more relieved than he hoped showed. "*I* am certainly entirely satisfied. I only hope that your cross can, indeed, provide the help we need. Otherwise, all of us may end up involved in remedial action after the fact, rather than preventive medicine now."

He went on to furnish a concise account of the theft of Solomon's Seal and all the information he and his companions had been able to garner since embarking on their investigation.

"By now, I have no doubt that the Seal is an artifact of power," he said at the conclusion of his narrative. "My friend Nathan Fiennes had become convinced that its misuse could activate a particular and deadly danger, but we don't know what that danger is, or the Seal's specific function, or what else may be involved. I begin to suspect that Solomon himself may have had a hand in the original structure of whatever power the Seal controls."

He told him then about his dream of Solomon and the Crown, and Peregrine's corroborating evidence of a crown connected with John Grahame of Claverhouse. Sir John did not bat an eye at the revelation regarding Peregrine's artistic talents.

"The Crown may be a second part of whatever binds this power or evil or whatever it is that the Seal controls," Adam finished. "Peregrine's vision also tends to support our theory that knowledge of the Seal and the burden it represented once resided in the Masters of the Knights of the Temple, and came here with the Seal and what it guarded when members of the Order fled to Scotland. After that, we believe that the secret was passed to subsequent Scottish Grand Priors until it apparently was lost with the death of John Grahame of Claverhouse, who was wearing your cross when he died.''

''I see,'' Sir John said. ''Then what you hope to do with the cross is to use it as a link and focus to do what? To contact the spirit of Claverhouse?''

''That's correct. We have some experience in this sort of thing. Noel is a first-rate medium. It's our hope that through him, we may be able to bring Claverhouse through for long enough to find out directly from him what the Seal guards and how, not only so that we know what we have to fear, but also so that we have some idea what countermeasures to take.''

Nodding, Sir John briefly considered what he had just been told, then turned his gaze on Peregrine.

''This ring with the lock of hair—you're certain it's Dundee's?''

''As certain as I can be, under the circumstances, sir,'' the artist replied. ''I'm confident that my vision of the burial was accurate, based on prior experiences of this sort. Obviously, I have no physical proof that the lock of hair in the ring and the one I saw cut are one and the same—but I believe that they are.''

''Then why do you think the resonances were confused when you examined the ring?'' Sir John asked Adam.

''Believe me, I've asked myself the same question,'' Adam said. ''My guess is that the ring itself generates stronger resonances than the lock of hair, which is shielded behind a piece of rock crystal. I considered trying to remove the crystal, to gain direct access to the hair, but the ring isn't mine to tamper with. I would be breaking faith with its owner if I risked damaging it.''

''I understand,'' Sir John said. ''May I see the ring?''

Wordlessly Adam delved into a pocket of his suit coat and brought out the Dundee ring, setting it on the table in front of Sir John. The general laid his stick alongside his chair, then donned a pair of silver-rimmed reading glasses from the breast pocket of his blazer and bent down to inspect the ring from several angles.

After a moment, he picked it up and turned it to and fro, looking especially at the lock of hair imprisoned under the piece of rock crystal, then enclosed it in his right fist and briefly closed his eyes. When he opened them, he looked at the ring again, then set it back on the table's glass top.

"Interesting," he remarked, removing his glasses and returning them to his pocket. "See what you make of this."

So saying, he reached into another pocket and brought out a flat black jeweller's case about four inches square, which he set on the table before Adam. At a gesture of encouragement from their host, Adam picked up the box and opened it. Inside, pillowed on a bed of black velvet, was a cross *formée* of red enamel over gold, obviously of some antiquity, perhaps three inches long and with a small ring at the top end to take a chain or cord or ribbon.

"I can assure you that this is the cross worn by Dundee at the time of his death," Sir John said confidently. "An ancestor of mine received it from a French priest named Dom Calmet, who'd gotten it from Dundee's brother David. My ancestor was from a collateral branch of the family, of course; neither Claverhouse nor his brother left any heirs. There's family tradition that it was used in 1745 to invest Prince Charles Edward Stuart as Grand Prior of Scotland, when he was received into the Order of the Temple at Holyrood Palace; but knowing it was a precious relic, if only of Dundee, and knowing that he was about to set out on a gruelling campaign in which it might be lost, he returned it into the keeping of the then guardian, Sir Malcolm Grahame. But, by all means, feel free to make your own additional assessment."

"Thank you," Adam said. He picked up the cross briefly to examine it, then passed it in its box across to Peregrine. "What do you think?"

Peregrine stared at the cross but did not touch it. "It

certainly looks like the one I've been seeing," he told his superior, passing it on to McLeod.

"Noel?"

The inspector adjusted his aviator spectacles for a closer look as he brought the box to eye level, but also did not touch the cross.

"It does look old," he offered. "But I'll refrain from any close contact until I can handle it in a ritual setting. I wouldn't want to blunt whatever punch it's got for helping us bring Dundee through."

He set it back on the table in front of Sir John and met his gaze directly.

"Will you permit us to try that, sir?" he asked.

"Of course," the general replied. "My only condition is that the cross not be taken from these premises."

"That's understood, of course," Adam said.

"I can certainly provide you with a suitable place to work," Sir John went on, "if you'd care to acquaint me with your requirements. Naturally, I should like to be present, if only as an observer, but I will certainly understand if you require privacy for what you intend."

Adam had already been impressed with the protection he had sensed around the gazebo, even without a formal warding being worked. He had come to Oakwood with no preconceptions, but it was an unlooked-for benefice to discover that he both liked and—more important—trusted the formidable figure in black seated beside him. The discovery that he and Philippa had worked together during the war—and Adam was quite certain that the claim was true—only served to confirm that he and Sir John were working toward a common unified goal, sanctified by the Light, even though their respective traditions might differ according to practice.

"Actually," Adam said, "I would welcome your advice and support for the work I have in mind. Noel is one of the finest trance-mediums I've ever encountered, and very good at what he does, but up until now, most of our experience in this area has had to do with facilitating contact with entities already desiring to communicate. That's a fairly passive process. In this instance, we'll be attempting to summon a specific soul who may not be expecting or welcoming our call, depending upon its present situation. For that matter, we don't even know if the soul in question is presently incarnate.''

Sir John's gaze strayed briefly to the cross in its box on the table before them, his expression deeply thoughtful. When he lifted his head, his hazel eyes held a new warmth that had not been there a few moments before.

''Philippa must be very proud of you, my boy,'' he said with a smile that shattered the former sobriety of his demeanor like a shaft of sunlight cleaving through cloud. ''I'd be honored and delighted to assist you. If I may, however, I'll suggest that we postpone the actual work until later this evening. Since, as you've pointed out, we don't know whether or not the spirit of Claverhouse is presently in incarnation, we stand our best chance for success if you attempt to make contact at a time when we can reasonably hope that any present body will be asleep. That assumes, of course, that a present incarnation lives in roughly the same part of the world, and therefore, in a similar time zone,'' he added wryly. ''If not, and if any complications should happen to arise, we of course would be morally bound to break off and await a more appropriate moment.''

Adam nodded, recalling his own experience and that of the Hunting Lodge in repairing damage caused to an innocent soul kept too long separated from its body.

''I quite agree,'' he said. ''My associates and I have had occasion to see at close hand what can happen to a soul when a summoning is abused. I hasten to add that the original separation was not of our doing, and that eventually we were able to alleviate the damage done.''

''It had not occurred to me to doubt that,'' Sir John replied. ''But back to practicalities. We should discuss the general form for what you propose. The three of you obviously will be most comfortable working in your own tradition, which somewhat differs from my own. This presents no problem for me, if it presents none for you. I have worked in a variety of esoteric traditions, over the years.''

"So have I,'' Adam said with a nod.

"I thought that might be the case. Having said that, then, and because I will not be personally involved in the night's work, perhaps it might be most helpful if I devise a ritual setting that will accommodate both our preferred traditions—if you agree. Weather permitting, this is the sacred space we use for most of our work here at Oakwood.'' He indicated the interior of the gazebo with a sweep of his hand. "You may already have sensed that the resonances are—somewhat different from what you are accustomed to. That can be adjusted.''

Adam smiled in his turn. "You anticipate me. I had been hoping I might find the boldness to ask what you have already freely offered. The benefit of your wisdom and experience is beyond reckoning. In your house, and under your protection, we place ourselves unreservedly under your guidance.''

"Thank you,'' the general said, as he closed the box with the cross and slipped it back into his pocket. "On that note, then, I suggest that we all adjourn to the library. Caitlin will be very cross if I keep you to myself much longer. We can discuss further details over tea. After that, I'll have you shown to rooms where you can rest for a few hours before we embark upon tonight's work.''

CHAPTER SIXTEEN

SIR John led the way back out of the maze, moving briskly despite his stick. The psychic thrum of power did not accompany them on the way out, perhaps because they were in his company. As they set out across the lawn toward the house, he and Adam fell into step like two friends of long standing, conversing companionably about commonplaces. Bringing up the rear with McLeod, Peregrine paused briefly to give his head a shake, for just as they emerged from the maze's gate, he had been assailed by a tantalizing whirl of impressions centered on their host. The action cleared his head, but also cleared away most of the details of what he had glimpsed.

"Noel, what do you make of him?" he whispered to the inspector, with a nod in Sir John's direction.

The inspector's blue eyes glinted with wry humor behind his aviator spectacles as he glanced sidelong at Peregrine. "Why ask me, when you can Look for yourself?"

"I did," Peregrine said, "but there's too much to See, and the images won't stay put. I daresay I might be able to get some of it down on paper if I got the chance to try some sketching, but frankly, I wouldn't dare try it without first asking permission. . . ."

"I wouldn't even ask, on his own turf," McLeod murmured. "He's—ah—a *very* senior Adept, Peregrine. Maybe even more senior than Adam. Certainly no less accomplished. Different tradition, though. Still, the two of them do seem to understand one another well enough. With any luck, we should get some interesting results before this night is out."

As they approached the French doors leading back into the library, McLeod and Peregrine still trailing several yards behind their seniors, they saw Caitlin Jordan curled up with a book in one of the window seats overlooking the garden. As soon as she caught sight of them, she laid her reading aside and came to greet them at the doors. After saluting Sir John with a fond kiss on the cheek, she turned to Adam with a smile playing about the corners of her mouth.

"Well, you appear to have survived the labyrinth without too much difficulty," she said, as Sir John turned back to usher McLeod and Peregrine inside. "How do you like our maze?"

"It has a character all its own," Adam said with a droll smile. "Or perhaps I should say that, like this house, it reflects the character of its owners."

Caitlin's deep brown eyes registered a flicker of wry amusement. "I hope we may take that as a compliment."

"Never doubt it," Adam returned readily. "What has been achieved here is greatly to be admired."

As their eyes met, he knew that she understood he was not speaking only of the architecture.

"I'm glad you approve," she said, slipping her arm through her great-grandfather's. "The maze can be daunting to those who aren't at home here."

Sir John's low chuckle turned all their attention back to him.

"Well, they *are* at home, my dear, and I daresay that when they've had a chance to experience the maze in its full configuration, they'll realize just how much at home they are. We'll be working tonight."

"Ah."

"And I do hope you'll stay the night afterwards, Adam," Sir John went on. "I don't know what plans you'd made, but of necessity, it's apt to be rather late by the time we finish."

"We're entirely flexible," Adam replied. "And if you're certain it's no trouble, we'll certainly accept your invitation. But we can book a hotel or bed-and-breakfast in the area if that's more convenient."

"Nonsense. It's settled, then. Caitlin, will you make the arrangements with Linton? They'll want to rest for a few hours and refresh themselves after tea as well. Why don't you put them in the east wing, if those rooms are made up? That way, they can have two baths to themselves.''

''Of course.''

Even as she turned to see to it, a discreet knock at the door heralded the arrival of Linton himself, pushing an elegant walnut service trolley on which reposed a fine tea set of translucent bone china. Peregrine, who had started to feel decidedly peckish, was gratified to see that refreshments included a selection of cakes and sandwiches. As Caitlin drew aside with the butler to give him her instructions, Peregrine moved in to inspect the offerings, helping himself to an egg sandwich at Sir John's indulgent gesture.

They lingered over tea for perhaps half an hour, Adam and Sir John comparing theories of reincarnation and McLeod occasionally joining in with observations from his own experience as a medium. Caitlin mainly listened, so Peregrine, not being the focus of the conversation or its reason, had ample opportunity to study both her and their host. He still could not fathom Sir John, who seemed to blur before his eyes when he tried to focus his Sight on him, but Caitlin continued to intrigue him. He mentioned her to Adam as they followed Linton up the stairs to be shown to their rooms.

''I'd love to sketch her, Adam. Do you think she'd allow it?''

''Unless you mean to do it over breakfast in the morning, I don't know where you'd find the time,'' Adam said with a chuckle. ''I doubt you'll be up to it after we've worked tonight, and I want all of us to try to catch a nap between now and then.''

They had reached the east-wing landing, and Linton led them along a carpeted corridor hung with Victorian wallpaper and a series of eighteenth-century hunting prints.

''These are the rooms Miss Caitlin thought might be most suitable, gentlemen,'' the butler said impassively, opening a bedroom door and the one directly opposite it. ''This one has a bath en suite, Sir Adam, so I've put you in there. Inspector McLeod and Mr. Lovat will be in the two rooms directly across the hall, with the bath next to you, Inspector." He had opened another bedroom door and now indicated a door beyond that. "I've had your bags brought up, and I believe you'll find everything you require; but if not, please ring."

"I'm sure everything will be satisfactory," Adam replied. "Thank you, Linton."

As the butler bowed and retreated back down the corridor, leaving the three of them congregated outside their rooms, McLeod glanced at his watch and moved into the doorway of the room he had been allotted.

"We'd better see about getting some sleep," he muttered, glancing sternly at Peregrine. "And you, laddie—you've no business casting calf's eyes at Miss Caitlin. Are you forgetting you're engaged to be married?"

So taken aback was Peregrine by this comment that a snort of embarrassed laughter escaped him.

"Of course I haven't forgotten. Julia's a super girl. I assure you that my interest in the lovely Caitlin is entirely chaste. I'm more fascinated by her past than by her present."

"Well, if you're going to dwell on the past, you'd be better advised to concentrate on Bonnie Dundee," McLeod said, and closed his door behind him.

The abruptness of his retreat left Peregrine speechless, and he glanced at Adam for reassurance.

"Don't take it personally," Adam said. "He's getting a bit nervous, and who can blame him? He doesn't often have advance warning that he's going to have to function as a medium, or knowledge of who it's likely to be. No matter how experienced one is, it has to be somewhat daunting to know that, if we achieve what we're setting out to do, an alien intelligence is going to take him over, body and soul. After all, what if the 'guest' chose not to leave? It isn't likely, I'll grant you, but the part of the human mind that isn't rational—simply isn't rational."

Peregrine nodded. "I hadn't thought about that aspect of it. I guess I'd be edgy too." He glanced at his watch. "What time do you think we'll start?"

"Probably not until ten or eleven," Adam replied, "so you have time for a substantial nap. I expect someone will be around to knock on our doors about half an hour before. Incidentally, in Sir John's tradition, it's customary to bathe before embarking upon a ritual, as much to cleanse the mind of inappropriate thoughts and distractions as to cleanse the body. It's possible the bath will be lit by candlelight, so don't be surprised. It's intended to help create the proper mind-set."

Peregrine nodded. "Fair enough. I guess I'll see you later, then."

"You will, indeed. Do try to sleep."

Peregrine's room was directly opposite Adam's, a pleasant, airy chamber with walls panelled halfway up in seasoned oak the shade of dark honey. As he closed the door behind him, he saw that his overnight bag and his artist's satchel had been set on a carved chest at the foot of the elaborate tester bed. He loosened his tie as he walked over to the wide, bowfront window, glancing out at the walled Elizabethan herb garden below, fragrant with beds of sage and rosemary and thyme, planted around a green bay tree at the center. Even from two floors up, Peregrine could hear the drone of bees among the patches of sweet lavender along the borders.

Breathing deeply of the garden's sweetness, he doffed his blazer and draped it on the back of a chair. Then he closed the curtains on the bow window and kicked off his shoes before lying down on the bed, setting his glasses on the table beside. With so much to think about, he was inclined to lie awake, but mindful of Adam's instructions, he touched the stone of his dragon ring briefly to his lips, then closed his eyes and set himself to go through a series of breathing exercises designed to compose the mind and relax the body. After a while, his brain began to clear of questions and images. Not long after, he settled into dreamless and restful suspension between sleep and trance.

He was roused some time later to a knock at the door.

"Who is it?" he called, sitting up and groping for his glasses, for the room was dark now.

"It's Noel. I'm done in the bath, and yours is running."

"Thanks, I'll be right there," he replied.

He turned on the bedside light to discover that someone, probably Linton, had been in the room while he slept, and had laid out a light blue terry-cloth robe at the foot of the bed. Taking that as a hint, he stripped down and donned it before poking his head into the corridor and then padding past McLeod's door to the bathroom. It was, indeed, lit by a candle, and while he lay back briefly in the warm water, he spent several minutes gazing into its flame and letting the flicker focus his thoughts toward the work ahead.

When he returned to his room a quarter hour later, he found it lit by candlelight as well, his own clothes hung up in the wardrobe and a dark swath of black silk laid out on the bed that turned out to be a caftan-like robe with a hood. The cincture beside it, when he held it closer to the candlelight, proved to be red.

Since he clearly was intended to wear the garment, Peregrine doffed the terry-cloth robe and slipped on the black one, shivering slightly at the slither of the silk against bare flesh. Except for the hood and the color, it was similar in style to the soutanes of sapphire blue that members of the Hunting Lodge wore when working formal ritual in the chapel in Strathmourne's cellar, but he was not sure he liked wearing black for working ritual. As he was knotting the cincture around his waist to close the robe, a light rap at the door made him look up. At his word of acknowledgement, the door opened and Adam entered, also robed in black.

"I see you're about ready," he said. "I expect we'll be called downstairs very shortly. Have you any questions before we go?"

"None that I can think of offhand," Peregrine said. He indicated the cincture around his waist and added, "Does the red cord mean the same thing here that it does for us?"

"The scarlet cord of the Initiate," Adam said, nodding. "That's common to a number of esoteric traditions. You don't look too happy about it."

"I think it's the black robe, actually," Peregrine admitted. "Adam, is this all right? To wear black, I mean."

Adam smiled. "Christian priests wear black cassocks all the time. Is that all right?"

"Well, of course, but—"

"Relax, Peregrine. I promise you, we aren't violating any taboos in departing from our usual working regalia. Think of the robes we wear as frames around a picture. They don't change the picture itself, but different frames can enhance the picture in different ways. What really matters in any ritual is the reality that underlies the symbolism."

"I realize that," Peregrine said somewhat ruefully. "I suppose I'm just feeling a bit out of my depth here."

"Don't worry, you aren't going to get in over your head," Adam said. "This is mainly Noel's show tonight. I don't expect that your part will be that different from what you've done dozens of times."

As Peregrine finished running a comb through his damp hair, they were joined by a black-robed McLeod, who seemed to have recovered his customary sang-froid.

"Sorry I barked at you earlier," he rumbled, hands thrust deep into the pockets of his robe. "It's the premeditation. I cope a lot better when I don't get to think about it ahead of time."

"He knows that," Adam murmured, laying a reassuring hand on the inspector's shoulder.

Leaving the door slightly ajar, he then bade them sit to either side of him on the edge of the bed and close their eyes while he talked them through a short centering exercise. The sound of soft footsteps approaching in the hall ended the exercise, bringing them to their feet as the door swung wider and Caitlin appeared in the opening, candlelight spilling from her hand to light her face and the dark cloud of her hair falling loose around her shoulders. Like them she was clothed in black, with the scarlet cord.

"Oh, good, I see you're ready," she said quietly. "Come with me, please."

Together the three men followed her down to the library, Peregrine bringing along his art satchel. As they entered, Sir John rose from a wing-back leather chair that gave almost the impression of a throne, his walking stick resting between his bare feet. Bright moonlight spilled through the French doors that led out to the garden, so brightly illuminating the library that Caitlin was able to put out her candle.

"Unless anyone has any questions, I think we can proceed to the temple," Sir John said, his gaze sweeping the three of them. "Here at Oakwood, we ordinarily use temple names when we work, but in this instance, if no one has any objection, I suggest we simply use first names. Incidentally, my close friends generally call me 'Gray' rather than 'John.' Please feel free to do the same."

So saying, he gestured for Caitlin to lead out into the moonlight, allowing his guests to fall in behind her before following.

They required no additional light to make their way across the lawns, heading once again toward the entrance to the maze. The close-clipped grass under their feet was cool and smooth; the night was balmy and almost warm. Beyond the darker bulk of the maze's hedges, the roof of the gazebo gleamed silver in the moonlight.

"You'll notice a difference in the maze when you walk it this time," Caitlin said, turning to face them as she set one hand on the gate. "We can change the pattern by changing the configurations of the gates inside. Tonight's pattern is for warding and protection, and to contain whatever power we may raise in the course of our work. You'll utilize it best—and contribute most—if you simply maintain an inner stillness and let yourselves be carried along by the pattern as it builds. When we reach the center, Gray and I will enter the temple first. The three of you will follow when called, in order of seniority. The ritual framework will be quite clear. All you have to do is follow."

Without further ado, she turned and opened the gate, herself leading their small procession through the twining corridors of leaves. The gravel underfoot was smooth, but necessitated going more slowly than when shod.

And the feel was, indeed, different from when they had walked the maze in the afternoon. Changing the pattern had the effect of opening a set of floodgates. Power seemed to be flowing out of the very ground, rising up in a mounting tide to gather in a shimmering cone high above their heads. With every step they proceeded deeper into the maze, the sense of power grew more intense.

Peregrine waited for the sense of bepuzzlement to recur—though all three of them wore their rings—but there was no such effect. Instead, linked in as he and his companions were with the keepers of the maze, Peregrine found his will creatively at one with theirs. His mind was clear, and his heart was at ease. By the time they reached the final turning, he was feeling ready, even eager, for the night's work.

They emerged into the bright moonlight of the maze's flagstoned center, Adam and his companions pausing just inside as Caitlin and Sir John proceeded up the steps into the gazebo. The moonlight set the white trellising aglow and silvered the rose leaves twined over it. The gazebo inside was lit by lanterns set along the inner perimeter at the four quarters. The table had been covered with a white cloth upon which burned two candles, one white and the other black, to either side of a red votive light set slightly back from them to form a triangle.

In silence Caitlin and Sir John took places before the table that had become a kind of altar, Peregrine realized. Distance masked what they said and their movements were shielded behind their bodies, but even so, it was not difficult to deduce that the two were establishing a formal focus to the working circle, according to their own tradition. After a moment, they turned as one and came to stand in the doorway of the gazebo, Sir John reaching for something hidden behind the frame of the doorway to his right. Moonlight glimmered like quicksilver on the blade of the slender sword that emerged in his hand, its point raising as his other hand beckoned Adam forward.

With a graceful inclination of his head, Adam moved forward to mount the four weathered steps, halting at the top as he was arrested at swordpoint, the tip of the blade lightly pressing at the hollow of his throat.

"Who comes?" Sir John demanded, loud enough that

McLeod and Peregrine could hear the challenge quite clearly.

Lifting his eyes to meet the other's unflinching gaze, Adam responded boldly, "Adam, Master of the Hunt and a servant of the Light, duly sworn."

"Enter and be welcome in this company, Adam, Master of the Hunt and servant of the Light," Sir John replied with a satisfied smile, lifting the swordpoint.

The warmth of his bidding was undeniable, as was Caitlin's, as she laid a guiding hand on Adam's sleeve. At the same time, she stretched up to kiss him on the mouth as she drew him into the gazebo. Her perfume mingled with that of the roses, heady and sweet, but even so, he felt the change of atmosphere as he passed into the further protection of their circle. None of it was totally unexpected except the sheer potency of what now surrounded him, underlined as she drew back and Sir John solemnly laid the sword across Adam's two hands.

"You may admit your Huntsmen," he said quietly.

With a slight bow, Adam turned to face outward again. The hilt of the sword tingled in his grasp, alive with energy focused through a different lens but for a common purpose. Directing that energy from his own perspective, Adam raised the sword before him and summoned McLeod with a glance. The inspector looked a little pale as he came across the short expanse of stone flags and mounted the four steps, to halt against the point of the sword at his throat.

"Who comes?" Adam demanded.

"Noel, a Huntsman and servant of the Light, duly sworn."

With a nod, Adam raised the swordpoint and stepped aside.

"Enter and be welcome in this company, Noel, Huntsman and servant of the Light."

As McLeod was admitted by Caitlin's kiss, Adam likewise bade Peregrine come forward. The young artist looked very solemn and wide-eyed as he approached, his sketchbox in his left hand, but he mounted the four steps bravely. Still, he gasped as the swordpoint brought him up short.

"Who comes?"

"Peregrine, a Hunstman and servant of the Light, duly sworn," Peregrine said, following the others' pattern.

With a nod of approval, Adam raised the sword and beckoned Peregrine to pass.

"Enter and be welcome in this company, Peregrine, Huntsman and servant of the Light."

He stood aside for Peregrine to be drawn inside by Caitlin, the sword still borne upright before him, then glanced askance at Sir John, for he sensed what should come next. At the general's nod toward the open doorway, confirming his expectation, Adam drew the tip of the sword three times across the threshold they had just crossed, left to right, envisioning the sealing of the opening they had used. He was familiar with the symbolism, and heartened to feel the wall of power rise up in response to his command, as biddable as in his own temple.

When he had finished, he crouched briefly to lay the sword across the threshold to reinforce the imagery, turning then to where the others were gathering around the round table, which he now could see bore the Dundee ring and cross, the latter now with a length of silky black cord threaded through the ring at the top.

Wordlessly Sir John reached out to join hands with Caitlin and Adam, bidding them take McLeod's and Peregrine's hands.

"Before we begin, we'll take a few minutes to center," he said quietly.

Drawing a slow breath to continue what he had been doing since he entered the maze, Adam fixed his gaze on the red votive light flanked by the black and white candles—in Qabalistic terms, the Middle Pillar balanced between the twin pillars of Severity and Mercy. They all must strive for balance tonight, regardless of how each individual went about it. After a moment, the squeeze of Sir John's hand on his left told Adam that they were ready to begin. As they dropped hands, Caitlin and Sir John turned briefly to begin pulling chairs closer, that had been set against the inside perimeter of the gazebo by each of the lanterns. A fifth chair had been added since their afternoon visit.

"Adam, I'll suggest that you and Noel sit facing one another, here in front of the altar," Sir John said. "I'll back you—and Peregrine, why don't you come around here, between them and the doorway, so you'll have a clear view of their faces while you're drawing? Caitlin will monitor the lot of us, from over behind Noel."

Nodding, Adam helped adjust the chairs as their host had indicated, positioning himself and McLeod so that their knees were nearly touching. Peregrine settled in a chair to Adam's right, with the shimmer of the gazebo doorway behind him, a sketch pad balanced on his knees and a handful of sharpened pencils in his left hand. Sir John was to Adam's left and slightly behind him, Caitlin behind McLeod.

As Adam turned his attention to his Second, the inspector removed his aviator spectacles and set them on the altar table, then settled back into his chair and turned his gaze to Adam's, briefly touching his sapphire to his lips before setting his hands on his thighs with a resigned sigh.

"Ready?" Adam asked quietly.

"Ready as I ever am."

"Close your eyes, then, and take a deep breath, and be prepared to go deep on my signal."

Without speaking, McLeod closed his eyes and inhaled to the depth of his lungs. As he began to exhale, Adam reached across and pressed his fingers lightly to his Second's right wrist. McLeod's breath became a sigh as he relaxed visibly in his chair, head lolling slightly forward on his chest.

"Good," Adam murmured. "Now, breathe in and out again, and go deeper still . . . and once more. As deep as you can go and still hear my voice . . . and hear *only* my voice. . . ."

So guided, and aided by long experience, McLeod settled readily into the desired level of trance—balanced, passive, receptive. That accomplished, Adam reached over to the altar table and took up the Templar cross, clasping it lightly between his two hands as he sat back in his chair and closed his eyes. He was now ready to embark upon his own part of the preparations, and the actual summoning of the former owner of the cross.

His first impression, as he sank into trance, was of the shimmering net of power woven over and above the precincts of the gazebo and the maze—star-white lines of singing energy whose remote echoes thrilled him with a sense of calm delight. Retreating deeper into trance, and trailing the strands of energy behind him, he found himself at the threshold of the Inner Planes. He could feel the warming presence of the cross between his palms, palpable as the glow from a bonfire, and he focused on that glow as he framed the words of a petitioning summons, speaking them aloud as well as in spirit, so that his companions' intent might reinforce his own.

"John Grahame of Claverhouse, Viscount Dundee and Grand Prior of Scotland. By this cross, token of your pledge to the Order of the Temple of Jerusalem, I charge you to hear me, and entreat you to respond."

He repeated the invocation three times without gaining any response. Shifting his grasp to the cross's cord, a few inches from where it passed through the ring on the top, he rested his elbows on the arms of his chair and let the cross dangle before his entranced gaze, also giving his companions a visual focus as he repeated the call, now drawing on the power of the maze to amplify his request. Minutes spun themselves out as he continued to broadcast his appeal until, out of the sidereal light of the Inner Planes, came the response he had been waiting for, strong in his mind.

Who calls?

CHAPTER SEVENTEEN

WHO calls?

The question reverberated in the charged atmosphere of the gazebo, heralding a new presence among them. Cautious, lest his sense of relief dispel his focus, Adam kept his gaze fixed on the Templar cross.

"A Master of the Hunt desires contact with that one who once was John Grahame of Claverhouse. Have you a current incarnation?"

The response was a clear negative.

"Then my request presents you no peril," Adam said. "By the power of the Light we both serve, I entreat you to come forth and speak with me. Grave matters concerning the Temple require resolution, and I would seek guidance from you, who last knew concerning these matters. A willing vessel stands ready to receive you as guest. He invites you to enter the temple of his body and speak with his voice. Will you enter?"

At once the spiritual presence manifested itself as a shimmering glow that flickered like heat lightning within the confines of the gazebo, reflecting from the edges of the Templar cross in Adam's hand. With it came a simultaneous injunction that Adam should place the cross around McLeod's neck.

Still balanced in trance, Adam complied, slipping the black cord over McLeod's head so that the enamelled cross hung on his breast, briefly pressing a hand to McLeod's forehead with whispered reinforcement to relax and offer no resistance. As he sat back again, his gaze fixed on McLeod's face to watch for the shift, the shimmering flicker around them shrank briefly to a single, glowing point centered in the heart of the Templar cross, then expanded once again to envelop McLeod in a luminous aura.

Gradually the brightness of its essence merged with his living flesh and then faded. After a few more seconds, his grizzled head rolled back, then straightened up with a snap. When his eyelids lifted, the presence looking out of his eyes was no longer McLeod's own.

"I was Grahame of Claverhouse, Viscount Dundee," said the presence now inhabiting McLeod's body, the voice virile and resonant but lighter than McLeod's own. "What need of the Temple impels you to summon me from contemplation of the Light?"

Drawing a deep breath, Adam kept eye contact with the eyes that no longer mirrored the soul of Noel McLeod.

"I require information about the Seal of Solomon," he said. "The need is urgent."

The blue eyes registered shock.

"By whose authority do you ask me this?"

"By my own authority, as Master of the Hunt and a justiciar of the Inner Planes," Adam said. "He whose guest you are also represents the Law. One who disregards the Law and spurns the Light has stolen the Seal and taken the life of him who had its keeping. I am given to understand that great harm will be done if the thief discovers and releases what it guards. So I ask again, *have* you any knowledge of this artifact?"

"The secret of the Seal is known to me," Dundee acknowledged, "but you do not know what you ask." The borrowed voice held a note of sorrow. "I was the last of my Order to carry the burden of that knowledge, and through pride I failed to provide for its transmittal. Too late I waited, and took my secret to my grave—not only that which you seek now but many others besides. Now my failure holds me anchored to this present identity, forbidden to progress in my quest toward union with the Light, sentenced to observe it only from afar."

There was grief and guilt in his revelation, a bleak resignation to what this tortured soul believed must be its fate. Failure there might have been, but Adam, well accustomed to diagnosing the ills attendant on the human psyche, suddenly wondered whether the spiritual restriction by which Dundee felt himself bound was self-imposed, the consequence of harsh self-judgement rather than any decree of Divine justice.

"What makes you so certain," he asked softly, "that these 'failings' of yours are beyond redress? I submit to you, John Grahame of Claverhouse, that if you would be free to resume your quest toward the Light, you have only to find it within you to forgive yourself for what you see as these derelictions of duty."

A grimace of anguished longing distorted McLeod's passive face.

"How can I pardon the wrongs I have done, when my duty remains undischarged?"

"How else, except by proxy?" Adam countered calmly. "If you will share with me the secret of the Seal, I will promise to guard it as faithfully as you have done, using that knowledge only to safeguard what was given you in trust."

"How can I dare what you ask, Master of the Hunt?" Dundee said. "I sense in you the tongue of good report, but I am oath-bound not to reveal the Seal's secrets to anyone who is not a brother of the knightly Order which I was privileged to serve as Grand Prior."

"Then rest easy, for I *am* of the Order," Adam said. "More than three centuries before your birth, I swore obedience to him who then was Master of the Temple, and gave that life in fidelity to the Temple. By blood am I bound as well, through Sinclair ancestors who served the Temple. I pledge you, by that Light which you seek still to serve, that authority resides in me to receive your confidence in good faith. Since you cannot alone attain that which you most desire, I invite you to receive me as your spiritual successor; to pass your burden on to me, and let yourself be free."

He fell silent and waited. The air was charged with tense expectancy. McLeod's head turned from side to side, the alien intelligence scanning and assessing, then returned its gaze to Adam.

"Others are present, Master of the Hunt," Dundee said. "Will you vouch for their integrity? For if I give this knowledge and they prove not worthy, I am forsworn, my soul condemned to further punishment for my failings.''

''All have made unreserved dedication to the Light, through many lives,'' Adam returned quietly, knowing it was true. ''Speak, I entreat you, before the vessel grows fatigued.''

Adam could see the indecision churning behind McLeod's blue eyes, but then the grizzled head nodded.

''Very well, Master of the Hunt. I will put my trust in your pledge, and my soul in your keeping—and may you and yours share my fate, if ye be forsworn.''

''I accept that condition,'' Adam said.

''Then hear what was told to me,'' Dundee said, his tone gaining strength as his confidence grew. ''The secret is said to date from the time of Solomon himself, who was our spiritual founder and father. Legend speaks of him rightly as a master magician, the master of men and demons. That reputation is well merited, for it was Solomon the Wise who, by his magical skills, subdued and captured the demons Gog and Magog and, in his wisdom, locked them away in a casket, which he buried deep in the cellars under the Temple in Jerusalem.''

Adam found himself nodding as he listened avidly. Off to his right, he could sense Peregrine sketching furiously. Sir John was a bulwark of reassuring strength behind him, and Caitlin had become almost psychically invisible.

''The Temple was destroyed in A.D. 70,'' Dundee went on. ''Centuries later, when Hugh de Payens and his fellow-founders of our Order came to defend the Holy City, the King of Jerusalem gave them leave to make their headquarters in an old part of the ruined Temple thought to have been the previous location of King Solomon's stables. In preparing the ground for rebuilding, the founders discovered a casket secreted in a hidden vault beneath the ruins—a casket fast-shut with a Seal that bore the imprinted symbols of Solomon, along with arcane wardings.

''Respecting the Seal of Solomon as a sign of warning, Hugh de Payens and his companions forbore even attempting to open the casket until they could learn more about it,''

Dundee continued. "After nearly a century, their successors eventually found what they sought through an unlikely alliance with the mysterious Assassin-Lord known as the Old Man of the Mountain, whose mountain citadel retained records of ancient legends associated with the casket, which had been believed lost. Thus it was that they learned what the casket contained—and likewise, that the demons imprisoned in the casket could only be safely controlled by means of three 'hallows': Solomon's Seal itself, Solomon's Crown, and the Sceptre of King David."

All at once Adam flashed on his dream the night after Nathan's death—King Solomon enthroned, wearing the Crown and wielding the Seal and the Sceptre. The clues had been before him from the beginning, and he had not realized.

"The three hallows are of vital importance," Dundee went on. "The imprint of the Seal is, of course, what binds the casket shut. Without it, the casket can neither be opened nor closed. But it *must* be used in conjunction with the Crown and the Sceptre. The Crown confers upon its wearer the wisdom to resist the madness of evil. The Sceptre, similarly, gives power to place that evil under restraint. If a man were to open the casket without the full protection of the hallows, the demons would escape and overwhelm him. Once free, there would be nothing to stop them from ravening across the land."

The entity regarding Adam through McLeod's eyes lifted a hand to lay across the Templar cross hanging on its host's breast, the tone of the voice becoming more thoughtful.

"Our predecessors should have taken steps to destroy the demons, or at least ensure that they could never be released," he continued. "Instead, they determined to reacquire the three hallows, against the time when it might be needful to turn the power of the demons against the Temple's enemies. The hallows were recovered, one by one, and given into the custody of three trusted knights, bound by terrible oaths, with the Master retaining the guardianship of the casket. Only he and his closest officers knew the casket's true secret, and the identities of those who held the hallows.

"When the Order withdrew from the Holy Land after the fall of Acre, they took the casket and the hallows with them to the Paris Temple and there guarded them until advance warning came of a planned suppression of the Order. Though tempted to unleash the demons against the Pope and the French King, who had betrayed the Order, the last Grand Master sent the casket and the hallows to Scotland for safety, where the casket was again hidden and the hallows dispersed to separate hiding places under separate guardianships. Much knowledge was lost in the centuries that followed, but the Crown eventually came into my keeping, along with the legend I have just conveyed to you."

Adam gave an involuntary gasp and raised a hand to his forehead as Dundee said "you," for with Dundee's mention of the Crown had come a series of vivid images of it, and an insistent buzzing at the edge of his senses. It nagged at his concentration like the sound of conversation overheard but not quite decipherable in an adjoining room, but he could neither focus it nor make it go away, even when he shook his head in an attempt to clear it.

"Adam, what is it?" Sir John demanded, his strong hand clasping Adam's shoulder from behind, on the left.

Increasingly disoriented, Adam sensed Peregrine also leaning forward in concern, and he clung to the lifeline of the general's hand even as he made himself try to seek out that other's presence.

"I—don't know," he murmured. "Images, almost memories—something to do with the Crown. I can't shut them out, but I can't make them focus, either."

Eagle-keen, Sir John shifted his attention to the presence housed in McLeod's body.

"I speak as deputy for the Master of the Hunt," he said. "I ask you to bear with us and abide a while longer. I believe this has bearing on your situation."

Dundee was staring at Adam oddly, and gave a careful nod.

"I will abide. A friend desires to communicate."

"What does that mean?" Peregrine whispered. "Adam isn't a medium."

"Are you?" Sir John demanded of Adam.

"I never *have* been."

"Then perhaps this is a previous incarnation of your own attempting to surface," Sir John said, watching him intently. "Are you aware of a particular past life with a pertinence to this situation?"

"No," Adam whispered, shaking his head.

"Well, perhaps there hasn't been a need for it to surface before now," Sir John murmured. "I must confess, this is beyond *my* experience—a past personality desiring to communicate with a discarnate soul ensconced in a medium's body. It's obviously needed, though. Would you like me to guide you back to bring it in, if that's what it is? Trying it solo could be a bit tricky, while still maintaining the Dundee contact."

"Are you always such a master of understatement?" Adam breathed, glancing back at McLeod, through whose eyes he was being avidly watched. "You sound like a man with past experience at this sort of thing."

"Far more than I would have liked," Sir John replied, as he shifted forward to crouch beside Adam. "Will you trust me to take you back?"

"Certainly."

"Thank you. I'm going to assume that you've keyed yourself to respond to the same cues that I watched you use on Noel," the general said, laying a hand on Adam's wrist. "Relax. Draw a deep breath and let it out—and when I touch your forehead, I want you to go very, very deep. Close your eyes and relax, and go deeper—now."

Adam had already been at a working level of trance, which he had not left since their work began, but the elder Adept's hand across his forehead plunged him as deep as he had ever gone for anyone else, even during therapy connected with his psychiatric training, so many years before. The vague rush of vertigo as the other took him deeper yet was a sensation he had learned to associate with sure and absolute control, and the certainty that Brigadier General Sir John Graham knew exactly what he was doing.

"Good," the older man's voice whispered. "Start casting back now . . . back to your adolescence, back to childhood, back to infancy, and beyond. . . ."

Guided by Sir John's quiet voice, Adam felt himself slipping effortlessly backwards in time, only the touch of the other's hand on his wrist anchoring a detached part of him to the here and now. Like a raft swept downstream by deep currents, he was borne swiftly in and out of patches of shadowy obscurity, moving toward a distant bright island in the midst of the flood. The island seemed to be moving upstream to meet him.

Then he saw that it was no island at all, but the converging image of a woman's face. . . .

Keeping close watch at Adam's other side, pencil poised above his sketch pad, Peregrine heard his mentor give a faint gasp and saw him stiffen slightly in his chair. As he himself leaned in, his view of Adam's face underwent a sudden, flickering transformation. The strong male features, stern even in response, yielded in fluttering succession to the image of a woman's more delicate profile. As the images strobed before Peregrine's startled gaze, it suddenly occurred to him that he had seen this face before, in conjunction with his vision of Solomon's Crown.

The realization hit him like a punch to the midriff. Even as Peregrine struggled to master his surprise, Adam relaxed and opened his eyes, his wide-eyed gaze darting round to the faces of all those present with an expression of urgent inquiry.

"This place is Oakwood Manor, in Kent, and you are among friends," Sir John informed the presence gazing out of Adam's eyes. "Can you tell us your name?"

Adam's lips moved, but no sound came out. His left hand lifted in entreaty toward the altar, starting to reach toward it. In a flash of sudden insight, Peregrine understood.

"The ring!" he whispered. "The Dundee ring is the focus!"

Nodding his agreement, Sir John picked up the ring and

captured Adam's left hand to slip the ring onto the third finger.

"Tell us your name, please," he repeated softly.

A slight shudder passed through Adam's frame as his hand closed and lifted to touch the ring's crystal to his lips and then against his cheek in caress, the eyes still searching restlessly; but this time, when the lips parted to speak, the voice that issued was a woman's bright contralto.

"I know thee not, sir. I am Lady Jean Seton, younger daughter of the Earl of Dunfermline. I seek John Grahame of Claverhouse. Pray, tell me which one of you is he?"

For Peregrine, the complete change of voice was accompanied by the transparent overlay of image which he had come to associate with historic personality resonance. The effect was both eerie and fascinating. Adam had once told him that any soul, by the time it reached the level of an Adept, would have experienced previous lives both as men and women, and had assured him that both he and Peregrine had lived past lives as women. Until now, however, Peregrine had never seen direct evidence of that truth. Hardly daring to breathe for fear of intruding, he pulled back slightly to surreptitiously turn to a fresh sheet of drawing paper.

Meanwhile, in response to Jean Seton's question, McLeod's head had tilted slightly to stare searchingly at Adam, a note of tenderness softening the inspector's bluff countenance.

"Dear lass, I am here," the spirit of Dundee declared quietly, "though 'tis a strange turn of Providence that brings us together now, after so long a time. Never did I think to hear your voice again after our last parting. Tell me how you and your brave sister fared in the days that followed."

Adam's face had lit at the sound of his voice, but now grew shadowed by Lady Jean's sorrow as he shook his head, his voice both sad and wistful.

"We fared both well and ill, my lord. The Crown was safely hidden, as you charged us to do, but Grizel perished to preserve the secret of its resting place."

Peregrine, glancing up as his pencil flew across the page,

capturing the images, caught just the briefest ghost-image of a second woman overlooking Adam's shoulder, in her hands an ancient diadem with six sharp points of beaten gold. It was memory, not vision, he quickly realized—a flashback to the images he had never quite been able to capture before, of his vision sparked by the Dundee ring. But it tended to confirm that this alter ego of Adam's must have been the other, younger woman—and Dundee had given them the Crown! No wonder the image of Solomon's Crown had fascinated Adam from the first. Even as Peregrine tried to sketch what he could recall of both women's faces, the spirits embodied in the persons of Adam and McLeod were continuing their odd reunion.

"Grizel perished? How did this come to pass?" Dundee asked, leaning forward.

Tears glistened in Adam's dark eyes as Jean recalled her sorrow.

"It was after your death, my lord. In those sad days that followed, our bitter loss blunting your victory, Grizel took the Crown north to our father's castle of Fyvie, there to hide it in a secret place prepared for it. I was to make haste toward St. Andrews, there to take ship for France. She was to sail from Aberdeen, where our father was to join us.

"But before Grizel could be quit of Fyvie, Covenanters came—mercenaries, searching for booty. No doubt they sought treasure of the common kind, of which there was none left at Fyvie, our father having cast his fortune with the Stuart cause. But they tortured her nonetheless, convinced that she was hiding the castle's treasure. Surrendering the Crown might have satisfied their greed and saved her life, my lord, but she died in torment, rather than break faith with you and betray our charge."

"The fiends, so to take sweet Grizel's life!" Dundee whispered, McLeod's body shuddering as the spirit housed within it registered its grief and outrage at the crime.

"Rest easy, my lord, they will have paid!" Sir John murmured, setting a restraining hand on McLeod's as he shifted his focus back to Adam's alter ego.

"Lady Jean, we would like to speak with Grizel, if we

may," he said gently. "Will you call her and ask her to join us?"

"I will call her if you wish," came the reply, "but she will not come, not even to me."

"Why not?"

"Because her spirit abides still with the Crown, watching over its resting place. She has no leave to quit her charge."

"And where is this resting place?" Sir John asked.

"In the same room at Fyvie where her blood was spilled."

"The Green Lady!" Caitlin murmured in a startled undertone, speaking for the first time since they had begun. At Peregrine's glance of inquiry, she added, "I collect ghost stories. One of the rooms at Fyvie Castle is supposedly haunted by a ghost known as the Green Lady. Gray, you don't suppose she might be Grizel Seton?"

Returning his attention to Adam, Sir John nodded distractedly.

"This begins to follow a pattern. Lady Jean, what if you were to go to her?" he inquired of Adam's alter ego. "Would your sister be willing to show you where the Crown is hidden?"

Adam gazed at him, uncertainty in the dark eyes. "While we lived and breathed, there was nothing she would not confide in me," he said. "But this secret is not hers alone to disclose."

"No," said the voice of Dundee, "it is mine. Ah, faithful Grizel," he continued, shaking his head on a note of somber tenderness. "In committing the Crown to her care, I little thought that her faithfulness would be tested even unto death. This much and more do I owe her—to release her from that charge. Say you will go to her, Jean, as my appointed messenger. Show her the ring upon your hand, and take the cross I wore unto my death, and instruct her in my name to relinquish the Crown to you. Give her my loving thanks and bid her depart in peace, for others now are prepared to take up the burden of guardianship."

Adam inclined his head in grave assent, answering again in Jean Seton's voice.

"I will do as you bid me, my lord, and with right goodwill."

"Sweet Jean . . . ," Dundee murmured.

But McLeod's bluff face was beginning to show signs of strain, his breathing quicker than it had been. At Sir John's beckoning glance, Caitlin bent to set a hand to the inspector's wrist while her great-grandfather murmured a few words in Adam's ear that closed his eyes and set him drifting passively.

"His pulse is a little unsteady," Caitlin murmured, after a silent few seconds of assessment. "We probably ought to bring this interview to a close."

"I agree," Sir John replied. "I think we've learned what's needed." Addressing himself then to Dundee, he said, "The body in which you are guest grows tired. Will it please you to release it now?"

"Yes, with my heartfelt thanks to him and to the one who now bears the burden of my charge."

"It is we who thank you," said Sir John. "Armed with your knowledge, we will find the means to keep bound the evil you and your Order have sought to contain all these long centuries," He reached across and set his free hand on McLeod's wrist. "Return now in peace to the realms of the Light, and may all bright blessings attend you."

McLeod's eyes rolled upward in their sockets, a long-drawn sigh escaping his lips as he slumped forward bone-lessly in his chair, head lolling. Abandoning Adam for the moment, Sir John leaned closer to remove the Templar cross from around McLeod's neck, then traced a sign above the bridge of McLeod's nose before laying a blue-veined hand lightly across his eyes.

"The guest has departed, Noel; you may now return," he said quietly. "When you feel ready, take a deep breath and let it out slowly, and find yourself here and now, grounded and in full control again, feeling relaxed and refreshed."

As Sir John took his hand away, McLeod drew a deep breath and exhaled audibly, then opened his eyes. Like a man newly roused from a sound night's sleep, he blinked and shook himself upright.

"Not half-bad," he mumbled drowsily. "Wish it were always that easy. . . ."

His wandering gaze focused on Adam's passive form, curious rather than alarmed, and he looked first to Peregrine, then to Sir John for enlightenment.

"You're not the only one who's been playing host tonight to a shade from the past," Sir John said.

Leaving McLeod to complete the inferences for himself, he laid the Templar cross back on the altar, then took Adam's hand and removed the Dundee ring, addressing himself once again to Lady Jean Seton.

"John Grahame of Claverhouse has returned unto the Light," he informed her gravely, "and we have much work to do in his behalf. Lady Jean Seton may return whence she came, to come again when the ring is placed on your finger. Go deep now, Adam, and begin coming forward in time. . . . Return to Adam Sinclair, gently . . . when you are ready. . . ."

CHAPTER EIGHTEEN

DRIFTING passively in the midst of pearly seas, Adam was conscious of nothing beyond a sense of peace until a voice called him by name. Drawn back toward self-awareness, he oriented toward the voice, swimming languidly upward through milky layers of translucent light toward a distant point of brightness which was the present moment in time. The sensation was effortless, even agreeable. He broke the surface with a slight start and opened his eyes to find Sir John Graham crouching at his knees, gazing up at him.

"Welcome back," said his counterpart. "How do you feel?"

"All right," he said, darting a glance at McLeod to assure himself that the inspector likewise was all right. "Good Lord, you must have taken me deep! I don't remember a thing."

"I thought that might be the case," Sir John said, reaching out a hand to Caitlin, who put a tiny tape recorder in it. "We routinely tape our sessions when we know we're apt to get past-life regressions—and this time, it's particularly fortunate that we did so. Sometimes it's difficult enough for four people to remember what one subject was saying; but for three people to remember the words of two, especially given the nature of your conversation, begins to get even more complicated. You can both listen to the tape while we have some supper.

"And what, I wonder, did Peregrine get during our little exchange?" he went on, turning a look of question in the artist's direction as he stood and shook the kinks from his knees from crouching down. "You looked very busy, son."

For answer, Peregrine leaned forward with a grin to

tender his sketch pad. Adam glanced through the sketches, tilting them toward the light of the nearest lantern, then shook his head, covering a yawn.

"I'm sure this will make more sense when I've had something to eat and heard the tape," he said, returning his gaze to Sir John. "I'll have to ask you whether we accomplished what was needed."

"I think so," Sir John replied. "Let's join hands for a few minutes to make certain everyone is grounded, and then we'll close everything down. After that, we'll return to the house for a change of clothes and a bite to eat, and then we'll review tonight's proceedings and see what's to be done."

Twenty minutes later, reclad in more conventional clothing, the group gathered in the library for hearty soup and sandwiches. While Sir John and Caitlin began delving into the library's extensive shelves, interspersing their research with food, Adam and McLeod listened to the tape, Peregrine correlating the dialogue with the sketches he had made. Satisfaction with what they had accomplished was mingled with amazement, for neither could remember much of what they had said. Peregrine, for his part, was still finding it a little difficult to reconcile his sketches of the very feminine Lady Jean Seton with what he knew of the undeniably masculine Adam Sinclair.

When the tape had finished, Adam switched off the recorder and glanced up at Peregrine, who was surreptitiously comparing one of his sketches with Adam's present appearance. Controlling a smile, Adam turned the sketch pad for a better look at the study of the fair Lady Jean.

"Do you find that perplexing?" he asked with a forbearing lift to one eyebrow.

"Well, I wasn't exactly expecting it," Peregrine began.

"Why ever not? I did tell you, the first time we discussed reincarnation, that some of my historic identities were female. Obviously, I didn't know about this particular one before tonight, but we're fortunate that we have this link to Dundee."

"I know that, and you did tell me," Peregrine agreed,

"but that was still theoretical, until I'd actually seen one. She was a beautiful, petite little brunette, Adam. I—suppose what surprised me more than anything else was the completeness of the gender shift from one persona to the next."

"I don't know why that should come as a surprise," Adam said. "You got used to the idea that Michael Scot and young Gillian Talbot were aspects of one and the same soul, despite the difference in gender."

"True," Peregrine said. "But I didn't know either of them the way I've come to know you. I mean," he went on somewhat lamely, "Lady Jean Seton was *completely* female, and you're—"

"Like everyone else, a mixture of qualities, some feminine, some masculine," Adam said lightly, smiling as McLeod rolled his eyes and bit into another sandwich. "Putting on my psychiatrist's hat for a moment—C. G. Jung rightly defined the totality of the self as a *conjunctio oppositorum,* a marriage of opposites. It's largely a question of balance, the balance usually being tipped one way or the other by the biological factor. Two X chromosomes produce a female body, a physical environment which encourages the feminine aspects of the psyche to take the ascendancy. Substitute a Y for one of the X's and you get the reverse effect. But the potential for either is always there.

"This means that every man has his *anima*—his female principle," he continued, "while every woman conversely has her *animus*. Occasionally you get someone like Lindsay in whom, for a variety of reasons, the psychological imperative is so powerful that it outweighs the physical disposition of the body. That it happens now and then is no cause for either shame or condemnation. It's simply a fact of human existence."

"I'm sure you're right," Peregrine said with a sheepish little smile, "and I'm not disputing any of this in principle. It's just that the proofs of the practice take a little getting used to."

In fact, the events of the past few hours had reawakened Peregrine's curiosity concerning his own past lives. He resolved to explore the matter further, once the present crisis was over, for it now occurred to him that it would be interesting, not to say enlightening, to discover what life was like from a woman's point of view. Thinking of Julia, he could see how such an experience might, at the very least, be uniquely instructive within the framework of a marriage.

As Peregrine helped himself to another piece of cake, Sir John came to join them, his reading glasses perched on his nose again, bearing a stack of books with bits of paper bristling from them as place-markers.

"You asked for information connected with the names Gog and Magog? I believe I can safely say that I'm now prepared to tell you far more than you ever wanted to know."

He set the books on the library table and eased into one of the chairs around it. As they settled in around him, he steepled his fingers in front of him with the unsparing air of a military commander about to deliver a staff briefing.

"If Gog and Magog *are* names to be equated with demons—then what we have here is a very ancient evil," he informed his listeners gravely. "Assuming that Dundee's testimony is an accurate reflection of the truth regarding the origin of these demons, and given that the historical King Solomon is generally acknowledged to have died somewhere around 925 B.C., it follows that these evil beings— whatever they are—have been locked away for nearly three millennia."

He paused to let the impact of this statement sink in before continuing.

"By the time we find biblical mention of Gog and Magog in the Ezekiel prophesies, around 592 to 570 B.C., the names remain associated with intimations of danger, but we find that they've been conflated to describe a dreaded King Gog of Magog whose armies were threatening to invade Israel. Almost a millennium later, the Koran speaks of them as *spoiling the land*."

"In other words," McLeod said, "Gog and Magog are names of evil repute in more than one tradition."

"So it would seem," Adam agreed. "That would tend to suggest some common origin to the association."

"The tale grows in the telling," said Sir John. "By the time the names pass into British legend, Gog and Magog have attained the status of giants."

He paused to open one of the books on the table before him, consulting the text as he continued.

"Geoffrey of Monmouth, writing in the twelfth century, reports that Britain was originally inhabited by a race of giants who were conquered by Brutus and his Trojan warriors around 1200 B.C., when Corineus was made ruler of Cornwall. After killing every other giant in the area, Corineus wrestled with the twelve-foot giant Gogmagog and threw him to his death in the sea.

"This Cornish connection comes through three centuries later, when Caxton identifies Gog and Magog as the last surviving sons of the thirty-three daughters of the Emperor Diocletian, women infamous for having murdered their husbands. As a punishment for their crimes, these women are said to have been cast adrift in a boat which eventually landed in Cornwall, where they cohabited with demons—so legend claims. All the resulting giant offspring eventually were killed off except Gog and Magog, who were captured and taken to London, where they're said to have been kept chained to the gates of a royal palace belonging to Brutus, that stood on the site of the present-day Guildhall."

"You know," Caitlin interjected from atop a library ladder, "a possible literary connection has just occurred to me." As the others all glanced in her direction, she came down to join them.

"Some aspects of this story remind me of the Grendel monsters from the legend of Beowulf," she said. "Grendel and his mother are described as hybrid creatures, part giant, part demon, who feed on human flesh. Beowulf, the hero of the piece, is not only a queller of monsters; he's also a sage King—an attribute which links him in with the pattern of esoteric traditions associated with Solomon. One might almost say that Solomon is the prototype for such folk heroes—but I suppose this constitutes something of a digression.''

''Digression or not, it's consistent with the demon legends we've heard so far,'' Adam said, pulling out a chair for her at the table. ''The common element is that it takes someone of exceptional strength and wisdom to subdue such creatures. Gray, what became of the giants in Caxton's account?''

''Eventually they died and were replaced by effigies,'' Sir John replied. ''And here we begin to enter the realm of verifiable history. We know that effigies were, indeed, erected in London's Guildhall in the fifteenth century. Most accounts identify them with Monmouth's Gogmagog and Corineus, but some sources take the Caxton slant and call them Gog and Magog. Whichever names you prefer, the effigies burned in the Great Fire of 1666; but apparently there was enough life left in the legend that a new set of effigies was erected in 1708. By then, general opinion had returned to Caxton's assertion that they were Gog and Magog, the last of the British giants. These effigies of 1708 remained in position until they were destroyed in an air raid in 1940. Here endeth the lesson.''

Adam was nodding thoughtfully as Sir John took off his glasses.

''I've seen photographs of that last set,'' he said.

''I'll go you one better than that,'' Sir John countered. ''I remember being taken to see them, as a small boy, and I remember walking over the rubble after the air raid that took them out. But the effigies are only the most recent surfacing of a corpus of lore stretching back at least three millennia. If we discard what can be categorized as quaintly fantastical and chip away the matrix of dross, what's left is a hard core of information that does not change, from one version to the next: first, that the names Gog and Magog have a persistent association with extreme evil; second, this association goes back at least as far as biblical times, when Ezekiel himself may have conflated the two names to frighten his people with the threat that a past evil was about to return. I would even venture to speculate that the racial memory of so great an evil could have been carried outward as civilization expanded into the Mediterranean, thus accounting for the Trojan legends that eventually found their way into British folklore.''

''And meanwhile, the actual demons were buried all that time under the Temple at Jerusalem,'' McLeod said.

''Apparently so,'' Sir John agreed. ''I also find it interesting that the first effigies of Gog and Magog were erected within a hundred years after the arrival of the real demons on British soil—if, indeed, that is what the casket contained, that the Templars had been charged to guard. But the legends had been around for centuries, so why erect the effigies at that particular point in time?''

''Perhaps because their mere presence on the island stirred some profound residue of racial memory,'' Adam said. ''When all is said and done, we know far less than we care to admit about the depth and complexity of the human psyche. The very existence of the effigies attests to the potency of the tradition. The single accounts might be regarded as circumstantial, and dismissible by themselves. But taken as a whole, they do tend to substantiate Dundee's assertion that Gog and Magog are demons of some kind, together with his contention that it is the age-old function of the Templar treasures to contain and control them.''

There was a flat pause.

''Wonderful,'' McLeod said sourly. ''We're dealing with demons that it took the wisdom of Solomon to subdue—and whoever stole Nathan Fiennes' Seal can release them on the world.''

''We've got to stop him,'' Peregrine said. ''But how?''

Sir John glanced aside at Adam, his hazel eyes agleam beneath his level brows. ''I think Adam already knows *his* mandate in that regard.''

''Aye, it does seem inescapable,'' Adam replied. ''It appears we're meant to go to Fyvie tomorrow, and ask my 'sister,' the Green Lady, to help us recover the Crown from its hiding place.''

''Do we really want to do that?'' Peregrine asked,

looking dubious. "I mean, if the Crown is safe where it is, wouldn't it be better to leave it hidden?"

"It would be," said Sir John, "were it not for the fact that the thief who stole the Seal is certainly after the casket, probably under the mistaken impression that it contains a treasure rather than a danger. If he knew what the Seal represented, beyond its value as an object of antiquity, he almost certainly has the skill to use it as a psychic link to help him locate the casket. Whether or not he'll have picked up on the need for the other two hallows, I couldn't say. But if you can get to the Crown before he does, Adam, you ought to be able to use it to locate both the Sceptre and the casket—hopefully, before he gets to the casket with the Seal."

"Good Lord, you don't *really* think he'd be stupid enough to just open the casket, do you?" Peregrine asked, wide-eyed.

"People who do these kind of things are stupid enough to try almost anything, laddie," McLeod rumbled, running a knotty fingertip around the rim of his cup. "He doesn't know it, but he's in mortal danger. If we don't get there first, he's apt to end up dead or mad—and God knows who else will suffer."

"That's why *we* must be prepared," Adam said. "And that means that we acquire the Crown and the Sceptre before we set foot near the casket. Dundee told us that the Crown confers essential wisdom on the wearer—presumably of how to wield the power that the Sceptre focuses—and also protects the wearer from the madness of evil. So our task not only is to attempt to stop the thief from releasing the demons; we have to be certain that if he succeeds in doing that before we can stop him, we must be able to undo what he's done: put the genie back in the bottle, so to speak. We have to assume that the demons can't be destroyed by means of the Seal and Crown and Sceptre, or Solomon would have done so. But merely reimprisoning the demons may be sufficient—so long as we can avoid becoming demon fodder in the process. . . ."

CHAPTER NINETEEN

AFTER another hour of discussion there in the library, they all retired. Adam felt his fatigue washing over him in waves as he climbed the stairs with McLeod and Peregrine, almost as if it lay waiting for him on the floor above, wrapping him more closely with each upward step he took. He readied for bed with a mechanical preoccupation that skirted but did not address the vast bulk of information he had taken in earlier—certain indicator that his work was not yet finished for the night; his unconscious was dutifully assimilating what he had learned, beginning to formulate their next strategy. He fell deeply and heavily asleep almost as soon as his head touched the pillow.

Initially, his profound need for physical restoration took him deep below the threshold of dreaming. But as his body started to recover its spent energies, his spirit-self began to stir, spiraling slowly upward out of the limbo of deep sleep toward levels of visionary awareness. For a time, this psychic aspect of his being merely drifted without apparent purpose through galleries of recent memory, like a traveller on holiday making a leisurely tour of a picture gallery. Scene by scene passed him by until at last he came upon a sumptuous painting encompassed by an antique gold frame.

Dominating the canvas was a bearded figure seated on a royal throne, whom Adam recognized at once as King Solomon. The great King of Israel was arrayed as Adam had seen him in his earlier dream, in flowing robes of scarlet embroidered with Qabalistic symbols, but this time he wore the Seal hung about his neck on a heavy golden chain. His flowing silver hair was confined by a golden diadem in the shape of a star with six upturned points, and he held in his right hand the Sceptre of his authority, aglow with latent power. At his feet lay a golden casket, perhaps half the size of a man, its lid ornately surmounted by four winged figures that recalled to Adam the apocalyptic visions of Ezekiel and descriptions of the Ark of the Covenant.

As he gazed in wonder at the painting, the scene itself seemed suddenly to come to life, expanding to draw Adam into the midst of it. Suddenly he was standing before the great King's throne, garbed in the sapphire blue of his usual working attire as he bent his head in respect. But as he straightened, a gust of sulphurous wind darkened the air above them, and the ground beneath his feet was rocked with a sudden crack of thunder.

Swiftly Solomon rose from his throne, glancing upward. Following his gaze, Adam saw roiling clouds of sickly yellow converging on the dais, charged with venomous flickers of greenish flame. To his horror and dismay, the clouds resolved into two monstrous humanoid shapes with writhing, tentacular limbs, each limb ending in a blind mouth gaping with fangs. The creatures bore down on the great King as if to rend him to pieces, spitting and shrieking their defiance.

Dark eyes flashing, Solomon raised the Sceptre and pointed it in an imperious gesture of command. Purifying lightning blazed skyward from the Sceptre's tip, flaring outward in a web of radiant energy to catch the two demon-things in midair, trapping them in a constricting lacework of fiery threads. Transfixed, they fetched up short, howling with pain and brute fury.

Still holding the Sceptre aloft, Solomon half knelt to raise the casket lid on its hinges with his free hand. Drawing himself up again to his full height, he spoke a Word of royal authority and pointed with the Sceptre toward the open casket at his feet. Instantly the two demon-things began to shrink within the compass of the net that held them, drawn irresistibly downward and forced into the casket.

Deaf to their howls, his bearded face set like iron, Solomon leaned over and shut the lid with a slam that reverberated in the air around him. A touch of the Sceptre's tip laid a lozenge of liquid gold across the gap where the lid met the base, like a hot iron set to solder. Doffing the chain about his neck, the great King then took the Seal itself in hand and pressed it firmly into the molten metal. When he took the Seal away again, its imprint was clearly visible before Adam's astonished eyes, as if limned in fire—a six-pointed star of interlocking triangles, surrounded by a scroll of Qabalistic symbols, each one fraught with power to capture and bind.

The symbol flared out with sudden, brilliant intensity. Dazzled, Adam flung up an arm before his face and reeled back. As he stumbled to his knees, he seemed to hear a deep voice speaking, the words ringing in his ears like a prophecy.

> *Ashrei adam matsah chokmah.*
> *Eits chaim hi la'machazikim.*
> *Bah ve tomchehah meooshar. . . .*

A sense of urgency dragged him partway to consciousness—just aware enough to recognize the impetus, edging on compulsion, that drew him upright in his bed and guided him to grope for the pocket notebook and pen he had left on the bedside table before retiring. The moonlight still streaming through the window was just sufficient to orient pen to paper, and his hand began to move of its own volition as he hovered in that twilight state between waking and sleeping that often gave access to inner wisdom.

He did not try to make out what his hand was writing, for to analyze the process was possibly to interrupt it. He kept the image of Solomon before him until his hand had spent its energy, pen and notebook falling away unheeded then as consciousness again receded to the inner realms. As he crumpled back on his pillow, haunting visions of a golden casket and a fiery Seal accompanied him as he spiralled downward into sleep again. . . .

The Seal seemed to grow even brighter as Henri Gerard fixed his gaze upon it where it lay cradled between his two outstretched hands. A few inches farther away from where he knelt, a fist-sized ball of rock crystal glowed against a square of black velvet spread on the floor of his Edinburgh bed-and-breakfast room, whose rather tawdry furnishings had all been pushed back and covered with new white sheets. By candlelight, he could imagine that it was a proper temple in which he worked. In any case, it was serving its purpose.

Gerard had fasted and prepared himself for three days before making this venture; now his efforts were being rewarded. Rainbow lights began to dance like wildfire around the room's four walls, refracted from the sphere's interior. When Gerard at last diverted his gaze to the heart of the sphere, a hazy image began to form in the crystal depths.

Gradually the image sharpened to show him a close-up view of a six-pointed star imprinted in pure gold, wreathed in scrollwork executed in Hebrew characters—the mirror image of the Seal he held in his hands.

Scarcely daring to breathe, Gerard willed his focus to broaden—for without a reference point, the mere vision of the Seal's imprint was useless. He could feel the drain on his energy, but the effort yielded results. Before his rapt gaze, the image slowly began to recede, at the same time revealing the Seal's placement on the side of a large, ark-like casket made of gold, its lid surmounted by four winged golden creatures.

Gerard's eyes widened in almost feverish avarice as the scene in the sphere continued to expand, torchlight flickering on the golden figures so that they almost seemed endowed with life. The casket was being borne forward by four white-mantled Templar knights who supported its weight on a pair of long wooden poles, carrying it toward a rounded stone gate arch. Two more knights, also mantled, followed close behind the casket, their faces set like iron in the glow of the torches they carried.

As Gerard watched, the Templars carried the casket through the arch and down a massive flight of stone steps. Another stone passageway opened up at the foot of the stair, off to the right, and the knightly procession carried on along the passageway to its end. Here two stonemasons in dusty aprons presided over a pile of building stones heaped around a partially walled-up doorway in the left-hand wall.

The four carrier knights turned left, bearing their burden past the waiting workmen through the remaining gap. The two escorting knights hung back, stationing themselves to the left and the right of the door. Their air of anticipation drew Gerard's scrying eyes to the implements they now drew forth from underneath their mantles. One of the implements was easily recognizable as the Seal; the other was a metallic rod tipped with a heavy knob and a hand-sized star made of two interlaced triangles of gold— some sort of sceptre, Gerard decided, of a strange and antique design.

The Sceptre drew Gerard's gaze like a magnet. As he continued to study it, willing further intelligence concerning the Sceptre, his fingers unconsciously tightened their grip on the Seal. Its latent power set the nerve ends tingling in his fingertips. He drew a deep, hoarse breath and closed his eyes, retreating still deeper into trance as he extended himself, struggling to touch the Sceptre with a questioning finger of the mind.

The effort taxed him to the very limits of his reach. The strain verged on physical pain. Bowing low over the Seal and stretching himself to the utmost, he made a last blind grab and bought himself a precious instant of discernment. Then, like a man teetering perilously on the edge of a precipice, he yanked himself back to palpitating safety.

The blood pounded in his temples, and his ears were ringing. His hands were cramped from their sustained grip on the Seal, and he groaned a little at the pain of returning circulation as he opened them enough to lay the Seal on the black velvet surrounding the crystal sphere. As he shakily straightened back to his kneeling position, sitting on his haunches, he discovered that his efforts had cost him a nosebleed as well, and he clamped a handkerchief to his nose and tilted back his head as he willed himself back to balance, trying not to think of the red stain now marring the white robe he wore. Sick and trembling, he forced himself to sit very still for several minutes while his breathing gradually righted itself and the racing of his heart subsided. Eventually he roused himself enough to draw a slow, deep breath and open his eyes.

For a moment everything around him was a blur. Then his vision stabilized to show him the mundane confines of his room at the guesthouse, ordinary and a little squalid beyond the boundaries of the circle he had laid out in tape on the tatty carpet. Candles burned at the points of the six-pointed star he had outlined inside the circle, and he and his black velvet and crystal and the Seal occupied the center hexagon.

Catching a glimpse of his own blanched reflection in the mirror on the wardrobe door, as he got shakily to his feet, Gerard pulled a pallid grin of triumph. Though he still felt decidedly unwell, the lingering agitation he was feeling was a relatively small price to pay for the knowledge he had just gained by the experience. Still grinning, he pulled folds of black velvet over the Seal and sphere, then set about releasing the safeguards he had erected around himself before beginning his work. When all traces had been obliterated—the candles doused, the tape pulled up, the furniture uncovered and returned to its proper places—only then did he allow himself to collapse on the bed, the Seal once more in hand, to inspect the contents of a plastic carrier bag, purchased several days before.

The stack of Ordnance Survey maps covered most of southern Scotland, but he had guessed, before beginning tonight's work, that the one he wanted was of the local Mid-Lothian Region. He spent the next few minutes poring avidly across its detailed surface till he found what he was looking for. Then he reached for the telephone on the bedside table.

Adam roused again shortly after daybreak, feeling mostly restored in body, but restive in mind. Sitting up in bed, his first thought was to grope for the notebook in which he knew he had written *something* during the night. He found it and his pen on the floor beside the bed, and was somewhat startled to discover that he had recorded the lines not in English, but in Hebrew.

He stared down at the alien script, mentally shifting gears. His knowledge of Hebrew was rudimentary at best, but enough came to mind to puzzle out the basic meaning of what he had written, especially having refreshed his memory at Nathan's funeral a mere week before. Haltingly he jotted down a rough translation on the page opposite, then murmured aloud what he had written.

> *Happy is the man who finds wisdom.*
> *She is a tree of life to those who grasp her*
> *And those who hold her fast are happy. . . .*

Even in what surely must be a clumsy translation, the words had the formal ring of verse. More to the point, he was certain he had come across the lines before—most likely in the book of Proverbs, said to be a compendium of King Solomon's own words. Recalling that there had been several Bibles on the shelves downstairs in Oakwood's spacious library, Adam decided it would be well worth checking out his hypothesis before breakfast. From what he had learned so far of Sir John Graham, he suspected he might well find Hebrew sources there as well.

Galvanized into action by this prospect, he sprang out of bed and padded swiftly through to the adjoining bathroom for a quick shower and shave, after which he dressed and slipped downstairs. As he had hoped and expected, the library was empty. Closing the door quietly behind him, he switched on an overhead light and went to work.

It did not take him long to find what he required. To his no great surprise, there were several volumes of biblical commentary as well as a concordance on the shelf adjacent to four or five different translations of the Bible. Working from the concordance, a King James translation, a Latin Vulgate edition, and a Hebrew Old Testament, he soon discovered that the lines he had recorded the previous night were, indeed, from the book of Proverbs, the thirteenth and eighteenth verses of the third chapter. Propping the texts open before him on the tabletop, he stared at the slightly different translations while he pondered their relationship to the dream.

Another vision of Solomon featuring the hallows and, this time, the casket. And a direct quotation from a book of sayings said to be the words of King Solomon himself. The more Adam thought about it, the more certain he became that the resonant voice he had heard in his vision had, indeed, been direct instruction from the great King. He was still considering the possible import of this when the library door swung open behind him.

"Good heavens, you're up early!" exclaimed a surprised female voice. "After last night, I expected you to sleep in."

Adam turned around. The slim figure in the doorway was Caitlin Jordan, her chestnut hair burnished to auburn in the early morning sunlight, her brown eyes inquiring. Rising from his chair, Adam pulled a wry smile and said, "Good morning. I hope I didn't startle you. If I did, I'm sorry."

"Not at all. It's only that I'm generally the first person up around here." Noting the books on the tabletop before him, she added, "More research, I see. I gather that things continued to percolate while you slept."

Adam saw no reason to dissemble.

"I had a rather intense dream, shortly after I fell asleep," he told her. "Another 'visitation' from or to King Solomon. I must confess, I find it a little daunting to be receiving guidance from so sage an entity as the great Solomon, who is probably the embodiment of wisdom—but there you are. That's who it was."

Chuckling lightly, Caitlin came to sit beside him in the chair he pulled out for her.

"I'm sure it's got to be daunting, in the middle of the night," she agreed. "Would you like to bounce it off me in the clear light of day? Two heads are bound to be better than one."

"I'd welcome your assessment," Adam replied. "It's hardly pre-breakfast fare, but here's what happened."

As she sat there beside him, listening avidly, he related the details of this second vision of Solomon.

''Finally, I surfaced long enough to write this down—just the Hebrew, at that point.'' He handed her the notebook. ''It has to have come from elsewhere, because I'm sure I couldn't have recalled the Hebrew on my own. Reading and translating are one thing—and normally, I can only just squeak through in Hebrew, even with the aid of a dictionary. Writing this in Hebrew from the spoken words is quite another thing. Anyway, I scribbled out that rough translation this morning.''

''And you tracked it down to these?'' she asked, leaning over to look at the texts lying open on the table.

''Yes. The lines are from Proverbs, as I expected. Here's the King James translation, and here's the Vulgate for comparison.''

> *Happy is the man that findeth wisdom.*
> *She is a tree of life to them that lay hold upon her:*
> *and happy is every one that retaineth her.*

> *Beatus homo qui invenit sapientiam.*
> *Lignum vitae est his qui apprehenderint eam,*
> *et qui tenuerit eam beatus.*

Caitlin scanned the verses, taking her time.

''Well, the first line is fairly unambiguous,'' she said, after reflection. ''*Happy is the man that findeth wisdom.* If we take *wisdom* as a synonym for *knowledge,* then it might simply be referring to all the information you've been able to glean so far regarding the casket and the hallows.''

''No, I think it refers to the Crown,'' Adam said positively. ''Dundee said that the Crown conferred the *wisdom* to resist the madness of evil.'' He cocked his head. ''Now, *there's* a thought that just occurred to me. Judeo-Christian tradition quite often personifies Wisdom as a woman, holy Sophia. One of the charges levelled against the Templars was that they supposedly worshipped a head of some kind—quite possibly a female head. I wonder if that could have come from a misinterpretation of their venera-

tion for the Crown of Solomon and the wisdom it represented?''

"The Crown of Wisdom," Caitlin said, nodding. "You
may well be right. In any case, I'd say it's fairly clear that
you've been given formal license from Solomon himself to
reclaim his Crown.''

Meeting her eyes, Adam drew a deep breath. It was a
heady realization, but the burden was likewise a daunting
one.

"If you're right about the Crown," Caitlin went on,
"then perhaps the other part refers to the Sceptre. The King
James translation refers to a 'tree of life,' but the Latin
lignum has more of the feel of wood, timber, a staff—or, by
extension, a rod of rule, a sceptre. *A staff of life to him who
grasps her, and whoso holds her fast is safe. . . .*" She
gave a perplexed sigh. "I don't want to be alarmist, but it
rather sounds to me like an additional warning that the
Crown by itself is not enough to see you through whatever
lies ahead.''

"Which tends to reinforce what Dundee said—that both
the Crown and the Sceptre are necessary to control the
demons in safety," Adam agreed. "And I have the impression that the Sceptre is involved in setting the Seal. It
certainly seemed to work that way for Solomon.''

"Which means that even once you've secured the Crown,
you mustn't dare try to go to the casket until you've found
the Sceptre as well," Caitlin said. "To do so would be folly,
if the Seal's been used to open the casket and the demons
are free.''

Adam nodded. "It makes our task that much more
daunting, because I'll have to go directly from whatever's
needed to retrieve the Crown into another difficult working
to locate both the casket and the Sceptre. But we'll worry
about that when the time comes.''

"Well, the time has come for breakfast, just now," said
a new voice from the doorway.

Both Adam and Caitlin turned around to find Sir John
smiling at them from the threshold, his hands resting on the
head of his walking stick.

"Good morning, all," he said.

Laughing delightedly, Caitlin rolled her eyes in mock consternation as she rose.

"Now you can see why Gray did so well in intelligence work," she said to Adam, going to greet her great-grandfather with a fond kiss. "He still comes and goes like the Cheshire Cat!"

"Nonsense," said Sir John, slipping an arm around her waist. "The pair of you were simply deeply absorbed in what seemed to be a very intriguing conversation. No, don't tell me about it now," he went on, when Adam would have spoken. "If you like, we'll confer after breakfast—which Linton informs me is being served in the dining room. You're welcome to linger here if you like, but I think I ought to warn you that young Peregrine has already set a covetous eye on the scones."

"In that case, we'd better come at once," Adam said with a smile, pocketing his notebook and pen. "My young friend is normally the soul of courtesy and moderation, but I'm afraid scones are a fatal weakness of his. . . ."

The party at breakfast was nearly twice the size of their group the night before. On entering the dining room, Adam found himself presented first to Caitlin's grandparents, the Earl and Countess of Selwyn, then to her mother, Lady Jordan. Bowing gravely over the hands of both ladies in turn, Adam thought he could see where Caitlin had come by her looks.

"We've heard a great deal about you, Sir Adam," said Lord Selwyn. He was a robust, silver-haired man in his early seventies, with a firm and vigorous handshake. "I'm sorry we weren't on hand to greet you when you arrived. Caitlin's father sits in Commons, you know, and Audrey and Sarah and I had been up to London for the weekend to attend a reception; didn't get home until quite late last night. I trust the rest of the household were able to make you feel welcome in our absence."

"The hospitality was unimpeachable," Adam assured him, "all the more so in view of the fact that we made so bold as to accept lodgings for the night on rather short notice. I hope we haven't thrown the domestic staff into an uproar.''

"The staff, I venture to say, are well up to dealing with far greater crises than unexpected guests,'' said Lady Selwyn. "Linton alone has seen us through more storms than a Yankee clipper on the China run round Cape Horn.''

Over breakfast, to which they helped themselves from a sumptuous sideboard, she went on to regale them with a succession of anecdotes illustrative of their butler's redoubtable sang-froid in the face of household disaster. Listening and laughing with the rest of the company, Adam was moved to furnish one or two tales of his own from the domestic annals of Strathmourne.

"It sounds to me as if Linton and my man Humphrey belong to the same rare breed,'' he concluded with a reminiscent grin. "The next time you have an occasion to stray north of Hadrian's Wall, you must call by Strathmourne and see for yourself.''

Breakfast concluded on a note of congeniality. While Caitlin and her mother took Peregrine and McLeod on a last tour of the rose gardens, Sir John drew Adam back into the library for a final assessment of all that had transpired.

"I would have to concur with what you and Caitlin worked out regarding the Solomonic pronouncement,'' Sir John said, when he had heard Adam out. "And the point about the head the Templars are said to have worshipped makes good sense. I know some scholars have tried to tie it in with one of the numerous cults of the head, but those mainly come from Celtic sources, and I've always felt that the Templar head connection was Middle Eastern in origin. Solomon's Crown would fit that hypothesis.

"Still, it's the Crown's present use that concerns us now,'' he went on, reaching into his pocket and withdrawing the jeweller's case with the Templar cross, which he passed to Adam. "Mustn't forget this, either. Aside from being your passport to get the Green Lady to help you, you may find it of use as additional protection, since it's a badge long associated with the Templar Order and its function as guardian. I'd advise you to wear it, especially when you go to deal with the casket.''

Nodding, Adam slipped the case into a coat pocket. "I'll do that. And thank you for all your help. I hope you realize that mere words are totally inadequate.''

"But words are what we have to work with," Sir John said with a wistful smile. "I'm only sorry that we didn't meet sooner, and that this meeting was under such conditions of urgency. Still, I suppose there's nothing like urgency to cut through the dross and focus on what's really important. In the normal course of things, it probably would have taken years to achieve the level of trust we shared last night, across our differences of tradition—and at ninety-two, I don't expect I have that many more years, this time around.''

"Then it's good that we skipped over all those intervening years," Adam said, smiling, "because as far as I'm concerned, our differences are very superficial—except that I see in you a glimpse of what's still to come, as I continue my own progression toward the Light. I feel privileged to have met you, Gray—and honored to have worked with you. Do you suppose I might ask for your blessing before we part?''

Sir John looked a little startled, then pleased. "You're sure?''

"Very sure.''

As Adam bowed his head, eyes closing as his hands dropped to his sides, he felt the touch of the general's hands lightly on his hair, and then the heady weight of benison filling him from head to toes.

"I give you the blessing of all the gods and goddesses whom I have been privileged to serve," Sir John murmured, "and I invoke upon you their wisdom to guide you and their strength to sustain and defend you and yours. May their bright blessings be with you and remain with you as you go forth in the service of the Light. Amen. Selah. So mote it be.''

"So mote it be," Adam repeated, lifting his head as Sir John's hands fell away. "Thank you.''

"Thank *you*."

The general's eyes were a little brighter as he glanced out the French doors where McLeod and Peregrine were returning in the company of Caitlin and Lady Selwyn.

"I think Linton's probably brought your things down to the car by now," he said brusquely. "You probably ought to be on your way. You wouldn't want to miss your flight."

"No, we should be off," Adam agreed. "Saying we'll go up to Fyvie is all well and good, but there are practicalities involved. Realistically, I don't think we can get up there before tomorrow night. There's groundwork to be laid. We can't very well show up on their doorstep and tell them why we're really there."

"Well, the Crown has to be first," Sir John agreed. "Without it, you can't even find out where the casket is, much less do anything if your man's gotten there first. Move as quickly as you can, though. And don't take any needless risks."

"Sound advice," Adam said lightly. "And I'll ring you as soon as we've wrapped things up—and give you an in-person report, as soon after that as I can. After all," he added, patting the pocket with the jeweller's box, "I have this cross to return."

Chapter Twenty

INSTEAD of returning the way they had come, McLeod headed them north out of Ashford to pick up the M20 motorway, skirting south of London on the M25 ring road and then dropping down to Gatwick on the M23. Their return flight touched down in Edinburgh shortly after two, slightly late because of heavy rain. Humphrey was not at the gate to meet them, but they found him waiting for them at curbside, standing beside the blue Range Rover. As he saw them approaching, he moved around to open up the rear for their luggage.

"Welcome home, sir," he said, as he took Adam's bag and stashed it in the back. "Before you ask, a package arrived for you from York this morning by special courier. I thought it might be urgent, so I took the liberty of bringing it along. It's in the glove box."

"Well done, indeed, Humphrey!" Adam murmured, exchanging a glance with Peregrine and McLeod. "That will be from Peter Fiennes. I wonder what he found."

While Humphrey continued stowing McLeod's and Peregrine's bags, Adam slid into the passenger seat and opened the glove box. The parcel was a paper-wrapped box about the size of a thick paperback book, heavy for its size. He had it opened by the time the others had piled in and Humphrey was pulling away from the curb. Inside, swathed in layers of tissue paper, was something hard and heavy, like a stone paperweight.

There was a note from Peter resting on top. Adam picked it up and read it aloud for the benefit of McLeod and Peregrine, listening avidly from the backseat.

"'Dear Adam: Found this yesterday, while I was clearing out Dad's office at the university. It seems to

be an impression of the Seal. I thought you might as
well have it, on the off chance it might be of some use
to you in your investigation. Thanks again for all your
help and support. Peter Fiennes.'

"Well, then."

While Peregrine and McLeod looked on, Adam gingerly
lifted the object free of its wrappings and turned it over. It
proved to be a square lump of thick red sealing wax a little
larger than a man's palm. Pressed into the wax was the clear
image of a six-pointed star of interlocking triangles encircled by a scroll of Qabalistic characters.

"An imprint of the Seal," Peregrine murmured, leaning
in closer between the two front seats to stare at it, his hazel
eyes narrowed behind his gold-framed spectacles. "If I look
the right way, I can actually see a hand pressing a metal seal
into the wax—maybe Nathan Fiennes' hand."

"I wonder why he did it," McLeod said.

"He probably was curious to see what the positive image
looked like in three dimensions," Adam said. "Or perhaps
he anticipated submitting the design to someone for analysis. Either way, it could be very useful indeed, since it
represents our first clear physical link with the missing
object. This actually touched the Seal, and carries its mirror
image."

As he spoke, he saw again in his mind's eye the image of
King Solomon setting his Seal to the casket containing a
pair of demon-spirits. The memory brought a sympathetic
tingle to Adam's fingertips from the Seal imprint he held in
his hands. The residue of power was palpable. He did not
doubt that the object which had made the imprint was the
Seal itself, not a copy.

Peregrine's voice recalled him.

"What are you planning to do with it?"

"For now, nothing," Adam said. "Ask me again after
we've seen what we can learn at Fyvie."

They dropped McLeod off at his house in Ormidale
Terrace and stayed long enough for a quick cup of tea while
the inspector put in a call to police headquarters.

"Yes. Well, thanks anyway, Donald," he said, just before he hung up. "Yes, definitely keep working on it. See you tomorrow."

He pulled a glum face, then glanced at Adam.

"Still nothing on Gerard," he said. "Looks like we continue to do this the hard way."

"Well, at least we're better prepared for that now than we were this time yesterday," Adam said resignedly. "Come on, Peregrine. I need you to give me a hand with some homework back at Strathmourne. Noel, we'll get back to you later this evening, when we've sorted out something on Fyvie."

Back home at the manor house, he and Peregrine repaired to the library, where they spent the next two hours sifting through the books in the Scottish collection in search of material pertaining to Fyvie Castle. While Adam pored over volumes on history and folklore, Peregrine concentrated his attention on commentaries dealing with the castle's layout and structure.

He found what he was looking for in Volume II of a work entitled *Castellated and Domestic Architecture of Scotland,* by Macgibbon and Ross. The section on Fyvie Castle was reasonably detailed, and included not only floor plans but a number of illustrations.

"This may be exactly what we need, Adam," he reported over his shoulder. "It's all pretty technical—no mention of any 'Green Lady'—but there's plenty of other stuff having to do with the way the place is constructed. Here, have a look for yourself."

He passed Adam the tan volume. Inspecting the layout of the rooms detailed in black and white, Adam nodded his satisfaction.

"That's useful," he told his young associate. "I've unearthed some interesting information as well. Between us, we should be able to work out where Grizel Seton was murdered."

"What have you got, then?" Peregrine asked, edging closer.

"To start with, a few tidbits of local folklore that may be

pertinent. There appears to be a long-standing tradition that 'the Devil' is supposed to reside at Fyvie, walled up in a secret room.''

"The Devil!" Peregrine murmured, going a little pale.

"Now, just relax," Adam returned. "I don't anticipate having to come face-to-face with the Prince of Darkness. A few of his minions, perhaps—"

"Adam, that isn't funny!"

Giving Peregrine a droll sidelong glance, Adam returned his attention to the notes he had jotted down.

"The room in question appears to be in the Meldrum Tower, just below the Charter Room—here on your floor plan. Macgibbon and Ross even label it as being sealed. Any attempt to open this room is said to operate an otherwise latent curse, bringing death to the laird and blindness to his wife.''

"Good Lord, has anyone ever attempted to test the curse?" Peregrine asked, wide-eyed.

"Yes. Two lairds of the manor made exploratory incursions. Both died shortly thereafter, and their wives both became afflicted with eye trouble. One of them actually did go completely blind. It's probably no wonder that when the castle went up for sale in 1984, all prospective purchasers—including the National Trust for Scotland, which finally bought it—were enjoined to agree to a covenant undertaking not to open the room, allow it to be opened, or allow any X-rays or other high-tech imaging to be done there.''

"Just in case the Devil really *is* locked up at Fyvie," Peregrine said.

"Or something *like* a devil."

"You mean something like Gog and Magog." Peregrine caught his breath slightly, his eyes gone wide and round. "Adam," he breathed, "you don't suppose the *casket* might be there at Fyvie, as well as the Crown?"

"I shouldn't think so—though I'd venture to guess that it might well have been there at some time in the past," Adam said. "That could account for the 'devil' tradition, not to mention the lingering influence of malignancy that apparently still resonates there. But even if I'm right in that conjecture, the casket has almost certainly been moved since. Once the local legend had taken root, it no longer would have been safe to keep it there."

"Too right," Peregrine agreed. "And I don't imagine Dundee would have sent the Crown to Fyvie for safekeeping if the casket had been there as well."

"Not unless he didn't know the casket was there," Adam reminded him. "But I do think that it would have been moved by Dundee's time, even if he didn't know where it had ended up. The Crown is another matter."

"You think it might have been hidden in the secret room, then? If people really thought the Devil was walled up there, they wouldn't be likely to disturb it."

"No, but hiding it there in the first place would have been a tricky proposition, if there *is* something down there. No, we'll have a look at the vicinity of the Charter Room, just in case I'm wrong, but I think that we'll find what we're looking for up here, toward the top of the Gordon Tower."

As Adam pointed out the equivalent space on the floor plan, Peregrine squinted at the legend in small print.

"The Douglas Room," he read off. "Why there?"

"Because that's the room associated with the Green Lady," Adam said, "and if she's Grizel Seton, she's the one who can tell us where the Crown is, even if it isn't in that particular room. I haven't been able to find out anything more to connect the Green Lady with a particular name, but the room itself is sometimes referred to as the Murder Room—which would be quite apt, if that's where Grizel was killed. There's even supposed to be a bloodstain on the floor that can't be washed off."

Peregrine gave a nod, obviously impressed. "I can't argue with that logic," he agreed. "Now all we have to do is figure out a way to drop in for a look around, without anyone else being the wiser."

At his accompanying grimace, Adam sat back with a thoughtful sigh.

"I've been wondering about that myself," he said. "Merely gaining access is no problem, of course, since we're still in the tourist season, and Fyvie is open to visitors during the usual hours. But that alone makes it rather too public for our purposes. If we're to gain entry to the castle outside normal visiting hours, I think we shall have to resort to some other stratagem—ideally, something that doesn't involve breaking and entering.''

Peregrine snorted. ''Well, that's a relief. I'm not sure I'd care to try breaking and entering a castle.''

Nodding distractedly, Adam continued to consider, then said, ''Correct me if I'm wrong, but aren't you on the books of the National Trust as someone they can call on, if they need an expert to authenticate a given work in their possession?''

''That's right,'' Peregrine answered. ''My special area of expertise is the works of Sir Henry Raeburn. They've got more than a dozen at Fyvie, you know. I've also done some minor restorations of paintings for the Trust—but I'm only one of a whole army of qualified people they can call upon.''

''That doesn't much matter,'' Adam said. ''Have you ever done any work on any of the portraits housed at Fyvie?''

''Not in any official capacity,'' Peregrine said. ''I'm familiar with the Raeburns, of course. But that's only because they were among the many works of his that I surveyed in detail while I was working on my thesis.''

''Did you survey them firsthand?''

''Yes, of course. You can't work from photographs or copies if you're learning to distinguish particular features of an artist's distinctive style.''

''Who arranged your surveying visits for you?''

''My academic supervisor worked it out with the castle administrator,'' Peregrine said. He peered owlishly at Adam and added, ''Is this important?''

''It could be,'' Adam said, ''depending on whether or not the castle administrator would still remember you.''

''I expect he would. I spent quite a few hours under his nose while I was going over the Raeburns,'' Peregrine said. ''That's assuming, of course, that he hasn't been replaced since I was last there. I'll be happy to telephone Fyvie and inquire, but before I do, could you tell me what all this is leading up to?"

The baffled appeal in his expression moved Adam to smile in spite of himself.

"Of course. We need a good excuse for getting inside Fyvie Castle outside normal visiting hours. With any luck, you're going to supply us with that excuse."

The ruse he went on to describe was relatively simple. Peregrine's response was a scandalized grin.

"Sounds deliciously devious to me," he said. "Do you really think it will work?"

"Our success or failure in the long run will depend largely on Noel's ability to brazen out an imposture," Adam replied with a smile. "In the short term, though, it's going to be up to you to sell the administrator on the initial idea."

"I'm game to try," Peregrine said. "Mr. Lauder was always pretty flexible—he used to let me in at all kinds of odd hours, when I was doing my research—but he may not much like the idea of having after-hours visitors descending on him at such short notice."

"The time factor can't be helped. Time is one thing we are desperately short on," Adam reminded him.

"I know," Peregrine said. "But let me see what I can do—though if Lauder's been replaced, all bets may be off."

The telephone number for Fyvie Castle was listed in one of the guidebooks Adam had been consulting. Taking the booklet with him for reference, Peregrine went over to Adam's desk and reached for the telephone, turning to pull a wry face at Adam as he dialled the number at Fyvie.

"Hello, I wonder if I could speak to Mr. Frederick Lauder, please," he said. "It's Peregrine Lovat calling."

There was a brief delay while the call was transferred to the administration office.

"Mr. Lauder, this is Peregrine Lovat—Mr. Bottomley's student," Peregrine said, when the line had picked up. "Yes, that's right—the one who was studying the Raeburns. No, I'm working out of Edinburgh these days. Yes, doing very well, thank you. I'm ringing up to ask if I might impose on you for a favor. . . ."

He went on to explain himself. Listening to the young artist's half of the conversation, Adam was relieved to hear that Lauder seemed to be not too resistant to what Peregrine was suggesting. When the young artist at length set down the receiver, he was flushed with triumph.

"We're in!" he announced jubilantly. "Lauder and his wife will be expecting us to turn up around eight o'clock tomorrow night."

"Excellent!"

"There *is* one minor inconvenience."

"How minor?"

"Well, to increase its revenue, the Trust hires out premises in a number of its historic properties," Peregrine said. "There's a do scheduled at Fyvie for tomorrow night—a black-tie dinner-dance for some consortium of North Sea oil executives from Aberdeen. It shouldn't be a problem," he hastened to add. "We'll just have to take care to stay out of their way."

Rolling his eyes, Adam consulted the floor plans again.

"Well, if they confine themselves to the Dining Room and Drawing Room, I shouldn't think they'd have any business where we need to be," he decided. "Actually, this could be a distraction that will work to our advantage. For one thing, it means your Mr. Lauder and his good lady will probably be too occupied with their guests to pay much heed to what the three of us might be doing. All that remains is to prime Noel as to what he's got to do to put on a convincing front as an expert in seventeenth-century plaster ceilings."

He telephoned McLeod himself. Apprised of the plan, the inspector displayed understandable reservations.

"Why me?" he grumbled plaintively. "What I *don't* know about art would fill an encyclopaedia. Wouldn't Peregrine be better suited?"

"Not this time," Adam said. "The castle administrator already knows him for his work with portraiture."

"All right," McLeod allowed grudgingly. "But why *ceilings,* for God's sake?"

"We need you to be expert in something that can't be

moved out of the room we need to look at,'' Adam said. ''Also, our excuse for this visit on such short notice is that you're going to be in the neighborhood only for the day, and want to make optimum use of the time. You're advising me on the ceiling restorations at Templemor.''

''You think of everything, don't you,'' McLeod said with a sigh of resignation. ''All right. If you want me to be a ceiling expert by tomorrow, I'd better hustle my hips over to the library before it closes, and pick up a book or two on ornamental plasterwork.''

''You can do that if you want,'' Adam said with a laugh, ''but I'll plan to have Peregrine give you a full briefing on the way up. Your time would be better spent working on the whereabouts of Henri Gerard.''

''Fair enough,'' McLeod conceded, ''though I'm not having much luck on that so far. What time did you want me at the house, then? I can take the whole day if I need to, but I've already had a lot of time off in the last couple of weeks.''

''Could you be here by three?'' Adam replied.

''All right. I sure hope we know what we're doing. . . .''

CHAPTER TWENTY-ONE

THE inspector proved to be as good as his word, arriving punctually on the dot of three o'clock the following afternoon. In deference to the fact that he was going to be posing as a scholar, he had traded his familiar black zipper bag with POLICE stencilled on the side for a plain, smaller version in brown. It still held the usual collection of police paraphernalia, including a high-powered torch with extra batteries, a cellular phone, and his Browning Hi-Power automatic, together with spare ammo clips. He also had three heavy books on architectural ornamentation and a crabbed assemblage of notes.

"The Gerard investigation wasn't going anywhere, so I decided to read about plaster after all," he remarked, as he shifted his bag into Adam's Range Rover. "You should have seen Jane's face when I lugged these tomes into the house last night. When she asked me what I wanted with them, I told her I was thinking about retiring from the police force and taking up a new career as an interior decorator. She said, fine, I could make a start on the back bedroom first thing tomorrow morning."

Adam chuckled. "That sounds like Jane. She's not worried, is she?"

"Not that I could see," McLeod answered. "Should she be?"

"No more than usual," Adam said. "At least not right now. Come on in and have a bite to eat before we get on the road."

Humphrey had set out a substantial snack of sandwiches and soup on the table where Adam's books were still laid out in the library. Even though Peregrine knew full well that there would be no time on the road to stop for a proper meal, he was unable to repress a pained grimace as soon as Humphrey's back was turned.

"I'm beginning to wish matters would come to a head," he sighed, eyeing his plate with disfavor. "I feel as if we've been living on sandwiches for *days* now."

"Careful what you wish for, laddie," McLeod said thickly through a mouthful of bread and ham. "Wish for trouble, and you just might get it sooner than you bargained for."

Adam was standing at the window gazing out into the grey afternoon as he also chewed on a sandwich, but at this exchange he turned around.

"Noel's right," he said. "If we can help it, we don't want anything to happen before we're as well prepared as we can be."

"Well, I just hope this enterprise comes off as planned," Peregrine said. "I'd hate for Julia to get a call later on tonight to tell her I've been gaoled in Aberdeen on suspicion of vandalism and attempted robbery."

"I don't think you need to worry about *that,* laddie," McLeod said lightly. "The last I heard, impersonating a plaster expert wasn't listed on the books as a viable offense. If you're determined to worry, worry about what Henri Gerard might be doing while we're poking our noses around in Fyvie's dark corners."

The rest of their impromptu meal concluded in thoughtful silence, broken only by the faint country sounds intruding from the garden outside. As they headed out to the car, Humphrey came to see them off, watching as Peregrine stashed his art satchel in the backseat, Adam's medical bag joining it. Waxed jackets and rubber wellie boots had been added to the paraphernalia as well, for the weather looked to be worsening rather than improving, off to the north.

"Sir," said Humphrey, "I've taken the liberty of putting a large flask of hot tea in the back of the car, along with a smaller one containing coffee. Is there anything else you think you might require?"

"Not that I can think of, but thank you, Humphrey," Adam said. "We may stay the night in Aberdeen, if the weather gets too bad, and come back tomorrow. So don't wait up.''

"Very good, sir," Humphrey said, and added softly, "You *will* be careful, won't you, sir?"

"Have no fear on that account," Adam said reassuringly. "We'll take no unnecessary risks."

But he knew even as he spoke that circumstances might well force them to take grave risks, indeed.

Dusk came early that afternoon, for they drove into pelting rain as they headed north with Adam at the wheel. Peregrine and McLeod spent the first hour reviewing the inspector's notes on ornamental plaster, Peregrine augmenting what McLeod had learned with information from his own experience. Once past Dundee, however, they had covered just about all McLeod could be expected to retain from so short a study. As the big Range Rover sped up the A94 toward Aberdeen and Fyvie Castle, conversation gradually died, each of them wrapped in his own thoughts and fears.

It was just after six when they hit Aberdeen, busy center of the North Sea oil industry. Traffic was still heavy, made worse by the rain, as Adam threaded the Range Rover westerly around the city, but it thinned as they headed out on the A96, making for the refuge of the low-lying hills. At Inverurie, they struck out northward toward Oldmeldrum, carrying on through a gradually darkening landscape of woods and fields until at last they were approaching the village of Fyvie. Just past the village center, McLeod spotted a sign sporting the familiar blue logo of the National Trust for Scotland, together with an arrow pointing the way to Fyvie Castle.

"There's our turn," he told Adam, pointing, and glanced down at the chronometer on the dash. "We're early, though. You want to pull over and kill time for a few minutes?"

Nodding, Adam pulled the Rover into a lay-by and cut the engine. "I need to organize myself anyway," he said. "I can't very well take my medical bag into the castle without raising eyebrows. Peregrine, would you hand it up, please? And have some tea or coffee if you want it, both of you."

Neither of them did, but they both watched avidly as, in the dimness of the car's cockpit, Adam opened the black bag Peregrine handed forward and delved into its depths. From the black jeweller's box came Dundee's Templar cross, whose black silk cord Adam looped over his head, tucking the cross itself inside the burgundy V-necked sweater he wore under his navy blazer. The cord became invisible, tucked close under the collar of his tattersall shirt.

The Dundee ring went into his left-hand jacket pocket, his *skean dubh* into his right. He was wearing his signet ring, but the others were not, lest the coincidence be marked by their incipient host. Just before Adam closed the bag, he handed McLeod the impression of the Seal, wrapped in a burgundy silk handkerchief with white spots.

"I don't know that we're going to need that tonight," he said, "but if we do, we can't use it if we don't have it with us. Peregrine, have you got a sketch pad?"

"A small one, in my pocket," Peregrine said. "I've got a pocket torch too. Nights like this, you never know when the power's going to go out, especially in these old properties. When I was working here as a student, I used to carry a cigarette lighter, even though I don't smoke. Needed it more than once too."

For answer, McLeod held up a blue disposable lighter and a pocket Maglite, as Adam passed his bag back to Peregrine.

"I'm right with ye, laddie," the inspector said. "On *that* front, I think we're well prepared."

They sat there for another quarter hour, Peregrine rehearsing McLeod one more time on his bona fides as a plaster expert, Adam oddly silent. Then, as Peregrine mostly cleared out his art satchel to make room for the Crown they hoped to bring out of Fyvie, they headed on along the curving road that led to the castle entrance.

Fyvie Castle was visible from the road as five tall towers standing above the trees of the surrounding park, glimpsed only intermittently between scudding clouds when the watery moonlight could silver the towers. As they drew nearer, details emerged of an imposing structure combining the strength of a baronial fortress with the architectural grace of a manor house. The narrow rectangular windows on the lower floors were ablaze with lights, bright enough to lay long swatches of light across the attendant sweeps of lawn. Lively snatches of music could be heard floating out across the forecourt from somewhere inside the building, proclaiming the presence of a formal function in progress. The rain had stopped, but the sky presaged more rain to come, and soon.

The car park adjoining the castle's east entrance was full to overflowing with executive automobiles belonging to the guests attending the evening's festivities. Adam swung the Range Rover off the gravel a short distance up the drive and cut the ignition, giving himself a few seconds to let any mental impressions register as he gazed up at the floodlit façade. He registered a glance at his two companions, and the three of them got out of the car, Peregrine grabbing up his art satchel, before they proceeded up the drive on foot toward the castle entrance. McLeod found the bellpull to the right of the doorway and gave it a vigorous tug.

A metallic jangle sounded beyond the heavy door. A moment later, the door swung wide, opened by a middle-aged man in the severe black and white formal attire of a serving butler. His welcoming expression turned politely quizzical when he saw that the three men on the doorstep were not in evening dress, but Adam moved smoothly to take command of the situation.

"Good evening," he said pleasantly, handing the man one of the cards he used on purely social occasions that said, simply, *Sir Adam Sinclair, Bt., F.R.C. PSYCH.* "My colleagues and I are here to see Mr. Lauder. I wonder if you'd be good enough to let him know that Mr. Lovat's party has arrived?"

His manner, though genial, was weighted with cultivated authority. The butler, glancing at the card, executed a respectful bow and said, "Certainly, Sir Adam. I'm not entirely certain where Mr. Lauder is at the moment, but if you gentlemen would care to step inside, I shall endeavor to find him for you."

He disappeared up the passageway, returning a few

minutes later in the company of a tall man in dinner clothes, with grey hair and high coloring. Shrewd grey eyes behind bottle-glass spectacles lighted on Peregrine, and the mouth that went with them framed a grin.

"Hullo there, Mr. Lovat!" he exclaimed heartily. "Welcome back to Fyvie! I hope you haven't been kept waiting overlong."

"Hardly any time at all—we've only just arrived," Peregrine said, returning the grin. "I'd like you to meet Sir Adam Sinclair of Strathmourne—"

"A pleasure, Sir Adam," Lauder said, shaking his hand.

"—and this," Peregrine said, indicating the inspector, "is Professor Noel McLeod."

"Aye, the gentleman who's interested in our ceilings," Lauder acknowledged with a sapient nod, also exchanging handshakes with McLeod. "It's nice to have you with us as well. Am I right that you come from America?"

"It's where I live and work," McLeod said with a straight face, "but I was born and bred in Edinburgh. Fortunately, my research brings me back here now and again," he added, "if only for a week or two at a time."

"Aye, Mr. Lovat did say you were scheduled to fly back to the States in the next day or two," Lauder acknowledged. "Glad we managed to fit you in at such short notice."

"Thank you for making the effort," McLeod said. "We appreciate it."

"Not at all. Now, tell me again which rooms you wanted to see." He glanced at Adam. "I understand that you're restoring a tower house, and you want some advice on plasterwork."

"That's correct," Adam agreed. "The core of the structure goes back to the twelfth century, I suspect, but I've decided to put it back to about what it was in the late seventeenth century. Much earlier than that, and it wouldn't be particularly comfortable to live in."

"Sir Adam is nearly ready to begin reinstating the ceilings," McLeod offered, "and Mr. Lovat told us there are some ceilings here that are similar in scale to Templemor. Work by Robert White, I believe."

Lauder nodded. "You'll want to see the Douglas Room, then, for certain, and also the Charter Room, for comparison. I'd also suggest you take a look at the Morning Room, but that may be a bit larger than you had in mind. Unfortunately, I can't let you see the Drawing Room or the Gallery, because that's where the party is set up."

"They'd be too big anyway," McLeod said, making a gesture of dismissal as he shook his head. "We'll be perfectly happy with the smaller rooms. We looked at the Vine Room at Kellie Castle earlier today, but it just wasn't what Sir Adam had in mind."

Lauder nodded knowingly. "Interesting work, that, but I think we've got better here at Fyvie."

"I agree," Peregrine replied. "Anyway, if Sir Adam likes what he sees, I thought I'd make some trial sketches to give to the stuccadores before they start on the ceilings at Templemor." He patted the satchel slung over his shoulder. "We won't get the craftsmanship you've got here at Fyvie, but at least they'll have something to aspire to."

Lauder beamed at the compliment. "Well, you couldn't have come to a better place for inspiration. The Charter Room alone—"

He was interrupted by a sudden loud crash from the corridor at his back, accompanied by the dissonant clatter of breaking dishes. Voices rose in a babble of dismay. Lauder winced and rolled his eyes toward the ceiling. A moment later, a middle-aged woman in a starched waitress's apron over her black skirt and white blouse popped around the corner with dismay writ large on her face.

"Mr. Lauder—"

"What is it this time?" Lauder demanded. "No, wait, don't tell me—I'll come and see for myself."

He turned apologetically to Adam and his companions, but before he could speak, Peregrine moved in to seize the initiative.

"Mr. Lauder, would it help if I went ahead and took them around?" he asked. "I'm already feeling guilty, to be imposing on you at such short notice on a night when you're obviously busy. I remember my way around. We'll be fine, honestly. And we'll be out of your hair before you know it."

The hubbub from the kitchen quarters was mounting. Lauder cast a harried glance over his shoulder, then capitulated.

"Och, it's this mob that'll be the death of me tonight," he muttered. "I doubt they'll be out of here till well after midnight, but you're welcome to stay as long as you like. I do ask that you come in and see me again before you leave, let me know how you've gotten on."

After receiving assurances from both Peregrine and Adam, the castle administrator hurried off to take charge of events in the kitchen. McLeod watched him go, then heaved a sigh of guarded relief.

"That was very well done, laddie," he told Peregrine under his breath. "Thank God there's this diversion of the dinner-dance. Otherwise, I think he would have been in our back pockets all night, and we couldn't get anything done. We made ourselves too interesting. Where to now?" he asked Adam. "The Douglas Room?"

"Not immediately," Adam said. "Before we do anything else, I want to have a look around the Charter Room."

"What are you expecting to find there?" McLeod asked, frowning.

"If we're lucky, nothing worse than some unpleasant resonances from the secret room beneath it," Adam said. "But since we're here, I want to check it out. It will also give Lauder's party a chance to get fully under way. Which way, Peregrine?"

"Down this corridor and up the stairs in the Meldrum Tower," Peregrine said, leading them out. "Just follow me and I'll cut in the lights as we go."

The Meldrum Stair was a tight turnpike spiral of steps, narrow enough that the three of them were obliged to ascend in single file. The door to the Charter Room opened directly off the stairwell into a small vestibule. It was not locked. Pushing the door open, Peregrine boldly set his foot across the darkened threshold, then stopped dead in his tracks.

"It's bloody freezing in there!" he whispered.

"All right, come back," Adam said quietly. He spoke calmly, but there was a steely undertone in his voice that had not been there a moment before.

Peregrine did not wait to be told twice. Retreating onto the little landing, he flattened himself to the wall to let Adam take his place on the threshold. McLeod pressed past him as well but stopped at Adam's elbow, shining his pocket torch into a blackness that almost seemed to drink up the light.

"I don't like the feel of this," the inspector murmured.

"Nor do I," Adam replied.

Cautiously he extended his right hand palm-down and slid it forward until it made contact with the shadows. It was like dipping his fingers into an icy pool of dirty water, and the signet on his finger became colder still. Drawing his hand back, he took a silk handkerchief from the breast pocket of his blazer and gave his fingertips a careful wipe.

"*Is* there something there?" Peregrine asked in a hushed voice.

Adam was still gazing into the darkness, his mouth drawn tight in a scowl of concentration.

"*Something*, yes. I'm getting some very chaotic impressions," he muttered. "Very turbulent. Very black. But I can't tell if what I'm sensing is past, present, or future. The resonances themselves seem out of phase with linear time."

McLeod's blue eyes narrowed sharply behind his spectacles, but he said nothing.

"Want me to try and have a look?" Peregrine suggested, starting to press forward.

"On no account!" Adam's voice, though low, was vehement. He stood at the doorway a moment longer, then drew back with a deep breath.

"We'll check it out, since we're here, but no one is going in without taking a few basic precautions," he said.

Reaching into the right-hand pocket of his blazer, he brought out his *skean dubh* held by the sheath. The blue stone set in its pommel seemed to glow slightly with a light of its own, and he touched it reverently to his lips as he bowed his head.

"Blessed be the Name of the Most High, for that Name shall be exalted above all others," he intoned softly. *"Blessed is he who dwells in the Light of the Most High, for the darkness shall not encompass him."*

With the faintly glowing blue stone, he signed himself with a symbol of warding, then beckoned his two companions to step forward. McLeod was first, slipping on his own sapphire ring before bowing his head to be signed in his turn with Adam's symbol of protection, traced in the air above his head with the pommel of the *skean dubh*. Taking his cue from the inspector, Peregrine likewise put on his ring, lowering his head as he presented himself to Adam with hands folded together at his breast in an attitude of trusting submission. As he sensed Adam's hand moving above his head, the air around him seemed all at once to quicken. A subtle warmth that was charged with power enfolded him like a mantle, and he clasped its protection round him and squared his shoulders as he looked up, prepared to brave whatever might lie ahead.

"Now, *don't* open, either of you," Adam ordered, preparing to move into the room. "Just back me. I don't want to stir up whatever it is; I just want to get a general impression of *what* it is."

CHAPTER TWENTY-TWO

SO fortified, Adam led the way past the threshold into the Charter Room, McLeod and Peregrine at his back, the pommel of his *skean dubh* held slightly aloft before him like a torch. The uncanny chill in the air gave back before him, as if deflected by an invisible shield. Glancing around him, following the questing beam of McLeod's electric torch, he spotted a light switch on the right-hand wall and nodded to him to turn it on. The visible blackness dissolved in the wink of an eye, showing him a square chamber lined with stout, deeply carved panels of dark polished wood. Plasterwork shields and heraldic crests were let into the cream-colored walls above the panelling, and more heraldic carving embellished much of the wood

Adam shifted his attention back to the panelling itself. Many of the panels would be movable, cunningly interlocked to conceal the presence of strong vaults he knew were built into the fabric of the masonry and stonework behind. The window bays looked to be at least nine feet deep, the corresponding walls easily thick enough to conceal a hidden closet or a secret passage.

Or the hidden entrance to a prison cell to contain something too dangerous ever to be let loose on the outside world.

Cautiously he advanced farther into the room. McLeod and Peregrine followed close behind him, both of them wary, guarded, ready at need to join their strength to his. The atmosphere seemed preternaturally thick and heavy. Undiminished by mere physical light, a subtler darkness that was not of the material world hung about the room like an invisible miasma.

Adam brought the group to a halt at a small, round table

in the middle of the floor. Here he paused to take a deep breath, poised on the edge of trance. The floor beneath his feet gave him a solid sense of grounding. Aware that he might be opening himself to no small risk, he turned his attention on the dark.

It was only the briefest of brushes beyond the wardings he had erected around himself and his allies, but impressions assaulted him like blows—impressions of something huge, dark, and brooding, something pent up in some congruent dimension to which the material precincts of the Charter Room were only an antechamber. The air was suddenly full of gusting psychic winds, buffeting up at him out of great chasms of darkness under the floor. Somewhere down in those depths, far, far beneath the physical confines of the house, a dark presence tossed and turned in restless cyclopaean sleep. . . .

He snapped himself out of trance to find his hands and face beaded with cold sweat, his hand clenching the *skean dubh* in a warding-off gesture to dispel the encroaching darkness. In the pounding silences between his own heart-beats he could almost still hear the blackness breathing. He gulped air, and became aware of Peregrine and McLeod staring at him in mute inquiry, bordering on alarm.

"Out!" he whispered, his voice reduced to a breath. "This isn't what we're after. Let's leave well enough alone, before we risk rousing something better left to lie!"

He gestured vehemently toward the doorway, and both Peregrine and McLeod backed out with alacrity. Only when back in the closer confines of the stairwell did Adam allow himself a careful sigh of relief.

"What did you see?" McLeod demanded.

"I didn't *see* anything," Adam said. "What I *felt* is . . . something probably better left undefined."

"Some kind of entity?"

"That—would be granting it too much," Adam said, pocketing the *skean dubh*. "The impressions were only barely comprehensible. Whatever is sleeping under this part of the castle, it seems to be flickering in and out of existence—

neither in this world nor out of it, but somewhere adjacent to both.''

"What are we going to do about it?" Peregrine asked, glancing around him a shade wildly.

"We aren't going to *do* anything," Adam said, reaching back into the room long enough to turn off the light. "Whatever the 'devil' of Fyvie may be, that question is no concern of ours at this moment. It has nothing to do with the casket or the Crown. Suffice it to say that it is confined and dormant, at least for the time being, and best let it stay that way. This means, too, that what we're after is almost certainly in the Douglas Room. We'd better press on before our Mr. Lauder finds an excuse to come and be congenial.''

The Douglas Room lay at the opposite end of the castle, directly above where the party was going on. With Peregrine leading the way, they headed back down the Meldrum Stair to the floor below, then made their way quietly along a long straight corridor to the lighted well of Fyvie's great Wheel Stair.

"These treads must be ten feet wide," Peregrine said, as they started up the sweeping stone steps. "When I was working here before, I was told that some Gordons once rode their horses up these stairs for a wager. Can you imagine?"

"I'm trying to imagine how they got back *down* without breaking legs," Adam murmured.

As they climbed, music drifted down from the Drawing Room and Gallery above, and warmth and the rich fragrance of roast pheasant wafted up from the kitchens below, harking back to the days when Fyvie had been an earl's residence and played host to royalty. But after what Adam had sensed in the Charter Room, neither he nor his two fellow-Huntsmen were likely to forget the more sinister aspects of Fyvie's long history.

The stairwell was well lit, enabling them to inspect some of the exquisite heraldic decoration adorning the newel post and the supporting arches that sprang periodically across the staircase. Peregrine further illuminated some of them with the beam of his pocket torch as they climbed, and paused to allow more thorough inspection of an oak panel set into one wall near the top, which read:

> *Alexander Seton, Lord Fyvie.*
> *Dame Gressel Leslie, Ladie Fyvie. 1603.*

Crescents and cinquefoils separated the four words of the earl's name, representing his paternal and maternal descent, and Leslie buckles adorned his lady's name.

"There's where your Grizel Seton probably got her name," Peregrine whispered, continuing on and pointing out more coats of arms, most surmounted by the Seton red crescent crest.

The murmur of voices and the clink of cutlery and glass grew louder as they approached the second-floor landing, its curtained doorway leading into the Drawing Room, where Lauder's dinner was taking place in the Gallery beyond. They slipped past it quickly, hoping no one would come out until they were out of sight beyond the turn of the stair. Half a floor up, just at the top of the stairwell, heavy doors faced onto either side of the final landing.

"That's the entrance to Lauder's apartments," Peregrine whispered, pointing out the left-hand one with the beam of his torch. "It's a good thing he's otherwise occupied. This other one is the Douglas Room."

His torch picked out the red crescent crest on the door just before he opened it, and Adam paused a moment to trace the curve of the crescent with his fingertips before following Peregrine across the threshold. As he did so, he experienced once again the moth-like flutter of Jean Seton's presence deep below the surface of his conscious mind.

No threatening atmosphere greeted their entrance here. The air was cold but quiescent, redolent of nothing more menacing than wood polish and potpourri.

"Now, where's that light?" Peregrine murmured, casting to the right with his torch and then leaning down to turn on a small table lamp directly beside an archaic-looking telephone. "Here we are."

The subdued light showed them a snug, neatly panelled

chamber not much more than eight or ten feet square, with a curtained window bay in the left-hand wall containing a wooden armchair. The wall opposite the door featured two smallish portraits, one above a drop-leaf desk with another lamp and the other above a small fireplace, its hearth cavity filled in with panelling above an ornamental plaque. The right-hand wall was dominated by a handsome eighteenth-century pine chest, tall and with many numbered drawers. A straight-backed chair was set between the fireplace and the chest of drawers, and another against the wall immediately to the right of the door, just beyond the table with the lamp and telephone.

Last to enter, McLeod scanned the room from the doorway, running his gaze around the walls and across the figured Persian rugs on the wooden floor.

"What are you looking for?" Peregrine asked, moving on into the room to bend and turn back several corners of the rugs.

"I'm just looking," McLeod grunted. "Policeman's force of habit."

"Well, you can look at this," Peregrine said, pointing out a dark stain he had uncovered on the floor boards just before the drop-leaf desk. "It's supposed to be blood. They say it won't scrub out. Do you think it *is* blood?"

McLeod knelt to inspect the stain, briefly running his fingertips across it, then got to his feet, still looking around.

"If it is, it's been here a long time," he said. "Adam, are you sure about this location? If your Green Lady is here, she's keeping very quiet about it."

"She's here." Adam sounded certain. "Just close the door and let me ward us. I don't like what I touched before, and with all those people making merry downstairs, I wouldn't want any hint of what we're doing here to cause reverberations elsewhere in the building."

The sound of distant music receded as McLeod word-lessly swung the door shut and stepped farther into the center of the room, drawing Peregrine with him. Glancing around him, Adam took out his *skean dubh* again, unsheathing it this time but grasping it lightly by the blade, with the pommel stone held before him, as he turned to face the wall with the chest of drawers, which was in the east. To perform the Banishing Ritual of the Lesser Pentagram as he now proposed to do was to invoke divine protection of a most potent sort; but with the blade in his hand, pointed toward himself, it was also a pledge on his part to accept the fullest measure of divine retribution, should he misuse the protection so invoked.

Briefly he clasped the blade between his two hands, the pommel stone pressed to his lips as he bowed his head over it, knowing that for this invocation and intent, he must use the Hebrew words rather than the English translation. Then, lightly clasping the blade in his right hand again, his left hand pressed to his breast, he raised the pommel stone to his forehead in salute and began to trace the Qabalistic Cross with it over his body.

"Ateh," he whispered, as the stone touched his forehead. Unto Thee, O God . . .

"Malkuth." The Kingdom. The stone moved to touch his solar plexus.

"Ve Geburah," to the right shoulder. *"Ve Gedulah,"* to the left shoulder. The Power and the Glory . . .

"Le Olahm." Forever and ever . . .

The hands came together again to clasp the blade between them, the head bowing once more as he whispered, "Amen."

"Amen," McLeod and Peregrine murmured in response.

Extending his arms wide to either side then, the *skean dubh* now lying in his upturned right hand with the blade pointed toward him, Adam closed his eyes and let his head tilt back slightly, strongly visualizing the images he now called forth: mighty archangels facing inward, spreading the protection of their pinioned wings out and over the room and all it contained.

"Before me, Raphael," he whispered. "Behind me, Gabriel. At my right hand, Michael. At my left hand, Uriel."

Opening his eyes, he closed his hand around the blade of the *skean dubh* and brought the weapon to center in salute, then extended its pommel upward and before him, toward the east, as he silently traced a pentagram with the blue stone—down toward the left, up and to the right, across, down and to the right, back to the starting point.

He could just see the vague after-image of a blue trail hanging on the air as he turned by the right, to face the door, and repeated the process, again tracing a pentagram before moving on to do the same in the west and the north. Returning then to the east, he extended his arms to either side again, aware both of the blade pointed at him and of the circle of protection hanging on the air where the *skean dubh*'s stone had traced, like a crown surmounted by four stars—apt imagery for what he hoped to accomplish before he left this room.

"In the name of Adonai, may we be protected from all evil approaching from the East, West, South, and North," he murmured. "And may my powers turn against me if I misuse the trust reposing in me. About me flame the Pentagrams. Behind me shines the six-rayed star. And above my head is the Glory of God, in Whose hands is the Kingdom, and the Power, and the Glory, forever and ever. Amen."

His second recitation of the divine attributes was accompanied by a repetition of the Qabalistic Cross, echoed solemnly by his two companions. After Adam had bowed his head over the *skean dubh* once more, he resheathed it and handed it to McLeod.

"I'll let you hold onto this," he said quietly. "What I just did may have confused our Green Lady, but I needed to do it because of what we sensed down there." He pointed at the floor. "Hopefully, any local entities will realize that our intentions are defensive but not hostile. As for would-be physical intruders," he went on, as McLeod slipped the *skean dubh* into a pocket, "Peregrine, I'd be obliged if you'd stand guard at the threshold and make sure we're not interrupted."

"Aye," said McLeod. "We don't want any errant partygoers wandering in here by mistake, looking for the gents' toilet."

The comment got a thin smile out of Peregrine, who had been looking very solemn after the preceding ritual, and he duly set his back to the door and pulled a sketchbook and a pencil out of his art satchel. Adam, meanwhile, moved over to the chair in the window bay and sat down in it, facing into the room toward the chest of drawers. Taking the Dundee ring out of his pocket, he handed it to McLeod, then likewise pulled Dundee's Templar cross out from under his sweater, touching the ancient artifact lightly to his lips before settling it on his breast.

"Ready whenever you are," he murmured, glancing up at McLeod as he settled back in the chair.

Pulling out his lighter, McLeod lit one of the pair of candles on the mantel ledge above the fireplace, then came back to Adam, setting both hands on his chair arms as he bent briefly to speak to him. Peregrine had never had opportunity to see the inspector work in this capacity before; but as soon as he began, crouching now at the left of Adam's chair, it became evident that he was well versed and confident in the techniques of hypnotic regression. Peregrine could not quite make out what he was saying to Adam, whose gaze was now fixed on the burning candle; but as he watched, he saw Adam close his eyes and tilt his head against the high chair back, apparently going deeply into trance. McLeod's touch on his forehead seemed to send him deeper yet, his head lolling slightly to one side as he went deeper, deeper. . . .

Utterly compliant to McLeod's quietly worded direction, Adam turned his back on the present moment and began his retreat into the past. At first a part of him remained dimly aware of his surroundings, of the glow of the lamp and candle behind closed eyelids; but then a moment of not unpleasant vertigo gave way to a vision of a doorway marking the backward boundary of his present lifetime. Passing through it, he found himself in a wilderness of mirrors surrounded by astral reflections of himself, increasingly buffeted by a rising wind.

Tossed back and forth from mirror to mirror, the reflections showed him glimpses of his spirit clothed in many different guises, some familiar, some less so—an Egyptian priest-king, a Greek matron, a Templar knight in chain mail and white mantle—but he could not seem to fasten on any of them. Simultaneously, from far, far away, he was vaguely aware of someone touching his left hand, lifting it, slipping a ring onto the third finger, shoving it home with a word of command.

At that touch, as the time frames whirled and danced around him, he found himself all at once face-to-face with an image of a dark-haired young woman in the sweeping gown of a Jacobite lady. The image drew him forward, and as he reached out the hand with the ring, the mirror swung inward like a door, inviting him to enter. . . .

Looking on anxiously from his post by the door, Peregrine all at once became aware of a dull shimmer in the center of the room. McLeod seemed to see it too, and drew back warily in the window bay where he crouched beside Adam, for there was no place farther to retreat without first going closer to the shimmer. As Peregrine stared, the shimmer brightened and quickened, exploding into a ghostly jumble of violent resonances. Determined to bring them to focus, Peregrine opened his inner sight to deeper perception, and gradually began to resolve three figures out of the initial visual chaos. Two of the figures were big men in the coarse garments of common soldiers, but the third—

Peregrine gasped and flinched, for the figure slumped heavily in the grasp of the two soldiers was a slender young woman with long dark hair, her green gown torn and bloodied. They had bound her wrists behind her, and the bare soles of her feet were burned and blistered. Her half-averted face was so battered, as she raised her head, that it took a moment to recognize her as the same woman he had seen in his earlier vision sparked by the Dundee ring.

Grizel Seton.

Even as the name registered in the back of his mind, the ornaments on the ledge above the fireplace gave a sudden rattle, the unlit candlestick toppling off the mantelpiece onto the floor. In the same instant, an icy blast of foul air rushed through the room, extinguishing the remaining candle and striking Peregrine full in the face like a heavy backhand slap. The force of it dashed his spectacles off his nose and slammed his back hard against the closed door. Flailing to keep his balance, he lost his grip on his sketchbook and almost fell, barely remaining upright on one knee. The paintings on the walls began to jutter violently on their hooks. McLeod had shrunk back hard against the side of the window bay, his gaze raking the room.

"Jesus, what's happening?" he rasped.

Peregrine, cringing against the door, found himself without the breath to answer. All at once, the soldiers disappeared and the tormented image of Grizel Seton shattered before him like a pane of glass, a haggard female shape rising up out of the glitter of flying shards with streaming hair and blazing eyes. Pages of Peregrine's sketchbook went flying into the air, whirling around like a storm of confetti. The second candlestick clattered and fell, and a brass bowl full of dried flower heads and potpourri tipped off the drop-leaf desk and spilled across the Persian carpets. With a piercing banshee moan, the ghost of Grizel Seton rocketed up off the floor, her burning eyes now turning toward Peregrine as she lunged for his face.

He ducked low, flinging up both arms to ward her off. Light flashed blue from the ring on his hand, deflecting a raking gash that glanced off the door behind him. The backlash buffeted him sideways, jarring the table with the lamp and setting it teetering. As he scrambled to keep his balance and also save the lamp from falling, a voice cried out sharply, *"Grizel! Stop!"*

The voice was a woman's, high and clear and imperative. At the sound of it, the angry presence in the room faltered and fell back. As Peregrine peered cautiously out from behind his crossed arms, he saw the hag-shape turn toward Adam, who had risen to his feet. But now, to Peregrine's wondering gaze, Adam's physical form seemed overcast by a transparent projection of that surprising past persona that had manifested itself at Oakwood: Lady Jean Seton.

Confronted by this image of her sister, the shade of Grizel Seton lost her fierce and bloody aspect. Her burning eyes softened, their fire quenched in sudden uncertainty. Before Peregrine's very gaze, she shrank and subsided. Even as he blinked, she was as he first remembered—a slender, dark-haired woman with the quiet beauty of a fallow doe.

A hush seemed suddenly to envelop the room. Then Grizel spoke, her voice tremulous with incredulity.

Who are you? I charge you to tell me truly.

"Truly I am your sister, Jean Seton," came Adam's whispered response, "reborn in the flesh as the man you see before you."

How do I know that you are not some foul shade sent to deceive me?

Adam lifted his hand to display the Dundee ring. "By this token," said the voice of Jean Seton, "given to me by our father after we fled to France. You knew it when he wore it unadorned. Now it contains a relic of my Lord Dundee, taken before our father helped lay him in his grave."

Boldly Adam extended his hand. Grizel Seton reached out to touch the ring with fingers translucent as seashell, her presence trembling like a candle flame in the wind.

Yes. I know you now for my own Bonnie Jean, she murmured softly. And all at once, tears seemed to glitter in her eyes. *Ah, sweet sister, when we parted so long ago in the Forest of Mar—and from* him *as well,* she continued wonderingly, *I never looked for us to meet again. What brings you back to me now, in this strange fashion, after so many years gone by?*

"The needs of this present day and time." Jean's voice was grave. "The charge of the Knights Templar has been violated. The Seal that was lost has come to light, stolen from its keeper by a thief in the night, and we have reason to fear that even now he is seeking the casket. If he should succeed in finding it, nothing less than Solomon's own wisdom will suffice to avert disaster. That being so, I have come to implore you to hand over to me the Crown which our Bonnie Dundee entrusted to your care."

Solomon's Crown? Grizel's voice registered troubled surprise. *This is a weighty request you make of me, dearest Jean. You were there beside me when our Dark John of the*

Battles enjoined me never to surrender it, even at the cost of my own life. My presence here is proof that I have never yet broken faith with him.

"And so I told him when we met again just two days past," said Jean.

There was a wondering pause. *You have spoken with his lordship?* Grizel asked eagerly.

"Yes, even as I am speaking to you here," came the response from Jean. "These two worthies with me will bear witness that he lives on in spirit, even as we."

How fares he, then?

"Less happy than he might, for knowing of the manner of your death," Jean answered. "Likewise, it gives him great sorrow that you should have been detained here so long, in exile from the Light. I am to convey to you his thanks and his blessing. I am also to tell you that, in the person of this latter self, I have his authority to take the Crown into my custody, to avert the present danger and to give you your liberty. He bade me show you this cross, which he wore that last time we saw him in the flesh, as earnest of his most urgent entreaty. You have only to show me where the Crown lies hidden."

To be free at last. . . . Grizel's words were a longing sigh as she reached out a hand to lightly touch the cross on Adam's breast. *Yes, I will show you, dearest Jean. But your companions likewise must pledge to keep sacred this trust that I bequeath to you.*

Her gaze turned to Peregrine and McLeod. The inspector had gotten to his feet as Adam and the ghost conversed, and now he made her a slight bow, right hand upon his heart.

"You have my solemn oath, Lady," he told her. "All of us are sworn to the service of the Light. We will keep faith with the trust you give to us—and with Lord Dundee."

"I give you my oath as well," Peregrine said, wide-eyed.

Very well, said Grizel. *I am satisfied.*

She drifted over to the fireplace and stroked across the panelling in the opening with a slender hand the texture of gossamer.

The Crown is there, she declared. *Though my captors*

*knew it not, this fireplace has never known a fire, for it has
no chimney breast. It houses instead a secret compartment
behind a screen of masonry. They thought to bring me here,
but they did not think to look far enough. All I had to do was
hold my tongue. . . .*

CHAPTER TWENTY-THREE

THE ghost of Grizel Seton shuddered slightly, as if at the memory of old pain. Peregrine stooped to retrieve his spectacles, then edged closer to McLeod.

"That panelling looks jolly solid," he muttered, "not to mention any depth of masonry beyond. How the devil are we going to get the Crown out of there without making a mess of the whole wall?"

"Damned if I know," McLeod replied. "But we're going to have to figure out a way."

Even as he spoke, Grizel Seton drifted closer to Adam.

Give me your hands, she instructed quietly.

She ducked beneath his shoulder as he raised his hands, rising again within the compass of his arms, her hands outstretched to overlay and merge with his. The shared contact gave Adam a cool butterfly sensation in his palms and fingertips. At the same time, he understood that she required control of his body. Confident that she would do him no harm, he relaxed and closed his eyes, allowing her the freedom to guide him.

The cool butterfly tingle in Adam's hands spread up his arms and down his legs. Yielding passively to Grizel's gentle influence, he allowed himself to be propelled forward three steps in the direction of the fireplace. Still responsive to her touch, he crouched and reached out. Just before he touched the panelling, his extended hands encountered an elastic area of resistance, as if he were pushing his fingers through a stiff block of gelatin. . . .

Grizel's guiding presence was investing the whole of Adam's body with a soft shimmer. As his and Grizel's superimposed hands reached *through* the panelling that covered the fireplace, McLeod breathed an incredulous

"Good God!" Peregrine could only nod by way of acknowledgement, watching in dumbstruck astonishment.

Adam himself appeared oblivious to what was happening, eyes closed, face serenely intent. Shifting easily onto both knees, he leaned farther forward, his arms disappearing almost to the shoulders as, for a breathless moment, he seemed to feel around for something beyond. When he moved to withdraw, still guided by Grizel, Peregrine could tell by the set of his shoulders that Adam now was carrying something. His eyes opened abruptly as his hands emerged from the panelling, and widened in wonder as light from the lamp by the door touched off a warm glint of precious metal between his fingers.

As soon as they were clear of the panelling, Grizel separated and drew back. Adam drew a deep breath, then gathered himself to his feet and turned to show Peregrine and McLeod the golden star diadem of six upturned points that he now held.

Peregrine could not repress a gasp. McLeod looked a little pale. Adam smiled, his own expression rapt with half-dreaming wonder as he turned the Crown over in his hands. Beside him, the filmy presence of Grizel Seton resolved once more into womanly shape.

This is the Crown once guarded for the Temple by John Grahame of Claverhouse, she told them. *Legend has it that Solomon the King invested it with his wisdom long ago.*

Her words seemed to call Adam back to himself. Looking up, he said quietly, in his own voice, "Thank you, Grizel. Be sure I will guard this with my very life."

If you fail in your mission, she replied, *you imperil not only your life but your soul as well. As keeper of the Crown, you have the great King's leave to use it. But I am bound to warn you that to do so, unless in the presence of both the Seal and the Sceptre, is to court gravest danger to yourself.*

"How so?" Adam asked.

Solomon divided his potency among the three hallows, intending them to be used together, Grizel informed him. *If one or the other of these hallows is missing, the user himself must compensate for the ensuing imbalance in power.*

Should you contemplate donning the Crown, for whatever reason, I urge you first to examine your own mind and conscience and see that you find yourself in no way lacking. To those already strong and wise, the Crown brings even greater wisdom. But to those who are not, it brings madness.

This warning shed further light on the dream Adam had had at Oakwood. It seemed that Caitlin had been right in her supposition that the Crown by itself might not be enough to see him through whatever perils lay ahead.

"You are not the first to warn me that the hallows are dangerous," he said to Grizel. "Two nights ago, I had a dream urging me to recover the Sceptre as well as the Crown. Do you know where it is?"

Grizel's response was a regretful shake of her head. *If my Lord of Claverhouse knew, he did not share that knowledge with me. I am sorry.*

Greatly daring, McLeod edged forward. "What about the casket, Lady? Can you tell us where it lies?"

Grizel shook her head again. *That knowledge was lost to the Masters of the Templar Order long before my time.*

"Then we must proceed armed only with the knowledge that we—"

Adam stopped short as a sudden idea occurred to him. McLeod was quick to catch the arrested expression on his face.

"You've thought of something, haven't you?"

"Perhaps," Adam said. "A stratagem worth trying, anyway."

As McLeod and Peregrine came closer, Adam went on to explain.

"From what Lady Grizel tells us, the three hallows are integrally related to one another. That being so, it may be possible to scry out the current location of the Sceptre by using the Crown as a focus. Obviously, our chances of success would be doubled if we were in possession of the Seal as well, but we have something almost as good——the imprint of it. Noel?"

Nodding, McLeod took from his pocket the silk-wrapped

bundle that was the Seal's imprint and passed it to Adam without comment. Peregrine looked mystified, but Adam proceeded to explain as he knelt to deposit the Crown on the floor in the center of the room and began unwrapping the wax.

"This piece of sealing wax carries not only the physical impression of Solomon's Seal but also the psychic impression of its potency," he informed his companions. "Since we haven't got the Seal itself, its imprint may be the next best thing. But it's still going to cost us considerable effort to make a scrying attempt. That being so, I hope Lady Grizel may be persuaded to assist us with her support."

He directed a questioning look to the ghostly presence of the woman who had been his sister in another lifetime, and she gravely nodded her consent.

I am ready to do whatever you require, she told him.

"Thank you," Adam said. "Your support will be most welcome. All that remains is for me to make the necessary preparations."

He set the wax impression of the Seal carefully within the compass of the Crown, then folded himself to sit cross-legged before the sigil so arranged, directing his colleagues to sit as well. As Peregrine settled to his right and McLeod across from him, Grizel Seton drifted across the floor to take up her station in the remaining quadrant of the circle, just to Adam's left.

"All right, support me in this, as best you can," he said. "I expect I may have to go quite deep."

So saying, he spread his hands over the Crown and what it encircled, curling his fingers over the six upturned points and letting his thumbs rest on the wax imprint of the Seal. As he began pushing himself down into trance and his awareness of the room receded, he became correspondingly more conscious of the supporting presences of McLeod, Peregrine, and Grizel Seton. Closing his eyes, he sank ever deeper, centering his attention on what lay beneath his hands. In his mind's eye, the Crown gradually began to glow with the hidden power of its own internal radiance.

The glow coalesced into a whirling spindle of golden

flame. The spinning flame gave rise to a skein of light like a thin golden thread stretching away from Adam into a labyrinthine mist. Aware of Grizel Seton's presence with him on the Astral and the others anchoring the silver cord of his own soul, he rose out of himself and set off to follow the golden thread back to its source.

Twisting and turning, the burning thread became a flying dart. Racing after it, Adam was catapulted suddenly out of the mists into a darkness full of moonlight and rushing winds. A shadowy landscape of hills and glens unfolded beneath him with frightening speed. Hurtling forward, he saw a panorama of lights spread out before him like a galaxy of stars.

The lights resolved into a grid of lines and squares—an aerial view of a large city. Shooting over the housetops like a comet, Adam recognized enough of the layout to realize he was passing over the city of Dundee. His vision impelled him on across the breadth of the Tay and south with dizzying speed over the fields and townships of Fife. Soaring over the turrets of the Forth Bridge, he overshot the sprawling lights of Edinburgh and plummeted earthward toward an architectural blur on the west bank of the River Esk that materialized at close range into an ecclesiastical structure of stone and brick.

Rosslyn Chapel, whispered a voice he recognized as Grizel's.

It was a place associated not only with the Templars but also with distant Sinclair relatives—in Midlothian, not far south of Edinburgh. As the chapel's exterior seemed to melt away before him, Adam found himself drawn past a shining beacon that, in its physical aspects, was known as the Apprentice Pillar, then downward to gaze at a blank area of bricked-up wall. The image brought with it the certain conviction that the Sceptre lay hidden in a vault beyond.

He started forward, hoping to penetrate the vault's interior. In the same instant, his astral self was violently wrenched loose from Grizel's stabilizing rapport. A sickening whirl of vertigo seized him as the world turned end over end and spat him into limbo. Tumbling blindly through space, he crashed through a barrier into the forefront of another living mind.

Henri Gerard!

Gerard's attention was focused not inward, but outward—on the Sceptre. Gerard was not physically present with the Sceptre, but in that brief instant of psychic contact, Adam realized that Gerard knew its location, and probably that of the casket as well. At the risk of exposing himself, he made an effort to read through the chaos of the other man's consciousness to grasp the other half of the secret. But in that selfsame heartbeat, Gerard became aware of him and turned savagely to attack the psychic intruder he sensed in his own mind.

A vicious blast of raw power pitched Adam backwards in time. Buffeted by hot breezes, he struggled to break free and discovered that chains bound him hand and foot to a cruel stake. Fire was crackling up around him in winding sheets, licking hungrily at his bare arms and legs. Choking with pain, he looked wildly around and saw through a wreath of rising smoke the bitter, smiling face of an old enemy.

Guillaume de Nogaret, called the Templars' bane, who had helped trump up the charges that led to the suppression of the Order of the Temple and sent so many Templars to their deaths.

With that part of his mind still rooted in the present, Adam suddenly realized that Gerard and de Nogaret were one and the same individual. In the next instant, his mind-link with Gerard was wiped out in a roar of billowing flames and a wave of pure agony. Adam's Templar-self cried out in anguish. But as the blaze rose to overwhelm him, strong hands reached out to pluck him from the corrosive grip of the flames.

He grounded with a jolt and lay there panting, too winded for a moment to move or speak. Gradually he became aware that he was lying on the carpeted floor of the Douglas Room, curled onto his side. Responding to urgent hands on his shoulders, he rolled heavily onto his back and opened his eyes to find himself gazing blearily up into the concerned face of McLeod, with Peregrine peering worriedly over his shoulder and Grizel Seton hovering anxiously in the background.

"Are you all right?" McLeod demanded. "Jesus Christ, what happened?"

Peregrine's face was blanched white. "I could see fire all around you," he said shakily. "You were . . . burning—"

His voice cracked. Adam gulped air and groped for words of reassurance.

"Those were just images," he told Peregrine with all the firmness he could muster. "Flashbacks of yet another earlier incarnation that connects with our adversary. The fires you saw might once have injured me, but not in this present lifetime. You can see for yourself, I've taken no real harm."

Gently disentangling himself from McLeod's supporting grip, he sat up and went on to relay what he had learned from that painful episode of contact.

"Actually, I've picked up some valuable information," he told them. "You remember I wondered whether our Mr. Gerard had a psychic past that could somehow account for his current behavior?"

"Yes," McLeod said.

"Well, it seems my suspicions were justified. He was one of Philippe le Bel's chief advisors. Knowing that, a lot of what's been happening begins to make sense, that didn't before."

McLeod was nodding. "When Gerard learned the truth about your friend Nathan's Seal, that knowledge must have activated all the latent ambitions of his previous life. Do you know if he knows where the Sceptre is?"

"I'm afraid so," Adam said grimly. "And the casket as well, I think. Fortunately, before he became aware of me, Grizel and I were at least able to resolve half the puzzle. I still don't know where the casket is, but the Sceptre is hidden in a secret vault at Rosslyn Chapel."

"Rosslyn . . . ," Peregrine murmured.

As an artist, he was familiar with Rosslyn as a treasury of Late Gothic stonework. Commissioned in the mid-fifteenth century by Sir William St. Clair, another scion of Adam's own family, Rosslyn Chapel was renowned throughout Scotland for the unique richness of its carvings. The church in its entirety had never been finished; but perhaps it had never been intended as anything other than a hiding place for an even more valuable treasure.

"Adam," Peregrine said urgently, "you've just told us that Gerard knows where both the casket and the Sceptre are! If he can recover the Sceptre before we do, he'll be better than halfway to recovering the Templar treasure he's coveted for centuries."

"Probably never suspecting what's *really* in the box," said McLeod. "We'd better hope we can get to Rosslyn ahead of him!"

"Indeed," Adam said grimly, letting the inspector help him to his feet. "Dear Grizel, I must thank you for accompanying me on the Astral. Your presence strengthened me. I owe you a great debt."

There is no debt, Grizel replied, smiling. *Do not forget that we were once of one blood, and one purpose.*

"I am not forgetting," Adam said, "not least, the fact that you have waited long enough for your liberty."

As he spoke, his face was overcast once more by the ghostly change of aspect that signalled the emergence of his persona as Lady Jean. When he spoke again, it was with her voice.

"May the blessings of the Light be always upon you, Grizel, for all your pains and service. Whatever happens to us from this point onward, I shall rejoice in the knowledge that you at least are free."

Grizel's presence was fading even as he spoke. In the last instant, she reached out and touched translucent fingers to Adam's lips.

Farewell, little sister, came her fading whisper. *Be strong, for the sake of all we both hold dear.*

Then she was gone.

A brief silence fell. Then McLeod drew himself up. "Well, what are we waiting for?" he muttered. "The game's afoot!"

CHAPTER TWENTY-FOUR

ADAM deposited the Crown in Peregrine's art satchel for safekeeping. Then he and his two subordinates set swiftly about erasing all traces of their evening's work before heading back down the Great Stair in search of Mr. Lauder. He came out of the Drawing Room with an expression of some relief, but they cut short their leave-taking with the excuse that Adam's beeper had gone off, and he was required back in Edinburgh for a medical emergency.

"I took the liberty of calling in on that phone in the Douglas Room," he told the castle keeper, "but I reversed the charges. Fortunately, we'd pretty much seen what we came to look at. I want to thank you again for letting us intrude on such a busy evening."

Lauder made a gesture of disclaimer. "Think nothing of it. It's the usual chaos around here, when we've got outside guests. I don't suppose I can tempt you to delay long enough for a bite to eat? They always overcater these affairs, and we've got several pheasants going begging."

"Ah, I wish we could," Adam said with genuine regret, as much for Peregrine as for himself and McLeod. "Unfortunately, we've still got a three-to-four-hour run back to Edinburgh, and I don't know how much the rain will slow us down. Thanks very much for your offer, though."

Peregrine said nothing as they made their dash back to the car and piled in, but as Adam shrugged out of a now sodden blazer and handed it back to the artist to lay out across the back, he gave him a sympathetic smile.

"Sorry about the missed meal, but we really shouldn't eat now, even if we could spare the time."

"I know that," Peregrine said glumly, as Adam started

the engine. "It's just that, after breathing the aroma of roast pheasant off and on for several hours, my stomach did a momentary leap of joy when we were actually offered some."

"Give yourself half an hour, and you may be glad there's nothing in it," McLeod retorted, consulting their road atlas. "Hand up that cellular phone, would you? I'm going to try to get us a chopper out of Aberdeen; and if I do, it's bound to be a rough ride, in this weather. I can't think of a faster way to Rosslyn, though. Head us toward the airport, Adam."

The general availability of helicopters in the Aberdeen area was a given, since helicopters were widely used to service the offshore oil rigs, but whether or not they could find one this late, and willing to fly them down to Rosslyn in this weather, was another question. As they headed back through the village of Fyvie, McLeod spoke with directory inquiries, jotting down the numbers of several helicopter charter services operating out of Aberdeen Airport.

Unfortunately, the airport proved to be a dead end, for the companies servicing the oil rigs only ran commercial flights. But by the time they were passing back through Oldmeldrum, McLeod had been able to obtain the number of a small private charter service based farther north on the main road back to Aberdeen.

"Now we're getting somewhere," McLeod said, as he began dialling the new number. "This one's just beyond Pitcaple. You'll want to go north on the A96 at Inverurie—if I can raise them at this hour."

Grampian Helicopter Service apparently was hungry for business, because within the space of five minutes, McLeod had secured the promise of a chopper and pilot standing by for takeoff as soon as they arrived.

"Right, we should be there in ten or fifteen minutes," he said. "Thanks very much."

As he disconnected and began to dial again, he glanced at Adam and grinned.

"We've got one. They'll even take a credit card. Now let's see if all that training I've been putting into young

Donald Cochrane will pay off. Hello, Donald?'' he said, when the call was answered. ''Yes, sorry to ring you up at home, but I need a personal favor. Yes. I've been Hunting up by Aberdeen with Sir Adam and Mr. Lovat. We're on our way to pick up a helicopter. We've had a tip that our Henri Gerard chap may be making for Roslin. Yes, down by Loanhead.

''No, I don't want you to go there. The charter service tells us that the nearest helipad is at Dalhousie Castle. We should be there in about two hours. Can you be there with a car to meet us when we land? That's right, Dalhousie Castle, at about midnight. No, no backup,'' he added with a glance at Adam, who shook his head. ''If our man is going to turn up, we'll have a better chance of apprehending him if the police keep a low profile.''

''In other words,'' said Peregrine, when the inspector had rung off, ''you think Gerard may be too dangerous for a conventional police force to handle.''

''Too right,'' McLeod grumbled. ''If we blow this thing, and Gerard does set Gog and Magog on the loose, numbers aren't going to matter except as potential casualties.''

Shaken by the revelation that he was being sought by adversaries other than the police, Henri Gerard had lost no time getting to the rendezvous point where he had arranged to meet his hired henchman. No one seemed to be there yet, but when Gerard flashed his lights and pulled into the agreed lay-by, just off the A7 road to Galashiels, Ritchie Logan made a lithe run for the car. Seen by the glare of the headlights, he was wearing an artistically begrimed set of workman's coveralls under a scruffy rain slicker, and carrying a heavy canvas tool-bag.

''Evening, Mr. Gerard,'' he said, as he slung the bag into the backseat. ''You're right on time.''

''I could say the same for you,'' Gerard replied coolly.

When Logan had piled into the front seat and slammed the door against the rain, he took a closer look at Gerard's taut face, close-set eyes narrowing at what he read there.

''What's the matter?'' he demanded.

Gerard gave a testy shrug of his shoulders and rammed the car into gear. "Nothing that I care to discuss with you," he said shortly, whipping their vehicle out onto the road again.

Logan gave him a sidelong look, obviously not impressed. "Look, Mr. Gerard. If your trouble's something personal, fair enough. But if it's got anything to do with this job tonight, I want to know about it."

Gerard considered the demand, then gave a nod of brittle indulgence.

"Very well. If you really must know, I have just learned that we are being followed."

Logan started up in his seat and darted an instinctive look over his shoulder.

"Who is it?" he inquired sharply. "The police?"

"No, a—competitor of mine."

Logan turned to stare at the Frenchman in some incredulity. "A *competitor*? What is he, another historian like yourself?"

"I don't know what he is," Gerard said. "But he is after the same thing I am."

"You mean you don't even know his name?" Logan's incredulity gave way to a snort of laughter. "That's rich, that is. For a moment there you had me worried." As he settled insolently back in his seat, Gerard gave him a scathing glance.

"You may scoff if you like," he snapped, "but I have reason to believe that this man, whoever he may be, poses a far greater threat to us than the conventional authorities. He possesses a knowledge and training at least equal to my own, and a comparable degree of power. If you were any less ignorant than you are, you would understand what that means."

"I know my job, Mr. Gerard," Logan said with tolerant scorn. "But if you want to worry about him, you go right ahead. He'd just better not get in my way."

"If he does," Gerard said tersely, "you may not even be aware until it is too late."

Logan settled into sullen silence after that, though more

apprehensive than he had been. He had suspected from the very beginning that Gerard might not be too mentally stable. Since then, the Frenchman's speech and behavior had become increasingly erratic. Logan thought it quite possible that Gerard was on his way to a breakdown—and Logan didn't propose to be around when the man finally cracked. On the contrary, he intended to be as far away as possible, taking the lion's share of the spoils with him.

Assuming, of course, that Gerard was onto something of real value. Logan had not ruled out the possibility that tonight's venture was anything other than a madman's wild-goose chase. But since he was being well paid for his services, and had profited handsomely from the jewels taken in their last job together, he was prepared to play the Frenchman's game for now, secure in the knowledge that he himself could change the rules anytime he chose. Either way, he stood to make a killing at Gerard's expense. . . .

Gerard, for his part, maintained an austere silence for the rest of the drive. Logan's patent skepticism mattered far less to him than the memory of that brief, betraying episode of mind-touch with a rival intellect—an intellect tainted, moreover, with the stamp of Templar wisdom and the clear intention to know the location of the casket. Once before, the Templars had balked him of fulfilling his ambitions. He was determined that history should not repeat itself in the present.

It was in a mood of rising tension that he and Logan drove quietly through the sleeping village of Roslin. The signs pointing to Rosslyn Chapel were hard to spot in the mist, but eventually they found the correct turn.

The chapel itself lay just beyond the village, perched on the west bank of the Esk behind an encircling wall. Quietly Gerard eased the car into the unpaved car park that bordered the wall on one side and turned it around before parking in the shadow of some overhanging trees. He was wearing what he fancied a cat burglar should wear—a black leather jacket over a black polo shirt and black trousers and running shoes—and he noted that Logan was dressed much the same, once he had zipped out of his coverall and donned a black nylon windbreaker from his tool-bag.

Gerard had a kit-bag too, and slung it over his shoulder as he silently followed his hired professional toward the wall. He found himself casting around him in the darkness for any psychic traces of his earlier adversary, but he found none. Still, the silence did nothing to abate his own sense of urgency.

They had to climb the wall to get into the grounds surrounding the chapel, and then kept to the wet grass as much as possible, to avoid the sounds of footsteps on gravel. All the doors were locked fast as expected, but Logan decided that the one at the chapel's western end would yield most readily to his skills. The dull clunk of ancient mechanisms moving sounded preternaturally loud in the surrounding hush, but the door swung open almost silently.

"After you," Logan murmured, waving his employer forward with sardonic deference.

He left Gerard to close the door behind them while he rummaged in the bag for a powerful electric lantern to augment the smaller pocket torch he had used on the lock.

"Here," he whispered, handing the lantern to Gerard. "Just keep the beam low, away from the windows."

The two men made their way stealthily up the central aisle between two rows of stone columns, Gerard leading. The discoloring flare of their lantern slid like a greasy hand over carvings intricate and exquisite as lace. Skirting to the right of the sanctuary, Gerard led the way around the base of a fat column carved in a lacy spiral—Rosslyn's famous Apprentice Pillar, legendarily embellished by an apprentice stone-carver whose master subsequently had murdered him out of envy. Beyond the pillar, hard against the south side of the chancel, a flight of stone steps descended into the chapel's crypt. With a little gasp of excitement, Gerard led the way down, shining his torch left and right as they went.

"All right," said Logan in a low voice. "Where's the entrance to this vault of yours?"

"There." Gerard shone the lantern to the left, following into an opening that led into a small, vaulted room with a dirt floor. As he played his light over the far wall, Logan was able to make out a telltale discrepancy in the screening brickwork indicating the former presence of a narrow, oblong opening.

"You did warn me we were going to have to do some excavating," the thief allowed sourly. "All I've got to say is there'd better be something more worthwhile than dead men's bones on the other side of this wall. I'm not about to dig it out by hand, either."

He threw open his tool-bag and lifted out a small tackle box, together with a mat of bunting. The upper tier of the box contained shaped quantities of plastic explosive. The compartments beneath held an assortment of detonators.

"Go back upstairs and wait for me," he told Gerard. "I'll join you as soon as I've rigged the charge."

"No, wait!" Gerard sounded peremptory. "Let me ward the chamber first so that the noise won't carry."

"There isn't going to *be* much noise—"

"There won't be *any*, if you'll just stand aside for a moment. Do it!"

To Logan this sounded like sheer lunacy, but he acceded with a shrug.

"Whatever you say, Mr. Gerard."

While the thief looked on in mute cynicism, Gerard opened his own bag and took out an assortment of implements including a plastic bottle of swine's blood, an aspergill of boar's bristles, and a small bowl hammered out of iron. Muttering invocations darkly to himself, he poured a measure of the blood into the bowl and offered it round the four corners of the room. Then, wetting the aspergill in the blood, he bent to paint a warding symbol on the floor at the base of three of the four walls. He left the wall with the door from the stair until last.

"You may set your explosives now," he told Logan. "I will close off the way behind us."

Logan shot his employer a wary look, now convinced that Gerard was a complete nutter, but rather than waste valuable time arguing, it seemed most expedient to comply. When he had finished, he stepped out of the room and watched uneasily as Gerard stooped low to paint a final symbol on the floor just beyond the threshold of the vaulted chamber. Then they both hurried up the stairs to the safety of the sanctuary.

Crouching low behind the Apprentice Pillar, Logan counted off the time on a stopwatch he pulled from his pocket. As the final second ticked away, he braced himself for the rumble of a muffled explosion. A faint shudder reverberated through the floor beneath him and rained down a shower of dust from the transoms overhead, but there was no audible sound.

Scarcely able to believe his ears, Logan turned to stare at Gerard in blank astonishment. Arrested in the act of removing the Seal of Solomon from his bag of equipment, the Frenchman glared back at him.

"I told you no sound would escape," he said tartly. "Now, let us get on with our business."

Slipping the Seal into a black nylon waist pouch, he led the way back down into the crypt, pausing to smear over the still-wet symbol he had drawn with a sweep of his foot. The floor beyond was littered with broken bricks and scorched bunting. Peering over his employer's shoulder, Logan saw that there was now a gaping black hole in the wall opposite the entrance. When Gerard shone the lantern inside the cavity, the beam showed up a low-ceilinged passageway of dressed stones beyond.

Gerard was first to enter the passage, ducking low to traverse the three or four yards to its end, where a low groined archway in the right-hand wall gave access to a shadowy chamber beyond.

The stagnant air stank of damp and old decay. Entering behind Gerard, Logan fetched up short with a curse at the sight of two long rows of stone tomb slabs, each holding a mouldering corpse in full armor. Gerard gave the thief a fleeting death's-head grin over one shoulder.

"Behold the former Barons of Rosslyn," he murmured. "It was their custom to go armed to their graves, perhaps as guardians of what we seek."

Logan was only half listening. As Gerard shone the

lantern around the confines of the chamber, the swath of yellowish light picked up here and there the colored glint of precious jewels in sword hilts and belts. A gemmed dagger caught Logan's eye, gripped in the gauntleted hand of the skeletal figure immediately to his right. Avarice supplanting his initial revulsion, he reached out to take it.

Gerard's hand fell heavily upon his wrist. "Don't burden yourself with trifles," he told Logan. "The real prize lies there."

He gestured with the lantern toward the far end of the vault. The broad "V" of light showed up a large mural covering most of the wall. As the two men advanced between the tomb slabs, the mural resolved into a large shield bearing the St. Clair arms: *argent,* a cross engrailed *sable,* surmounted by the family crest in the form of a crowing cock. As supporters, the shield was borne up by the life-sized figures of two kneeling Templar knights wearing the cross-emblazoned white mantles of their Order.

Gerard unzipped the pouch at his waist and took out the Seal. Walking up to the right-hand figure, he applied the Seal firmly to the center of the cross on the mantle. With a rusty grinding noise, the section of wall with the shield pivoted round like a door. Beyond the opening it revealed lay a whitewashed inner chamber into which Gerard and then Logan quietly passed and then stopped stock-still.

The life-sized figures standing vigil all around the room were only painted Templars, but the two kneeling to either side of a small, child-sized stone sarcophagus in the center of the chamber were real, though long dead—perhaps the very men depicted in the mural outside. Clad in suits of chain mail, mail-coifed heads bowed over their swords, the threadbare remnants of once-white mantles still trailed from their shoulders. The lid of the sarcophagus was crested both with the Templar cross and with the St. Clair arms.

Breathing hard with excitement, Gerard set the lantern on the floor and approached the sarcophagus, slipping the Seal back into his belt pouch. Stone grated against stone as he set his fingers to the edge of the stone lid, but the weight was more than he could shift unaided.

"Here! Help me!" he rasped at Logan.

Logan darted forward to comply. In moving closer, his feet caught in the remnants of one of the mouldering mantles and pulled over its wearer in a startling clatter of collapsing chain mail and separating bones. The skull skittered almost under Logan's feet, and the thief kicked it aside with a grimace of disgust as he got a grip on the edge of the lid opposite Gerard. Grunting and straining, the two of them were just able to shift it off and lean it on edge against the side of the sarcophagus. At Gerard's gesture, Logan snatched up the lantern again and shone it inside.

Within lay something long and narrow, wrapped in a pall of purple silk whose color remained miraculously undimmed by age. Fingers trembling, Gerard bent over and lifted away the top folds. Beneath, pillowed on more silk, lay a slender rod of rich, untarnished gold. One end was capped with a decorative knob supporting a three-dimensional star of interlocking triangles nearly the size of a man's palm—surely the sign of Solomon—and the other had a miniature version of the Seal carved into the flat, so that it, too, could be used as a seal.

Gerard gave a wordless moan of triumph as he allowed one trembling forefinger to stroke down the shaft. Then, with an ecstatic sigh, he rewrapped the Sceptre in its silken shroud and reverently lifted it from its resting place. While his attention was so diverted, Logan's gaze strayed toward the gleam of the fallen knight's fallen sword. But as he made a move to pick it up, Gerard rounded on him, flushed with hectic pride.

"Leave that piece of trash where it is!" the Frenchman ordered. "Now that we have the Seal and the Sceptre, the true treasure of Solomon is only waiting for us to claim it!"

CHAPTER TWENTY-FIVE

M IDNIGHT was fast approaching when the helicopter carrying Adam, McLeod, and Peregrine touched down on the helipad at Dalhousie Castle in a light rain. Parked at the edge of the tarmac beside the landing circle, a dark grey VW Passat Estate flashed its headlights once as the pilot cut the engine.

"There's our next ride," McLeod said, as they disembarked from the chopper. "Thanks very much, Mr. Pearson. Someone will be up to collect the car in the next day or two."

Clutching their bags and ducking low under the still-turning rotors, the three of them made a dash for the car. Before leaving Adam's Range Rover at the heliport, they had changed blazers and tweed jackets for the ubiquitous green waxed jackets that were more suitable for the weather and their probable activities. Detective Donald Cochrane threw open the front passenger door as they approached, a quizzical look on his face as they piled in, McLeod and Peregrine in the back and Adam up front.

"Good to see you, Donald," McLeod said. "Now see how fast you can get us to Roslin. Sir Adam will direct you."

Acknowledging the order with a wordless nod, Cochrane popped the car into gear and punched the accelerator. As they roared out of the car park to the departing chuff of helicopter rotors behind them, Adam opened the road atlas he had brought along and breathed a silent prayer that he and his companions would be arriving in time. Ahead of them, the Midlothian landscape was flooded with watery moonlight, bright enough to show him individual sheep dotting the fields on either side of them.

Turning right out of the car park, Cochrane sent the Passat shooting like an arrow up the deserted highway, only slowing to turn southerly again at the crossroads in Bonnyrigg. A long, straight run of about two miles brought them to Rosewell, whence they wove more westerly until they were creeping through the outskirts of Roslin itself. As they turned down an unpaved road that was signposted to Rosslyn Chapel, Adam instructed the younger detective to kill their headlamps and proceed very slowly, turning then to speak to Peregrine. McLeod was pulling the Browning Hi-Power out of his bag, slapping a clip into the butt, slipping the weapon into the waistband of his trousers.

"Keep your eyes open," Adam advised in a tight undertone, handing Peregrine a small torch. "If you See anything out of the ordinary, let us know at once."

The great wall surrounding Rosslyn Chapel loomed ahead, the pointed Gothic spires of the chapel itself glistening beyond in the moonlight.

"Pull over there," Adam instructed their driver. "And just wait for us here."

With a glance back over his shoulder at McLeod, Cochrane did as he was bidden, parking in the shadow of a weeping cherry tree and killing the engine.

"If we're not back in an hour, call for reinforcements," McLeod murmured, handing Cochrane his cell phone as he and his companions got out of the car.

"Are you sure you don't want me to come with you, sir?" Cochrane asked hopefully.

"Quite sure, thank you. I want you to stay here with the car in case somebody has to give chase."

"Whatever you say, sir," Cochrane sighed. He added plaintively, "I wouldn't mind somebody telling me what's going on."

McLeod reached over and gave the younger man a clap on the shoulder. "Later," he said with gruff firmness. "Right now, you're right where you're most likely to be needed."

Carrying his medical bag, which now housed the Crown, Adam led the way up to the actual entrance through the

surrounding wall and tested at the door, but it was firmly
locked.

"Unfortunately, that doesn't mean a thing," McLeod
muttered. "Our friends could have climbed over the wall
just as easily as we're going to do."

Adam was already testing his weight on the copestones
farther to the right, and turned to hand Peregrine the medical
bag.

"Hold this until I get on top."

Watching as the taller man swung himself up onto the
wallhead as easily as mounting a horse, Peregrine glanced
down at his legs and grimaced.

"There goes another pair of perfectly good trousers."

He passed the medical bag up at Adam's gesture, then
scrambled after him. McLeod joined them a moment later,
and together they made their way over to the chapel itself.
The side door was secure, but the great door at the west end
was standing ajar.

"Damn!" McLeod mouthed silently.

Drawing the Browning, he gave the door a nudge and
cat-stepped across the threshold, dropping warily to a
crouch as soon as he was inside. After a twenty-second span
of silence, he eased his stance and beckoned his companions
forward. Padding after Adam, Peregrine found himself in
near-total darkness.

Not daring to switch on his torch until one of his
superiors gave the word, he instinctively drew a breath and
narrowed his eyes in an effort to see. The surrounding
darkness gave back shadowy impressions of Gothic stonework. Then his deeper sight picked up a ghost-glimmer of
movement among the columns ahead. The breath caught in
his throat.

"What is it?" Adam's voice hissed in his ear.

"I thought I saw something," Peregrine whispered back.
"Over there to our right."

All three men stood still and listened intently. "I don't
hear anything," McLeod muttered.

"It may have been just a visual resonance," Peregrine
allowed in an undertone.

"If Gerard were still here, we would have been aware of it by now," Adam decided. "Let's have a bit of light."

He switched on his torch. Peregrine did the same. The crossplay of the beams threw fantastic shadows round the walls, but the chapel itself seemed to be empty. They pressed forward up the aisle, making for the distinctive Apprentice Pillar. Just beyond it and to the right, at the top of the stairs leading down to the crypt, McLeod came to an abrupt halt.

"Gerard's been here all right," he said quietly. "And Jesus, what a mess he's made!"

He pointed his torch down the stairs to the level below and started down. Hurrying to join him, Peregrine and Adam saw that the floor of the crypt was strewn with rubble from a controlled explosion, fanned outward from an opening to the left. McLeod fetched up short before he reached the threshold, his craggy face contorting in a grimace of disgust.

"Ugh, Black Wards!" he said shortly, shining his light among a number of dark smears on the floor. "Our boy left in such a hurry, he didn't bother to neutralize them properly."

Coming to stand beside McLeod in the doorway, Adam could sense the murky pulse of malignant energies.

"We'll have to deal with them before we attempt to go any farther," he murmured.

He handed his bag to Peregrine to hold, then opened it up and took out a vial of salt and a small, silk-wrapped bundle. Inside the bundle was a long, narrow piece of magnetized lodestone, the size and shape of a wolf's tooth, that Peregrine had seen several times before. Palming this in his right hand, Adam took the vial in his left hand and sprinkled salt over the blood-sign immediately across the threshold. The ring on his right hand flared blue as he reached out with the toothstone.

"The Light shineth in the darkness," he intoned in a low voice, *"and the darkness comprehendeth it not. Blessed be the true Light which lighteth every man that cometh into the world, for the darkness shall not abide in its presence."*

Before the power Adam had invoked, the Black Ward guttered and died like a snuffed candle flame. Proceeding around the chamber to the left, he dealt with each of the remaining three wards in turn. Peregrine was aware of the toothstone drawing off the dark energies Adam's words had unbound. By the time the older man had finished, the atmosphere in the chamber was empty, neutral. As Adam beckoned Peregrine to enter the chamber, pocketing the salt and the toothstone, McLeod went over to inspect the gaping hole in the adjacent wall.

"I don't think we missed our boy by much. These stones are still warm from the blast," he reported over his shoulder.

"Well, let's see if he got what he came for," Adam replied. "I don't doubt that he did, but we're going to have to hunt for some clue to where he's gone next."

The Frenchman's trail was heartbreakingly easy to follow. Inside the burial vault, with its generations of long-dead Barons of Rosslyn laid out on their biers—some of them perhaps Adam's distant ancestors—Adam and his companions came to the yawning entrance to the inner chamber, passing between the guarding Templars painted on the wall. The empty stone sarcophagus told the tale, with the bones of one of its last guardians strewn beside it. Adam gave the other one respectful distance as he wearily leaned both hands on the edges, trying to decide what to do next.

"It was *here*," Peregrine murmured forlornly. "I can almost see its afterimage. If only we could have gotten here half an hour sooner!"

"Wishing won't help," McLeod said a little impatiently. "What I want to know is where Gerard and his pal may be planning to go from here."

"His pal?" Peregrine looked to the inspector in surprise.

"Aye. If you take the trouble to look, you'll see there are *two* sets of footprints in the dust on the floor. Furthermore, whoever set that explosion knew what he was doing— probably the same thieving professional who helped Gerard turn over the Fiennes house. It wouldn't surprise me to learn he was the one who did the killing."

Peregrine sighed heavily, casting a dejected glance over the remaining Templar.

"If only our friend there could talk," he murmured. "Maybe *he* knows where the casket is."

Following Peregrine's glance with his own, Adam pulled a thoughtful frown.

"If only our friend could talk . . . ," he mused, then abruptly straightened and grinned. "Maybe he can. Peregrine, you're brilliant!"

Beckoning for the artist to bring him his bag, Adam dropped to one knee beside the skeletal figure of the remaining dead Templar and lifted out the Crown of Solomon.

"What are you going to do with that?" McLeod demanded. "You know what Lady Grizel said about wearing it."

"*I'm* not going to wear it," Adam said.

Clasping the Crown between his hands, he closed his eyes in a brief, silent prayer, then reached out and set the diadem gingerly on the dead knight's mailed head, at the same time plunging into trance and allowing his own submerged Templar persona to overshadow him with past memories.

"*Non nobis, Domine, non nobis, sed Nomini Tuo da gloriam,*" he murmured, using the ancient Templar motto as a seal upon his intention. Not to us, Lord, not unto us but unto Thy Name be the glory. . . .

"Assist me, my brother," he went on softly. "Let me take up your burden. The despoiler of your rest has taken what you guarded, and goes now to awaken that which should never be freed. Tell me where it lies, that I may stop him."

There was an electrifying pause, during which Peregrine felt the hairs on the back of his neck begin to bristle. Then the Templar's mummified skull shifted upright with a creaking of dry neck bones. Beneath the Crown, twin points of pale light gleamed within the sunken sockets of the eyes, and the fleshless jaw moved.

"*Stop him . . . ,*" said a voice both heard and sensed. "*Stop the enemy of our Order. . . .*"

"The casket," Adam pressed urgently. "Tell me where to find it, I beg of you."

The ghost-light flamed up with sudden vehemence within the dead man's skull. *"Our preceptory at Balantrodoch!"* came the sepulchral response. *"There it lies. Go now, before it is too late. . . ."*

"Balantrodoch?" McLeod's voice was almost as harsh as that of the dead knight. "Where is *that*?"

Peregrine was trembling visibly with fearful excitement, but this answer, at least, he knew.

"Not far!" he whispered. "I remember it from Adam's maps. The place is called Temple now, and it's only a few miles from here!"

His hazel eyes widened as he realized the import of what he had just said. "Adam, Gerard could be there already!"

Even as he spoke, and before McLeod could forestall him, the young artist reached out an eager hand to grasp Adam's shoulder in emphasis. His peremptory touch snapped Adam back out of the past with a dizzying wrench, eliciting a choked exclamation as Adam clutched at his head. In the same instant, the bones of the Templar clattered apart and collapsed into a heap of mouldering rags and broken bits of armor.

"You bloody fool!" McLeod snapped, springing to Adam's aid. "Don't you know better by now than to jerk somebody out of a trance like that?"

"I'm—I'm sorry," Peregrine whispered. "I wasn't thinking. . . ."

"Let it pass, Noel." Adam got his legs under him with the inspector's assistance and staggered upright, clapping a hand to the nape of his neck as he gulped air and willed his nausea to recede. "I'm all right," he assured them. "He didn't mean it. I'll get myself in hand on the way to Temple. In the meantime, Peregrine's right. We'd better move fast."

Retrieving the Crown from the tangle of brittle bones at his feet, he fumbled it away in his bag with McLeod's help. As he did so, his pain-bleared eyes lighted on the two Templar long-swords lying in the dust among the scattered bones and mail.

"You'd better bring those," he instructed, pointing. "I don't like despoiling the dead, but I don't think the Brethren will mind—and the weapons may offer you some slight protection if the demons are allowed to get loose."

Wordlessly Peregrine gathered the two swords in his arms, wide-eyed.

"Now back to the car as fast as we can make it," Adam said. "And from there, on to Temple. . . ."

CHAPTER TWENTY-SIX

THE tiny village of Temple had only one main street. The tidy rows of stone-built cottages flanking it stood blind and deaf as gravestones in the dead of this rainy September night, when all decent folk could be expected to be in their beds—and were, in Temple. In a wide field behind one of the rows of cottages, accessible only via an unpaved lane, the area's sole reminder of former Templar eminence stood alone and aloof just behind the local primary school—a round-topped stone archway, dog-toothed and ancient, said to be all that remained of the former preceptory of Balantro-doch. Beyond the arch, between Gerard and a rectangular depression now occupied by the school's playground, a slight mound marked the probable foundations of some of the structures formerly standing there. Stark as a cenotaph, the arch itself glimmered in the fitful moonlight like tarnished silver, casting faint shadows across the tall grass.

Henri Gerard was scarcely aware of these niceties of his surroundings. As he stood in the moonlight beneath the tall horseshoe sweep of the arch, oblivious to the lightly falling rain, he felt as if he had somehow stepped outside of time. His link with his own psychic past had never seemed more vivid to him than it did at this moment—as if only the thinnest of temporal membranes separated him now from that greater self, Guillaume de Nogaret. He could almost taste the moment—so exquisitely imminent now—when at last he would come into possession of the wealth and power that had so long been denied him.

Half-intoxicated with anticipation, he drew himself up to his full height, the Sceptre gripped in his right hand, the Seal cradled in his left. Oblivious to Logan, hunkered down in the shadows over his canvas tool-bag, he basked in the light of the moon while bright fantasies of triumphs yet to come paraded themselves before his mind's eye.

But these glorious visions faded prematurely before the brief, intrusive image of Nathan Fiennes. The elderly Jewish scholar presented himself on his knees, hands clasped before him in mute appeal, as if imploring Gerard to turn back. . . .

A cold thrill of fear touched the back of Gerard's neck. Rather than yield to it, he banished the vision with a jarring bark of a laugh and a wave of the Sceptre in his hand, at the same time hugging the Seal closer to his breast. Then, eyes feverishly bright in his thin face, he took a firmer grip on the Seal he was holding in his left hand as, with his right, he brandished the Sceptre defiantly over his head and pronounced the potent opening words of an incantation as ancient as the rod itself.

The star of interlocking triangles at the head of the Sceptre began to glow. As the glow brightened, the star became a blur of golden flame. Gerard's voice rose in crescendo until, with a sudden hoarse outcry, he swung the Sceptre downward to smite the ground in front of the arch with a final, raw Word of command.

Fire flared up and scorched the grass in a golden line running away from Gerard, accompanied by a faint subterranean rumble as of distant thunder. As Logan gaped in astonishment, a crack opened up along the scorch line on the far side of the arch, yawning and widening to disclose a dark passageway into which descended a massive flight of stone steps.

Elated, himself hardly able to believe what he had done, Gerard replaced the Seal in his belt pouch, then thrust the Sceptre through his belt like a sword before half turning to beckon to Logan. Setting his jaw, the thief picked up his tool-bag and moved to join the Frenchman at the top of the stair. Gerard had told him to have the big electric lantern ready—ridiculous in the moon-drenched field, Logan had thought at the time—but now it was evident why. Refusing to let himself be unnerved, Logan switched on the lantern and shone it down the stairs, following somewhat hesitantly at the Frenchman's impatient gesture.

The stairs led down under the mound. At the bottom, a stone passageway led off to the right, with doorways opening from the left side. Gerard caught his breath as, peering ahead by the light of Logan's lantern, he recognized the corridor he had seen while scrying with the aid of his crystal ball. Heart pounding, he quickened his pace to a trot, outstripping his accomplice.

The doors to the side chambers sagged drunkenly on rusty hinges, revealing chill cavities of darkness beyond, but true to Gerard's vision, the last one on the left had been filled in with stones and mortar. Beckoning Logan closer with the lantern, the Frenchman ran his hands over the stonework, brushing aside dust and cobwebs like heavy gauze until, at eye level, he uncovered a lozenge of mortar that bore the stamped impression of a six-pointed star surrounded by a wreath of Hebrew characters.

Quite involuntarily, Gerard let out a little cry of joyful anticipation. Removing the Seal itself from its waist pouch, he applied it firmly over the imprint. When there was no response, he put the Seal away again and turned to Logan with a look of wild-eyed impatience.

"A pickax, *here!*" he ordered. "Explosives could bring everything down."

Logan's thin lips tightened resentfully at his employer's imperious tone of voice, but he thrust the lantern into Gerard's hands and opened his tool-bag without comment, lifting out a short-handled pick.

"Keep the light on where I'm working," he said, as he limbered up his shoulders in preparation to begin. "And give me plenty of room if you don't want to get hit."

Gerard gave him a gimlet look from under scowling brows, then backed away to the opposite wall. Setting his teeth, Logan hefted the pick and let swing the first blow. Shards of stone and ancient mortar flew back in a growing cloud of dust as he fell to his task. He would have stopped when he had cleared a hole large enough to admit them, but Gerard made him keep working until most of the original doorway was open. After nearly fifteen minutes, the French-man pronounced himself satisfied.

Logan fell back to wipe the sweat from his face. Time enough to exact his revenge for being treated like a serf by this oaf of a Frenchman. Gerard, meanwhile, had shouldered his way past the other man and darted through the opening, his pale face ablaze with anticipation.

Once inside, he stumbled to an abrupt halt, eyes wide with greedy awe. For set in the center of the round vaulted room, glitteringly revealed in the garish glare of the lantern, was a golden ark-shaped casket, sealed shut with a wafer of gold that bore the imprint of Solomon's Seal. The lid of the casket was surmounted by four winged creatures facing outward toward the four quarters in unsleeping vigilance. Flanking the casket on either side was a pair of stout wooden carrying poles, once again recalling Gerard's scry-ing vision.

As he continued to feast his gaze on the prize, one hand pressed to the Seal at his waist, the other caressing the star on the Sceptre, he became belatedly aware of other shapes in the room. Tearing his gaze away, he swung the beam of his lantern around and saw that this chamber had been left better guarded than the last he had violated.

These were no painted sentinels. Around the circular perimeter of the vault had been placed thirteen tall, straight-backed chairs with arms. Twelve of the thirteen chairs were occupied by the mummified remains of as many white-mantled Templar warriors. The guardians sat with their mail-coifed heads bowed low over gauntleted hands that clasped the quillons of their standing swords. The thirteenth seat, directly opposite the casket, stood vacant.

Entering behind the Frenchman, still carrying his pickax, Logan took a long, uneasy look around him and muttered a wondering imprecation.

"Jesus, Gerard, these people must have been as crazy as you are!"

Gerard rounded on him with a fierce contempt that made the thief recoil.

"*Ah, que vous êtes bêtes!*" he spat. "Having eyes, can

you see nothing beyond the base material world? Even these accursed heretics knew that this life is merely a shadowy adjunct to the realms of the higher powers.''

He indicated the quiet forms of the dead Templars. Meeting the Frenchman's hollow, burning gaze, Logan threw up his free hand in an ironic gesture of disclaimer.

"Okay, you can have your higher powers," he allowed. "Forget I said anything. All I'm interested in is that box over there.''

He took a step toward the casket, but Gerard made a noise between his teeth and put himself squarely in the thief's way.

"Fool!'' he whispered. "You will get nothing from that casket without first reckoning with those higher powers you are so disposed to mock! Now, hold the light and be silent while I do what must be done to ensure our safety.''

Logan thought about bashing the Frenchman in the head then and there, but his memory of how the ground had opened to admit them where they now stood made him give a grudging nod instead, as he took the lantern and backed off a few paces. Satisfied, Gerard turned his back on the thief, and so missed seeing the way the other man surreptitiously tested the weight of his pickax. Oblivious to the dangerous gleam in his accomplice's eyes, the Frenchman approached the casket with the reverent attitude of a priest entering a sanctuary. After carefully shifting aside the wooden staves, he reached into the breast pocket of his black jacket and took out a stick of compressed charcoal wrapped in a twist of thin white paper.

There were Hebraic symbols inscribed on the paper. Dropping down on one knee, Gerard raised both hands above his head and bowed his head. His lips moved, framing words whose echoes seemed to Logan to be too guttural to be either French or English. Having uttered them, the Frenchman took the charcoal stick and began to draw lines on the floor.

Curious in spite of himself, Logan edged closer in order to see better, following as Gerard's sketching gradually went farther afield. By degrees, the Frenchman's charcoal marks took the form of a double circle enclosing the casket, augmented by a running scrawl of writing between the two lines that the thief suspected might be Hebrew. His patience wearing thin, Logan overstepped the unfinished circle and stared down at the back of the other man's bent head. His hand tightened on the pickax as he debated whether to strike now or after the casket was open.

Gerard seemed suddenly to become aware of him and turned sharply around. Standing his ground, Logan demanded, "How much longer is this going to take?"

"As long as is necessary," Gerard snapped. "Now be silent!"

Another minute saw the circle closed off around them with an elaborate knot-flourish. Rocking back on his heels, Gerard took out the Seal and raised it above his head while he spoke more of the language he had uttered before. Then, getting to his feet, he slipped the Sceptre from his belt and raised it above his head, at the same time extending the Seal as he leaned forward and fitted it to its golden imprint on the casket.

For a moment nothing happened. Then the casket lid clicked upward a fraction with a slight, metallic ping. The ping was followed by a thin plume of sulphurous smoke. Then came the sound of a sibilant, long-drawn sigh.

A look of uncertainty crossed Gerard's taut face, and he hugged the Seal to his breast as he considered what to do next. Lowering the Sceptre, he used the tip of it to prod the casket lid open a fraction farther. Very softly, something inside gave a chitter of malevolent laughter. Then, all at once, the lid slammed back as a sudden blast of noisome vapor rocketed upward out of the box.

Gerard recoiled with a strangled cry. Above his head the expanding vapor cloud writhed and began to separate into two loathly humanoid shapes. . . .

As Adam and his associates raced toward Temple, an unquestioning Donald Cochrane at the wheel, Adam lowered his head and pressed his sapphire ring lightly to his forehead, letting McLeod and Peregrine navigate while he tried to regain the psychic equilibrium that the too-quick awakening in the burial vault at Rosslyn had cost him. For the next few minutes, he was only dimly conscious of the big estate car's rushing momentum. But as they bore down on the outskirts of Temple, to McLeod's low-voiced directions, he became aware of a building disturbance in the atmosphere overhanging the village. Ripples of dark energy battered past him like psychic shock waves, leaving few doubts as to their source.

Huddled contritely in the backseat with the Templar swords braced with one hand between him and McLeod, Peregrine was likewise aware of the rising storm of rebellious powers. Leaning forward in his seat, he asked in a subdued voice, "Adam, are we too late?"

"Yes and no," Adam replied grimly, opening his eyes. "I very much fear that the genies are out of the bottle, but we may well be in time to put them back in. It will be at a cost, though."

Dragging his medical bag up onto his knees, he took out the Crown, then slipped a couple of pre-loaded syringes into an outer pocket of his waxed jacket.

"What are those for?" Peregrine asked.

"Sedatives," Adam said with bleak candor. "Even if, by some miracle, Gerard and his partner manage to survive tonight's ill-judged venture, I wouldn't want to vouch for their state of mind."

Peregrine gulped and subsided. Peering over Adam's shoulder through the windscreen, he scanned the lay of the land ahead of them as they slowed to nose along the narrow, twisting road into Temple. Not far past an old, ruined church standing stark and silent in the moonlight on their right, Adam spotted a break in the rows of interconnected cottages that lined both sides of the main street, opening off to the left.

"Donald, cut the engine and the lights, and park just beyond that lane," he said softly, laying a hand on Cochrane's sleeve.

The young detective complied, letting the Passat coast for another thirty yards before bringing it to a halt where Adam had indicated. Catching McLeod's eye in the rearview mirror, he said, "Do I get to come along this time, sir?"

Adam and McLeod traded swift glances, and Adam shook his head minutely.

"Not this time, old son," McLeod murmured, clapping his subordinate briefly on the shoulder. "You're to wait with the car and keep your eyes and ears open—nothing more." He took the Browning Hi-Power out of his waistband and handed it up to Cochrane. "If Henri Gerard should come running out that lane, do whatever you need to do to take him into custody, but otherwise, do *not*, under *any* circumstances, come down that lane until I give you leave. Do I make myself clear? Disobey that last order and you'll find yourself tending parking meters for the rest of your professional life!"

Adam and Peregrine had gotten out of the car while McLeod briefed his young assistant, Peregrine taking out the swords. Now the artist handed one to the inspector.

"We're to take on demons with *these*?" he murmured.

McLeod gave him a sly grin.

"Don't sell them short, laddie. Unless I miss my guess, these weapons have more virtues to them than a sharp cutting edge."

Peregrine took his own weapon in hand and hefted it. For all its length and weight, the sword seemed less unwieldy than he would have expected. And he knew, from prior experience, that however much his current body might lack skill with such weapons, his spirit appeared to know them well.

Adam had gone on ahead, and was already waiting for them at the mouth of the lane, keeping to the grassy verge so his footsteps could not be heard. He had secreted Solomon's Crown in the capacious inner pocket of his waxed jacket, close to his body, but he was holding his *skean dubh* in his right hand, the naked blade close along the side of his leg, the blue stone in its hilt a close match for the one in his ring. His left hand held an unlit pocket torch.

Leading them quietly a few yards farther along the lane, so they were no longer directly between the cottages flanking the opening to the lane, Adam drew them close to sign himself and each of them with a sign of warding, the flat of the *skean dubh*'s blade touched momentarily to each forehead.

"Though the darkness come upon me in the valley of the shadow," he whispered, *"my feet shall never falter. For the Daystar goes before me to enlighten all my ways."*

With a final salute to the Light, flourishing the *skean dubh*'s blade in the moonlight, he led them farther along the lane. Off to the left, a school playground occupied a large, rectangular depression, and beyond it, gleaming in the moonlight, stood the rounded curve of the arch that was all still remaining of the old Templar preceptory.

Skirting the corner of the playground, they struck out through tall, wet grass toward the arch. As they drew nearer, Peregrine saw that its weathered grey stones were underlit by a pale, eldritch glow discernible even in the moonlight. The source of that glow was a gaping hole at the base of the grassy mound just before the arch's shadow.

Even as that fact registered, a thin, long-drawn scream came echoing up out of the womb of the mound, almost more felt than heard. As Adam and his companions started forward, the voice screamed again on a shriller note of mindless terror.

CHAPTER TWENTY-SEVEN

HOLDING his *skean dubh* uplifted before him, Adam circled round the arch and went through it, plunging down the steps. Torch in one hand, sword in the other, McLeod followed hard on his heels, Peregrine bringing up the rear with his own sword brandished two-handed. At the bottom of the stair, a stone-walled corridor stretched off to the right, with a ghastly radiance leaking out into the passageway at the far end through a jagged hole in the left-hand wall.

The air reeked of rampant corruption. From inside the lighted chamber came obscene noises of gobbling and slavering, punctuated by a wet, tearing sound and a grinding crack like the snap of bone between carnivore teeth. Amidst the noise of frenzied feeding, Adam could hear halting whimpers that might have been human.

Steeling himself for the worst, he sprinted forward to the gap in the wall. As he reached the threshold, a hot gust of air raked his face like a set of talons, harsh as a blast of volcanic wind, stinking of brimstone and carrion. Eyes narrowed to smarting chinks, Adam beat the fumes away with a wave of his *skean dubh* and found himself confronted by a scene from an inferno.

The chamber beyond was dominated by the roiling presence of two nightmare shapes, half-fog, half-fire. Crooning and chuckling, they were hunched down over a grisly pile of torn flesh and broken bones that Adam realized must once have been a human body. At the center of the room stood a golden casket, its lid gaping wide. On the floor on the farther side of the casket cowered the trembling figure of Henri Gerard.

The Seal was lying on the floor beside him. Tightly

clutched in his right hand was a slender rod of burnished gold that Adam recognized at a single glance as Solomon's Sceptre. Oblivious to Adam's arrival, Gerard was brandishing it weakly in the direction of the two demon-shapes while he haltingly mouthed a warding incantation through chattering teeth. So far, the influence of the Sceptre seemed to be holding, but Adam knew that its protection would last only as long as Gerard could maintain his faltering self-control.

At least the Frenchman had had sufficient forethought to draw a magic circle on the floor before opening the casket. The spidery black wheel of lines and symbols gleamed like wet tar in the phosphorescent demon-glow. Preoccupied with feeding for the first time in three millennia, the demons apparently had not yet tested the strength—or weakness—of that fragile-looking boundary. But Adam doubted that the existing circle would prove potent enough to contain them for more than a matter of minutes once they had disposed of their present victim—or the next.

A clatter of footsteps announced the arrival of McLeod, with Peregrine following close behind. Craning past Adam's shoulder to see into the room, the inspector managed to murmur, "Sweet Jesus." Peregrine gasped and went white, all but gagging as he half turned away.

The energy generated by the magic circle was like an invisible curtain wall. By narrowing his eyes and calling up his deep sight, Peregrine could See it as an opalescent screen of shimmering filaments. Inside the circle, Gog and Magog were gleefully continuing to pick over the reeking remnants of their kill, their drooling tentacle-mouths smeared with blood and venomous saliva. Visibly denser than they had been only a moment before, the two demons appeared to be taking on added strength and substance from their feast on human flesh.

"The more they eat, the stronger they're going to get," Adam whispered, as he realized what was happening. "We've got to contain them here and now, whatever the cost. If these creatures get loose to carry on feeding, there may be no stopping them."

McLeod braced himself resolutely, shifting his grip on the hilt of his sword.

"What do you want us to do?"

Before Adam could respond, the nearer of the two creatures appeared to notice Gerard for the first time. Slewing its featureless head around, it hissed at him with its Medusa-like cluster of mouths. Gerard cowered farther backwards, only to overbalance and sit hard, stopped by the barrier of his own making. His eyes suddenly went wild as he realized he was trapped.

Slavering over a last gobbet of flesh, the other demon turned on its haunches. Eyes like gouts of balefire blazed in the gloom with sudden and renewed appetite as it regarded Gerard. Gaping back at them in stricken horror, the French-man gave an incoherent shriek of denial. The Sceptre faltered in his trembling grasp.

"Can't we do something?" Peregrine whispered urgently.

"I'm thinking," Adam murmured back.

Merciless as basilisks, the two demons separated and began to converge on Gerard from either side around the casket. The Frenchman made a feeble attempt to wave them back with the Sceptre, but his quaking arm and will lacked the strength to give the gesture any real authority. With throaty gurgles of anticipation, the demons edged closer.

"You'd better think fast," McLeod muttered.

"I know."

Glancing around the chamber, Adam finally noticed the long-dead Templar guardians seated around the perimeter of the chamber. The sight brought a single desperate recourse to mind.

"Try to create a diversion," he whispered to his two fellow Huntsmen. "I'll see what I can do."

So saying, he faded swiftly away from them to the left, into the murky dark along the edge of the wall, skirting the seated sentinels. Behind him, McLeod and Peregrine began shouting and clashing their swords together in the doorway. Sharp and bright despite their antiquity, the Templar blades rang out in the demon-gloom with almost supernatural clarity. Like the peal of cathedral bells, the blade-music echoed and reechoed in that confined space in soaring counterpoint to Gerard's terrified whimpering.

Arrested by the chime of consecrated steel, both demons halted in their tracks. Cringing and snarling as if stung by the sound, they seemed briefly to lose sight of their intended victim. Fiery eyes swiveled around, probing in the direction of the two gesticulating figures in the doorway. Still writhing, they whipped about and surged forward as if to hurl themselves at their tormentors.

The magic circle absorbed the impact of their charge, but only just. Adam could sense that the containment field would not hold against too many such assaults. While the two demons were still foundering about in dismay, he made his way around to Gerard's side of the circle and dropped to a crouch at the feet of one of the sentinels, deep in shadow. Determined to maintain his calm, he slipped his left hand into the inner pocket where Solomon's Crown lay secreted and took two deep breaths in succession, retreating inward to seek a vantage point among the Inner Planes. As he hovered briefly between waking and trance, a prayer of petition rose spontaneously to his lips in the words of an ancient King of Israel, son to the great King whose Crown lay beneath his hand:

O send out Thy light and Thy truth: let them lead me; let them bring me unto Thy holy hill, and to Thy tabernacles. Then will I go unto the altar of God, unto God my exceeding joy: yea, upon the harp will I praise Thee, O God my God. . . .

The words resonated throughout his inner being, filling his spirit with strength and certainty. Convinced now that he was acting in accordance with a Will higher than his own, he stood up in the shadows and pulled the Crown from his pocket. Right hand to his breast, closed around the hilt of the *skean dubh,* he closed his eyes and put on the Crown of Solomon.

The circlet seemed to adjust of its own accord, settling gently but firmly about his temples. In the selfsame instant, he experienced a sudden dizziness, as if he were being

plucked out of his corporeal body. Set free from the
confines of normal time and space, all at once he was flying,
soaring upward on wings of air and fire like an eagle
seeking union with the sun. Above him blazed an ever-
unfolding glory that burned his sublunary sight away and
gave it back to him as vision purified.

With new eyes, he saw before him the image of a great
city built upon a mountaintop. Rising tier upon jewelled tier,
the city shimmered like an opal against a firmament of stars,
all towers, gates, and crystal-welling fountains. Adam
alighted before the city's eastern wall, facing three lofty
gates of topaz, emerald, and sardonyx. As he paused there in
spirit, the central gate swung open to allow a great company
in armor to begin pouring out.

At the forefront of the company was a regal silver-haired
figure whose flowing crimson robes and imperial bearing
proclaimed him, even at a distance, as King Solomon. The
host at his back was made up of warriors from every age,
Israelite swordsmen marching shoulder-to-shoulder with
Templar knights. Prominent among them was a tall figure
wearing a buff cavalry jacket under a white-plumed chapeau. The handsome, firm-lipped face above the lace jabot
belonged to John Grahame of Claverhouse, Bonnie Dundee.
Smiling as he met Adam's gaze, the viscount gave a nod in
salute.

The company came to a halt at a sign from the King, who
beckoned Adam to approach. Awed but unafraid, Adam
obeyed, sinking down on one knee to bow his head before
the wisdom and power the King represented.

*"Blessed is the man unto whom the Lord imputeth not
iniquity, and in whose spirit there is no guile,"* he seemed
to hear the great King say, as strong hands were laid on his
shoulders. "Receive the blessings of Wisdom in the name
of the Most High, knowing that the might and authority of
the King and all this company go with thee."

The Crown on Adam's head came to life in a burst of
white light. Impressions flooded in upon him from all sides,
honed to a cosmic acuity he had never known before. For a
fleeting instant, he was minutely aware of the sidereal dance

of atoms and elements, building like a symphony into larger patterns of shape and form.

Then the dimensions of the created universe folded round him like a box, and he found himself back in the confines of the underground vault of a former Templar preceptory without passage of time, with King Solomon's Crown upon his head and holding his *skean dubh* clenched tightly to his breast.

Reduced to human proportions, his senses retained their heightened sensitivity. Willing himself to filter out the noise and stench generated by the presence of the two demons, he threw a glance around the room in search of inspiration for his own next move. Like a magnet, the golden Sceptre waving feebly in Gerard's hand drew his gaze, and he realized that, if he hoped to dictate terms to the demons, he would first have to wrest control of the Sceptre from the terrified Frenchman.

Fortunately, he had the means to do that. The steel of the *skean dubh*'s blade was forged from meteoric iron, starborn, like the toothstone he had used at Rosslyn. Advancing boldly to within an arm's length of the circle's barrier, just behind Gerard, Adam made the *skean dubh* the focus of all his own accumulated will and wisdom, feeling the power blaze up within the compass of his right hand like a flaming sword. Then, like lancing a boil with a needle, he made a quick stabbing motion with the *skean dubh* just above Gerard's head, puncturing the circle.

The barrier imploded with a psionic concussion that shivered the surrounding stonework. Already in motion, Adam reached forward and plucked the Sceptre from Gerard's nerveless fingers. Narrowly avoiding a lashing blow from a demon tentacle, he stepped astride the Frenchman's half-fainting form and drew himself up to his full height, shifting the *skean dubh* and Sceptre so that he held the Sceptre aloft in his right hand.

"*Gog and Magog of the children of Lucifer!*" he called out sharply. "*I command you in the name of Adonai and of Solomon the Wise to listen and attend to my words!*"

Poised to strike again, the demon nearest him hissed and

recoiled. The other mantled like a cobra and spat a jet of venom that scored the floor at Adam's feet. Gerard gave a thin, mewling cry and tried to squirm away. Regally oblivious to both the Frenchman's whimpering and the rising reek of acid smoke, Adam brought the *skean dubh* and the Sceptre together across his chest and fixed the two demons with a steely stare of absolute and unwinking authority.

"You cannot harm me," he stated coldly. "Behold the Crown and Sceptre of Solomon the King, whom the Lord of Hosts invested with power over all unclean spirits. By virtue of that selfsame power, and in the great Name of the Lord Jehovah, I order you to return to your prison-house. And by His authority, *I will be obeyed*!"

His voice cracked like a whip. The demons' response was a bull-throated roar of rage and defiance. Over by the doorway, Peregrine winced and clapped a hand to one ringing ear. Half-choked by the noisome fumes wafting outward from the center of the room, he peered over at Adam through stinging eyes, then caught his breath in sudden wonder.

For his mentor's aspect had undergone a striking metamorphosis. Superimposed over Adam's familiar face and form had come the striking likeness of an Egyptian priest-king in flowing robes of translucent linen. The Sceptre and the *skean dubh* were overshadowed by the images of the crook and the flail, the two royal symbols of Egyptian authority. Likewise, the golden circlet upon his head now bore the dual aspect of Hebrew diadem and the double crown of Thebes and Memphis, both images wedded to one another in a shimmer of authority derived from the Divine.

His fear all but forgotten in his astonishment, Peregrine realized that the Crown itself must be the focus of the transformation, eliciting past manifestations of Adam's power from ages gone by to enhance his present authority. Even as that thought crossed his mind, Adam made a sudden move, imperiously indicating the open casket with the Sceptre.

"Go!" he commanded. *"I charge you to return to the prison which is your only lawful place in this world!"*

Howling and frothing, Gog and Magog fought to hold their ground. Implacable, his lean face set like iron, Adam brought the added compulsion of the *skean dubh* to bear, stepping forward as he adamantly directed the two demons toward the casket. When the creatures separated and tried to bolt, Peregrine saw twin arcs of scintillating energy lash out from the implements Adam held in his hands. It caught the demons in a cross-net of white fire, driving them back shrieking in the direction Adam had marked out for them.

They shrank as they retreated before him, screaming in impotent rage before Adam's compulsion. Relentless, he continued to drive them backwards toward the casket, his dark eyes ablaze with uncompromising authority. Sputtering like spent flares, now chittering almost pitiably, the creatures hovered briefly like so much dirty smoke over the opening until, with a final lash of power, Adam forced them down inside.

As soon as they vanished from view, McLeod cast down his sword and darted forward to slam the lid on the casket.

"Quick! Get the Seal!" he shouted to Peregrine, as he leaned on the lid with all his weight. "Hurry up, man! Don't just stand there!"

Abandoning his own sword with a clatter, Peregrine lunged to snatch the Seal off the floor where Gerard had dropped it, slipping a little in the gore besmirching the stone.

"What do I do with it now?" he cried wildly.

Adam made no response, all his powers of concentration focused through the Sceptre and *skean dubh* pointed at the casket as something struck the underside of the casket lid with force enough to lift it up a chink. Wrestling it back down with panting effort, McLeod nodded stiffly toward the broken mark of the Seal on the side of the box.

"Set the Seal *there*!" he gasped.

Mentally commending himself to the Light, Peregrine threw himself down on his knees and jammed the Seal down hard over its previous impression in gold. There was a shrill, ululating howl from inside the casket, which was shaking and vibrating, but Peregrine continued to hold the Seal in place, desperately willing the impression to take. McLeod set his hand on it as well, joining his concentration to Peregrine's. Majestically, still caught up in his overshadowing, Adam stepped close enough to touch the tip of the Sceptre to the gold beside the Seal.

Under their combined force of will, the broken impression softened like putty, the metal liquefying to spread over the gap. In that brief instant, Peregrine felt the Seal settle under his hand and renew itself. A moment more he held it, then eased the Seal cautiously from the gold. The side of the casket now showed an unbroken imprint of the Seal of Solomon, and all movement inside the casket seemed to have ceased.

"We've done it!" Peregrine announced breathlessly. "At least, I *think* we've done it."

With a side glance at Adam, McLeod warily eased his weight off the lid.

CHAPTER TWENTY-EIGHT

THE silence was broken only by the sound of harsh breathing as McLeod and Peregrine tried to get their wind back. When no new sound intruded from the casket, McLeod allowed himself a guarded sigh of relief and straightened up.

"I think it's going to hold," he announced, still wary.

Adam merely nodded, swaying a little on his feet in momentary light-headedness. With the containment of the twin horrors of Gog and Magog, the astral overlay of Egyptian priest-king had wavered and faded, the aura of power and authority he had wielded only seconds before giving place to a white-lipped pallor born of near exhaustion.

Aware of his two subordinates' concerned glances, Adam summoned a ragged smile of reassurance and wordlessly handed the Sceptre over to McLeod, then sheathed his *skean dubh* and slipped it back into a pocket. He was reaching up with both hands to remove the Crown when, behind him, Henri Gerard gave a sudden low moan and twitched convulsively. As Adam turned, the distraught man clapped both hands to his ears and uttered a piercing, wild-eyed wail.

"I'd wondered how long that would take," Adam murmured, as, now whimpering and beginning to sob, Gerard curled into a fetal ball and began banging his forehead against the stone floor. "Noel, I'm going to need a hand with this."

Passing the Crown and Sceptre to Peregrine, the two of them moved quickly to the Frenchman's side, Adam seizing him by the shoulders and turning him so that McLeod could get a strong, restraining grip on his wrists.

"Steady on, Mr. Gerard," Adam said in a low, soothing voice, rummaging in a pocket for one of the pre-loaded syringes. "The danger's all over. There's nothing more to be afraid of."

As he pulled off the needle's plastic protector with his teeth, the Frenchman gave him a haggard, wild-eyed stare, then flinched away with an anguished howl, bucking convulsively even when McLeod threw his weight upon him to pin him to the floor. Between them, physician and policeman managed to hold their hysterical patient quiet enough for Adam to administer the drug. The Frenchman continued to flop and struggle for several seconds, but then, very suddenly, his body went limp and the terror-stricken eyes rolled upward into merciful oblivion. With a last bubbling moan, he slumped back and was still.

"Hard case!" McLeod breathed, cautiously releasing his grip and getting up off Gerard as Adam monitored the unconscious man's pulse. "I've seen hard-core crack addicts saner than this poor bastard."

"So have I," Adam said soberly. "He isn't going to come out of it, either, without some serious professional help."

Peregrine's gaze was troubled as he stared down at the now-sleeping Gerard. "Was it the demons that did this to him?"

"His fear of them certainly helped push him over the edge," Adam said. "And I'm sure it didn't help to see his accomplice ripped apart and eaten before his very eyes." His glance strayed involuntarily to the shattered torso and the smear of entrails and gore that were all that remained of Gerard's companion. "But he didn't get to the breaking point overnight. If I had to guess, I'd say his present collapse is the result of a growing complex of obsessions that may be rooted in a past beyond his present lifetime— though if I said that to most psychiatrists, I'd be laughed out of the profession. Whoever gets the job of putting his psyche back together again is going to be in for an interesting time of it."

Staring down at Gerard, Peregrine was somewhat surprised to discover that he felt more pity than anger for the man who had almost succeeded in loosing two powerful demons upon an unsuspecting world.

"Then you think he can be cured?" he ventured.

"Given time and patience and an open-minded therapist, it's possible," Adam allowed. "But I wouldn't care to even speculate how long it might take."

He drew a deep breath and squared his shoulders. "In the meantime, our most immediate priority is to decide what's to be done about these Templar treasures, to ensure that they never again become a source of dangerous temptation."

Somewhat dubiously, Peregrine shifted his attention to the Crown and Sceptre he still held in his hands. "I don't suppose we can simply hide them in some safe place," he said doubtfully.

"You tell *me* what constitutes a safe place," McLeod retorted.

Adam nodded slowly, biting at his lip. "Noel's right. And it isn't merely a matter of hiding the hallows; there's the casket itself to be dealt with. Fortunately, we have wiser counsel than our own at our disposal."

Standing, he surveyed the surrounding circle of knightly sentinels until his regard lighted upon the thirteenth chair that stood empty. Following the direction of Adam's gaze, Peregrine noticed for the first time that the unoccupied chair was loftier than the other twelve, showing rich and intricate patterns of carving on the arms and high back. Intrigued by this discovery, he realized only belatedly that his mentor was reaching out to relieve him of the Sceptre and the Crown.

"I'm afraid I'll have to have those back," Adam told him with a wry smile. "They're going to be necessary for what remains to be done."

Suppressing a pang of rising curiosity, Peregrine surrendered the two golden artifacts without question. The Crown Adam took and laid carefully on the empty chair; the Sceptre he set on the floor in front of the chair, turning then to fetch the Seal from where it lay beside the casket.

"Let's get Mr. Gerard out of here, at least as far as the

doorway,'' he said, gesturing for his two colleagues to take charge of the unconscious Frenchman. ''You're both free to watch what I'm about to do—in fact, I'd welcome your support on the Inner Planes—but please don't do anything that might interfere, except in the unlikely event of some interruption from outside.''

Shifting a shoulder each under Gerard's limp arms, McLeod and Peregrine dragged him over to the doorway and just outside, where they propped him against the corridor wall. Adam, meanwhile, had bent to lay the Seal on the floor beside the Sceptre, and now straightened to face the unoccupied chair. Behind him in the doorway, McLeod and Peregrine took up their Templar swords again and knelt at vigil.

Folding his right hand over his left across his breast, Adam took several slow, deep breaths to center and focus again. As he did so, the physical confines of the room seemed to fade and recede, an astral reality beginning to overlay both the horror and the wonder of what literally surrounded him. The throne became one of a circle of thirteen seats suspended in the midst of a firmament of stars, and as his gaze took in the sparkling, blue-white swirl of astral constellations, he became aware of the sapphire on his right hand as a source of kindred light. Focusing his intent on reflecting that light back to its source, he bowed low before the empty throne as he framed a wordless plea for an audience with one he knew only as the Master.

Kneeling next to McLeod in the doorway, opening himself to follow where Adam led, Peregrine felt the faint twinge of vertigo and the momentary rushing sensation that he had learned to associate with soul-flight and the shift of perspective from the physical to the Astral. His vision blurred, his sight briefly confounded by speed and distances until, with a slight jar, his spirit found its grounding amid the Inner Planes.

As Peregrine's vision cleared again, he found himself still kneeling shoulder-to-shoulder with McLeod, but now at the edge of a circle of thirteen throne-like chairs set out in an open space full of silver light, like a temple open to the stars. The spectral forms of twelve white-mantled Templar preceptors now overlaid the mummified husks that Peregrine knew still occupied the physical reality of the twelve lesser chairs, ghostly gauntleted hands shifting slightly on the hilts of grounded swords as their golden-glowing eyes sought a bright-spinning spindle of purest white light hovering within the confines of the thirteenth chair. Before it the astral Adam stood, now garbed in a sapphire-blue soutane.

Gradually, the white light became a white-clad figure seated there, white-bearded and noble, the Crown of Solomon now resting on white-draped knees and compassed by pale, graceful hands, the Sceptre and Seal at his sandal-shod feet. That the Master had chosen to reveal himself in the chapel garb of a Templar Grand Master seemed altogether appropriate in this august company. Even expecting the visitation, Peregrine felt familiar awe and joy leap up in his breast, and he found himself wishing he dared take out a sketch pad and pencil; but he could not seem to summon sufficient will to do it.

As Adam straightened from his bow, his gaze lifting to the Master's, the blue soutane of his astral image shifted to a white Templar mantle and robes like those worn by the others.

Well met, Master of the Hunt, came the Master's greeting, like the mellow music of a hunting horn. *Be welcome in this company, and your Huntsmen with you. This night's work has been well done. Do you require further assistance?*

"I entreat your counsel, Worshipful Master," Adam responded. "Though we have returned the demons Gog and Magog to the place fashioned to contain them, yet would I see them banished once and for all from the face of the earth, and the hallows dispersed so that henceforth they will be neither a burden nor a temptation to any human creature."

The Master nodded, a smile perhaps curving the lips obscured by the beard. *You have freely offered what would*

*have been required. Thus shall the knowledge be freely
given. But there is more you would ask of us.*

Adam inclined his head in agreement. ''In my office as
physician, I likewise desire to know what may be done to
bring healing to the soul of Henri Gerard—and whether
some duty remains to the soul of the man slain by the
demons. Truly, I believe neither man sought to serve the
Darkness. They are young souls, led astray by the glamour
of greed.''

You plead eloquently for your foolish younger brethren,
the Master replied, *and wisely you temper justice with
mercy. What you desire is within the mandate permitted.
Approach and kneel.*

Adam obeyed, briefly bowing his head as the Master took
up King Solomon's Crown and stood. The twelve preceptors rose with him, giving solemn salute with their swords as
the Master elevated the Crown in mute acknowledgement of
the Divine Wisdom it embodied. As it began to descend,
Adam closed his eyes, offering himself as a vessel to be
filled.

The touch of the Crown on his brow let loose a wellspring
of sudden knowledge rising up within him, like a vast and
shining fountain bursting forth from among dry boulders in
a desert. Like a traveller long parched by thirst, he let the
flood overwhelm him, drinking deep of its grace with every
pore. . . .

Looking on, Peregrine saw his kneeling mentor sway
slightly and reel back on his haunches, half catching himself
on his hands, then grope blindly forward. As his hands
closed on the Sceptre and the Seal, he got his feet under him
and stood upright, crowned head raised as he elevated the
hallows at arm's length like an oblation. An answering blaze
of white light suddenly enwrapped him from all sides.

Dazzled and briefly startled, Peregrine braced himself
against another whirling rush of astral winds. When he
could see again, he was kneeling once more in the doorway
of the underground vault and the Master and his shining
company were gone. Beside him, McLeod heaved a relieved
sigh and gave his head a shake as if to clear his vision, then

turned his anxious gaze to where Adam now stood facing the empty thirteenth chair, the Crown on his head and the Sceptre and Seal in his upstretched hands. As his arms slowly lowered and he turned around, his dark gaze held a gleam of confidence.

"You'd better get our unfortunate friend out to the car," he said quietly, with a faint smile to reassure them. "What remains to be done, I must do alone, and there's some urgency. The balance just now is fragile."

With a nod for answer, McLeod leaned his sword against the doorjamb next to Peregrine's and turned to set a shoulder under one of Gerard's arms as Peregrine took the other and helped hoist the Frenchman's dead weight to a standing position. Supporting him heavily between them, they started slowly back along the passageway toward the stairs. Adam slid the Seal into his pocket as they left, his hand emerging with the vial of salt he had used at Rosslyn. This he uncapped and sprinkled on what the demons had left of the butchered thief, at the same time whispering an invocation to frame his intent.

"Go forth, thou wayward child of God, known only to Him, and be freed of the snares of Evil, that you be not bound to this place. With contrite heart may you be received into the Presence of Him Whose never-failing love surpasses all human imperfections. Amen. Selah. So be it."

Pocketing the empty vial, he lightly touched the head of the Sceptre to the dead man's shattered torso, lifting it then to trace first a cross and then a circle over the remains, then put him out of mind and moved closer to the casket. Doffing the Crown, he set it squarely on top of the casket lid, with a murmured exhortation for Divine attendance as he retrieved McLeod's torch and backed out the door, breaking then to dash back along the passageway toward the stairs.

He could smell the fresh scent of wet earth as he scrambled upward. A light rain still was falling, and the steps toward the top were mud-slick and a little treacherous. Emerging into the open air, Adam stumbled back to the standing arch, the Sceptre still in his right hand, and paused within the arch to scuff away enough grass and earth to lay bare a small patch of rock in the middle of the threshold. Turning back then to face the gaping blackness of the stairwell, he set the torch aside and drew out the Seal from his pocket, bending to set it carefully in the center of the cleared space. As he tightened his grasp on the Sceptre and straightened, he called up memory of what had been imparted to him, then boldly stretched forth the Sceptre to touch the left-hand side of the arch.

"Creature of earth, thy name is Boaz," he whispered, focusing his intent through the hallow in his hand. "Thou art the symbol of that holy darkness which is the night of the soul's blind quest for its Creator."

A fresh breath of air puffed past him with a heavier spat of rain, scented with dew and wet grass. Drawing another breath, he shifted the Sceptre to touch the right-hand side of the arch.

"Creature of earth, thy name is Jachin," he whispered. "Thou art the symbol of that holy Light which is the illumination of the mind and the consummation of the heart." Lifting the Sceptre to touch the center of the arch, he continued. "Light and dark together are the pillars of Creation. Be thou steadfast in this world and the next, according to the manifold names of Him Who ordains thee: *Yod He Vau He, Adonai, Elohim, Eheieh, Shaddai el Chai, Jehovah Sabaoth, Elohim Sabaoth, Shekinah. . . .*"

The holy Names seemed to resonate soundlessly across the night air, lingering as a perfume with Adam's final whisper. In the taut stillness, pregnant with anticipation, Adam slowly lowered the Sceptre, bowed his head in homage to What he had called upon and asking indulgence for any liberties taken, then tossed the Sceptre underhanded through the arch, between the Pillars, into the dark mouth of the passageway beyond.

It caught the watery moonlight as it tumbled end over end through the air, very like an old World War I German stick grenade in the way it moved—and in the result it produced. It disappeared into the stairwell opening and struck stone several steps down, chiming as it continued bouncing downward. The final distant ping was swallowed up in a sudden deep rumble from far underground, accompanied by a burst of dazzling light that lit up the arch like a solar flare. As Adam threw up a hand before his eyes, the earth beneath him was jolted by a heavy boom that threw him to his knees.

A secondary series of shocks ripped briefly through the ground beneath him, and he made a scrambling further retreat on hands and knees as, above him, the standing arch of stones shuddered and threatened to collapse. Blinking away the lurid afterimages, he stayed down until the last rumbles had subsided, then groped in the grass for the torch.

He found it in the grass a few feet from the right-hand side of the arch, and aimed its beam through the archway with trembling hands. No trace remained of Sceptre, Seal, or stair passage. It was as if the earth itself had swallowed them up, leaving no trace beyond a few faint scorches on a small patch of bare stone at his feet.

For the space of half a dozen heartbeats while he searched, the silence was profound. Then the hush was broken by the sharp, interrogative barking of a dog, swelling to a chorus as other local animals took up the inquiry. The dark houses adjoining the field showed a sudden rash of lights.

Switching off the torch, Adam scrambled to his feet and made for the end of the playground, keeping low, heading through the tall grass for the lane. As he gained the rutted track, two dark figures detached themselves from the shadows and approached him, one slender and one burly.

"Adam?" came McLeod's whispered query from out of the gloom. "We heard what sounded like an explosion."

"That was the passageway closing in," Adam said, urging them back toward the car. "Hopefully, the locals will think it was thunder."

"But what if someone should decide to excavate the site some day?" Peregrine asked, craning his neck back in the direction of the mound.

"He would find nothing but old stone," Adam said with grim conviction. "The authorities of the Inner Planes have ordained a new and final resting place for the Templar treasures which is not within the physical confines of this world.''

As they trotted toward the end of the lane, Cochrane's dark-colored Passat crept abreast of the opening, brake lights showing briefly, its low idle almost silent.

''Ah, there's Donald to whisk us out of here,'' Adam murmured. ''If no one suspects we were ever here, there will be nothing to explain in the morning. . . .''

CHAPTER TWENTY-NINE

"WHAT'S going to happen to Gerard?" Peregrine finally asked, as Donald Cochrane sped them away from the village of Temple, heading them back toward Edinburgh. "I mean, are we going to hand him over to the authorities down in York?"

Adam glanced aside at the unconscious Frenchman, slumped limp between him and Peregrine in the rear passenger seat.

"Do you think that's what we ought to do?"

Peregrine frowned perplexedly. "Technically, I suppose, the answer should be yes. But frankly, I don't see that it would do anybody much good."

"Why not?" Adam asked.

"Well, for one thing, he's in no fit state to stand trial for anything," Peregrine said with blunt honesty. "For another, the circumstances surrounding his crime are so outlandish, I don't see how the evidence could possibly be doctored to make it legally acceptable."

"All the same, he *did* steal the Seal, and was at least indirectly responsible for the death of Nathan Fiennes," Adam said.

"*We* know that," Peregrine replied. "But I wouldn't fancy trying to explain the facts to a jury. They'd probably advise the judge to have us locked away in the same mental hospital as Gerard."

"There's no arguing *that,*" McLeod agreed from his seat beside Cochrane. "I take it, then, that you're in favor of waiving the question of justice?"

"Not waiving it, exactly." Peregrine groped for the words to articulate his feelings. "It seems to me that justice of a kind has already been done. The other man is dead—I don't suppose we'll ever even know who he was—and I certainly can't think of any worse punishment for Gerard than the one he's suffering at the moment, being literally terrified out of his mind.''

"I couldn't agree with you more," Adam said. "Perhaps Karma itself has decreed a fitting end to Gerard's place in this affair.''

"Then what are *you* suggesting that we do?" Peregrine asked, caught slightly off guard by his mentor's abrupt change of tactics.

Adam worried at his signet ring as he pondered the practicalities of his answer.

"Nathan Fiennes' family, at least, deserve to be told a version of the truth, if only to reassure them that the killer is not still at large," he said after a moment. "I make myself responsible for accomplishing that. As for Gerard himself—"

He glanced at the Frenchman and sighed. "He doesn't know any of us by name, and probably wouldn't recognize us if he were to see us again. I doubt he has any clear recollection of what happened down in the crypt, but anything he might be likely to say on that account will simply be taken as further proof of his mental disorder. That being the case, I would say that the kindest thing we could do for him is to find a safe place to leave him where he's certain to be found and taken into care for treatment."

"But who could help him?" Peregrine asked. "If, as you've suggested, the source of his problem springs from past-life guilt—"

At Adam's droll sidelong glance, Peregrine broke off in sudden comprehension. "You think he'll end up as *your* patient!" he murmured. "And you can make sure he does, can't you? But—do you really think he can be helped?"

"I did say it would take time and patience," Adam replied. "And I like to fancy that I'm reasonably open-minded. As I mentioned before, his obsessions appear to stem from guilt left over from a previous lifetime. What I didn't realize until tonight, back at Fyvie, is that Gerard's guilt is directly traceable to the period surrounding the suppression of the Templars. His previous incarnation from that time is known to history as Guillaume de Nogaret.''

''I've heard of *him*!'' Cochrane said, speaking for the first time since leaving Temple. ''This ties in with Masonic history. Isn't he the one who incited Philippe le Bel to carry out the suppression of the Templars!''

''That's right,'' Adam said grimly. ''He was one of Philippe's principal courtiers. Philippe harbored a grudge against the Templars not only because of their wealth but because they had denied him membership in the Order. De Nogaret nurtured that resentment with lies to serve his own ambitions. He was probably responsible for promulgating some of the worst charges against the Templars, including the assertion that they practiced a form of idolatry by worshipping a head of some kind.''

McLeod turned to stare at Adam over the back of the seat.

''You don't suppose he had some inkling, even then, that some of the Templars' secrets tied in with Solomon's Crown. . . .''

''Difficult to say,'' Adam replied. ''Whether or not de Nogaret was involved, what does seem clear to me now, knowing what we do about the hallows and the casket, is that the Templars treasured the Crown, in particular, because of its power to keep evil at bay. If their respect were perceived by the unknowing as veneration of a mysterious relic—it's only a short leap of logic from a crown to a head—it's easy to see how enemies of the Order could have distorted the truth and come up with a charge of idolatry— worshipping a head.

''A convenient little frame-up,'' McLeod observed. ''If that's what really happened, they could have cleared themselves at any time by disclosing the true nature of the hallows. But if they had, men like de Nogaret might have tried to seize the power the hallows represented, and to misuse the threat of what lay hidden in the casket.''

''So the Templars elected to keep their secret intact, even at the cost of their own lives,'' Peregrine finished. He sighed. ''Well, at least it wasn't for nothing. We managed to uphold the charge they'd been given. Maybe in time, Gerard will be able to face up to the folly of what de Nogaret was trying to do, and find the courage to start over again.''

"We can only hope,'' Adam said. "But in the meanwhile, gentlemen, we've done a good night's work—with some help from some extraordinary friends.''

Smiling wearily, he pulled the cord of the Dundee Templar cross over his head, glancing wistfully at the glint of red enamel, then reached into his pocket and drew out the Dundee ring, holding both so that they reflected light from the instrument panel up front.

"I intend to write a very complimentary article about the Templar connections of John Grahame of Claverhouse," he said quietly. "It's unfortunate that the whole story of his contributions can't be told—though his name will certainly live on as one of Scotland's great patriots.''

With a jaunty flourish, he tossed the ring into the air and caught it in his fist, then slipped it and the cross back into his pocket.

"The whole story of *our* contributions won't be told either,'' McLeod observed drily. "But that isn't why we got into this business anyway, is it? And frankly, I'll be just as well pleased to be able to close the book on this particular case without trailing too many loose ends behind me. There's nothing I hate worse than having to invent explanations to satisfy official curiosity. Other than that break-in at Rosslyn, which can be passed off as grave-robbing, there's no inconvenient evidence left behind for us to cover up.''

"True,'' Peregrine said with a sigh. "All the same, it seems a pity we never seem to end up with any physical proof that we've accomplished anything. I mean, after all our running around tonight, all we've got to show for our pains is Mr. Gerard—and we're going to be ditching *him* on the doorstep of the first convenient hospital we come to!''

This observation produced a sly backwards glance and a deep chuckle from McLeod.

"Actually, laddie, that's not quite true,'' he said with a grin. As both Peregrine and Adam stared at him blankly, the inspector bent over and reached down under the front seat.

When he straightened up, his companions saw that he was clutching the hilts of a pair of Templar swords.

"I grabbed them before we started manhandling Gerard up the stairs," he explained to Peregrine, obviously enjoying the fact that he had taken even Adam by surprise. "You obviously were preoccupied trying to keep him on his feet and get him out of there. At the time, I was thinking we might return them to Rosslyn, where they came from, but it's since occurred to me that there's no way we can do that without generating far more paperwork than I care to deal with—not to mention creating a stir that's bound to bring the newshounds sniffing around."

As Adam rolled his eyes heavenward, nodding in silent agreement, McLeod continued.

"So it looks like we've become custodians of a pair of Templar swords. It might be that Templemor would be a good home for them, it being a Templar site and Adam having been a Templar. I was thinking, too, Mr. Peregrine Lovat, that they might provide a rather impressive sword arch at your wedding. Given your role in tonight's work, I don't think the former owners would mind. And if you ask Adam *very* nicely, he might even let you hold the wedding reception in the great hall at Templemor."

HISTORICAL AFTERWORD

THE background on the suppression of the Order of the Temple of Jerusalem is essentially accurate, barring the existence of the casket and the three hallows that guarded it. Since the Templars were accused of worshipping a head, a crown/relic such as we describe could have been the basis for such an accusation.

The background on Bonnie Dundee is historically accurate other than his association with the Crown of Solomon. The neck cross he is said to have been wearing at his death at Killiecrankie disappeared after David Grahame conveyed it to the French theologian and historian Dom Calmet, but it easily could have ended up in the hands of cadet Grahams as postulated, and might well have been used to invest Prince Charles Edward Stuart at Holyrood Palace in 1745. A ring containing a lock of Dundee's hair is known to have existed, but its present whereabouts is unknown.

James Seton, fourth Earl of Dunfermline, is a likely candidate to have cut the lock of hair, since he was one of Dundee's most tried and trusted officers, a close personal friend, and is known to have been present at his burial. He was the owner of Fyvie Castle at that time, and came from a line of Setons whose antecedents included Knights Hospitallers—and who possibly were secret Templars as well, after the suppression of the Order. The names of Seton's two daughters are unknown, as is their fate, but they probably would have been in their twenties at the time of

Dundee's death. Seton's wife was named Jean, as was an earlier Seton daughter, and the name Grizel also appears twice in earlier generations of Seton women. James Seton died in exile in 1674, and the Dunfermline title became extinct.

The references cited are genuine.

—*K.K.*
Bray, Co. Wicklow, Ireland